*HOW TO
ALIGN
THE
STARS*

SHAKESPEARE PROJECT

HOW TO ALIGN THE STARS
a novel

AMY DRESSLER

EGRET LAKE BOOKS
SEATTLE

Copyright © 2024 Amy Dressler

All rights reserved. No part of this publication may be reproduced, distributed, or transmitted in any form or by any means, including photocopying, recording, or other electronic or mechanical methods, without the prior written permission of the publisher, except in the case of brief quotations embodied in critical reviews and certain other noncommercial uses permitted by copyright law. For permission requests, write to the publisher via the contact information found on the website below.

This is a work of fiction. Unless otherwise indicated, all the names, characters, businesses, places, events and incidents in this book are either the product of the author's imagination or used in a fictitious manner. Any resemblance to actual persons, living or dead, or actual events is purely coincidental.

No AI Training: Without in any way limiting the author's [and publisher's] exclusive rights under copyright, any use of this publication to "train" generative artificial intelligence (AI) technologies to generate text is expressly prohibited. The author reserves all rights to license uses of this work for generative AI training and development of machine learning language models.

Egret Lake Books
www.egretlakebooks.com

All photographs, illustrations, graphics, designs, and text are copyrighted and used by permission. Please contact the publisher above for further information regarding copyrights.

Library of Congress Control Number: 2024932329

978-1-956498-10-3 ISBN (paperback)
978-1-956498-11-0 ISBN (epub)

First Edition
1 2 3 4 6 7 8 9 10

*For S, who utterly ruined my
plans to be a merry spinster.*

Chapter One

Bea

Beatrice and her bookcase were stuck. She'd come to campus yesterday with a tape measure to make sure the garage sale treasure — seven feet of mid-century teak that was going to look splendid against the exposed brick in her new office — would fit onto the seldom-used elevator. Although she was more accustomed to measuring the distances between planets and moons than the dimensions of secondhand furniture and creaky elevators, Bea's calculations were undoubtedly flawless.

This morning, Bea had manhandled the bookcase into the science building lobby, only to be confronted with an Out of Order sign taped to the stainless-steel elevator doors. Since it was fall move-in day, Messiman College's facilities staff would be busy helping students rearrange their dorm room furniture and politely explaining to parents why they couldn't drive their SUVs across the grass. There was no chance of the elevator being fixed any time soon.

Wrestling this thing back into her car was out of the question.

It was going into her office today, elevator or not. The bookcase was heavy, but the blankets she'd strapped around it to prevent scratches helped it slide easily. She could propel it up the stairs if she got a shoulder behind it and heaved.

Bea and her bookcase reached an impasse at the landing halfway to the second floor, turning the corner between flights. A hard shove caused it to pivot around the newel post with an unexpectedly forceful lurch, wedging her into the corner. Even when she braced her butt against the wall and gave it her all, the damn thing wouldn't budge another millimeter.

Sweaty tendrils of hair stuck to the back of her neck. Bea leaned against the wall in the small space her predicament afforded her, pulled the elastic from her sloppy bun, and used her fingers to rake her hair back into a more secure ponytail. She could call someone to come help her — if she hadn't left her phone in her car to avoid dropping or damaging it. For the thousandth time, she cursed unfavorable women's pocket capacity to phone size ratios.

It was fine. This building was empty right now, but campus was busy. Someone would come along. She hoped it was soon because she had just become acutely aware of how much coffee she'd had this morning. Bea fixed her eyes on the bottom of the stairwell, willing someone to walk by. She hummed to herself to pass the time and take her mind off her bladder. She was at seventy-three bottles of beer on the wall when she caught a glimpse of an unfortunately familiar battered Cubs cap bobbing through the lobby. A hat that almost certainly belonged to the last person on earth Bea wanted to ask for help.

But she was stuck.

And she really had to pee.

"Hello?" she called, projecting her best auditorium-lecture voice — direct from the diaphragm — toward the lobby. "Ben?" She tried not to sound begrudging. "Help."

Ben Addison appeared in the doorway at the bottom of the stairs. In addition to the hat, he wore what must have been one of a dozen stockpiled CBGB t-shirts, faded jeans, and a smirk.

"I had heard the administration is encouraging emotional support objects, but an entire bookcase seems a bit extreme, doesn't it Dr. Hayes?"

Bea bristled, interpreting his widened eyes as an expectation that she would laugh at his little joke, but she wasn't amused by the cheap shot at students who needed coping mechanisms.

"Funny," she replied without arranging her face into a smile. "I'm moving into my new office. I'm sure all the shelving in your fancy ass workspace was purchased and installed for you, but not all of us get that luxury."

Ben grinned and brandished a candy bar. "But there are better vending machine choices over here. You guys have Peanut Butter Twix." He opened it and ate half in three fast bites. Chewing, he asked, "Want the other half?" and waved the wrapper at Bea.

Unbelievable. "No. Thank you."

"Ah. Dieting, are we?"

"No. 'We' don't diet." Bea was long accustomed to the irksome assumption, every time she turned down sweets, ordered a salad or went for a run, that she was trying to lose weight. As long as she felt good (she did) and could climb the six flights to the rooftop telescopes without getting winded (she could), she believed it was a waste of energy to be bothered about her size. Bea had reached a truce with her body image, but there were certain people with a knack for making her self-conscious and it was hard to maintain her confidence in front of them — especially fucking *Ben* with his spectacular history of making her feel bad about herself. Bea could usually go along to get along, but once a line was crossed there was no coming back. Ben had been a citizen of enemy territory since they were students here together.

Her bladder began to twinge more insistently. If she didn't get out of here soon, she was risking humiliation. She'd had her fill of being embarrassed in front of Ben years ago, a repeat performance would be even worse than owing him a favor. "Can you just help me?"

"Oh." He stroked his chin. "So, this isn't on purpose, then?"

She glared. "No."

"I can probably help. What's the magic word?" He crossed his arms and waited, a lazy smile spreading across his face. He was eating this up.

"Please." She practically spat it at him.

"Was that so hard?" Ben examined the bookcase. "I think I should come around and pull from the top. If we can get it up and over the railing, we'll be golden."

"Yeah, I was trying that, but it's too heavy to lift so high by myself."

"No worries. I'll pop up the other stairs and be back in a flash. Don't go anywhere."

And he winked, the arrogant jerk.

Two minutes later, Ben appeared in the doorway on the second floor, chewing. He tucked the candy wrapper into the back pocket of his jeans and gripped the top of the bookshelf. "Okay, I'm gonna lift from here, you push from there. Ready?"

Bea nodded and braced to push as well as she could.

"One…two…three." Veins popped out against the muscles of Ben's forearms as they heaved the bookcase over the railing, Bea dividing her effort between propelling the bookcase and maintaining the integrity of her pelvic floor. It came to rest on its side, tilted up the stairs.

"It's a straight shot from here to the door," Bea said. "I can handle it now. Thanks."

"This thing is heavy. I'll help you get it the rest of the way."

Bea pressed her thighs together. She needed to get to the ladies' room as soon as possible. "That's okay. Really. Thanks."

"Not taking no for an answer." His words were friendly, but she detected resolve behind them. He knew she was dying to get rid of him and had no intention of obliging.

She didn't have time to argue. "Fine. Then hold on a minute." Squeezing past the bookshelf, she rushed up the rest of the stairs, coming face to face with a bemused Ben. "Excuse me."

He flattened himself against the wall, allowing her to pass into the hallway, where she waddle-darted to the restroom. She unbuttoned her jeans as soon as the heavy door closed behind her, slamming the stall door and sitting in one hasty motion.

Bea took several deep breaths after she washed her hands, steeling herself to continue the interaction. Even when Ben was being perfectly polite, she could never shake the feeling that beneath a thin patina of civility, he was mocking her. Maybe not, but since it would be consistent with his past behavior, she didn't feel obligated to give him the benefit of the doubt now.

When she came out, he was loitering in the hallway with the bookcase standing next to him. "With these blankets it was pretty easy to slide it right up."

"Yep. That was my plan. I could have done it just as easily."

"Well, I did it for you. Which one is your office?" He tipped the bookshelf back onto his shoulder as if preparing to scoot it down the hallway linoleum.

"Don't be ridiculous, we can at least carry it together." She moved to take hold of the top. "I don't want you to push too hard and loosen the joints."

"Splendid," said Ben, taking up the bottom. "Lead the way."

Bea unlocked the door to her office and Ben whistled. "Coming up in the world."

She wasn't going to let his sarcasm ruin this for her. After years in a glorified broom closet with a slit of a window overlooking the dumpsters, she finally—thanks to Dr. Stein's retirement last spring—had one of the spacious faculty offices facing the grounds. The science building, constructed in the seventies to a utilitarian aesthetic, lacked the ivy-encrusted neoclassical charm of the older structures on campus, but the faculty offices on this side were large and airy. Through the floor-to-ceiling window, they had a view of the quad filled with students moving into their dorms. Bea had even brought a rug in to brighten up the cumin-colored, Nixon-era industrial carpet. The new bookcase was a satisfyingly perfect fit on the wall next to the door. Bea dropped into her desk chair and swiveled to face Ben, who leaned a shoulder against the door frame.

It was silly, but picturing this space in her head—her own office in the building where she'd taken her first astronomy courses, a place to confer with colleagues and mentor students—had gotten her through the more grueling parts of her PhD program. Now it was a reality and the first person to see it was the only person on this campus she wouldn't have been delighted to welcome here.

"It's no *Librotory*," she said, emphasizing the ridiculous name of Ben's workspace, "but it will do."

"Oh, come on," Ben said. "You know I didn't name it that. The donor relations people thought it would 'resonate with alumni.' It's not my fault they consider my background an asset."

Ben was the special collections librarian, in charge of rare books, as well as a lecturer with the art department. Last year, Messiman had opened a lab in the library to house Ben's book repair facility and serve as the studio for Book Arts classes, where students could learn bookbinding and printing techniques, or create art pieces from existing books. The lab was easily fifteen times the size of Bea's new office and much fancier than her building's outdated classrooms.

"Background, ha. You don't even have a PhD." She'd worked her tail off to complete her doctorate, but it seemed like Ben had waltzed right into his comfortably-funded position. He wouldn't even have to apply for tenure.

Ben's face, already flushed from the effort of furniture moving, reddened more deeply. "I have two master's degrees."

"Ooh, fancy. Tell that to a dissertation board."

"At least I've spent time outside of the ivory tower. A dissertation review is a picnic compared to art critics."

"Well. Thanks for using your delicate artist's hands to help me move furniture."

"You're welcome. Where are your books?"

"Pardon?"

"Your books? Presumably you plan to put some" — he indicated the empty shelves with a lazy flourish — "here?"

"In the car."

"Let's go get them."

"I can certainly manage a few boxes of books myself."

"The elevator is broken. I insist."

"No, I insist. I can handle it." She settled her hips more firmly into her chair and crossed her arms.

"As you wish. Always a pleasure, Beatrice." He gave her a little salute, spun, and sauntered down the hall.

"Likewise." She injected saccharine into the reply and lobbed it at his retreating back. Once Bea heard the creak of the stairwell door and the sound of his feet on the steps, she exhaled to slide the tension out of her shoulders.

Heron

The window was dirty, but Heron had to admit her decision to clean it right this minute had more to do with the view she could get of her boyfriend unloading the truck. The August sun glinted off Charlie's sandy hair as he transferred her boxes and furniture from the truck bed to the lawn, stacking them to bring upstairs. His large frame, which made Heron feel tiny and cherished when his arms folded around her, allowed him to lift the big cartons she could barely get a grasp on.

He tossed a box of clothes out of the truck. It popped open and scattered sweaters across the dry brown lawn. She grimaced; she'd be picking twigs and bits of grass out of them for weeks. One deep breath in to acknowledge her annoyance, then out, focusing her intention on gratitude. She should feel fortunate to have Charlie's help. Music blasted out of the Sig-O-Delt house, and she knew he would rather be over there with the guys instead of helping her and Maggie move into their place.

The apartment was in a big old house that had been carved into rental units, and Heron's bedroom had a large dormer window through which she could see Charlie's corner room across the street. When they weren't together, they'd be able to see each other's lights through the poplars lining their block.

She watched Charlie stuff the sweaters back into their box, then pick up the little violet-painted nightstand she'd found browsing garage sales with Bea last weekend. A few minutes later she heard him set them down with a soft thump just inside the door of her bedroom. The ghost of his reflection appeared in the window as he came up behind her and wrapped his arms around her hips, turning her and lifting her down from her stepstool. He topped the gesture with a sweaty kiss that made her head swim.

"Hey," he said.

"Hey."

"Only the mattress left. I can get it, but it will be a little easier if you help me."

She set down her rag and spray bottle. "Let's go."

The double mattress was the only brand-new thing she'd splurged on, and she didn't want it dragged across the ground. The walnut staircase in the foyer, a leftover from grander days, was wide enough to make lugging the mattress an easy task. Heron guided from the top while Charlie, at the bottom, took most of the bulk. They settled it on the low platform frame and slid the bed into Heron's window nook. As soon as it was in position, Charlie flopped down.

"Just a sec," said Heron, grabbing the mattress cover and fitted sheet and gesturing for him to stand up. "You're getting it all sweaty." He was streaked with dust and perspiration. She could wash bedding, but once the ticking was soiled, it would be that way forever no matter how clean the sheets were.

"We can't get this sweaty?" Charlie put on a playful tone. "I thought that was the whole point."

"Charlie, please? Come on." He stood up, but annoyance flashed across his face. Oops. Should've just let it go. "The point," she said, as she wrestled with the elastic corners, "is that we don't have to sleep wedged into a twin bed in a dorm or frat house anymore."

When she finished, Charlie threw himself back down on the bed, turned onto his side and patted the spot in front of his stomach, where she curled up as his little spoon, head pillowed on his bicep. Lying on their sides, they faced the candles and framed photos Heron had already unboxed and arranged across the dresser.

"You're amazing, you know," he said. "You aren't even unpacked yet and this room already totally feels like you."

It was such a sweet observation, she let her lingering irritation at his carelessness float away. He really did get her. She squeezed his hand where it rested on her hip. "I've been thinking about it a long time, how my own space should be. The dorm rooms felt so institutional, I could never get the vibe right. And I love my dad so much, but his house hasn't felt like home since my mom…"

"I know." Charlie kissed the top of her head.

"I want a place where everything is just how I intend it to be," she said. "Where I always feel safe." Where nobody left.

If things were different, she'd have that with Charlie right now. They'd originally planned to live together senior year, but when Charlie was elected fraternity president, that all changed. Chapter bylaws required him to live in the frat house.

"Babe," he'd said, "I can't pass up this opportunity. Being a past president will get me so much farther in alumni circles."

She wanted to believe him, but a seed of doubt had taken root and grown all summer, fear creeping like ivy and crowding out the light. Charlie was a classic Gemini; she loved how gregarious and fun he was, but she worried about him keeping things from her. What if changing their housing plans was his first step toward making a clean break at graduation? It wouldn't be the first time a guy thought a girl was good enough for college, but not forever, and it wouldn't be the first time Heron drove someone who was supposed to love her away. She resolved to be her very best self: no nagging or clinging, helping him with his school and fraternity responsibilities, prove his life was better with her in it. She could do this; she was so much better than she used to be.

"It's only a year." Heron popped to her feet to hunt for pillows and the rest of the sheets. She kept her tone deliberately bright. "Not even that. Only nine months until graduation." The next time she moved into a place it would be a home shared with Charlie, she had to have faith in that. If she didn't believe in them, how could she expect him to?

Bea

Bea only had five boxes: four of books; one of miscellaneous items there hadn't been room for on the tiny desk in her old office. Still, after her tussle with the bookshelf, she was exhausted and grimy by the time she got them up the stairs and unpacked. She sat to rest and watch the activity out the window. It was hard to believe that it had been nearly two decades since she was one of these fresh-faced kids settling into the dorm, and six years since she'd returned, snagging a tenure-track position right after completing her PhD in a stroke of luck that still amazed her.

Securing tenure would mean she could stay here at Messiman for her entire career if she wanted to, and Bea desperately did. Since it was an undergrad-only school, there was less pressure to secure funding and more focus on teaching. She strongly preferred hands-on work with students to fussing with grant applications. And she wanted to stay in Millet. The night skies in eastern Washington, while they might not have rivaled Hawaii or Utah, felt like home to her. This was where she fell in love with the stars, after all. She had family ties here, too. As a student, Bea had earned pocket money babysitting her younger cousin. They'd developed a sisterly bond, becoming friends as Heron grew up. Heron would probably move away next summer, but Bea was close to her uncle Len and often spent evenings out at his winery. Since she wasn't especially close to her own parents, it was nice to be near extended family—especially when they came with free wine and acres of vineyard perfect for stargazing.

She was arranging her few paper files in the bottom desk drawer, when she heard a gentle rap on her half-open door. Rick Brown hovered in her doorway, holding a small potted cactus. Rick was nearly six and a half feet tall and as slender as a stalk of wheat. He was one of the kindest people she knew and had been her mentor since she'd first switched her major from pre-med to astronomy. As the chair of the two-person department, Rick was technically Bea's boss, but the role he filled in her life was more like something between grandfather and business partner.

"Looks like you're getting settled into the new space pretty well." Rick accordioned himself into one of the guest chairs and set the cactus on her desk. "A little office-warming gift."

"Thank you. It's perfect. I ought to put some more plants in here but I'm sure I'll kill them."

"You'd definitely kill them. Stick to succulents, kiddo."

She laughed and moved the cactus to the side of her desk nearest the window. "Hopefully I'll get to keep this office awhile."

"You will."

Rick's faith in her as an undergrad had given Bea the confidence to pursue her doctorate, but the thing she loved best about him was that his encouragement always came with sound practical advice.

"That's what I came to talk about. I reviewed your tenure file. Everything looks pretty good—publications, student evaluations, letters of recommendation—but I think to get approval from the faculty personnel committee and sign-off from President Phillips, you should boost your service to the college community a tad. It's been a few years since you did something outside of the science division."

Bea had avoided campus-wide initiatives since Ben's reappearance, not relishing the idea of bumping into him unexpectedly. Why did he have to be her only classmate who'd returned to work at the college?

⁓

Three years ago, it had been an unpleasant surprise for Bea to turn around to be introduced to the new special collections librarian and find herself looking into an annoyingly familiar pair of hazel eyes.

"Beatrice!" Ben had said with a mockingly jocular tone that

was also all too familiar. "Great to see you again."

They hadn't exactly been friends when they graduated, but she didn't think it was necessary for him to be sarcastic right out of the gate. "Hello, Ben." She tried to keep her tone cool, neutral. "The last I heard you were fully committed to the art world. Don't libraries seem a little cushy for you?"

Ben flashed a self-effacing grin that likely would have charmed anyone else into a puddle. "Bit of an age-limit on the starving artist lifestyle, especially when you're paying off MFA loans. I did a show using repurposed books and got to know one of the librarians at Northwestern, who suggested I get a second Master's in Library Science, and here I am."

Bea congratulated herself for refraining from scoffing at the "science" in "Library Science," saying instead, "I see. Welcome, then. I know Messiman appreciates having alumni on the staff."

"Faculty."

"Pardon?"

"Librarians are non-tenured faculty here even if they don't teach anything else, but as it happens, I'll also be teaching a Book Arts course offered by the art department."

"How nice. I'll recommend it to my cousin. She could probably use an easy credit to round out her schedule."

Ben caught the eye of someone across the room. "Nice to see you, Bea. Excuse me." He strutted away.

"Well," she told Rick now, "I've been focusing on my own students. And I guest-lecture in some of the philosophy and religion classes about the intersection of early astronomers and epistemology."

He slapped the desk in triumph. "That's why I put your name forward to represent Messiman at the Cascadia Undergraduate Education Symposium this fall. They want to do a roundtable panel on interdisciplinary pedagogy."

"Sure," she said, "I could definitely do that." What better way to avoid Ben than by going out of town?

"Great," Rick reassembled his implausible limbs into a standing position and ducked his head an inch to get through her doorway. Leaning back into the room, he said, "I'll let them know. We're sending two people, so you'll be working with that fellow from the library who teaches Book Arts. You'll want to get in touch with him to make a plan. See you tomorrow."

As soon as he was gone, Bea threw her head back in a groan. Of course. She'd never told Rick about her history with Ben or even mentioned an aversion. It would be unprofessional, the details were embarrassing, and amiable Rick would never believe anyone couldn't get along if they put a little effort into it. He was right about her tenure file, though. She did need to add something more outwardly focused. And this conference was her best chance to get it.

If Bea didn't get tenure this year, she could try again, but the bar for approval was always a bit higher the second time. And if she failed then, she'd be back on the job market, a daunting prospect. Tenure-track positions were in short supply, with many universities deciding to cut back on classes or rely on adjuncts instead of backfilling vacancies.

Bea was so close to getting everything she'd ever wanted. It would be beyond foolish to jeopardize it all with a grudge, even a valid one. For the sake of all that, she could suck it up and play nice. With any luck, she could continue to avoid Ben after the symposium. Forever.

Heron

The president's room was luxurious, as far as frat houses go. Charlie's desk sat in front of a wide, paned window. A table and chairs intended for officer meetings was strewn with Charlie's lacrosse gear. For the alcove that held the extra-long twin bed, Heron had sewn curtains out of navy fabric with a subtle constellation pattern in a lighter shade of blue, with a blackout lining. Charlie hated too much extra light when he slept. Maybe making these for him was over the top, but it had been a fun project and it was going to make Charlie's life just a little bit better.

She was using her handheld steamer to smooth out the wrinkles in the just-hung drapes. Charlie wrapped his arms around her waist and kissed her on the back of her neck. "Thanks so much, babe. These are cool. I like the little doodles."

"They aren't doodles," she said, "it's the Zodiac. Look, here's Taurus, that's me, and Gemini, that's you."

"Gemini is twins?"

"Yep. Twins and the bull."

"Kinky." The interjection came from Charlie's open doorway.

Heron turned in Charlie's arms so she could face the source of the voice. Jason. He was Charlie's fraternity brother, but Heron had known him longer. They'd been in Messiman's college prep program together as high school seniors and Heron had made an effort to be kind, but when he asked her to homecoming she declined because she already had a date. He'd acted strangely toward her ever since, seeming to alternate between hostility and innuendo, but no one else ever seemed to pick up on it. Sometimes she was oversensitive; maybe it was nothing. Still, she never felt at ease around Jason.

"Jace!" Charlie broke their embrace to step forward and thump Jason on the shoulder. "How was your summer, bro?"

Heron turned back to the curtains, wincing. Charlie was trying much too hard to be friendly, probably trying to make up for beating Jason out for the presidency during officer elections last spring.

Charlie and Jason launched into a discussion of membership recruitment strategies. "Academics sounds better to guys who want to please their parents," Charlie was saying, "but other frats have higher GPA rankings. We should invite a bunch of guys to our first football game."

Heron considered excusing herself, but she and Charlie planned to walk over to the quad soon to watch the annual move-in day ultimate frisbee game, and she wanted to be ready to go when he was. She might as well go ahead and unpack some of Charlie's things. When she grabbed a suitcase, he caught her eye and gave her a grateful smile. Charlie's smiles said so much. This one was *Thanks. Sorry. I'll try to wrap this up quickly.*

This suitcase was full of rolled socks and neatly folded boxer briefs. Heron began sorting everything into the top two drawers of Charlie's dresser. Her back was to the guys, but she could see them in the mirror. In one of the sock balls, she felt a hard lump. It was probably cuff links or something, but the feel of that little domed square made Heron's heart skip a beat. If this was what she thought, Charlie had no intention of ending things with her this year. Snooping was wrong, but she needed to know. Looking in the mirror to confirm that Charlie's back was still turned, she slipped it out of the sock and cracked it open. Inside, she saw the starry glitter of diamonds; a marquise cut in a white gold setting, surrounded by intricate art deco scrollwork and smaller stones. Heron stifled a gasp, slipped the box back into its sock, and placed everything in what she hoped was a random-looking arrangement in the dresser drawer. Feeling the pull of being watched, she flicked her eyes up to the mirror. Charlie wasn't looking, but she thought she caught a fleeting glimpse of Jason's gaze on her before he returned his attention to Charlie.

The sun had gone behind some clouds and the late August heat was beginning to relent. Breeze from the window fan hit the perspiration-dampened back of Heron's tank top, and a shiver tingled the skin of her upper arms.

"Babe, I think I'll go back to my place and do some more unpacking there," she said. "Pick me up when you're done?"

"Sure."

She slipped out of his room, jogged down the stairs and out into the sunlight. She drew in a big lungful of summer-warm air and exhaled, releasing the looming tangle of doubts. As she walked the half-block to her apartment building, it seemed like her sandals were six inches off the ground. She probably shouldn't have looked in the jewelry box, but even that was like something from a movie. And just like an actress in the romcoms she watched with Bea during their girls' nights, Heron knew their joy would compensate for any lack of surprise when Charlie gave it to her.

Images rushed through her head of the antique ring sliding onto her finger, white silk under her hands at her sewing machine, Charlie's sunlit face smiling down at her, a flower-covered arch behind his head. Everything she could ever want was just within reach.

Chapter Two

Heron

"I have to tell you something."

Heron paused *13 Going on 30* and told Bea about finding the ring in Charlie's socks. It had been a week and she thought she might burst if she didn't tell someone, but she didn't want it to get back to Charlie that she knew. Maggie would promise to keep it a secret but hung out with so many of the same people as Charlie, she might let something slip inadvertently. Movie night with Bea, just the two of them, was the perfect opportunity to get it off her chest. Anyway, in most ways Bea was her closest friend, despite the age difference.

Bea blinked, taking a long moment to speak. "Oh, Heron, are you sure that's what it was? You said you only got a quick look."

"It's pretty hard to mistake a diamond ring, Bea."

Bea took her feet off the coffee table and sat up straighter. "Oh. Okay. Wow. And you'll say yes if he asks you?"

"Of course I will. What else would I say?"

"I don't know, 'Let's wait a couple of years, I love you but I'm not sure I should marry my first serious boyfriend, if it's right now it will still be right later.'"

Heron refilled her glass from the pitcher of sangria sitting on the coffee table in front of them. "First of all, Charlie isn't my first serious boyfriend. Remember Dave? You called our decision to break up when he left for college in Seattle 'mature and sensible.' Second, if it's going to be right later, then it's right now." She twisted the afghan in her hands. She needed Bea to see how much better it would be for her when everything was settled with Charlie, after promises were made and she could relax and start looking forward to the future. "And third, well, can't you just be happy for me, Bea? Isn't this what every little girl dreams of, a perfect happily ever after?"

Bea answered only by scrunching up her face.

"Come on. You showed me all those Disney movies when I was little and said you loved them when you were my age. Didn't you want your own handsome prince to sweep you off your feet?"

When Heron was a teenager, they'd switched to rom-coms. She had once asked what the appeal was for Bea, with her cynicism about things like love at first sight. Bea said she spent so much time thinking about the grand machinations of the universe, sometimes it was nice to watch something lighthearted, silly, and guaranteed to have a happy ending. Understandable, but Heron wondered if her cousin might be a closet romantic after all. No one watches *Sleepless in Seattle* that many times if they don't believe in love.

Bea shrugged. "Maybe I saw myself in those stories when I was very young. But pretty soon it became clear that everyone thought I had more in common with the hippo from *Fantasia*."

"Bea. That's not true. You're lovely and smart and anyone would be lucky to have you."

"It is, and it's fine. That hippo is doing great. She's happy. She has a flourishing ballet career. And you know, I did date quite a bit in grad school."

"You never told me."

"It wasn't worth mentioning. Mostly guys who were happy to fool around but didn't seem to want to be seen out with me. There was one guy in my doctoral program who clearly just wanted to pair up with someone who'd help keep his notes in order. Honestly, who needs it? Herschel is all the male energy I need around here." Bea turned to scratch the chin of the burly orange tabby sprawled across the back of the couch.

Her cousin said things like this often, but this house must feel empty sometimes with Bea and the cat as the only occupants. Next year, when Heron wasn't around for evenings like this, wouldn't Bea be terribly lonely? It sounded like she'd run into a few duds, but that wasn't a reason to stop trying. She'd stopped fretting about her dad since he'd fallen for Toni, and she never worried about her mother, but Bea was another story. Bea was so formidable, but she had a tender side few besides Heron ever saw. She needed someone who made her as happy as Charlie made Heron.

Bea pressed play. They watched a few more minutes of the movie before she gestured at Mark Ruffalo's character and said, "Look at this smug jackass, for instance. Totally stuck in perpetual adolescence. Not even movie boyfriends are worth the trouble."

"Huh. He looks a bit like Professor Addison."

"'Professor' Addison. Yeah, he does. Right down to the hipster t-shirt." Bea snorted. "Speaking of perpetual adolescents."

"I like him."

"You don't know him the way I do." Bea's eyebrows lowered, darkening her expression. She'd been snarky about Ben ever since he started working at the library. Heron knew Bea and Ben had been students together and she'd always had the impression there was a deeper history, but her cousin had never elaborated. Now that Heron knew Bea had been cagey about her romantic history, a possible explanation occurred to her.

"Bea! You didn't have, like, a thing with Ben Addison. Did you?"

Bea's eruption of laughter drowned out the movie, but there was a bitter edge to it. "A thing? No. Absolutely not. Far from it. Why would you think that?"

"I don't know. Just asking, gosh. Let's keep watching the movie." Heron picked up the remote and rewound the bit they'd missed.

But she did know what had given her the idea. It was abundantly clear to Heron that Bea had strong feelings about Ben Addison. When his name came up, she always had a biting comment. She wouldn't behave that way if she were simply ambivalent toward him. If Heron could get to the bottom of what, exactly, those feelings were, and get Bea to admit to it, maybe Bea would back off from being so judgmental about Charlie. Besides, on the off chance there was some fondness buried under all the vitriol, maybe it wouldn't be such a bad thing to try to tease it out.

Bea

Bea considered Heron's question as she got ready for bed. The truth was, there had been a time, years ago, when she did have feelings for Ben Addison. Maybe she should have been more open with Heron about her history with him, but every time she considered explaining it, she shied away. Bea talked a good game about self-acceptance, but a small piece of her was embarrassed it had happened at all — and that it hurt her badly enough to still want to avoid the person responsible. She'd also withheld the information to protect Heron. Her cousin's sensitivity and capacity for empathy were some of her best qualities, but Bea knew she would be upset and there was just no reason to unnecessarily distress her.

Up until their senior year, Bea'd been under the impression that she got along fine with Ben and his fraternity brothers. Her sorority often paired with the SODs for social events, and Bea had been in several classes with Ben because they were both history minors. He was funny and cute in a scruffy way, driven and smart, a straight-A student and president of the fraternity, but also artsy and acerbic. Bea found this combination of qualities intriguing.

As they studied together for a test on gender in ancient Greece, she even thought he'd been flirting with her a little. She'd been harshly disabused of the notion when Trish Elm, the president of her sorority and a pearl-clutching go-getter she'd never especially liked, flung Bea's dorm room door open while she napped off an all-nighter and declared, "I'm so sorry about all of this, Bea, you must be absolutely crushed. Don't worry, I've already demanded a formal apology."

Bea rubbed the daytime sleep out of her eyes. "What?"

Trish thrust a bright yellow photocopy of the SOD's monthly newsletter under Bea's nose. The photocopied letter was often illustrated with little doodles. On the calendar, next to an event scheduled with Bea's sorority, there was a cartoon of a cow in a dress among a pile of beer cans and pizza slices, with the caption, "Maybe you can drink her cute, but you can't drink her skinny." The cow wore cat-eye glasses with stars in the corners, just like Bea's.

At the sorority's next chapter meeting, Ben stood in front of the group to deliver a vague, wooden apology read from an index card while Bea, burning with humiliation, willed the powder-blue carpet to open and swallow her. It seemed each pair of eyes in the room effortlessly looked anywhere but at her. She felt the harsh glare of their attention anyway, and it was awful.

It wasn't the first or last time someone had tried to make Bea feel bad about her body, but it was the most public. She would never forget what it felt like to be the object of everyone's rubbernecking pity. Although she knew she'd be able to dredge up enough cold courtesy to work with Ben, she could never forgive him for being the cause. She could be civil, but forgiveness wasn't on the table.

By Sunday evening, when Bea left to pick Heron up for family dinner, she'd put Ben and the committee assignment temporarily out of her mind. She wanted to talk to Heron about her next steps after senior year: grad school applications, internships, career paths. Heron had been withdrawn all summer. Charlie spent school breaks back east with his family, and she tended to get edgy when they were separated, but this time had been worse than usual. Now that he was back, Heron was coming out of her funk and Bea didn't want to wait much longer to talk about post-graduation plans. The drive out to the vineyard would be the perfect opportunity.

She'd been making this drive on Sundays for many years now. When Bea was an undergrad, her Uncle Len and his first wife, Felicia, would occasionally invite her out to their place—at that time just a simple farmhouse—for dinner and to sample Len's first batches of wine. Even though she was at the farm often to babysit preschool-aged Heron, the dinners were a nice gesture, giving Bea a break from dining hall food.

When she'd returned to Millet after grad school, Sunday dinners became a weekly event, only it was Bea who handled the food, turning up with a pot of soup or a lasagna. It had only been a few months since Felicia's departure, and even though no one had died the house had taken on a funereal aura of shocked sadness. Bea felt obligated to make sure Len and Heron were eating something resembling a real meal at least once a week. It seemed important to get them sitting down together at their own table.

They'd continued the tradition after Heron enrolled at Messiman. At first it was the three of them, but then Heron started inviting the winery's new chef, Toni, to join them, telling Bea that she missed her mom, but she'd picked up on a spark and didn't want her dad to be alone. Since Toni and Len's wedding a year ago, it had been the four of them gathered around the table with good wine and better food.

Tonight was going to be perfect. The air had a late-summer cider wash, golden and crisp. With a week of classes behind them, Heron and Bea were settled into their respective routines but not totally wrapped up in academic stress yet.

Bea pulled up to the curb at the columned hulk of Heron's apartment building. While she waited, she let herself drift into the dreamy lyrics of her folk-pop playlist. She was yanked out of her musical reverie when both passenger-side doors of her car opened. Charlie plopped into the front next to her and scooted the seat all the way back with all the space-taking confidence of a twenty-two-year-old man, an unruly collection of floppy blonde hair, tanned hairy knees, elbows, and aftershave. Heron climbed into the backseat, laying a garment bag down on the empty half.

In the rearview mirror, Bea caught her eye and raised a brow.

At least Heron had the grace to look sheepish. "Sorry. I forgot to tell you Charlie was invited this week."

"Great!" Bea pushed a bright tone into her voice. "Hi, Charlie." Charlie's galumphing presence was going to put a damper on her plan to discuss Heron's future.

"Hi, Dr. Hayes," Charlie said with a guileless grin. "I heard you got Dr. Stein's old office. Congratulations. That must be a nice change."

Bea rolled her eyes at Charlie's attempt to suck up. He'd been in her entry-level class two years ago and had visited her old, closet-sized office to ask a question about chemical differentiation. Bea suspected he understood the concept just fine but thought it was a good idea to ingratiate himself with his girlfriend's family.

"Thanks. It is. I even have room for a coffee maker." One trait Bea and Charlie shared was a teasing disdain for the caffeinated beverage habits of Heron and Len, who only drank tea (loose leaf if at all possible) and could wax poetic for several minutes at a time about the different flavor profiles of blends which, to Bea, all tasted exactly the same and more like dishwater than something she might want to drink on purpose. At least Charlie liked coffee.

Heron leaned forward and squeezed Charlie's shoulder. "Charlie's been great, helping Maggie and me get settled in. He even installed some shelves in the kitchen. And you should see the lights he put up in my window. They make the room look enchanted."

"It's just a set of string lights. My parents bought them for their gazebo but then decided they'd rather have something hardwired." Charlie's words were humble, but he sounded pleased with himself.

"I'm sure they're lovely," Bea said, glancing again at Heron in the rearview mirror. Her elbow was propped on the car door, chin resting in her hand, and she'd rolled the window down half an inch, creating a breeze that ruffled the top of her sable-brown hair.

They were outside of town now, ripples of bronze wheat rushing past the windows, the sun just starting to make its way toward the horizon. Turning under the arch announcing Heron Acres Vineyards, they passed a few cars with Oregon plates on their way out. No doubt last-minute tasters who'd stayed until closing.

Charlie was out of the car before she even engaged the parking brake. "Think your dad's in the cellars? I want to ask him about some stuff." Not waiting for an answer, he pecked Heron on the cheek and loped across the gravel lot to the winery building.

Bea caught Heron's eye across the roof of the car. Heron's expression was neutral, but there was a grin in her voice. "Could be about anything."

"Sure it could." While Heron skipped upstairs clutching her garment bag, Bea went to the kitchen to find Toni, smiling despite her misgivings about Charlie. Heron's good mood was contagious.

Heron

Heron was at the sewing table in her childhood bedroom when her father came in from the cellars to find her. Aside from the things she'd taken for her apartment, not much about this room had changed for as long as she could remember. The brass daybed was still covered with a quilt her mother had made when she transitioned out of her crib, a broken star pattern in pink and yellow florals, as well as the stuffed animals she couldn't bear to put away in the closet. The sewing machine, a castoff from her mother, sat at its own table in the corner and the walls were decorated with Audrey Hepburn posters, the remnant of a preteen phase. While her friends had been tacking boy bands to their walls, Heron had been thrilled to find a poster from the original release of *My Fair Lady*.

"Hi, Birdie," her dad said, tapping on the threshold before he entered. "We're all having drinks on the patio."

"Be there in a minute. I just want to finish this hem."

"Ah. You and your mom, such marvels with sewing." He hadn't mentioned her mother in a long time. They usually avoided the subject by unspoken mutual agreement.

"Well. She likes what she's doing now," Heron said. For the past few years, Felicia had been working as a seamstress for an upscale Seattle department store.

"I suppose it suits her."

"Sure. Me too. This was the first dress I made on my own, remember?"

Finished, she disengaged it from the machine and held it up for him to see—silvery silk with a trailing botanical pattern in inky indigo thread. Heron had worn it to homecoming her senior year of high school and was transforming it into something she could wear as a more grown-up cocktail dress, shortening the skirt and reworking the bodice. It had been strapless, but the material she removed to make it knee-length had been enough to add cap sleeves with a keyhole back, even after she cut around the grass stains. Heron wondered now if she'd even recognize the girl she'd been when she wore the first version; hiding her pain behind recklessness, tumbling through the night with a boy nothing like Charlie.

"I don't know anything about dresses, but that looks pretty to me."

"I thought it would be good for the reunion reception, if you still need me to come help. Charlie says he can help, too." Events were a new venture for the vineyard; next month they'd be hosting the fifteen-year reunion for Bea's graduating class.

"Thanks, honey. It's nice of Charlie to let us put him to work."

"I think he wants you to see him as part of the family." Charlie's earnest insistence on participating in her family business to get on her dad's good side was so endearing.

"He's a good kid," he said, "but I don't want you to settle down too fast, okay? You know your old Dad isn't too old-fashioned. I don't think there's anything wrong with living together before marriage and I'd rather you take your time to be sure."

Heron concentrated on zipping the dress into its garment bag so her father wouldn't see the irritation on her face. "Have you been talking to Bea?"

"A little. We just want you to think things through carefully."

"Dad. We've been together almost three years. You and mom had me by the time mom was my age, and you'd only been together—" Heron stopped talking when she saw her father's brows draw together abruptly, reminding her this bit of family lore wasn't a fairy tale anymore. But she and Charlie were nothing like her parents. Charlie was solid, she was constant. They made sense. No one was going to drive him away from her. Besides, Len had Toni now and Felicia seemed happy in the city. Everyone was all squared away; there was nothing to worry about. "Anyway, Charlie and I have been together long enough to know we're a good match."

"I know, sweetheart. Don't get so certain the path you're on is right that you forget to look around and wonder where the other ones go, okay?"

"Okay."

They'd had conversations like this before. Her dad was trying to take responsibility for his part in what had happened with her mother. He felt he'd tied Felicia down to a farm and a family too fast, and so when she left it was his fault. Heron supposed she could understand why he saw parallels with her and Charlie, but this was totally different. She knew exactly what she was choosing. Besides, although she could never tell him, she knew Felicia's reasons for leaving had nothing to do with how quickly they'd married.

Bea

The stars were out in full force by the time they were driving back into Millet. This far away from town, the Milky Way spilled across the sky like cream poured into coffee. Bea never got tired of this. When she bought her house in one of the tree-lined neighborhoods near Messiman, she'd wanted something close to campus for the sake of practicality, but even in a small town the lights were bright enough to obscure fainter stars. There were state-of-the-art telescopes on the roof of the science building, but sometimes she drove out into the surrounding farmland, simply to watch the naked sky. She'd fallen asleep in a random wheat field on more than one occasion.

The row of student houses was quiet, lights on in most of the windows. A few students sat on their porches with laptops. The computers were sleeker, but not much else had changed about Sunday nights since Bea's time as a student. This street would be a whirl of parties and music on Friday and Saturday, but by Sunday night the red plastic cups were picked up, hangovers nursed, and studies resumed.

She stopped the car in front of the SOD house. "Nice to see you, Charlie. Take care."

Charlie opened his mouth as if to protest, say he'd be spending the night at Heron's anyway, but when she gave him her best teacher look, he closed it abruptly and got out of the car. Bea continued down the block and found a parking place across from Heron's building.

"Do you want to come see my new place?" Heron said.

"Yes! My friend Louise lived in this building our senior year and I bet it looks exactly the same."

Heron wrinkled her nose. "Probably. I doubt it's changed since long before your time." As soon as they hit the foyer, the smell of musty carpet, old paint, and ramen seasoning transported Bea back in time. Heron ushered her up the ornate staircase and into her apartment. The living room was cavernous, tall ceilings with large windows on two sides, and decorative molding around the baseboards. The makeshift student furnishings — some battered seating, a few wire shelves, a card table with folding chairs — were dwarfed by the space.

Heron's roommate was curled on a papasan chair under a Mary Cassatt print, a highlighter clenched between her teeth as she squinted at a dog-eared copy of Moby Dick.

"Hi Bea," Maggie grinned. Like Charlie, Maggie took Bea's intro-level class as a freshman, but since then had tagged along with Heron to enough of their movie nights to be comfortable on a first-name basis. Bea had always liked Maggie for not treating her too much like a teacher.

"Hey, Maggie. A little light reading?"

Maggie grimaced. "For my thesis. I'm trying to get ahead of it before too many papers are due for my regular classes."

"Smart."

Bea followed Heron into a little galley kitchen that seemed to have been carved out of a hallway. "Do you want tea?" Heron was already filling the kettle. Bea shook her head. "Maggie, tea?" Heron called.

"Yes, please."

Heron busied herself scooping leaves from a tin into the basket of a turquoise teapot, Bea's Christmas gift to her last year. Bea picked up the tin and read, "Lavender coconut. This sounds more like a body wash than something I would want to ingest."

Heron laughed. "It's good. Lavender is a calming herb; you

should try it. My mom sent this—she said she found it in a little tea shop in Pike Place Market."

Of course Felicia had sent a care package. A simple, finite motherly task. But at least it was something. Instead of the snarky comment she wanted to make, Bea gestured at the rest of the kitchen and said, "This isn't bad for a first apartment. It's not stylish but it's everything you need." Heron hadn't been kidding about the datedness; the floor was rust-colored linoleum, and the stove and refrigerator were avocado green, but the beige countertops looked new. Heron and Maggie had decorated with vintage pasta and liquor ads. The olives in the martini glass on their vermouth poster picked up the green from the appliances.

She wandered further down the hall, knowing at a glance which room was Heron's. Six different tarot sets were stacked on top of the bookcase, along with a dish of crystals and semiprecious stones. The shelves were packed with textbooks—Heron was double-majoring in art and sociology, an amount of pressure that made Bea nervous for her, although Heron seemed to be handling the accompanying stress reasonably well. The walls were lined with Cezanne prints Heron had bought freshman year after learning how, because of his focus on balanced composition, Cezanne's landscapes could create a soothing environment.

Bea felt a surge of love for this sweet, starry-eyed young woman. With sixteen years between them, her affection for Heron hovered somewhere between motherly and sisterly with a dash of friendship thrown in for good measure. Now, the little kid who'd sat on her lap and demanded constant repeat performances of *The Rainbow Fish* was almost a fully-fledged adult. Maybe, Bea thought with a flicker of distaste, almost a wife.

Something un-Heronly caught her eye on the desk, and Bea picked it up. "LSAT?" she asked, flicking through the workbook.

"That's Charlie's. I'm helping him study."

Bea set the book down. "I hope you're doing your own studying first."

"I am." Heron sank onto the bed, pulling one of the velvet pillows into her lap. "But Charlie learns better when someone is quizzing him. It's kind of fun. And interesting. I didn't realize there were so many social science overlaps with legal studies."

"Sure. But have you thought about what you're going to do after graduation?" Bea pulled out the desk chair and sat.

"I'll go wherever Charlie picks for law school. New York if everything goes according to plan. And then, just see what job I can find, study for the GRE?"

"You know there are law schools all over the place, right? Is Charlie willing to be flexible about his plans based on what you want to do? You don't have to rush into tying yourself down to a dream that isn't yours."

Heron threw the pillow down and stood, pacing across the room. "I'm not rushing into anything. Why do people keep saying that? Three years of dating is not rushing in."

"All I want is for you to have a little time on your own in the real world, Birdie, before you decide the rest of your life."

Heron turned, squaring her stance. "Not everyone is like you, Bea. I know you love being on your own and that's great. I admire it. Everybody does. But Charlie helps me believe everything isn't going to fall apart. I need that. And I'm so lucky I have him."

Her eyes were bright with frustrated tears, and Bea relented. Heron was right, she hadn't had a major panic attack since she'd been with Charlie, and considering everything she'd been through in high school, that was something. Bea couldn't say he hadn't been good for her. She pulled Heron up into a hug, feeling her take the slow, measured breaths which had become her go-to coping technique.

"Okay, okay. I know, Bird. I know he makes you happy. Just...

think about what else you're going to do next year, all right? Now," she stepped back and patted Heron on the arm, "do your homework."

"Goodnight, Bea."

On her way out, Bea paused on the steps of the apartment building, listening to the muffled music coming from one of Heron's neighbors, someone's laugh spilling out of an open window. It had been a long time since she'd been like these kids, everything ahead of her. She loved her life the way it was, but for a moment she wished she could go back and do it all over again with the confidence she had now.

Chapter Three

Heron

Intent on applying her eye makeup, Heron didn't notice Charlie in the doorway of her room. When she finally saw him in the mirror behind her, she jumped and her eyeliner skipped, leaving a wobbly line. "Dangit!" she said and wet a cotton swab with micellar water to erase it, then started over.

It had been a month since she found the diamond ring in Charlie's things, and nothing. She was still excitedly anticipating his proposal, but it was beginning to feel like something that was lurking around the corner, waiting to spring out at her, and she'd started to doubt what she had seen. Maybe Charlie having a ring didn't mean what she thought it did. But what else could it be? She wished he would get it over with so they could move on to the next stage of planning their wedding and their future together. Poor Charlie, it wasn't his fault. He didn't have any idea she knew about the ring.

"Sorry babe. Maggie let me in."

She met his eyes in the reflection and smiled. "It's okay. Give me one sec." She finished her mascara and stood. "Can you do this up?" Her re-made dress was finished and Heron was pleased with it, but the fabric across the bust was a little too tight for her to easily fasten the button at the top of the keyhole in back. She could reach the zipper, but she'd left it for Charlie because she knew he liked to do it. His left hand wrapped around her hip, holding her steady as he slid the zipper up past the curve of her waist, bending to plant a kiss at the triangle of bare skin between her shoulder blades before he fumbled with the button at the back of her neck.

"You look so beautiful," he said. "I'm a lucky guy."

She spun, basking in his admiration. Her ballet flats made it easier to be graceful. The dress would look better with heels, but she was going to be on her feet all night. "Thanks for helping out tonight."

"I'm happy to." He grinned his affable, melting, Charlie grin. "I think it will be a good chance for me to network with some of the Sig-O-Delt alums. Besides, there will be a lot of eligible men there and I don't want you getting whisked away."

She wrinkled her nose. "They're *old*."

"Lots of men have a wife fifteen years younger. Plus, you're like best friends with Bea. They're her age."

"Yeah, but Bea is...Bea. She's not like other adults."

"Babe, *we're* adults."

"Well, technically. But we're not real-world adults quite yet."

"Sure. I guess some people that age are easier to relate to. Ben, for instance." Besides taking his Book Arts class, Charlie had been spending a lot of time with Ben Addison because he was the alumni advisor for the fraternity. He seemed to be developing a bit of a man-crush.

Heron locked her apartment door and they started down the stairs. "I do like Ben a lot. It's so weird that he and Bea aren't friends. I feel like they share a vibe, don't you?"

He nodded. "Yeah, like, cynic with a heart of gold?" Charlie opened the car door for her, and she slid into the seat.

"Exactly!" So, Charlie saw the spark of potential compatibility between Bea and Ben, too. Interesting. Very interesting.

Bea

Bea was having a ball. The wine flowed freely, the tasting room patio had been turned into a dance floor washed in torchlight and open to the September stars. Graduating classes at Messiman were fewer than five hundred. After four years in a place where there wasn't much to do besides study, hang out on the wide grassy quad, and go to parties, everyone pretty much knew each other. The reception was a gathering of old friends, and it was lovely to catch up. The magic of the evening had been enhanced for Bea by the fact that, in defiance of the odds, she had gotten through cocktail hour and dinner without getting stuck in a conversation with Ben.

She was wearing one of her favorite dresses, a fifties-style cocktail frock in the dusky periwinkle of an early evening sky. Whenever she deviated from her dark, boring teaching wardrobe, Bea chose this retro style because it felt like armor to her. The fitted bodice and full skirt cinched or hid everything she was least comfortable showing off, while the just-plunging-enough V-neck drew attention to the one area of her body that consistently drew positive attention. She'd pinned one side of her hair back, letting the other fall in loose waves, and forgone her usual clear lip balm in favor of a berry-colored lip stain. She'd been getting comments from her classmates all evening about how great the look was for her. Maybe when her tenure was approved and she didn't feel like she had to play it so safe, she'd change up her everyday wardrobe a bit; she should look for some similar styles in daytime fabrics. With higher necklines, she thought, as she picked a macaron crumb out of her cleavage.

The evening was beginning to wind down, as people with children left to retrieve them from the college-provided babysitting services. Bea settled at a table under the toasty umbrella of a propane heater, talking to her friend Louise, whose five-month-old daughter Ada was too little to watch movies in the athletic center with the bigger kids. Three-quarters of her attention was on Louise's story about her first day leaving Ada in daycare to go back to work, the rest was focused on the bar, where Louise's husband, Rob, stood with Ben. Rob's head tipped back in a guffaw at something Ben said. It looked like a courtesy laugh to Bea.

As the hip-hop beat gave way to the reggae organ strains of "No Woman, No Cry," the clusters of dancers began to separate into pairs. Rob set his beer down on the bar and started toward their table, trailed by Ben. Fantastic.

Louise saw them coming too. "Bea, would you hold her for me, please? I need to dance with my husband."

Bea was never comfortable with babies. She was good with preschoolers, a product of spending so much time with Heron at that age, and she got along great with kids once they were old enough to be mesmerized by a picture book or think her half-assed attempts at hide and seek were funny. Infants never seemed to like her very much despite, she often joked, having looked matronly since she was nineteen. But Ada would come in handy as a fifteen-pound shield against Ben, something to give her attention to if he sat down, and oh god, it looked like he was going to. Maybe she could fake the need to step away for a diaper change. "Sure," she held her arms out to accept Ada from Louise, and watched Rob chivalrously lead his wife to the dance floor.

"Wow, that's weird," Ben said with a mock-shudder, scraping a chair away from the table and plopping into it, eyes on Bea and Ada. "It's like seeing a velociraptor cuddle a puppy."

"Fuck off," she mouthed at him over the wispy little head, but there was something about the weight of the baby that couldn't quite keep a smile from the corner of her lips. Her solid, warm heft was comforting.

And, okay, under an objective assessment, Ben cleaned up pretty well. He'd swapped his t-shirt for an untucked white button-down and a gray blazer, both just rumpled enough to look all the better for never having seen an iron. His dark jeans looked new—no holes in sight, and for once he was without his Cubs hat. Even in the low light, Bea could make out the salty strands starting to thread through the dark hair at his temples; she was annoyed to note that they looked good, distinguished, like they'd been placed there on purpose. Of course, he was still wearing Chuck Taylors, leaving Bea's faith in the basically homogenous nature of his closet intact. She was wishing she'd worn sneakers herself. The pinup-style open-toe pumps she had on were reasonably comfortable but had begun to pinch after a couple of hours on the flagstones. Ben wasn't clean-shaven, but it looked like he'd tidied up his beard, leaving the right amount of scruff to contrast with the collar of his shirt. When he scooted closer, he brought the scent of hops and pine with him.

"Charming as always," he said with an arched brow, but he grinned and took a swig of his beer. "Too bad I can't ask you to dance."

"Indeed." She reached up to smooth Ada's blanket.

Like a benign guardian angel who appears right at the

moment you're about to get away with something, Jane Phillips, the Messiman College president, was at Bea's elbow. "Give me that baby," she said, "I've been dying to hold her all night. You two should dance and enjoy yourselves."

Well, shit. If it were anybody else making the suggestion, Bea would demur, but President Phillips would be the ultimate decision-maker on her tenure, and she couldn't afford the appearance of a bad attitude. Unfortunately, Ada, out cold, was all too happy to be passed around. The tiny traitor didn't make a peep when Bea handed her over and reluctantly followed Ben to the dance floor.

Bea's heels put them eye to eye, but she fixed her gaze between Ben's eyebrows as she settled her hands on his shoulders. When he placed his hands on the soft dip at her waist, she flinched, not used to feeling pressure there, worried he would make a snide comment about the squishiness of her midsection. "Sorry," he said softly, "is this better?" Ben slid his hands down a couple of inches to find surer purchase at the top of her hips, guiding her in swaying movements to the gentle reggae beat.

"Sure," she said, willing some of the tension out of her body so he wouldn't think she was uptight about basic human contact. Over Ben's shoulder she saw Heron and Charlie dancing, too. With Heron in flats, Charlie was more than a head taller, and he bent at a near-comical angle to bury his face in the hair at her neck.

Ben's mouth was near her ear. "We've danced to this song before, do you remember?"

She remembered, but she was surprised Ben did. A frat party junior year. Then, they'd been friendly, she'd thought Ben was funny and cool, and being close to him had been thrilling, the intense heat of his hands through her clothes and the gentler warmth building up in the space between their bodies igniting her with possibilities. Definitely not like tonight. Nope. No heat or possibilities here. It was only a few months after their long-ago dance that any bubble of infatuation she was harboring for Ben had been unceremoniously popped. Now, any heat she felt when she was in his proximity could be attributed to simple physics.

"Yeah," she said, pulling back to look him in the eye. "I didn't know you well enough yet."

His bark of laughter broke the couples near them out of their slow-dance reveries as they shot annoyed looks at Bea and Ben. "Right," he said. "Of course." He leaned in to pull her closer and they swayed in silence for a few measures before he said, "I'm probably lucky there weren't more dances. Saved me some tears, I'm sure." He sang along with Bob Marley, softly but with a pointed edge when he got to the chorus.

She let an indignant gasp break the tension. The absolute nerve. Saved him some tears? What about hers? She'd cried a few because of him. Besides, his interpretation of the lyrics was patently wrong. "That's not what he's saying. He's telling his love not to cry."

"Then why isn't the song 'don't cry?'" His mouth was at her ear and his grip on her hips had shifted to her lower back, narrowing the space between them so that their chests were touching. Bea's heart was thudding, and she hoped Ben couldn't feel it. If she couldn't feel his, she was probably safe, right?

"I don't know. I'm not an expert on patois."

"You're not?" he said. "I thought you were an expert in everything."

She snorted. "I thought that was your thing. 'Postmodern renaissance man' and so on." She pulled back to look him in the eyes, hands braced on his shoulders. "I guess I'd feel like I needed to compensate, too, if I were you."

Ben stepped away and the places on her body where his hands had been suddenly cooled. The song was over, and he had steered her neatly to the edge of the dance floor where he could deposit her at the bar.

"Right. I suppose you would," he said. "Thanks for the dance."

He picked a beer up from the bar, and when he turned back to her, the vulnerable crack in his demeanor was gone. And then, so was Ben. He turned and strode off toward Louise and Rob, who had retrieved Ada from President Phillips. He said something and they all laughed. Bea ordered a whisky from the bartender.

Heron

When the music slowed, Charlie reached for Heron. She nestled her cheek against his chest. She loved not having to cast her eyes around for a slow-dance partner. Here he was, right within reach. How amazing was that?

"Having a good time?" he murmured in her ear.

She tipped her head back to look at him. "The best. You?"

"Yeah. I got to talk to one of the Sig-O-Delt alums here with Bates Scanlon Lewis. They're one of the bigger conglomerate firms. This guy is with the Denver office, which would be awesome."

"That's great, babe." Charlie had been networking all night. She loved how even while he was working at the party, he was also looking for opportunities to advance his future. Their future.

"He gave me his card and told me to call him when I'm looking for summer internships. He said they like to meet stable upstanding young people to add to their team. He and his wife are still here. See them over there at the table next to the bar?"

Charlie guided Heron a little to the right so she could see the man, dressed in an expensive-looking suit, being handed a drink in a rocks glass by an immaculately groomed woman in a dark sheath dress and pearls.

"Maybe you can talk to him again later," she said.

He smoothed a strand of hair back into her bun. "I'd rather talk to you."

Heron let Charlie steer her along on the current of the music. His arms felt so strong around her. She had almost forgotten about the ring. It shouldn't matter, really. She knew he was here, her constant. He would ask when the moment felt right but it was already clear she'd be his forever.

Past Charlie's shoulder, she saw her cousin over by the bar. Bea and Ben had looked good dancing together; Bea relaxed and pretty in her dress, Ben laughing. Of course she adored Bea and the more she got to know Ben in class, the more she liked him, too. They were so similar — smart, witty, sarcastic on the surface but warm and caring underneath. There wasn't any good reason for them not to at least be friends.

Heron closed her eyes as Charlie guided her movements. The song was a ballad about being just kids when they fell in love and building a life together. It described how she felt about Charlie perfectly. They were young, but they knew exactly what they wanted. They were so lucky they hadn't had to wait to find it. Suddenly, the solid warmth of Charlie's arms was gone. She opened her eyes, surprised at the loss. Charlie lowered himself to one knee and pulled the diamond ring out of his pocket. He held it toward her like a tribute to a goddess.

The DJ lowered the music. Charlie's voice rang out at a volume the whole party would be able to hear. "Heron Hunter, you're amazing: your beauty, your warmth, your kindness, the way you take care of me and others. I want us to step into the next chapter of our lives together. Will you do me the extreme honor of being my wife?"

It was a good thing she found the ring weeks ago, because even though she'd expected this to happen and been desperate for it, she was stunned speechless. It was overwhelming. The starlight, the music, the wine, Charlie so handsome in his suit, everyone watching them. Her heart fluttered and her knees faltered. All she wanted was his arms around her again. Pressing her right hand to her heart, she nodded and gave him her left. Charlie slid the ring on as applause rang out around them. The gold was warm from Charlie's pocket, and it nestled comfortably at the base of her finger as if it had always belonged there. He pulled her hand to his lips to kiss it and she guided him up, sinking into him again as soon as he was upright.

She stood on tiptoe to whisper "I love you," into his ear, and then eased into his arms.

Bea

As she watched Heron and Charlie embrace, wistfulness welled behind Bea's eyes, mingled with relief. She'd been waiting for this ever since Heron had told her about the ring and had begun to wonder when he was going to get it over with already. It made her happy to see Heron happy. Her cousin was undeniably dancing on a cloud of bliss, melting into her newly minted fiancé's arms, but as the deep blue opacity of Charlie's suit eclipsed Heron's ethereal dress, Bea ached for the lost possibilities represented by the ring sparkling on her finger. She knew her cousin loved Charlie and was sure he loved her, too, but marriage was so final. At thirty-seven, Bea couldn't imagine wanting to tie herself to another person and all their plans for the future, forever. How could Heron be sure at only twenty-two?

Heron and Charlie finished their dance and as the next up-tempo song began, they accumulated an entourage; men clapping Charlie on the back and joking about the old ball and chain, women clutching at Heron's hand to examine the ring. Bea ordered another whisky and followed them over to where Len and Toni were in excited conversation with Ben, Louise, Rob, and

President Phillips. As she joined the fringes of their group, Bea picked up the thread of the conversation.

"It's so romantic," Louise said, as she bent to examine Heron's hand. Bea made a mental note to say something complimentary about the ring later.

"Lovely," said President Phillips. "Did you know seventy-five percent of Messiman alumni marry other Messiman alums?"

"It worked out for us," said Rob, kissing his wife on the cheek. "You're smart to stake your claim on this one, Charlie."

"I know," Charlie said, sliding his arm around Heron's waist. "She's the sweetest girl in the world."

"Certainly the sweetest in her family," Ben said, "present company excluded, Toni." He winked at Heron's stepmom before cutting his eyes toward Bea. "If you all will excuse me, I can't handle any more acid burns tonight." Ben retrieved his beer from the table and strode off to the edge of the party, where the horizon of the lantern-lit dance floor bled into the inky abyss of the vineyard.

Heron gave Bea a questioning eyebrow raise, and Bea answered with a slight shake of her head to say it was nothing, reaching her arms out. "Congratulations, Birdie," she said, encompassing Heron in a hug. "You too, Charlie." Charlie was a surprisingly earnest hugger, not squeezing her too tightly or giving the kind of light, perfunctory embrace that is mostly for show. "I hope you both have many happy years together."

"We just have to get you settled down, Bea," said Toni.

Toni was still in the dewy, newlywed stage, where all she wanted was for everyone to be as happily coupled as she was. Len was still in the throes of newlywed bliss too, but he knew Bea well enough not to suggest she abandon spinsterhood.

Bea snorted. "Hell no. I am far too set in my curmudgeonly ways. Anyone who is age-appropriate for me and is not also set in his own curmudgeonly ways simply isn't someone I would care to associate with. No," — she continued amidst the group's laughter—"the only person who would put up with me at this point would be a complete doormat, and I"—she sipped her drink for emphasis—"can't imagine a worse fate than living with a doormat. Fortunately for me, I don't need one. I have my family." She beamed at Heron, Len and Toni, and Charlie, for he was going to be her family now, too, and she'd better get used to it. She cast her gaze upward. "I have the stars. I have my students. I have a beautiful house. I have a cat and I may eventually acquire six or seven more. Half the neighborhood children are convinced I'm a witch, which is great. By the time I'm fifty I'm sure all of them will be and then Halloween will be a total blast. How could any of that be improved by a man? And even if I thought it could, who on earth would have me?"

President Phillips patted her on the shoulder. "Never say never. I didn't get married until I was forty-five."

Yes, but Jane Phillips was married to a woman, an entirely different circumstance and one Bea sometimes wished was an option for her. But as appealing as the idea of a marriage to a career-oriented, like-minded woman was—Jane's wife, Kelly, was a surgeon; they were a real power couple—Bea had never found herself attracted to women. Besides, President Phillips' marriage had its own complications. Her stepson Jason was a frequent topic of faculty grumbling. Even sweet Heron didn't have anything nice to say about him. Bea was glad the little snot was graduating this year, although she supposed the completion of his degree was no guarantee he'd be out of Jane's hair come June. Even perfect matches sometimes came with strings.

Looking at the cluster of bemused candlelit faces around her, five married people and two only minutes into their engagement, Bea realized she may not exactly have a sympathetic audience.

In a softer tone than she'd used before, consciously avoiding any edge of bitterness, she said, "I'm merely saying marriage isn't for everyone, and isn't for me." She chuckled. "To the great relief of the male population of Millet, I am sure. Will you all excuse me?"

Under a chorus of nods and murmured pleasantries, Bea departed with a slight stumble.

Heron

"Have you two thought about setting a date?" Louise asked. "Rob and I got engaged at graduation, but we lived together for a couple of years before the actual wedding. We wanted to finish grad school first."

Heron felt a blush rise in her cheeks. She'd been thinking about this since she found the ring, but of course they hadn't had a chance to talk about it. She gave Charlie a questioning look.

"Soon?" Charlie said.

"Soon," she answered, glad he didn't want to wait until after he was done with law school.

"Certainly not until after graduation." Her father's tone was firm.

"No sir," said Charlie.

"What about graduation weekend, then?" said Heron. "I'm sure our friends will come no matter when it is, but it would be nice to do it when they're all still here."

"That sounds good to me," said Charlie. "I'll talk to my folks."

Right, Charlie's parents. She was going to have in-laws soon. When she'd met them at parents' weekend, they seemed like perfectly nice people, if a little stiff, but the idea that they were about to be her family members was strange.

"Well, congratulations, you two." President Phillips stood, gathering her handbag and wrap. "This has been a lovely event, Len, Toni. You have a beautiful facility here. Messiman is lucky to have your family as part of our community. And Beatrice! I knew she was a great teacher, but I had no idea she was so funny."

"Funny if you like misandry," said Rob, under his breath.

Louise's brows drew together, "What do you mean, honey?"

"Look, I like Bea, but she's always been pretty snide about men. It gets a bit old."

Heron flinched. This wasn't a fair assessment of Bea at all. She had plenty of male friends. She could be a little prickly, that was all. Rob was probably biased because he was friends with Ben.

While Heron was formulating a defense of her cousin, Louise spoke up to say, "She prefers being single. There's nothing wrong with that."

"Hmm." President Phillips looked thoughtful. "What a shame. I saw her dancing with Ben Addison earlier and she looked like she was enjoying herself. I think they'd make a lovely couple."

"Ha!" Louise erupted, startling Ada. "They'd murder each other within a week."

"That's true," Heron said. "I've never known her to have it in for anyone the way she does for Ben. What's that all about?" If anyone knew, it would be Louise. This was her chance to find out more.

"Well," Louise said, "she never did forgive him for that ugly cartoon in the SOD newsletter."

This was the first Heron had heard of a cartoon. Could there be a concrete reason for Bea's grudge? If so, why hadn't Bea ever told her about it?

Before she could ask for more details, Rob said, "That's such crap. It was one guy who was responsible for the stupid thing, our social chair Mike, who was a total douche, and he only did it because—" Rob seemed to think better of what he was about to say and closed his mouth.

The others looked at him expectantly. Louise raised a brow.

"Well? Out with it, hon."

Rob sighed, clearly outnumbered. "Because he was giving Ben shit. He knew Ben had a thing for Bea."

Wow. Heron was so used to Bea speaking about Ben as an arch nemesis. This was it then, the something between them Heron had been picking up on. She should have been surprised, but somehow, it made sense.

Charlie didn't seem taken aback, either. "Maybe he still does." Now it was Charlie's turn on the hot seat, as all heads swiveled in his direction. He explained, "I met with Ben yesterday to talk about some SOD administrative stuff. He asked if I knew whether Bea was bringing a date tonight."

Interesting. The length and vigor of Bea's rant about how Ben had probably based his entire aesthetic on Mark Ruffalo's hipster movie character had been…remarkably detailed for someone who didn't like him much. Heron asked Louise, "Do you think Bea had a crush on Ben, too?"

"She definitely did." Louise was quick to answer. "Back then, at least. She never said it in so many words, but believe me, I know our Beatrice pretty well."

They all pondered this information for a moment. Except for Ada, who burbled out a little white froth of spit-up, then smacked her lips and went back to sleep.

"So…" said Toni, as everyone watched Rob dip a napkin in a water glass to wipe his daughter's face.

Heron would be wedding planning soon enough and wasn't looking forward to more cautionary lectures from Bea, like the one she'd gotten a few weeks ago. If Bea were absorbed in her own love affair, maybe she'd be distracted enough to ease up a bit. Besides, a companion might keep her from being too lonely after Heron left Millet next year. And if Bea and Ben had fallen out as students because of a silly misunderstanding, it wouldn't be a bad thing to try to set things right now, would it?

"What if we do something about it? Look. They're both stubborn." This was met with a murmur of agreement. "If they have feelings for each other, neither of them is going to make the first move. Unless—"

"Unless they each know the other is receptive." Charlie finished her sentence and she beamed at him. Of course he was on her page.

"I'm sure I can pique their interest."

"I bet you can," said her father. At his side, Toni winked at her.

Heron's matchmaking had become a bit of a family joke, but what was wrong with being good at bringing people together? Helping people avoid loneliness warmed Heron's heart. Who couldn't use a little more love? And who deserved it more than Bea? "We only have to plant a few seeds," she said.

"And nurture the soil, create the right conditions for them to grow," added her dad, predictably extending her agriculture metaphor.

"Exactly. Charlie and I are spending a lot of time with Ben in the Libratory this quarter, and I already see Bea a lot."

"You and I will both be spending some time with Bea, wedding planning, honey," Toni added, squeezing Heron's arm. "I'm sure we can drop a few hints."

President Phillips cleared her throat, bringing Heron back down to earth. She'd been carried away and forgotten the company they were in. Around the table, she saw the others rearrange their expressions into innocence. In the flicker of the candlelight there was still an air of mischief, but they all looked like naughty children expecting a scolding. Heron stifled a nervous giggle.

"What the hell," the college president said, setting her purse back down and leaning in. "They are both going to Portland next month for a higher education symposium. I've got a request on my desk from Ben to check out a college fleet vehicle. But" — her voice was merry — "it might be fiscally responsible of me to deny it since Beatrice is driving her own car and will be getting reimbursed for mileage. That will give them four hours in the car to work through their differences."

Heron's dad chuckled. "Jane, you dark horse."

President Phillips deadpanned, "It's simply responsible stewardship of college resources."

Heron made a conscious effort to keep her jaw from dropping open. Who would have guessed the stuffy college administrator had a mischievous streak?

"I'm sorry we have to go back to Seattle tomorrow and will miss all the fun," said Louise, "but maybe we can get the ball rolling this weekend. Starting with giving Miss Tipsy over there a ride home." She inclined her head toward Bea, who sat near the DJ, gazing into the middle distance with a glazed expression and slightly slumped posture Heron recognized from the time they'd split a magnum of champagne to celebrate her twenty-first birthday.

"Good plan," said Charlie. "I can drive her back here to get her car tomorrow."

Heron squeezed his hand. "Aw, thanks babe."

As Louise went to retrieve Bea, Heron leaned back against Charlie's chest. What a good team they made.

Chapter Four

Bea

Bea allowed Rob and Louise to guide her to their car. She was more intoxicated than she'd intended to be, and grateful for the ride home. The satin lining of her dress slid on the leather of their back seat as she fumbled to fasten her seatbelt.

Louise was buckling Ada into her car seat next to Bea. "You need me to do you next?"

"Very funny." Bea yanked the filmy layer of skirt that was getting in the way aside and slid the buckle home. "I have it."

Rob got into the passenger seat, sliding it toward her knees. "Enough room back there?"

"I'm fine." She'd only seen him have a couple of beers, but since Louise was breastfeeding and hadn't been drinking at all, it made sense for her to drive. So sensible. Bea felt a surge of affection for her practical friends, which she drunkenly articulated as, "So responsible. So nice. You're nice too, Rob."

Louise twisted in her seat after she started the car, and said, in a voice Bea had heard her use on Ada earlier in the evening. "Okay honey, why don't you just close your eyes and take a little nap?"

Bea stuck her tongue out.

The baby's sleepy gurgles made Bea feel sleepy too, and the headlight-lit fences and fields flashing past the window made her queasy, so she closed her eyes.

Louise and Rob must have thought she was asleep, because Louise said, "Nice to catch up with Ben."

"Yeah. He's a good guy."

"I didn't get to talk to him much. How's he doing?"

"Great. It's a nice fit for him here. More stable than what he'd been doing in Chicago, but he still gets to do some creative things. He mentioned it's been...interesting to see Bea around campus."

"Oh yeah?"

"I think he's still carrying a torch for her, after all these years."

Bea's eyes snapped open. Realizing Louise could probably see her in the rearview mirror, she closed them again and emitted a soft snore she hoped sounded convincing.

"Wow. That seems like him, though." Louise sounded pensive. "Just a solid guy, doesn't do things on whims."

Solid my ass. It took all of Bea's willpower to stay still and keep her eyes closed.

"Poor bastard. Obviously barking up the wrong tree," Rob said.

Louise laughed. "Bea's great, but she's not exactly the forgiving type. I think Ben's pretty much been dead to her since senior year."

Damn right he had, and for good reason.

"That's a shame."

"It really is."

Louise pulled up in front of Bea's house and turned back to shake Bea's knee. "Sweetie? You're home."

Bea thought she made a pretty good show of pretending to startle awake. She gathered her purse and shoes from the floorboards and made her way, barefoot, up her front walk. After she unlocked her door, she turned to wave at Louise and Rob. As they drove off, she heard Louise's giggle trickling from the driver's side window. For a moment, she longed for someone to laugh about a party with on the way home. She'd meant what she said earlier about being content on her own, wholeheartedly. What she sometimes missed was the platonic ideal of a partner. Pragmatically, she knew such a person didn't exist for her, and the wrong fit would be much worse than being occasionally lonesome.

Herschel met her in the entryway, winding himself around her legs. She filled his dish with kibble before changing into an ancient Messiman t-shirt and the galaxy-print cotton pajama pants Heron had made for her last year. Bea knew she would sleep better if she let herself sober up a little before she tried to go to bed. Grabbing a can of sparkling water from the fridge, she padded out onto her porch and settled onto her cushion-covered swing, draping an afghan over her legs and pulling her feet up under herself to keep them warm.

She'd left the door ajar and a few minutes later, Herschel followed her out, springing up next to her before placing first one front paw, then the second, onto her belly, leaning in for a few thorough kneads before he climbed the rest of the way onto her lap and settled in, purring. Bea reached up to scratch the extra-soft fur behind his ears. "Hi pal," she said, as he extended his nose to touch her chin.

As she waited for her head to clear, Bea stroked Herschel's

back, letting the rumble of his purrs relax her. A few leaves drifted from her maple onto the grass. Soon the nights would be too cold to be out here without bundling up, but for now the chill in the air was a pleasant balm for the flush from whisky, wine, dancing, and social unease. Bea knew she came off as outspoken and confident, but she could get carried away when she felt unsure of herself. She'd been on the defensive around Ben for so long she wasn't sure she had a handle on the difference between offensive and defensive anymore. Come to think of it, he didn't seem as game for trading barbs as he used to be. Oh lord, she probably owed him an apology, but it would be beyond awkward. She'd be nicer to him the next time she saw him. A *little* nicer—no need to go overboard.

Louise and Rob clearly had no idea what they were talking about. Ben wasn't carrying a torch for her. They were simply two people who didn't like each other very much, doing their best to work together. Right? And sure, there had been a time when they were students when she'd thought—even hoped—Ben might be interested in her as more than a study partner, but that was more than fifteen years ago. The idea that anything could, should, or would happen between them now was simply bananas. Bonkers. The two of them together now, what, canoodling on the quad? Lunching together in the campus cafe between classes? Ben cuddling here on this cozy porch swing with her? Completely out of the question.

Bea didn't realize she was nodding off until Herschel jumped down and chirped at her from the open front door. "Right, pal. Time for bed." She followed him inside.

Heron

The Librotory took up half of the fourth floor of the newly renovated Messiman library. Two glass walls carved out an office for Ben in one corner. The classroom and work area for students had tables and a workspace with cases of letterpress type and an old-fashioned printing press. Ben did his repair and restoration work in a section of the room that was only separated from the rest of the lab by an open wall of shelves, where books in various stages of rehabilitation could reside until they were ready to return to the stacks.

There were plenty of gaps between shelved books where a person could see and hear what was going on in the big room while remaining concealed. In fact, early in the semester, Heron and Charlie had been startled by Ben's throat-clearing emergence from this space, which they'd presumed to be empty. Charlie had booked three hours of printing time for them on Thursday at a time when Ben's calendar was blocked off for repairing bindings. He'd be back there. And if their acting skills were up to snuff, he'd believe Heron and Charlie didn't know he was listening to them.

Heron slipped her sandals off and tiptoed into the room, ducking down to confirm the presence of denim-clad legs and black Converse, visible between some old atlases on the shelf dividing the repair area from the classroom. She backed out of the room and gave Charlie a thumbs up.

Striding into the lab, Charlie, in what Heron liked to think of as his practicing-for-the-courtroom voice, said, "But that doesn't make any sense at all. Your cousin has been extremely vocal about her feelings."

"True." She followed him in. "But that's precisely my point. Don't you think it's a little strange that she talks about Ben so much, if she truly can't stand him?"

"Hmm," Charlie stroked his chin. "The lady doth protest too much?" Gilding the lily. With her back to the repair shelves, Heron rolled her eyes at Charlie to let him know he was going overboard. He continued, "Well, if it's true, poor Beatrice. It seems pretty obvious to me Ben thinks she's a bitch."

Heron flinched at the language, but from the repair room behind her, she heard a small, indignant huff.

She made a "keep going" motion and Charlie said, "Last week, when I mentioned you were having lunch with Bea, he said he was surprised you two were related because you're so pleasant. And when he talks about his old friends from school, he never, ever mentions her."

"Oh, that's awful, because Bea talks about him so much, he must be on her mind constantly. She wouldn't let him live rent-free in her head like that if she didn't have some feelings for him."

There was a clatter from behind the repair shelves. As if, perhaps, someone had knocked over a jar of tools. It was too loud to pretend they hadn't heard it. Heron widened her eyes at Charlie in mock surprise. "What on earth was that?"

"This building is haunted, haven't you heard? Maybe the ghosts are upset about the renovation."

Heron grinned at Charlie's quick thinking.

He elaborated. "Two students were planning to elope, but she ran off with someone else instead, and he came up here, to expire from a broken heart amongst the peer-reviewed journals."

He looked so cute and silly, with his put-upon expression of melancholy, Heron couldn't resist kissing him. They melted together, and as the heat built Charlie boosted her onto the typesetting counter.

He was running a hand up her leg when Heron remembered they weren't actually alone. She grabbed his wrist and said, "Babe, we'd better get to work, right?" She caught his eyes and then cut hers over to the repair area.

Charlie ran a hand through his hair and adjusted his khaki shorts, clearing his throat. "Right you are, my sweet little future wife. Grab the paper and I'll start mixing ink."

"Future wife! Aw." She started gathering supplies.

Their assignment had been to print postcards with a quotation in a typeface chosen to compliment the text. In the cases of old type, Heron found a font with elegant sans-serif simplicity. The upper case containing the capital letters was missing entirely, so she had chosen two stanzas of an E.E. Cummings poem. Heron was drawn to it for the spareness of the language, the way it spoke about how she felt for Charlie, eager anticipation of folding their lives together. Charlie only cared that it wasn't too many lines to render in the painstaking typesetting process, packing each letter in with slivers of metal until they were tight enough to withstand the pressure of the press.

They'd already set their type, but it still took more than an hour to run the postcards through the hulking printing press, adjusting the ink colors and amount of pressure as they went. The final cards bore the lines of poetry in rose-colored ink, with letters indented just enough to feel pleasant when she ran her finger over the poem.

Ben kept a tub of the kind of scrubbing soap used by auto mechanics at the workspace sink, saying it was the only thing that really worked to remove the oily printer's ink. Washing her hands with the pine-scented grit, Heron watched the ink run pink on the porcelain. As she dried them, she glanced at Ben's corner of the room. Through the space between an old set of encyclopedias and a stack of journals, she could see slices of sneakers and knees. Ben, stuck back there this whole time, was sitting cross-legged on the floor.

Heron dismissed a flash of guilt. This was going to be worth it, and it was for his own good. If the conversation Ben overheard hadn't seemed consequential to him, surely he would have come out of hiding? She grinned at Charlie, cocking her head toward the repair room. He wrapped his arm around her shoulders and they rushed for the stairwell, stifling their laughter until the door whooshed closed behind them.

Bea

The lecture on supernovas was one of Bea's favorites. Explosions impress students; that is a truth universally acknowledged by science educators across disciplines (well, okay, maybe not biologists). Bea started with what holds a star together—gravity and fuel—then moved into the instability occurring when those things start to wane. She always concluded her lecture with images of a supernova in Messier 82 from 2014, then turned the lights off in the classroom for the grand finale.

"You should look at this the same way you would regard an artist's rendering of anatomy," she said. "It looks like some of our still photographic images, but this is entirely a simulation." She pressed play and watched the students' mildly impressed faces at the mirror-image mushroom clouds give way to awe as the explosions shot across the screen.

"Next week we'll talk about the aftermath. Black holes. Cosmic rays. The reading is on the syllabus! And your night sky observations will be due as usual, so if you haven't signed up for telescope time, see me after class."

Bea flicked the lights back on and as her eyes adjusted to the fluorescents again, she noticed Ben sitting in the back row of the auditorium. With his cap, jeans and t-shirt, it hadn't been hard to mistake him for a student at a distance, and she rolled her eyes. They were both too old to be dressing like teenagers. Ben didn't ever seem to face any consequences for his sophomoric wardrobe, but Bea certainly would if she came to work wearing some of the more whimsical things that caught her eye when she shopped with her friend Sarah.

She'd have to see what Ben wanted, but Layla, one of her students, was standing in front of her. Students come first.

"Dr. Hayes?"

The poor kid seemed so nervous. This was an entry-level class, and she got a lot of first year students who were still getting their feet under them, but every once in a while, there was one who tugged her heartstrings more than most. That was Layla this year. She'd chosen a seat in the front row and wore crisp shirts buttoned and tucked neatly into her jeans, while the other students were sloppy in their hoodies and pajama bottoms. Her round glasses took up half of her face and gave her an owlish air.

"Hi Layla, what's up?"

"I need to talk to you about observation time. The slots only go from eight to midnight, then the lab assistants lock up the roof? And they're only on weekdays?"

"Mm-hmm."

"Well, I work weeknights until eleven. I deliver pizzas."

Behind Layla's glasses, Bea could see dark circles pressed into the pale skin under her eyes. It sounded like she was running herself ragged, but hands-on time with the telescopes was crucial to the curriculum. No matter how engaging her lectures were, they were no substitute for students seeing the stars and planets themselves, giving them a first-hand perspective on Earth's place in the universe.

Layla's voice wavered as she continued. "And I've been trying to get up to the roof right after work, but all the telescopes are taken and by the time I get one I don't have time to complete the observation. Is there any way I can get a different assignment? Or if I can have a key to the roof so I can go up there later—I promise I'll be super responsible. Otherwise, I think I might have to drop this class."

Bea felt a deep pang of sympathy. Messiman was replete with well-off students who didn't need jobs at all, and many others were able to get work-study gigs designed to accommodate class and study schedules. Bea herself counted her blessings constantly that the only job she'd needed to pay for her books and extras was babysitting Heron, which had hardly seemed like work at all and certainly hadn't interfered with any of her labs.

"Don't drop the class," she smiled, then lowered her voice to say, "no one else has asked any smart questions about white dwarfs." Bea winked, and Layla broke into a giggle. "I'll tell you what, you said you don't work Saturdays?"

"No, ma'am."

"Oh geez, please don't call me ma'am, it makes me feel like a difficult customer at the supermarket."

Layla laughed again.

"So here is what we're going to do. If you're willing to give up a little of your Saturday night, I can give up some of mine. I'll meet you here at eight on Saturdays. Sound okay?"

"Oh, that's perfect Dr. Hayes! Thank you so much! You won't regret it!" Layla shrugged into her enormous backpack and bounced out of the auditorium.

Ben said from his perch at the back of the room, "That was kind of you."

"What, no jokes about how spending Saturdays with a student is going to cut into my hot dates with my cat?"

"No." Ben stood and descended the steps, stopping when they were eye to eye. "Not many of the faculty members here would give up part of their weekends for a student like that. I don't know why you think I would joke about it."

Bea felt heat rise into her cheeks, and the impulse to back away. He was close enough for her to smell, once again, the evergreen of his...what was it? Soap? Cologne? The aftermath of cavorting with a forest sprite? Unfortunately, Bea had leaned against the table she used to arrange handouts and receive student assignments. There wasn't enough space between him and it for her to make moving away look casual. She had no choice but to hold her ground, doing her best to look anywhere but into his eyes, but he caught her glance and held it for a second. She felt a zing up the backs of her legs and was glad to have the table for support after all. Ben seemed to relent and backed up, perching on the edge of one of the desks in the front row.

"I came to speak with you about this interdisciplinary ed contingent thing," he said. "Since we'll be working on it together, should we sit down to spitball some ideas? I don't want to show up at the panel underprepared and I bet you don't, either."

She didn't. She'd jotted down a few ideas, but she'd been reluctant to reach out to Ben about discussing them after things had been so tense between them at the reunion. Something flashed through the back of her mind, Rob's voice saying, "carrying a torch," but she dismissed it now in the light of day as hastily as she had that night. Things had always been uncomfortable between her and Ben and always would. They were oil and water. But she was a professional and so was he, ratty t-shirts notwithstanding. Surely, they could set aside their past and their differences to work together for the betterment of the college. And for the sake of her tenure.

"That would be good, actually," she said with what she hoped came off as a cordial smile, "but I have a faculty meeting in" — she glanced at the clock — "twenty minutes. Can we set up a time to sit down next week?"

"Sure. Wednesday?"

"Wednesday's fine. I'm free midday."

"Great. Do you want to grab lunch, then? Or would you rather meet in one of our offices to keep things strictly professional?"

She rolled her eyes. "I can go to lunch."

"Good. I'll pick you up here. Now I'm going to go see if they still have the good Twix in your vending machine." He spun on one sneaker-clad heel, eliciting a squeak from the linoleum, and exited into the science building hallway.

After he was through the door, Bea chuckled. She'd been to the vending machine this morning in search of pretzels and noted the slot formerly occupied by Peanut Butter Twix had been full of granola bars. Not even a good kind — apple-cinnamon flavored. The mental image of Ben's disappointment almost got her over the chagrin of yet another awkward interaction.

Heron

"I have a surprise."

Heron's dad carried an unlabeled bottle and three of the glasses they used for dry white wines out to the patio. It was likely to be the last warm weekend in October. Heron and Charlie had gone to the vineyard early to enjoy the sunny afternoon and begin planning the wedding. Heron arranged the glasses while her father uncorked the bottle and poured an inch of pale yellow wine into each.

"This pinot gris is from grapes harvested six years ago. That was a tough year for both of us, Bird, but when I tasted this, I knew it was special, so I put some of it away to age a little longer. It'll be my first reserve vintage."

Heron felt herself beginning to choke up. This was the most she'd heard her dad talk about the year her mom left in a long time. Guilt skulked around the edges of her consciousness, but she ignored it, focusing instead on how happy they all were now.

He continued, "I think it proves something about waiting out the bad times. There's always a reward. I'm so proud of you, sweetie. And so happy to welcome you into the family, Charlie." He raised his glass.

Heron and Charlie followed suit and they all clinked their

glasses together, then drank. The wine was crisp and light, lemony with a hint of spice behind the tang.

"This is wonderful, Dad," she said.

"I'm glad you think so, because I have more than enough to serve about two hundred guests, especially if we also serve a red. I've been talking to my bottler, and I think he'll give me a deal on splits for favors. We can do a special label with your monogram and wedding date. What do you think?"

"It's perfect, Dad. I love it. Thank you! Charlie, what do you think?"

"Well...the wine is delicious, Mr. Hunter—"

"Call me Len, son."

"Len. The wine is very nice, but I've spoken to my parents, and they would like us to get married in their church. My mother says we can hold the reception at our country club."

Heron set her glass down. She knew Charlie intended to talk to his family about the wedding date and location, but he hadn't told her he'd already done it.

"Babe. Why didn't you tell me?"

"I was going to. I just hadn't gotten around to it yet."

Her dad looked hurt but recovered quickly. "I certainly know how to ship wine, if that's what you both want to do."

Heron glanced between her father and Charlie, both men expecting an answer from her. She could kick Charlie for putting her on the spot like this, but she needed to keep her annoyance in check. An open mind was important to the success of a relationship.

"I don't know," she said. "I hadn't really thought about having it anywhere but here. Isn't it traditional for the bride's family to host the wedding?"

"Yes," Charlie said, "but my parents want you to know, Len, they're happy to cover all the costs. No Brewster has been married anywhere but our family church since 1856. My mother has her heart set on it."

Heron had always pictured herself as a bride here in her family home, but weddings were about compromise, weren't they? She didn't want to start her marriage on the wrong foot with Charlie's family.

"Well," she said, "if it's so important to them. I'm sure it will be lovely. Is that okay with you, Dad?"

"Whatever you want, sweetie. We could still have a reception here after graduation if you like."

"Great." Charlie gave them both his most dazzling smile. "I'll call my mom tonight."

Toni, who was attending to the last of the weekend's visitors in the tasting room, had been put on the lookout for Bea's car coming up the drive. She texted Heron, "She's pulling in. Get ready."

"Ooh, it's time. Come on."

Heron and Charlie had one more try at piquing Bea's interest in Ben planned for tonight. They dashed through the vineyard, so they'd be next to Bea's car when she parked, separated by two rows of cabernet grapes. Harvested late in the fall, the vines still provided a good amount of cover. In the space under the trellis, they could see Bea's feet when she got out of her car.

"Oh, Charlie," Heron said, matching her walking pace to Bea's, "you must have misunderstood what Ben said. We all know he and Bea have never gotten along."

"I'm not kidding, babe. Ben told me his biggest regret is hurting a girl's feelings when he was my age. He said, 'If I could go back and undo it, things would be different now.' Who else could he be talking about?"

"Beats me." Heron continued along the row, watching through the leaves. Out of the corner of her eye, she saw the red and yellow plaid of Bea's shirt keeping pace with them. They'd hooked her. "If he does mean Bea, he'll be paying for it forever. I love her but she has no idea how to let go of things. Poor Ben."

From the other side of the hedge, they heard a dismissive snort. Heron stifled a giggle.

Charlie held up a cautioning arm to slow Heron as they reached the end of the field. Bea went into the house, and they turned to do a loop around the next row before going in to dinner.

He laced his fingers through hers and said, "Do you think that did the trick?"

"I think we got the point across. What gave you the idea for the line about Ben regretting something? I mean, it was perfect, but how did you come up with it?"

The only thing that could breach the armor of one of Bea's grudges was a sincere expression of regret. Heron knew that well, but she was surprised Charlie had picked up on it.

"I didn't." He squeezed her hand before dropping it to rake his hair back from his face. "Ben said it while we were going over SOD conduct standards. Jason sent out a…tasteless meme to the whole house with some first-year girls in it, and Ben got pretty mad. So far, he's been laid back about stuff, but not this. He made us suspend Jason's social event privileges for the rest of the semester."

"Wow." Heron felt a little of the tension between her shoulders release at this news. Jason tended to make her uncomfortable, although she could never pinpoint a specific thing he did to cause such a feeling. It was something about the way she caught him looking at her sometimes, an occasional innuendo or double-edged compliment. Even the ingratiating way he behaved around Charlie felt to her as if there was an agenda behind it. Heron wasn't exactly happy to hear about the meme and hoped it never got back to the girls, but it was nice to have confirmation that this wasn't all in her head.

Bea could be prickly, and she held grudges, but she didn't get upset without reason. Heron hoped her cousin could forgive Ben, because it was sounding more and more like her hunch about the potential between them was spot on.

Chapter Five

Bea

Once again, Ben was waiting in the back of the auditorium when Bea finished teaching. This time she was expecting him.

"Do you want to go off campus?" he asked. "It's the day half the drama department works in the cafe and I'm not sure I can bear another performance from *Rosencrantz and Guildenstern Are Dead* in the sandwich line."

"Should we walk to Mostarda? It's all fancy now but the turkey sandwich is still exactly the same as always." Like much of Millet, the cafe Bea suggested had gotten a facelift as the wine industry grew and the town became a popular tourist destination.

"Perfect."

Their walk across campus felt almost to Bea like it would have with any old college friend, taking turns remarking on changes to campus, laughing about Halloween their sophomore year when one of the bigger trees lining the quad was festooned so thoroughly with toilet paper that bits fluttered onto the walkway until graduation.

As they passed the student union and turned onto Main Street, the college buildings gave way to tasting rooms, boutiques and bistros. Ben said as they passed the second chain coffee shop, "Remember when we got the one Taco Bell on the edge of town, and it was a big deal?"

Bea laughed. "Yeah, I got roped into being the sober drive-thru chauffeur pretty often."

They passed a wine bar advertising "sangria slushies" and came to the wrought iron fence cordoning off Mostarda's sidewalk seating. The maroon and cream awning was new, but it harkened back to the old red and white one, when this place had been called The Mustard Jar. Back then, it was a quaint but no-frills deli. Now, the lighting was dim and inviting, the path to the register was lined with bottles of wine and carefully curated pantry staples, and the eagle-topped copper dome of an espresso machine loomed over the counter.

The balcony hadn't changed, though. While the dining area had been spruced up and extended onto the sidewalk, there was still a staircase in the back of the shop, if you knew to look for it, leading up to a second level where a hodgepodge of wobbly tables were occupied by students hunched over laptops, and professors graded papers in the careworn armchairs, sipping cappuccinos. It was open to the space below in a way that allowed the restaurant noise to carry upward, the clatter and conversation blending into a pleasant clamor. As a student, Bea had often found it easier to study here than in the oppressive quiet of the library.

Walking ahead of Ben, she found a table in the corner, where there would be enough room for them to spread out their notes. She shrugged out of her jacket.

Ben settled into the chair opposite. "So," he said, "interdisciplinary education."

"Right." She drew the memo from President Phillips out of her folder. "We'll be on the panel for a roundtable discussion on current measures, and should come back from the symposium with a plan for expanded 'cross-disciplinary curriculum development to enhance student learning outcomes' to implement next fall. She says she plans to involve more faculty in the spring."

Ben took a legal pad out of his bag and scrawled "Libraries" and "Science" at the top, then drew a line down the middle. "So, my entire job is cross disciplinary. The special collection is weighted toward humanities, but every department has books coded to their subject matter. But in the sciences, isn't what you teach pretty cut and dried? Gravity, orbits, and so on?"

"Not at all. The first assignment my entry-level students do is choose a constellation that interests them and write a paper on it; including the properties of the stars, but also the history of the figure. Who named the constellation, and why? What did it mean to them? I get a lot of students in that class who aren't science majors. I want them to understand how ancient peoples organized the stars into symbols to help the make sense of the universe and their place in it."

While she spoke, Ben wrote "history" and "research" under the science heading. "That's excellent. I've been thinking about something like that, too, for my Book Arts class next round — have the students start out researching some aspect of bookmaking: the medieval monastery environment, how the switch from vellum to paper changed the dissemination of information…" As he went on, Ben's ideas about contextualizing the course content were on point, but she found herself distracted as she watched his face, illuminated by passion for his work. She had thought librarianship was a career he'd settled for, but maybe he had only needed another try to find his calling.

Maybe she had misjudged him. Could what Charlie said on Sunday about Ben's regrets be true? Bea still wasn't sure, but she didn't want to become so set in her opinions that she couldn't see the person sitting in front of her for who they were. From now on, she would keep an open mind and do her best to be fair to Ben. If only he would lose the stupid ball cap that made it harder to see into his eyes.

Their work was interrupted by the cook yelling their order number.

"I'll go grab that." Ben was already pushing his chair back.

Bea started to protest that she could certainly fetch her own damn sandwich, but caught herself and smiled instead. It felt strange, smiling at Ben. "Thanks."

While he was gone, she sketched out a bubble diagram of cross-disciplinary assignment ideas, which they worked on together until Bea noticed she was late for her office hours.

"Shit. I have to run."

Ben joined her on a mad, merry dash back to campus. She didn't notice they'd passed the library and he'd continued on to the science building with her until they were at her office.

Fortunately, there weren't any students waiting outside her door. She opened her laptop to check her messages, hoping she hadn't missed anyone. While she did that, Ben leaned a shoulder against the door jamb.

"That was great," he said.

"It was. I think we have some solid ideas."

"Right. For the symposium." His demeanor downshifted.

She looked at him quizzically. Surely he had been talking about the work.

"Yes. Well, talk again soon."

"Sure." He looked at her for a second before he turned to go, like he wanted to say something more, but instead he left, throwing a "see ya" over his shoulder after he started down the hall.

Through the window, Bea saw him emerge from the building and head down the path back to the library. She studied his departing figure for clues about what he was thinking, but it offered none.

Heron

The return of more middle-class women to the workplace in the early 1960s was marked by streamlined silhouettes. Homemakers adopted the styles too, but in brighter prints and more delicate fabrics.

Heron stopped typing, pulled out the pencil she'd stuck in her hair, and made a tick mark on her notes. After a month of research, her thesis was starting to come together well enough to begin drafting, and she was on a roll. She thought she could have a rough draft of this section done today. Charlie was sprawled on her bed studying for a statistics test. The occasional mutter or rustle of pages was making it easier for her to focus; a tiny reassurance she wasn't in this alone, that was all she needed. After double-checking a reference in her folder of articles, Heron's fingers and mind were off again, words flying across the page.

Charlie sat up. "Babe," he said, "I'm getting hungry. Do you think you could possibly make me a turkey burger?"

"There are snacks in the kitchen." She was a little hungry too. "Can you bring me a string cheese when you come back?"

"I'm not snack hungry, I'm meal hungry."

She looked at her screen. She had a few paragraphs left to go.

"Just let me finish this section. You can get some chips while you wait—I have the barbecue kind you like."

"But it's almost six. And I have a chapter meeting at seven. I really should eat before."

"Can you eat at the frat house? I want to finish this."

Charlie screwed up his face. "It's fish stick night."

"Fine." She saved her file and closed her laptop, rising to go into the kitchen, assuming he'd follow her.

"I'll be out as soon as I finish this chapter. Thanks, babe. You're the best." He blew her a kiss.

Oh well. She could work while he was at his meeting. This was what partnership was, wasn't it? Setting your own work aside sometimes to take care of your person. And it was sweet how much he liked her cooking.

She pulled ground turkey out of the fridge, preheated the oven and countertop grill, and was shaking half a bag of frozen sweet potato fries onto a cookie sheet when Maggie clattered through the door, followed by Bryant "Bork" Hardy. He was another SOD brother, although he wasn't in Charlie's inner circle, and Heron usually only saw him at big functions.

Bork and Maggie had classes in the same building on Thursday afternoons, and usually walked back together afterward.

"Hey." Heron, knowing the answer to the question she was about to ask, was already dumping the rest of the fries into the pan. "You guys want turkey burgers?"

"Awesome," said Bork.

"Yes, please. Thanks, Mom," Maggie sing-songed.

Heron threw a fry at her.

Maggie said, "I'm gonna change. Be right back."

Bork hovered in the kitchen doorway. "Can I help?"

"Um…sure. Do you want to get toppings ready? There's lettuce and tomato in the fridge."

Heron's bedroom door opened, and Charlie appeared in the hallway with the sleepy, squinty look of a person adjusting to the real world after hours of staring at fine print. "This is cozy," he said.

Heron caught an edge to his voice but decided to pretend she hadn't. He was only tired and hungry. She stepped forward and kissed him, careful to hold her messy hands away from his sweater. "Isn't it? Bork is helping and Maggie will be out soon."

Becoming more himself, Charlie thumped Bork on the back and said, "Want a beer?" He leaned into the fridge.

Heron was about to tell him they didn't have any, but Bork said, "Nah, man, I have a test tomorrow."

Charlie emerged with one of Maggie's pear hard ciders, opened it to take a swig, and grimaced but kept drinking. Heron made a mental note to buy her roommate a replacement. She washed her hands and poured glasses of water for herself and Bork.

Maggie cleared her books from the table and set it while Heron finished cooking and Charlie and Bork had a loud conversation about…quarterbacks or something.

When they all sat down, it felt like the flimsy card table was levitating between the four of them, held aloft by Charlie and Bork's long legs. Bork told a story about his high school baseball team that made Maggie laugh so hard ginger ale came out her nose, and Charlie's hand rested on Heron's knee almost the whole time. It was one of those simple moments you want to capture and also a glimpse of the future; this was what it was going to be like next year, hosting friends in the home she shared with Charlie. By the time the guys left, they were already three minutes late for their fraternity meeting, but that was fine since the SODs couldn't start without Charlie.

"I'll help you clean up," Maggie said.

Heron waved her off. "I've got it. I made the mess."

"Oh, stop it. You don't have to take care of everything, you know."

"I don't take care of everything." Heron scowled.

Maggie sighed. "Cooking dinner for Charlie while he studies? Come on, Heron. That's a little Susie Homemaker even for you."

"It's only turkey burgers. And what do you mean, 'even for me?'" Heron set the stack of plates she was holding down a little harder than she'd intended to and winced at the noise they made clattering on the counter.

Maggie put the grill plates in the sink to soak before she answered. "It's just…sometimes it's like you're treating being with Charlie like a job interview. Like some sort of messed up wife audition. And I don't think you should feel like you have to do that."

"Maggie. It's just a quick dinner. We all needed to eat anyway. God."

Maggie put her hands up. "Okay, okay. I'm sorry. I don't mean to hurt your feelings. I just want you to know you can tell Charlie to order a damn pizza. Okay?"

"Of course." Heron made a concerted effort to make her smile reach her eyes.

After the kitchen was clean, they retreated to their own rooms to study, but Heron couldn't get her flow back. She was writing about the intersection of social change and fashion in the latter half of the twentieth century, but every time she started to think about the gender roles and clothes of the sixties, Maggie's comment popped into her head. A wife audition. Maggie knew how much she loved Charlie, and how much he loved her, but she was mistaking the little sacrifices that came along with love for something negative. It wasn't Maggie's fault—she simply didn't understand the give-and-take, compromise and selflessness that came with sustaining a years-long relationship. She'd never seen the consequences of taking people for granted the way Heron had.

Heron hadn't checked her horoscope yet today; that must be why she felt slightly off-kilter. Hers immediately made her feel better:

TAURUS: It will be tempting to lose sight of your end goal today. Don't let distractions steer you off course.

Obviously, Maggie's remarks were trying to distract from her happily married future. As always, she checked Charlie's:

GEMINI: Appreciating your loved ones today brings a deeper sense of security. You will soon have an opportunity to repay their kindness.

See? Charlie obviously appreciated the things she did for him, and he did nice things for her, too. For good measure, Heron checked Bea's sign:

SCORPIO: If you're in a rut, it might seem more comfortable to stay there, but an open mind will allow you to see all the opportunities in front of you.

Heron let out a little hum of satisfaction. Perfect. She'd set the wheels in motion to help Bea see Ben as an opportunity.

Bea

Bea took a sip of her old-fashioned, savoring the sweet, smoky bite. She liked wine—living where she did and being related to Len, she kind of had to—but nothing could beat a beautifully crafted cocktail. The aesthetics were better, too, the squat little glass, the curl of orange peel in its amber pool. Perfect. Sarah's glass of cabernet looked pedestrian by comparison.

Bea and Sarah became friends right here at the Venerable Grape's live music night, on a particularly crowded evening when a Portland-based performer she loved was doing an acoustic set. Bea had just moved back to Millet after grad school and didn't know anyone else in town who might like the show. She went by herself and was lucky to snag a small table. A woman in a violet coat with a wild mass of black curls came in, eyes casting around for a spot. Although she didn't mind being there alone, Bea felt guilty taking up a whole table for herself, so she waved the woman over and offered her the empty chair. She'd only been trying to be kind, but as they chatted between sets, they hit it off. Sarah was a couple of years older than Bea, had recently broken up with her girlfriend, and didn't have many friends in town either. They'd been close ever since, occasionally road-tripping to Seattle to see a show, singing along in the car to *Jagged Little Pill* and *Exile in Guyville* until their throats were raw.

The Grape perched like a terrarium in the tall-windowed second floor of one of downtown's old office buildings, exposed brick lined with tapestries and potted plants, scattered vintage lamps, mismatched rugs, and cafe tables. A postage-stamp sized stage was tucked into one corner and a counter along the back wall served a variety of complicated coffees and cocktails. Now Main Street was full of wine bars and cafes, but the Venerable Grape was the first. It had been around since Bea was a student, when it was the only alternative to the dive bars north of campus.

Tonight's act was a Messiman student, an earnest young man with an earnest guitar. He was decent, Bea supposed, if not quite her thing, but tonight's crowd wasn't listening with the rapt attention they usually gave to the bigger out-of-town acts. The room hummed with chatter broken occasionally by a particularly sincere wail from the performer. Over their cocktails and cheese board, Bea was filling Sarah in on Heron's engagement.

"It sounds like something out of a movie," Sarah said.

"Yeah, it was nice. Heron's thrilled."

"You sound...less thrilled."

Bea shook her head. "I'm happy she's so happy, but come on, who gets married at twenty-two anymore?"

"Not us!" Sarah laughed.

"Definitely not us. I just don't want her to dive into marriage too early. Especially after what happened with her mom."

Sarah's eyebrows drew together. "Do you mean, because Felicia regretted getting married young, or because Felicia leaving made Heron more likely to seek family security?"

Bea considered this for a moment before answering. "Both, I guess. I think Heron has a more sensible head on her shoulders than Felicia, but how can she not see the connection? I've always thought she was in a rush to grow up too fast. She likes for things to be settled and I'm afraid that will lead to mistakes."

"I think you could give her a little more credit. She's a smart young woman. It's okay for her to know what she wants. On the very small chance that it turns out to be a mistake, she knows better than most she can undo it, and she has a good support system."

Bea appreciated Sarah's honesty, even when it was galling to have her errors in judgement pointed out. She sliced a hard sliver of Manchego cheese and waited until she could detect the "notes of caramel" promised by the menu card before saying, "I suppose you're right. And even if you aren't, I shouldn't be the one to rain on her parade."

"Atta girl."

"I am taking her to a wedding show weekend after next, heaven help me. Toni is far more into this wedding planning stuff, but she can't leave the tasting room on a Saturday."

Sarah laughed. "I would pay good money to see Beatrice Hayes at a wedding show."

"You're more than welcome to tag along. I won't even

charge you."

Sarah sipped her wine. "Sadly, I'm working."

Bea was about to respond when a raucous burst of masculine laughter from behind them caught her ear. It was between sets now and the crowd noise had increased, but the sound still carried across the room and several people shot dirty looks toward the back of the bar. She turned and saw Ben at one of the high-top tables in a group of five or six guys who all appeared to be several beers deep. She caught his eye, and for a moment their gazes locked, a taut line connecting them past the other people in the room, over all the chatter. The rush of unspoken connection zipped down Bea's spine, taking her so by surprise she stifled a cough as the last sip of her drink caught in her throat.

This was not the sort of situation Bea was accustomed to finding herself in. Should she wave? Go over there to say hello? Before she could decide, one of Ben's friends shot off a one-liner and the entire table erupted in laughter again. Their eye contact was broken when Ben tipped his head back in a guffaw. Bea looked down at her empty glass, the orange peel beginning to dry out and turn brown around the edges. Well, if Ben wanted to talk to her, he could certainly walk over to say hello. His merry band of brothers over there probably wouldn't even notice he was gone. And it would be rude of her to leave Sarah sitting here all by herself, wouldn't it? Whatever.

She returned her attention to her friend. "Sorry, I missed what you just said."

"Samples. If the booths at the show are giving out samples, bring me back as many as you can. We can always use stuff like paper, ribbon, and tulle for the craft closet, and the residents love those soft mints. Most of their teeth can't handle Jordan almonds, but I freaking love those things so bring them all to me." Sarah, a social worker at a nursing home, was always doing small, extra things for her clients.

Bea chuckled. "You got it." Come to think of it, a non-matrimonial mission would make the entire outing far more fun for her, and she suspected Sarah knew that.

When the musician packed up his guitar and the sound system switched over to trip hop, Bea said, "I'm not quite ready to go home yet, are you?"

They switched from drinks to herbal tea for Sarah, a decaf cappuccino for Bea, and had an animated discussion about the latest antics of Sarah's clients and Bea's students. Bea's ears pricked up when, behind her, she heard Ben's table scrape their stools back and start a round of loud goodbyes. She guessed he would probably come over to say hello after his friends left, but when she turned to look, the back of the room was empty.

Bea gulped the last of her coffee. She had to pull it together. One pleasant working lunch and a couple of rumors had her behaving like a moony teenager. Pathetic.

Heron

Heron walked home from the library alone on Saturday evening. All around her classmates bustled across the quad, many heading back to their dorms or apartments to get ready for an evening out, or to the dining hall for dinner, some bundled in jackets and scarves. Some unfortunate souls were on their way into the library with a night of studying ahead of them.

Heron's head had been buzzing and her stomach queasy since yesterday. After suspecting she had bombed a bluebook test in her Criminal Justice class and a disappointing meeting with her thesis adviser, who expressed concern about her focus on mid-century gender roles not covering enough new ground, she was feeling academically precarious. By the time she met Charlie on the quad after their Friday afternoon classes, she'd been riding the edge of panic, shaky and scattered.

"I'm sure it's not as bad as you think," he'd said. "You haven't gotten anything lower than a B+ on a test since I've known you. And you have plenty of time to figure out your thesis — most people haven't even started yet."

She planned to use the weekend to regroup. She'd been in the library all day, searching the databases and reading articles. She was starting to see a way forward. By shifting her emphasis slightly to focus more on differences between trends in the domestic sphere and professional spaces, she could say something interesting about how women use clothes to code switch when they move between roles. It would be less about how women differentiated themselves from men, and more about how they differentiated between different versions of themselves. Heron was happy with the change. Deciding on a research topic that could apply to both her sociology and art majors had been a challenge, and the new focus on self-expression would help keep her research balanced between both fields of study.

She was also starving. This was one drawback of living off campus; if she still lived in the dorms, she could walk into the dining hall and be sitting down at a table with a tray of food within minutes. But her cozy little apartment was better. She'd much rather go home, put on her snuggliest pajamas, and order a pizza without the risk of having to sit on the awkward fringes of a random cluster of classmates. She and Charlie had started dating early freshman year and she'd spent so much time with him she hadn't made many close friends. The Lambdas, Maggie's sorority, had invited her to join twice, but she just didn't see the need when she was at so many SOD events. On days like today, she wondered if she was missing out on something.

She'd have the apartment to herself tonight. The SODs had a function with the Lambdas and Maggie and Charlie would both be there. Since it was an official Lambda/Sig-O-Delt event, only members of those groups were allowed to attend. She didn't mind; what she really needed was a quiet evening in. She was just disappointed it would be alone. Heron gazed upward at the crystalline sky, marred only by a few wispy clouds quickly turning from white to apricot. As she walked, she soaked up the last cold rays of October sun.

When she opened the door of her building, the scent of savory spices: coriander, garlic, cumin, chilis, filled her nose and Heron was hit with a wave of nostalgia for her mother. Felicia had stopped cooking long before she'd left and these smells retained an association with simpler times, from before she'd known how fragile happiness could be. One of her neighbors must be making dinner. Heron briefly considered fixing something for herself before discarding the idea; she was much too tired. It had taken her hours to fall asleep last night, only to be yanked awake in the early morning hours by a pounding heart and swimming head.

As she entered her apartment, the mouth-watering smell hit her full force along with the warmth that filled the apartment when the oven was on. Odd. Maybe Maggie wasn't at the party yet. As soon as she clicked the door shut, she heard the blender turn on with a whiz. Maggie, not a fan of cheap keg beer, must be making herself a pre-party daiquiri.

"Mags?" she called.

"Nope." Charlie emerged from the kitchen holding two glasses filled with thick, saffron-colored liquid. "It's me."

She dropped her bag and rushed forward to kiss him. His lips were sweet and cold, and he gingerly half-closed his arms around her, careful not to spill the drinks.

"Mm," she said, licking her lips. "Mango?"

"Mango margaritas for madame," he said with a bow, emphasizing the alliteration. He handed her a glass.

"What on earth did you rim these with?" The coating around the edge of her glass was sticky and red, and made the tip of her tongue tingle when she tasted it.

He laughed. "Crushed up Pop Rocks. Do you like it? My sister told me about it."

"Hmm, yeah, I do." She usually preferred her margaritas on the rocks, with salt, but this was sweet and fun, like Charlie. "But aren't you supposed to be at the Lambda function?"

"They won't miss me. You were pretty down yesterday, and I thought my girl needed me more than my brothers tonight."

"Aw." She leaned in to kiss him again. "Thanks, babe."

He grinned. "It's what I'm here for. Now go put your pajamas on because I know you'd be in them by now if I weren't here. Dinner will be ready in twenty minutes, but there's guacamole now."

The margaritas had been enough of a surprise. "You actually cooked? I thought you'd gone to the taco truck or something."

"Not exactly. I talked Pollo D'Oro into selling me a pan of enchiladas to bake here. The guacamole is from there, too. But I made the margaritas myself." Charlie looked so proud. Behind him, Heron could see a can of frozen concentrate mixer on the counter.

Half an hour later, Heron was in her coziest flannel pajamas (Charlie had laid them out on the bed for her, pleated into a heart shape), snuggled against Charlie under her softest blanket, watching *The Little Mermaid* with a warm plate of enchiladas balanced on her lap. It was all of her favorite, most comfortable things, all here on this couch. How did she get so lucky? The heaviness of the food and her second margarita spread through her limbs, and she felt herself nodding off, head nestled against Charlie's chest, right in her favorite spot where she could hear his heartbeat. She was asleep before Ariel even got her legs.

The trumpet fanfare of the finale roused her. "Hey." She blinked up at Charlie.

"Hey." He planted a kiss on her forehead.

"Go to your party."

"Nah. I'm here with you."

"Go on. Really, I'm just going to go to bed." She stood and stretched.

"Okay, how about this. Twenty minutes. A quick appearance, so no one can say I didn't show, and then I'll come right back here."

She handed him her keys. "Deal. But let yourself in. I might be in bed by the time you get here."

"Counting on it." He winked. Pretty cute—maybe she could try to stay awake until he got back.

Heron washed her face and brushed her teeth, crawled between the sheets—clean sheets; Charlie had also done a load of her laundry—and was drifting off when he slipped into bed behind her, wrapping an arm loosely around her waist and fitting his knees into the crook of her legs.

"'Night," she mumbled, already half asleep. She wanted to say, "I love you," but all she had the energy for was "love," which slid out like a sigh.

Chapter Six

Heron

Heron sat cross-legged on her bed, watching out the window for Bea's car. A Christmas-morning feeling buzzed through her folded limbs. Today was the day she would truly start to feel like a bride. When Bea pulled up in front of her building, she slid her feet into her running shoes and grabbed the bag she'd packed, which included a pair of heels for trying on dresses (she wore a half-size bigger than Bea, close enough to share in a pinch, and Bea wouldn't think to bring any), bottles of water, granola bars, and the wedding planning binder Toni had bought for her. And a bag of cheese puffs, a tradition for their road trips. The convention center was only about an hour away, but she wanted this day to be as much fun for her cousin as possible.

She climbed into the passenger seat. Bea was wearing cropped leggings, a sweatshirt emblazoned with the quote, "Not fragile like a flower, fragile like a bomb," (so Bea) and running shoes like Heron's. She was drinking from one of The Beanery's largest paper cups. The box for the number of espresso shots was marked with a six and circled emphatically, as if the barista couldn't quite believe it either. Oh boy, Bea was really fortifying herself for this day.

"I got you a chai," Bea said, indicating the cupholder.

"Thanks. And thank you for coming with me today. I know it's not exactly your idea of fun. Maggie would have come, but she has a rugby game."

Bea made a dismissive sound. "It will be an adventure. Before I forget, Sarah asked me to bring back some samples. Help me grab some for her, will you? Anything older people might like for crafting or activities."

"Sure," Heron said.

At a stoplight, Bea glanced over. "So do we have a game plan?"

"A game plan?" Leave it to Bea to want a strategy for this.

"Well, do you have certain vendors you especially want to talk to? Is Charlie in charge of anything?"

"Just to get some ideas, mostly. Charlie says he doesn't have strong opinions, but I'm supposed to talk to his mom soon about arranging details in Connecticut."

"I'm guessing she will have some opinions."

"I know she does." Heron watched a couple of farms blur past and then said, "Charlie says she has a favorite photographer, string quartet, and caterer. Might as well use them."

Bea laughed. "Imagine being the kind of person who has a favorite string quartet. Or caterer!"

"Or professional photographer," Heron added.

"Well," Bea put on a mid-Atlantic accent. "Darling, everyone

HOW TO ALIGN THE STARS 89

who's anyone needs one of those in case the fellow who does the life-sized oil portraits is otherwise engaged."

Heron laughed. "I know. It's all very different."

Here, Charlie was just…Charlie. He had nice clothes and a decent car, and he didn't have to worry about tuition or books the way some of their classmates did, but he didn't act snooty. Heron was aware she had more financial privilege than many, herself. She took summer jobs to help pay for her expenses, but they never worried about not being able to make a tuition payment. The way Charlie talked about his family back east sometimes made them sound like they existed in an entirely different world. Something out of an old movie, where people dressed for dinner and used finger bowls. She rubbed her sweaty palms on her jeans.

As usual, Bea had one of her playlists of nineties female singer-songwriters on. She was always trying to get Heron into these older artists and while she enjoyed Bea's taste, Heron wondered why Bea never played anything new. Had her cousin simply stuck with the music that had been popular when she was younger, or was it just that the music of the era suited Bea perfectly? As they turned off the highway, Bea's favorite song — upbeat, harmonious folk-pop with lyrics about astronomers and karma — came up in the rotation. Heron decided it was probably a little of both. Bea had always known what she wanted, and worked hard to get it, but she kept room in her heart for the people she loved. Heron admired that deeply; hopefully there was more of Bea in herself than she got credit for. She planned to approach her future with Charlie with the same gusto Bea had for studying the stars. Heron filled her lungs and joined in to sing the chorus.

They were both hoarse when they pulled into the convention center. The parking lot was nearly full, and Bea said, "Why don't you hop out and get us signed in. I'll park and meet you inside."

Heron grabbed her bag and exited the vehicle hastily because a line of cars had already built up behind Bea's. As she walked toward the building, she looked at the other women — the crowd contained only a few reluctant fathers or hands-on grooms — wondering who was betrothed and who was, as Bea put it, "pit crew."

A pang of regret crept in at the sight of so many brides here with their mothers, but Heron brushed it away, replaced with gratitude for Bea, and Toni and her dad and everyone else who was excited for her and wanted to be involved with wedding planning, even if her mom didn't. Bea had come with her today when she would literally rather be anywhere else. Who could ask for better support? So many others here were just as in love as she was, just as filled with anticipation for the future. With gratitude in place and her intention set, Heron pulled the door open and stepped inside.

Bea

Bea hustled across the windswept parking lot, where she'd finally been able to snag a spot in the far back corner. She was happy to have on a warm sweatshirt until she opened the heavy convention center doors to an immediate sensory assault of warm, moist air, perfume, and shrieks of feminine delight. The entire space, normally a perfectly sensible beige facility where Bea had once attended a Women in STEM conference, was thoroughly draped in shiny white polyester and tsunamis of tulle, accented by sprays of ribbons and silk flowers. What fresh, frilly hell was this?

"Bea!" Heron's voice was nearly drowned out by the din, but Bea moved toward it like a beacon. The sooner she found her cousin, the faster they'd be finished here and back home to relax with a movie marathon. Bea swam through the crowd, passing more than one group wearing matching pastel sweatsuits, before reuniting with Heron, who said, "Don't be mad."

"Bird, of course I'm not mad. It only took me five minutes to find you."

"No." Heron handed Bea a pink badge on a hot pink lanyard and a reusable canvas grocery bag in a matching lawn-flamingo shade. She said again, more emphatically, "Don't be mad."

Bea looked around. Heron's badge was pink, too, but most of the older women had lavender, and some of the younger women had yellow. She looked more closely at the lanyard and saw "Bride" running along the ribbon in a script so encumbered with curlicues and flourishes it was nearly illegible.

Heron smiled, a nervous grimace. "You said you wanted samples for Sarah. The lady at the counter said most vendors only give samples to brides. So...I registered both of us as brides. You also get a tiara." Heron handed her a tiny crown made of rhinestones, glued to a barrette, then clipped her own to the top of her head.

Bea turned it over in her hands as she scanned the room. It appeared that the yellow badges were for bridesmaids, purple was for mothers-of-the-bride, and there were a few white-haired ladies with blue badges — probably grandmothers. None of those would feel right, either. Acting as the mother-of-the-bride would emphasize the fact that Felicia wasn't here with her daughter. According to Len, Felicia had only called to offer Heron perfunctory congratulations, hanging up after five minutes. Heron had asked Bea to be a bridesmaid, along with Charlie's sister and Maggie, and Bea had agreed (only, she'd quipped, if her official title could be Old Maid of Honor). But all the women with yellow badges looked like they were in junior high to her. Perhaps this event didn't attract many sensible, subdued brides with sensible, subdued friends.

Bea huffed out a breath to steel herself. Might as well go for broke; it wasn't like she'd ever be attending one of these things to plan her own wedding. Besides, she could regale Sarah with the story later. She clipped the tiara into the top of her ponytail. "Lead on, fellow bride," she said.

"Yay!" Heron did a little jump of delight and dragged Bea into the hall of vendors.

If the lobby were purgatory, the exhibition hall was the ninth circle of hell. Booths turned the entire space into a labyrinth. They looked much like the vendor setups Bea was used to seeing at academic conferences, except that the acres of shiny white drapery skirting the tables and backdrops made it look like all the booths had joined the same cult. On a rectangular, pink-carpeted runway in the center of the room, an endless parade of models in bridal party fashions marched like automatons. Some of the wedding show attendees observed from white-draped folding chairs in the middle of the rectangle. How did they get in or out? Were they supposed to just wait for a space between flower girls and make a break for it?

Over the loudspeaker, an emcee was leading a group of brides and bridesmaids through a practice bouquet toss in some unseen corner of the room, which didn't discourage one of his competitors from playing tired old party hits at top volume.

Bea took a deep breath. One lap around for Heron to get the information she needed; that was all. She looked at her cousin's face, rapt and wondrous. She was enjoying herself. Bea could suck it up for her sake. She should. She would.

"What do you want to look at first?" she yelled over the noise.

"Invitations?" Heron pointed toward a booth.

"Okay." Bea followed her over to a stationery booth, the draped tables laid out with heavy engraved card stock. While Heron examined a rose-printed square with elaborate cut-outs that opened like a wrought iron garden gate, Bea picked up a small box, startling when the sides fell away as she took the lid off. Inside, a cut-out silhouette of a bride and groom were marked with a simple "STD: MM-DD-YYYY."

A saleswoman set down the tablet she was working on and came over to say, "Those are quite popular with couples who have engagement parties, to hand out as favors. But they can also be mailed. When is your special day, dear?"

Bea remembered her bride badge. "I'm not sure yet." Didn't most people get married in the spring? "Spring, probably."

"Spring weekends fill up! You should get save-the-dates out as soon as possible. Would you like to look at our postcards?"

"Oh, that's okay." When the woman turned around to get a sample book, Bea grimaced at Heron who was deep in conversation with the other woman working the booth and didn't notice. "I'm really just here browsing with my cousin."

The woman picked her tablet up and tapped at it with a stylus. "Ah, well, maybe you want to wait until your engagement is a little more official. I notice you aren't wearing a ring."

Bea bristled, offense causing her to forget she wasn't, in fact, engaged. "What does my jewelry have to do with it?"

"Look, I've been doing this a long time and I've found that women who haven't gotten a ring yet end up cancelling a lot of orders. It's a simple fact."

"And I suppose the bigger the diamond, the bigger the order?"

The saleswoman shrugged elegantly. "It's merely an observation."

"Really. A little piece of carbon with nothing special about it at all. Did you know it rains diamonds on Saturn?" She could tell her voice had gotten louder, but she didn't care. "And they can easily be created in a lab. But all this" — she gestured to indicate the hall — "hype creates the high prices." Heron's eyes flicked up from the pile of floral-printed cards she was sorting through.

"It's simply traditional, dear."

"So is burning witches," Bea snapped.

Heron appeared at Bea's elbow. "Okay, I think I'm ready to move along. How about flowers? I know I'll use the Brewster's florist; I only want to get a few ideas."

Bea nodded. Across from the florist, she saw a booth that did interest her. Oversized apothecary jars filled with pastel candy. Women with pink badges were using small silver scoops to fill little cellophane bags. She could get some almonds for Sarah and some bridge mints for the nursing home residents. Since Heron and Charlie would be giving mini bottles of Len's wine as favors, Heron wouldn't need to look there.

"I'll be over there," Bea said, inclining her head toward the candy.

By the time she was done with the candy jars, scoring some champagne-flavored gummy bears for movie night in addition to the treats for Sarah, Heron was seated at the florist's table clicking through pictures of bouquets on a large computer monitor.

"What do you think of peonies?" she asked, showing Bea baseball-sized riots of petals in myriad shades of pink.

"Pretty," Bea said. Each bouquet was nice enough, but they all looked nearly identical to Bea, whether they were roses or peonies or lilies. She'd never been big on cut flowers. If she ever got married, she might like to carry greenery or autumn leaves.

If she ever got married? Bea shook her head as if she'd been swimming and the idea was water she needed to clear out of her ear. Where the hell did that even come from? They must be pumping something in through the vents; that was clearly the only rational explanation. She had to get out of here. It was too hot and noisy, and she'd had too much caffeine.

She leaned over to speak into Heron's ear. "I'm going to go grab some air. Do you want to meet near the bridesmaid dresses in…an hour?" Hopefully an hour would be enough time for

Heron to make her way through the rest of these booths.

Heron dragged her gaze away from an image of a magenta cluster of roses. "Sure. Here." Like magic, she produced a cold bottle of water and a granola bar (peanut butter, Bea's favorite) from her bag and pressed them into Bea's hands. Bea started the arduous process of moving toward the exit against the flow of giddy women trying to move deeper into the hall, feeling like a cantankerous salmon swimming upstream.

Heron

With Bea gone, Heron felt freer to linger over things she knew her cousin would make fun of; matching *Mr.* and *Mrs.* coffee mugs and pillowcases, a fluffy white robe with "Bride" emblazoned across the back, a fancy pen for signing the wedding certificate.

The back third of the hall was devoted to gowns, and as Heron moved through them, she found herself wandering through a forest of dresses. Mannequins and dress racks rose on either side, fabrics in a range of colors between white and blush, the skirts spreading out like the lower branches of snow-draped trees. Heron stretched out a hand to run along the fabric, considering the textures ranging from the rough rustle of tulle to waterfalls of the slipperiest satin. She had a basic idea of what she wanted and had gathered a few patterns but immersing herself in all these gowns was helping to crystallize her vision. The way the wide straps of one bodice narrowed at the collarbone, then crossed over a bare upper back; a skirt lifted enough in front to show toe-tips and pooled into the barest hint of a train, embroidery drawing the eye to a focal point. Heron had never been a big fan of lace or beading. Aside from being difficult to work with, she thought they distracted from the lines of a well-constructed dress. She wanted her own gown to rely on beautiful fabric instead. She wondered if there were any vendors here selling fabric and had begun to look around for one when she bumped into Bea.

"Feeling better?" she asked.

"Much. Let's do this bridesmaid dress thing."

As they walked toward the corner of bridesmaid fashions, an island of color in the sea of whites and ivories, Heron told Bea her ideas about dresses.

"Maggie and I are so close to the same size, and have the same coloring, I think I can try on anything I like, and we will get a pretty good idea of how it will work for her. Charlie's sister told me not to worry too much about her — apparently, she's been in so many weddings she's stopped caring what the bridesmaid dress looks like. She has Charlie's height and coloring."

"Tall and blonde? Gee, wherever will we find something to flatter her?" Bea stopped walking so she could look Heron in the eye. "Listen, kiddo. You know I am not willowy and statuesque, or cute and petite like you and Maggie. If you can't find a dress you like that works for all of us, I'm perfectly happy to just be a guest, you know."

It was rare for Bea to speak frankly about her appearance. She was so confident and such a vocal proponent of body-acceptance. It was disheartening to hear her float the idea of not doing something merely because it might be hard to find the right clothes. What insecurities was Bea still harboring, and what else might she pass up because of them? Sometimes it was hard to tell which things Bea genuinely wasn't interested in, and which she brashly eschewed, rejecting them before they could reject her. She had most people fooled, but she wasn't as tough as she would have everyone believe.

"Bea," Heron said, "I can't imagine not having you up there with me. If we don't find a bridesmaid dress we like for you, you can wear whatever you want."

"Pajamas!"

"Um, maybe let's just look at some dresses," Heron said, laughing at Bea's mischievous pout.

As she began to flip through an assortment of satins, Heron was trying to work up the courage to tell Bea she wanted to go with something in a light shade of pink. A saleswoman approached Bea, who was flicking through the other side of the rack.

"Hello ladies," she said, with a pointed glance at Bea's bride badge. "Our size range is the same for attendants as it is for brides. I'm afraid we likely don't have much that will work for you available to try on. Our largest size might do, with alterations, but maybe you'd like to look at our Mother-of-the-Bride range? We have some beautiful suits perfect for...less conventional brides."

ough

"Actually," Bea said, "I'm getting married in a white bikini. A Vegas thing—you can have your ceremony in a dolphin tank. It's *so* romantic."

Oh my god. Leave it to Bea. Heron suddenly grew very interested in the beadwork on the dress in front of her, failing to maintain a straight face as Bea gushed and the saleswoman's expression grew increasingly incredulous.

Bea continued in a more serious tone, "In addition to being a 'less conventional' bride, myself, I am a bridesmaid for my lovely cousin here. So, let's see how something in your largest size works for me, all right?"

"Certainly." The saleswoman bit her lip. "We only have one sample in that size with us today but it's our most popular style."

"Thank you so much," Bea over-enthused, raising an eyebrow at Heron as the woman went to fetch the dress.

"Let's try somewhere else," Heron said. Maybe they could make a getaway before the saleswoman reappeared. While Bea could certainly hold her own, she shouldn't have to spend any more time around someone who was clearly bent on making her feel bad.

"No way," Bea winked at her. "I'm enjoying making her uncomfortable way too much."

Heron laughed. "Okay."

Fifteen minutes later, Bea stood on a pedestal in the dressing area. The strapless column had zipped past her ribs but not over her breasts, and a series of metal clips held it to her bra. The dress bunched around the curve of Bea's stomach, and she pressed her hands against her lower abdomen.

"Well," she said, sticking a toe out from under the hem, "the length is good? And I do like the color." It was deep teal; jewel tones always looked nice on Bea.

"Thank you so much," Heron said to the saleswoman as she climbed onto the podium to help Bea undo the clips and zipper. "I think we will keep looking."

The woman pursed her lips. "You might try the Spruce Room, downstairs. That's where you can find the vendors for people with more…alternative tastes."

In the mirror, Bea grinned at Heron. "Sounds perfect. Shall we look there?"

"Let's go." Heron hopped down and tossed Bea her sweatshirt. She'd be glad for a break from the overwhelming noise and crowds of the big exhibition hall, too. While it was exciting to finally be starting her planning and see all of this wedding stuff in one place, it was still sensory overload.

They weaved their way through the hall and down the staircase. The basement level of the convention center had lower ceilings and was far less crowded. Bea and Heron found the Spruce Room at the bottom of the stairs, a barer space where the folding tables were adorned more simply. Booths sold kits for making your own invitations or assembling wedding favors, chalkboards for signage, and handmade accessories like ring pillows and flower girl baskets. Along one wall, there were racks of dresses and a sign reading, "Old, New, Borrowed, Blue." Heron also spied bolts of fabric there and made a beeline for them.

A flyer on the table in front of the shop explained they were a new business getting ready to open a storefront in Seattle, specializing in "Custom-made gowns, refurbished vintage dresses, select rentals, and non-traditional styles." This might be perfect for both of them.

Looking through the fabric swatches, something caught Heron's eye immediately. A pale ivory dupioni silk, with a faint pattern of scrollwork and watercolor vines in a shade of blush that barely contrasted with the background. A dress made of this would look solid from far away, but the embellishment would be visible up close.

"Can you sell me this by the yard," she asked, "or do I have to order a gown?"

The saleswoman walked over, a young woman in a pinup-style dress, with a half sleeve of tattooed ferns adorning one arm.

"I'm Lucy, the owner," she said, extending a hand for Heron to shake. "What do you have in mind?"

Heron got out her phone to show some of her inspiration pictures. "Oh, and I made this dress," she showed the woman a picture from the night Charlie proposed. "Twice, actually," she scrolled through to find an older picture, from her homecoming dance.

"You seem like you know what you're doing," Lucy said. "We could probably sell you some fabric. Good choice. This is hand-painted and it's one of my favorites."

They began the calculations of how many yards Heron should buy. The material was expensive, but overall it would be cheaper than buying a dress already made.

"I'll tell you what," Lucy said. "Do you need bridesmaids dresses?"

"Yes." Heron nodded. "Three."

"If you buy them from me, I'll give you ten percent off and throw in an extra yard so you have a little more room for experimentation. Just in case."

"We'll take a look," Heron said, and scanned the room for Bea, surprised to see her buying a candle from a table on the opposite side of the room. "Bea!" Heron waved her over.

"Smell this," Bea said. "It's like the best part of Christmas." The candle Bea waved in front of Heron's nose smelled of evergreen layered with cinnamon and whisky. It did smell great.

"It's nice. But I thought you only liked vanilla candles."

"Tastes can change." Bea's tone was almost . . . coquettish.

Heron turned away to hide her satisfied smile. There was a simple explanation for her cousin's new aromatic interests. Ben's Librotory, with the spice of old paper and sharp tang of the pine scrubbing soap, had a similar smell.

Bea

The Spruce Room was much more Bea's style. No DJs with booming sound systems or walls of white polyester here. Ambient jazz played softly over the speakers. It smelled like a spa, and there were things here Bea might actually consider purchasing. The other shoppers were different, too; less shrill. When Heron made a beeline for the dresses, Bea drifted over to a booth advertising "clean-burning soy candles," picking up a few to sniff. Could she help it if the one she liked best smelled a bit like Ben? No. It was a nice smell. Nothing to feel weird about.

Heron beckoned her over to a portion of the room cordoned off for a dress shop, and she thought, *here we go again*. But this one was different from upstairs. The saleswoman looked like she belonged more at a rockabilly club than a wedding show. The fabrics here were richer colors, without so much beading and frippery. Heron had taken off her sweater and was draping a swatch of softly patterned ivory fabric around her torso. "This color is actually called candlelight," the saleswoman said. "It's perfect with your complexion." It would be a cliche to say Heron was glowing, but Heron was glowing. It would also be a cliche to say tears sprung to Bea's eyes at the sight of the young woman she'd watched play dress up as a little girl, beginning to look like a bride, but the tears were there anyway.

"That's lovely, Bird," she said, surreptitiously dabbing with the cuff of her sweatshirt under the guise of adjusting her glasses.

The saleswoman caught her eye and winked. "You must be bridesmaid number one. I'm Lucy." She pulled the tape measure from around her neck. "If I can get some quick measurements, I'll pull a few dresses for you to try on."

"Oh," Bea said, taking her bulky sweatshirt off to reveal her own tank top underneath. "You probably don't have anything that will work for me, I'm a size—"

"Ah-ah." Lucy stopped her. "We don't do anything by dress size here. They vary so much across brands and bridal sizes always run small. And"—she gave Bea the kind of up and down assessment that normally made her cringe—"I have lots of things in stock that will fit you."

"Shouldn't you have bought me dinner first?" Bea asked as Lucy ran the tape measure around her bust, making a pencil notation on a tiny notepad.

"Pfft, dinner for second base? Aren't we fancy? Don't suck in." With brisk, efficient motions, Lucy ran the tape measure around Bea's waist and hips.

Through the gap in the fitting room curtain, Bea watched Heron pull bridesmaid dresses she liked from the racks. "That seems to be a lot of pink, Bird," Bea called.

"Hmm, does it?" Heron widened her eyes in feigned innocence. "Just try them. Please?"

The fitting room was rigged out of pipe and drape, with a pedestal in the middle and a couple of mirrors. It was utilitarian, nothing like the showplace upstairs, but as Bea stood in the third dress she'd tried on, she was surprised to admit to herself she wouldn't hate standing up in front of two hundred people in it. It was indeed pink, but a muted dusty rose reminding her more of flower petals than cotton candy; sleeveless but cut at the right point on her shoulder to make her arms look strong. A high bateau neckline concealed her cleavage. A wide band of pink in a slightly darker shade ran around the narrowest part of Bea's waist, and a full skirt flared across her lower belly and hips. It wasn't anything Bea would ever pick for herself, but it was pretty. Heron looked adorable in the copy she'd tried on to see how it might look on Maggie.

"Wonderful, ladies," Lucy said, returning from the front with two plastic flutes of champagne. "Heron, we'll ship the dress to your future sister-in-law based on her measurements; she can either get it pinned and mail it back for any adjustments, or take it to a local tailor."

They changed back into their street clothes, and while Heron texted Charlie's sister about the dress, Bea sipped her champagne and absentmindedly perused the racks. It only took her half the glass to get a pleasant floaty feeling, and she remembered the legend about Dom Perignon comparing champagne to drinking the stars. A twinkle caught her eye from a shot of dark velvet among all the silks and laces. She pulled the dress out to look at it more closely. It was a deep, rich midnight, dark blue with the faintest hint of teal. While the other fabrics on the rack reflected the light, this seemed to absorb it, pulling her gaze in and then sparking it with delicate, random pinpoints of pale silver embroidery.

"Oh!" Lucy was returning with the paperwork. "You should try that on. I made three of those for a winter wedding, but one of the bridesmaids dropped out. It's on clearance."

Bea replaced the dress on the rack. "I don't think so. I don't have any place to wear it."

"Nonsense," said Lucy. "You can never find a great dress when you have the occasion for one. And velvet is versatile, you can dress it up or down depending on shoes and accessories. Just try it on. If you like it, I'll give you the same ten percent discount I'm giving Heron on top of the sale price."

So, Bea found herself back on the pedestal. This was not a typical bridesmaid dress in any way, nor was it even a typical cocktail dress. The velvet had enough give to it for Bea to move her arms easily in the fitted, elbow-length sleeves, and the wrapped neckline skimmed the top of her cleavage—sexy without being too much. Instead of the structured, flared-skirt silhouette she gravitated to because it camouflaged her butt, stomach and thighs, the draped fabric skimmed close to her body. It made her consider her belly in a way she hadn't before; material hugged rather than pulling or bunching as if it wanted to caress and decorate the curve instead of hiding it or trying to smash it flat.

"Bea," Heron gasped, "you have to buy that."

Lucy cast a critical eye. "It does look perfect. I don't think I would even try any alterations. And," she walked around the back of the pedestal, then handed Bea a small mirror, "turn around."

Bea started to step down. "No, I really don't think I need to check out my own ass, thank you."

"Bea. This is a totally weird thing for me to say, but you look *hot.*" Heron had moved around behind Bea to see the back of the dress. "Just look."

"Fine." Bea took the mirror from Lucy. She hadn't seen herself from behind in years. Her hair spilled down her back, the warm highlights threaded through the brown were set off by the rich blue of the velvet. If the curve between her waist and hips looked surprisingly good from the front, from the back it was a knockout, leading into the curve of her butt in a way she'd admired on other women without ever thinking of it as something she might see in herself. Below the hem, her calves were strong and shapely. Maybe it was the effect of the champagne, but she *did* look hot.

"Fine," she said. "Sold."

Honestly, the dress was worth buying for the fabric alone, which invoked the winter night sky she loved. If she never ended up wearing the dress, maybe she could get Heron to turn it into some throw pillows.

Chapter Seven

Bea

Campus was still dark when Bea pulled her car into one of the spots at the library loading dock, where she'd agreed to pick Ben up. This early, the only students out and about were probably still up from Thursday night. Ben emerged from the back door promptly at six, wearing dark jeans and a charcoal cable knit sweater. Bea was in her tried-and-true conference outfit; a fine-knit blue top, a black skirt that looked tailored but had enough stretch to be comfortable for long hours of sitting, with tights and flat knee-high boots. She'd thrown a hoodie on over everything, which she would trade for a blazer when they got to the conference.

Bea hadn't seen Ben since the night at the Venerable Grape.

She'd been turning that evening over in her head in the weeks since. She was sure he'd seen her, but maybe she was mistaken. Maybe what she'd overheard Charlie and Rob say about his regret and his feelings toward her were misunderstandings. The uncertainty about where she stood with Ben was making her edgy. She'd spent so long at odds with him, the newness of reframing her feelings, even to simply be cordial, had shaken her confidence. Being Ben's adversary was a familiar, comfortable role but she had no idea how to be his friend. On this trip, she was determined to be breezy and professional, without hinting that for the past two weeks, she'd been overthinking every little interaction with him.

Ben approached the car, and she popped the hatchback for him. There was plenty of room in the cargo area next to her tidy little wheeled suitcase, but he opened the side door to toss his duffle bag into the back seat before sliding into the car.

"Thanks for the ride. Guess it doesn't make sense for the school to pay for two separate cars to go."

"Well, duty calls, and I answer," she said. She hopped out to close the tailgate, glaring at the back of Ben's head. "At least until I've secured my tenure. Besides, we can't all be morally above car ownership." Bea's hybrid got excellent mileage and she walked to campus as much as she could, but Ben always biked or walked, and she'd heard him make a few snarky remarks about faculty who burned gas driving short distances to campus. Especially when here he was, cheerfully letting her consume fossil fuels on his behalf.

"Yeah." Ben pulled the lever under his seat to scoot back several inches. "Actually, I just can't afford a car payment on top of my student loans."

"Oh." Well, now she felt like an asshole. But why hadn't he simply said so?

The car was silent as Bea drove them down the empty Main Street. As they passed Mostarda, she was reminded that beyond a few emails they'd exchanged, they hadn't talked about the conference since their lunch there. "We should probably use this time to discuss our panel strategy."

"Yes," Ben said, "but it's so damn early. Can we swing through The Beanery?"

"Good idea." She'd had a cup of coffee at home, but with a four-hour drive followed by eight hours of conference schmoozing ahead of them, there was no such thing as too much coffee. She took the turn to lead them to the espresso bar's drive-through. She expected Ben to order some sort of hipstery pour-over, but he got an iced mocha and a bagel, and insisted on paying for her latte.

Soon they were on the highway headed toward Oregon. When they passed the grange hall, Ben laughed and said, "Remember the barn dance the SODs and Omegas had there sophomore year? Rob threw up on the sofa in the entryway. They still won't accept bookings from Messiman student groups."

"I remember. Louise and I were roommates that semester and Rob passed out in *my* bed. I had to sleep on our chapter room couch."

"Good times," Ben said.

"Well" — she pursed her lips — "better for some than for others." Overall, Bea'd had a fine time in college, but she wasn't going to let Ben off the hook for making part of her student time at Messiman difficult to bear.

Ben was quiet for a long time. Then he said, "Listen, Bea. I've always wanted to talk to you about that cartoon."

"Nope." Her tone was sharp and she put up a hand between them to ward off any further discussion. She shouldn't have alluded to it. It might have been the root of her dislike for him, but her feelings of antipathy had flourished so heartily that she rarely thought about the caricature anymore.

"It's water under the bridge. If you'll recall, you did apologize. As you were required to. Forget it. Let's pretend it never happened."

Ben made a sound halfway between laughter and indignant sputtering. "It's obviously not water under the bridge and you have quite clearly not forgotten it happened. You take great pains to remind me you're holding a grudge every time I see you."

"Oh, really?"

"Yes, really. And it's fine if you hear what I have to say and you still can't forgive me, but if we're going to work together, I think you owe it to me to hear me out."

Bea's disdainful snort was entirely involuntary, but she turned it into what she hoped was a casual-sounding laugh. "I don't owe you anything," she said. In the seat next to her, she could practically feel Ben's resolve harden, as he twisted in his seat to bore through her with his gaze.

"Fine," she relented, and Ben faced the windshield again. What could he possibly have to say that might make things better? And was he ever going to say it? "Go," she snapped.

"Okay, so. I didn't draw the cartoon."

"I suppose it materialized out of thin air, then?"

"Do you remember Mike, our social chair? He knew I kind of…had a thing for you. When we had that history class together, I thought you were so funny and charismatic. Like, 'here is a woman who is going to really take the world by the balls.' And Mike was a total dick about it because Mike was a total dick about almost everything. When it came out and our advisor said we had to issue a formal apology, I knew Mike would only make things worse. So, I wrote the apology, and I went to your meeting to deliver it. I thought that would hurt less."

"Oh." It was all she could say. She'd thought, back then, Ben might have been flirting while they studied together, but after she saw the cartoon, she reframed every single conversation they'd ever had into one where he was mocking her.

She let a half-dozen miles of road unspool in the silence between them before she said, "You were wrong, you know."

"I know. I was president, I was responsible for the things the other officers did, the whole thing was all my fault. It's one of the reasons I'm the advisor for the guys now, to make sure something like that doesn't happen again." When she didn't say anything else, he added, "I just wanted you to know the truth about what happened. I always have, but it's never seemed like quite the right time."

Bea gunned the engine to pass a row of three semis before she responded. "No. I mean, you were wrong about it hurting less coming from you. I couldn't have given two shits about Mike's opinion of me, but I liked you, Ben. I thought we were friends. I was used to guys being jerks about my size by then, but you seemed different. Thinking you would spend all those hours making jokes about Athenian gender politics with me, and then turn around and do something so cruel. That was a whammy because on top of everything else I was mad at myself for misjudging you."

He ran a hand through his hair and turned away, so when he said, "Well, shit," it was more to her passenger window and the scrubby hills whizzing past beyond it.

They'd come to the point in their drive where the highway ran parallel to the water, through the Columbia River Gorge. A few stubborn leaves still clung to the trees and the low November sun sparkled on the water. Bea reached for her sunglasses, using the cuff of her hoodie to surreptitiously dab a tear, and said, "Yeah, well."

He turned away from the window. "So. Just to reiterate. I am sorry."

She cut her eyes over to him. "I accept your apology. Friends?" She took a hand off the wheel, extending it toward him in an awkward sideways gesture.

He shook it. His hand was cool from holding his iced coffee, and rough, and a shiver zinged through her upper arms at the friction when their fingers slid past each other.

They'd gone through their panel talking points thoroughly by the time Bea pulled off the highway onto the little side road leading toward Multnomah Falls.

"Hope you don't mind," she said. "I always like to say hello to the falls when I pass. It's a little bit of a tradition." Bea had gone to Louise's house in Portland for school vacations almost as often as she'd gone to see her own parents in the Seattle suburbs. They'd always stopped to crane their necks up to watch the slender torrent of white water rushing down the rock face.

"Not at all. I'd like to stretch my legs."

The lot was crowded with people trying to catch the last of the leaves on a day without rain. Evergreens flanked the elegant mist drifting off the falls, but golds and oranges of maple and aspen dotted the hillside, not as full as they'd surely been weeks ago, but there were still enough leaves hanging on to provide a color contrast to the deep greens of the pines and mosses. The roar of the water drowned out the voices of other sightseers around them, though the view of the base was never free from the obstruction of people posing for selfies and group shots.

Ben tipped his head back. "Wow."

"Yeah."

"Want to take a picture to celebrate our truce?" He gestured at the queue with their phones out and ready.

She started to laugh as she turned to give a sarcastic answer but stopped short when she saw his expression. He looked completely sincere, no trace of the mockery she would have expected from him. Maybe she'd made more than one misjudgment of Ben Addison. Fine, one selfie wouldn't hurt.

They waited a few minutes in the crowd jockeying for a prime position in front of the plunge basin. Bea leaned in next to Ben as he held his phone at arm's length, keeping her hands in the pockets of her hoodie while he put an arm around her shoulder to pull her closer into the frame. The contact wasn't especially intimate, but the assured grip of his fingers on her upper arm and the warmth between their bodies made her realize how little, these days, she touched other people or allowed them to touch her. Obviously, that was why this felt strange and a little thrilling; it was only a novelty.

"Hey, take one with mine." Louise needed to see this. Bea handed Ben her phone. Right when he snapped the shot, a growl issued from his stomach loud enough to be heard over the roar of the falls. In the resulting picture, Bea's head was turned toward him with an expression of surprise, and Ben's mouth was open in the beginning of a laugh. They broke apart, erupting into hysterics driven more by the need to break the tension of the morning than Ben's rumbling stomach.

"Um, so," Bea said as soon as she had recovered, "are you hungry?" This set off another burst of laughter from both of them, drawing some curious stares and annoyed looks from the tourists around them. Right. They were disrupting the peaceful communion with nature and selfie sticks. She collected herself and checked the time. "We could get a bite here. We've made good time. I bet they're still serving breakfast at the lodge."

"That sounds good."

As they walked toward the little stone lodge set beside the base of the falls, Bea texted the photo to Louise with the caption:

"It's been a weird morning."

As they were talking to the hostess, her phone buzzed several times, but she didn't look at it until they were in the lobby waiting for their table. It was a text message from Louise, with Heron added to the chain, and it said "OMG I can't believe it worked!" Then: "Shit shit shit."

Then, after a moment, "Bea, honey, that message was meant for someone else. Texting while pumping, lol. Cute picture! There must be a story there and I can't wait to hear it. I have NO IDEA how that would have come about."

"Would you excuse me for a minute?" she said to Ben, then walked outside and dialed Louise's desk extension, knowing she might not pick up her personal cell but would always answer her work phone.

"Talk," she said when her friend picked up. Bea paced back and forth in front of the stone steps leading into the inn as Louise disgorged the details of Heron's little scheme, the explanation peppered with apologetic assurances about it being all in good fun and because they cared about her.

When the call was over, Bea wasn't sure whether she was more angry or humiliated. She was half-tempted not to tell Ben — wouldn't it be easier to simply pretend the whole thing had never happened? But they seemed to have reached an accord in the car, and she had the nagging feeling withholding this information would be against the terms. When she went back inside, she found Ben at a table in front of a large stone fireplace, stirring cream into a cup of coffee. A steaming mug waited at her spot.

"I went out on a limb." He grinned, looking pleased with himself.

"Good call. So, I have quite a story to tell you."

"Those little shits," he said, when she was done filling him in on her conversation with Louise. "Heron and Charlie had me trapped in the book repair room for an hour and a half after I overheard them talking about you."

"Oh? What did they say?"

A rosy flush appeared on Ben's neck, creeping from the collar of his sweater all the way up to his jawline. He took a sip of his coffee. Stalling, Bea thought.

"How about a deal," he said, "I don't tell you what they said about you, you don't tell me what they said about me."

It sounded great, since Bea was pretty sure, even after their frank talk this morning, she might die of humiliation if she had to tell Ben about skulking behind the trellis to eavesdrop on Heron and Charlie, or how what she heard them say had affected her.

"Deal."

Sitting across a table from Ben felt different from sitting next to him in the car. More intimate, even though they were farther apart. She'd been thinking all morning about their conversation, and she couldn't ignore the fact that the air wasn't quite clear between them yet.

"Listen," she said, "I think I owe you an apology, too."

Ben's brows knit together. "You didn't do anything you need to apologize for."

"Not back then, no. But I haven't exactly been fair to you in the meantime. It was just…Okay, so everything was exactly the way I wanted it—I worked my ass off to get my PhD in six years, the job at Messiman fell into place, and everything was great until the one person who could make me feel more like an awkward outcast than an astrophysics badass showed up. And, well, it made me kind of bitchy—" Ben started to interject, but she stopped him. "Let me finish. Please. I realize you didn't have any intention of making me feel that way. I probably always knew it. But it was easier to take it out on you than to be tough with myself about my insecurities, and that wasn't right. I'm sorry." She exhaled deeply when she finished, feeling the stone that had been sitting in her chest lift away.

"Wow. First of all, thank you, and it's fine, apology accepted, but I can't honestly say I'm totally innocent. I think I was hoping we could get the rapport we had before the cartoon back. We used to tease each other a lot, remember?"

She nodded, recalling the good-natured ribbing they'd engaged in when they studied together. She'd been telling herself for years she'd mistaken it for flirtation.

"You...didn't seem receptive to a sincere conversation," Ben tactfully understated. "So, I couldn't really think of another way to interact and for a while it was pretty satisfying to get a rise out of you, but lately it's stopped being fun."

"Dang, Ben."

He chuckled. "I have four sisters. Button-pushing is my love language."

While Bea was laughing, the server came with their breakfasts. She picked up her water glass and tipped it toward him, nodding up at the view of the falls to their left, where the cascade tumbled under a footbridge with a few hardy hikers crossing it. "Truly. Water under the bridge." They clinked glasses.

༄

Their panel was a success. They were paired with two professors from the state university, a political scientist and a historian. Bea spoke about the prompt for her own assignment on stargazing in antiquity and gave some examples of her guest lecture topics for classes in other disciplines, and Ben spoke more broadly about the intersections between research and critical thinking skills.

When the political scientist interrupted Bea's point about the through line from Galileo's defense of heliocentrism in front of the Inquisition, to challenges to science from conservative politicians, Ben reclaimed control of the conversation and returned the ball to her court.

"I believe that's what my colleague was saying," he said, friendly but firm. "There has always been ideological tension between science and religion. Correct, Dr. Hayes?"

"Yes," she'd said. She was used to this kind of showboating and didn't need Ben to come to her rescue, but it was nice to have an assist from a teammate. "It may be a little more nuanced now than it was in the seventeenth century, but I draw a direct line for students between Renaissance astronomers' conflicts with the Inquisition and today's struggles to get funding for things like maintaining our observatories. Although, fortunately, the National Science Foundation doesn't use thumbscrews."

As the room laughed, Ben caught Bea's eye and winked.

After the panel, they went their separate ways, each taking the opportunity to network with acquaintances in their own disciplines at the requisite rubber chicken, hotel ballroom dinner on Friday night. Bea rolled her eyes at Ben holding court at a table of giggling female librarians in novelty-print dresses and statement eyewear, but it felt more like the friendly ribbing of their early student days.

Bea spent most of Saturday in sessions focused on STEM disciplines, which meant she didn't see Ben again until she bumped into him at the coffee station during the final afternoon break.

"I was thinking about catching a movie tonight. Something with as many explosions and as little discussion of 're-envisioning the pedagogical paradigm' as possible," he said. "You in?"

"That sounds great, actually." After two days of intense discussions with other academics, sitting in a ridiculous action movie without having to talk to anyone sounded like a delight. "Unfortunately, I have plans already."

"Of course you do. It was foolish of me to assume you wouldn't be busy."

It felt strange not to assume she heard sarcasm in Ben's voice. She hated to admit she preferred him a little snarky, just as she preferred him with a five o'clock shadow.

"Ask around. I'm sure you can find someone who wants to go."

"Ha." Ben barked a laugh that drew a disapproving look from a tweedy gentleman examining the tea selection. "They'll probably toss me out of here if I ask the wrong person whether they enjoy The Rock's later works. I don't mind going alone."

Bea had balked at telling him what her evening plans were, still used to shielding herself from his mockery, but maybe if he'd go to a movie alone, he wouldn't think it so strange. "Actually, my plans are a reservation for one at Aspen. I do this sometimes when I travel for work, kind of…take myself out on a little date. I know it's silly." When he opened his mouth to speak, she felt like she had to get the admission in before he inserted a barb. "But I like exploring new places and doing something a little different and fancy. They always have those bulletin boards where you can find a dinner partner, but then you end up making awkward small talk all night and honestly, I prefer my own company."

As she spoke, his eyebrows had been gradually rising. Probably, she told herself, because he couldn't believe what a pathetic dork she was.

He said, "That's rad, I love it. And Aspen is supposed to be amazing. Enjoy your evening, Bea."

Once, against all her better judgement, Bea had bungee jumped off a bridge near Arecibo. It'd seemed like a once in a lifetime opportunity was presenting itself and she'd known she would be furious at herself later if she didn't take the plunge. As she stood at the edge, her heart pounding and her body pricked with nervous sweat, she knew she would only find the courage to step off if she pretended someone had pushed her. So she did. And as she flew above the ravine, all the fear and doubt had melted away in the sheer exhilaration of being unmoored from gravity as she merged with the sky.

Bea picked up a napkin and placed it between her sweaty palm and her coffee cup, then said in what she hoped was a this-just-seems-practical tone, "Do you want to come? I'm sure I can call and change my reservation."

A grin broke across Ben's face. "I'd love to."

"Great. We should leave the hotel at seven."

Bea felt a little dizzy as she walked back to the ballroom for the final half of her session on "Diversified Assessment Methods." Probably too much coffee. She shifted her thoughts toward hybrid essay and multiple-choice testing.

―――

Back in her hotel room, the blue velvet dress just hung there in the closet, *twinkling* at her. Bea had packed the dress with her dinner alone in mind. She'd never worn anything like this before and wanted a sort of test drive, to see how she felt in it out where other people could see her. People she didn't know and would never see again. But now, Ben was tagging along, and it would probably be more comfortable to stay in the businesslike, professorial top and skirt she'd worn to the conference. She tidied her hair, added a little smoky shadow to her eyelids, and was standing in her bra, boots, and tights, flicking her gaze back and forth between the blue dress and her taupe oxford shirt when Ben rapped on her door. It was seven already. The only thing worse than overdressing would be to seem like she spent so long primping she couldn't be ready at the appointed time.

"Fuck it," she muttered, and threw the dress over her head. No reason to change her plans because Ben was coming along, right? The cool velvet slipped over her body like a magic spell, feeling as good as the day she'd tried it on at the wedding show. She didn't have time to examine herself in front of the mirror, fretting about how the dress drew attention to her body in a way she wasn't used to or comfortable with before inevitably tearing it off and putting the safe shell of her familiar clothes back on. So, she didn't look in the mirror at all. She ran a hand down to make sure the velvet lay smooth—at least it felt good—and reached for the door.

The second she turned the knob, she regretted the dress. Ben was definitely going to think she was trying too hard to make this seem like some sort of date, instead of simply her, being herself, wearing the outfit she'd intended all along for a nice evening out. When she opened it, she saw his eyes widen and braced herself for the inevitable comment. She just wasn't sure whether it would be a joke, or if, more unbearably, he would try to say something nice.

Instead, he took his phone out of his pocket and said, "Should I get us a car?"

Bullet dodged. "It's only half a mile. I thought we could walk if that's okay with you." Her boots were comfortable, and it was a nice evening.

"Sounds great. Lead the way."

˜

The meal was a seven-plate tasting menu. The second course, a "deconstructed panzanella," consisted of four tiny cubes arranged on the plate. Ben said, "I'm not sure whether to eat this or build something with it."

Bea smiled and took a sip of the accompanying wine-pairing,

a woodsy chardonnay. But when the next course, gnocchi with peas and fresh mozzarella pearls, appeared and everything on the plate was spherical, they both laughed out loud.

"I can't wait to see how they turn the steak into tetrahedrons," Bea said, through giggles.

Noteworthy plating aside, the food was delectable, and the wines complemented it perfectly. They didn't talk about much else until they were finished with dessert (pyramids of passion-fruit mousse) and lingering over coffee. The warm, lazy feeling Bea felt from the food and wine gave her a little extra courage to ask about something that had been perplexing her. "I'm glad we're friends now," she said, "I would have enjoyed this on my own, but it was a lot more fun with company."

"Me too." A corner of Ben's mouth quirked into a half-smile.

"I thought we got along pretty well when we got into planning for the panel, didn't we?"

"Sure."

She fiddled with the handle of her cappuccino cup. "Okay, I'm just going to ask. I saw you at music night at the Grape last week, and I was pretty sure you saw me. I thought you might come over to say hello and was a bit puzzled when you didn't." With uncharacteristic vulnerability, she added, "It made me feel like you were fine being friendly with me when we were alone, but not where your buddies could see."

She hated how this made her sound, like an insecure girl in middle school. But, despite the effort she put into the shell of being confident and together, sometimes she did still feel that way. If they were going to be friends, they needed a truly clean slate.

Ben pinched the bridge of his nose. "Hell, Bea. I felt weird about that, too. I was with my poker buddies. Thursday night is usually our game, but the kid who played that night is one of my work study students."

Ah yes, the earnest young man with the earnest guitar.

"He's a sweet kid, I wanted to support him. So, I talked the guys into going to the Grape instead of our game, and they, uh, weren't on their best behavior. They were already giving me shit about the music and I didn't want to…expose you to that, especially given our history. I wasn't really sure you'd want to talk to me and figured you could've come over if you wanted to, although I was kind of glad you didn't."

"I see."

"Saying all that out loud sounds pretty bad. I was trying to spare your feelings, not hurt them further." He stared down into his coffee cup as he said this, then looked up, catching her eyes with his, asking for understanding.

She could tell Ben was sincere, and she could see where he was coming from, but it still stung. She felt pinned down by the eye contact.

"Well," she said, setting her cup back in its saucer harder than she intended to, splashing a little milk onto the table, "I guess it's at least nice to know you're not too embarrassed to be seen associating with me in places where nobody you know will see us."

Bea knew the bitterness in her words wasn't fair. She was sabotaging the conversation, not giving him the benefit of the doubt he'd been promised. But she also was eager to be safely alone again. She wondered how long it would take to get a rideshare and whether she would have to let him in the car with her. Would it be too mean to leave him to find his own way back to the hotel? She'd perhaps had enough bald honesty for one night.

From the look on his face, she might as well have slapped him. "My god, Bea, that's not it at all. It's just that most of those guys do nothing but complain about their wives. I've been single the whole time we've had this game going, and they all talk about how great I have it. I wouldn't want to talk to any woman I was

HOW TO ALIGN THE STARS

interested in around them. It has nothing to do with who you are. Besides" — he was visibly frustrated now, raking a hand through his hair — "you've always looked good to me. I guess I can understand why you'd have trouble hearing that, given the Mikes of the world, but I hope you believe me. It was true fifteen years ago, and it's true now."

If Bea'd had too much honesty before, now she was wondering if it was possible to actually *expire* from too much disclosure of things best left unspoken. Her heart had begun to pound hard, and she wondered if Ben could see it moving beneath her breast. With her napkin, she dabbed at some of the coffee she'd spilled on the tablecloth, trying to figure out how to respond.

Ben beat her to it. He reached across to put his hand over hers, resting it there lightly as if he didn't want to scare her. "I sure hope you're taking me seriously, because that dress is making me lose my mind."

Um. What? When she looked up and met his eyes, he seemed completely sincere and a little nervous, as if he had no idea how she was going to react to what he'd said.

"Oh." Too much, this was all too much. Bea rarely indulged in honesty with herself about Ben, but — well, *because* when she did, she had to acknowledge she'd been wild about him in college and still found him attractive in a way that was irritating to no end. Irritating because she thought he'd never return the feeling, though. Irritating because he wasn't a real option for her. But now here he was, right in front of her, being an option, and what the hell was she supposed to do about that? Deflect, obviously. Make a joke. Quick.

"This old thing? I just threw it on." She laughed and after a split-second of hesitation, he joined her. It felt good to break the tension, but as the laughter faded it came right back along with something new; the urge to see what it felt like to touch him and have him touch her.

~

When their car came, Ben opened her door, placing a hand lightly on the small of her back to guide her as she climbed in. She felt his thumb swoop in a tiny circle, as if he couldn't quite resist the luxe feel of the fabric, or of her beneath it, and heat rushed through her body. In the backseat of the car, she let her hand rest on the seat between them and his found it, his thumb tracing the same circular pattern on the soft skin of the back of her hand. During the short ride, they didn't speak, eyes straight ahead as if looking directly at the fragile thing happening between them might break it.

Ben took her hand again when they got out of the car, but the bar in the lobby of their hotel was filled with people from the conference, and she hastily pulled away. They hurried in tandem toward the elevator like children trying to get away with something. The elderly professor who'd been so absorbed with the tea selection in the afternoon boarded with them, and they finally made eye contact over his head as the three of them rode upward. The muted, string-section whine of the instrumental music was the only sound in the excruciatingly slow elevator. Bea stifled an ecstatic giggle, heart thumping. The gentleman wished them a good evening with a tip of his hat as he exited on the third floor. Bea didn't even let the elevator doors slide shut all the way before she reached for Ben. Then his hands were everywhere on the velvet, his lips on her neck, then her jaw, then her own lips as she buried her fingers in his hair to bring him where she wanted him.

"Holy shit, Bea," he murmured when he caught his breath.

So, this was a thing that was actually happening. Even as she was absorbed entirely by the physical reality of Ben, there was a tiny piece of herself watching from the distance, triumphant and bemused. She took his hand and pulled him off the elevator at their floor, down the hall to her room. Behind her, his hands ran over her hips, and he nuzzled the back of her neck. It took her three tries to get the door open because she kept pulling the keycard out of the reader too quickly, but finally they were in her room, the door closed behind them, and she was lifting his shirt to run her fingers over the skin underneath. He pulled it over his head, and they parted long enough for Bea to bend down to unzip her boots and step out of them. Ben's chest was pale, sprinkled with a dusting of dark hair, and his stomach had a touch of the softness to be expected from someone who spent most of his time bent over books, but his shoulders and biceps had rugged heft. She was already exceedingly familiar with the fine contour of muscle under the tawnier skin of his wrists and forearms, having been annoyed to find herself appreciating it on a number of previous occasions.

His hands found her hips again, inching the material of her dress upward as he murmured, "Okay?"

Feeling herself at a precipice again, she nodded and raised her arms so he could lift it over her head, then drew him toward the warm, newly exposed skin.

After a moment, she nudged him away, keenly aware that the way the waistband of her tights dug into the soft flesh around her middle was not the most flattering look for her. At least she had on nice underwear and her best black bra. "Avert your gaze," she said, in a way she hoped sounded carefree, then added "please," hoping he'd understand.

He rolled his eyes but obliged, turning around as she shimmied out of her tights. Once they were off, she pressed herself against his back, feeling his jeans rough against her bare legs and pressing her lips to the fox tattoo on his shoulder blade. He turned and yanked her into a kiss. She felt herself hurtling toward the edge of the cliff.

Ben stepped back and looked at her for a long time. A disconcertingly long time. She found herself resisting the urge to grab for her dress or the bedspread, make a dash for the light switch. But she felt a challenge in his gaze and met it, setting her shoulders back and remaining still. And, okay, holding her stomach muscles in because a gal could only confront so many insecurities in one evening.

Finally, Ben spoke, "Bea," he said, his eyes boring into hers in a way that made her feel much more vulnerable than she had when they were on her body, "you are so lovely."

"You don't have to say that, you know," she said with a little chuckle, picking her dress up off the floor and folding it into a tidy square. "I have many excellent qualities, but beauty isn't one of them."

"Why would you say that?" Ben sounded hurt, like she'd insulted him rather than herself.

"Western beauty standards, feedback from dates, sizes typically stocked by clothing retailers, men who like to yell things from pickup trucks…the opinions of most people, really." She'd ticked these off on her fingers; he seized her hand and kissed the base of her palm in a gesture which would have made her laugh if he didn't look so fucking earnest.

"Most people are idiots. I thought you knew that."

She knit her brow into sarcastic wonder, and said, "I do." The irony struck her — how ridiculous it was of her to dismiss so many opinions of others and take pride in following her own star — except when it came to an assessment of her appearance. Suddenly, this seemed totally, ridiculously, hilarious and she burst into laughter, forgetting to suck in her stomach.

And then they were both laughing again, and then they were on each other again, and then the rest of their clothes were on the floor, and she was all skin, cool against the white sheets and heated against Ben's, and her nerve endings sprung to life under his fingertips as she flew into the abyss, and she wasn't alone.

Bea dropped right into sleep but woke up sometime in the hours after midnight when she rolled over with a leg outstretched — something she was accustomed to doing from years of having a bed to herself — and her foot made contact with a hairy male leg. She winced on Ben's behalf and whispered "sorry," but he didn't stir. She rolled to her other side and tried to focus on going back to sleep, but suddenly she was keenly aware of the soft sound of his breathing and...was that also what the tickle on the back of her neck was? She pulled the covers up around her shoulders and Ben shifted, jarring the mattress, bringing sharp awareness to his motion and hers. Every time one of them moved, the other would feel it.

Finally, she gave up and slid out of bed. She fumbled around in her bag for her e-reader, pajama bottoms, and hoodie, then curled up in the armchair by the window. From here, she could see the lights of the city and the shivery glimmer of the river under a moon that was waxing gibbous, but still too far to the east to be seen. Maybe Ben would wake up and she could ask him to go back to his own room so they could both get some sleep for their drive in the morning, but the modest illumination from the digital page didn't make a dent in the darkness of the room.

Five chapters later, she was finally exhausted enough to feel her eyelids grow irresistibly heavy. She crawled back into bed as the plump moon hung over the western horizon and the river began to lighten with the first pearly hints of dawn.

She woke up to a day-bright room and a soft hand on her shoulder. Ben crouched in front of her, dressed. "Hey," he said,

"I'm going back to my room to shower and get my stuff packed up, and I'll meet you back here to go down to breakfast."

"Mmmparay," she said.

"Um," there was mirth in Ben's voice, "would you like me to bring you some coffee?"

Capable of articulate speech now, she flopped onto her back and said, "Hell yes," then added, "please."

"I'd kiss you," he said, "but I really need to brush my teeth. The situation is dire."

She chuckled. "It's fine. Me too. See you in a bit."

Although she woke easily when there was something interesting to see in the night sky, getting out of bed in the morning was always a struggle for Bea. This one was particularly special in its awfulness. As she wrestled herself out of the covers and staggered to the bathroom, she felt like Frankenstein's monster. Correction: Frankenstein's monster after an eventful weekend in Amsterdam. She winced at the bright lights around the white-tiled vanity, and again as the hot water of the shower reminded her of the previous evening's physical exertions.

It took longer than usual, and three-quarters of the extremely large cup of coffee Ben handed her through the cracked hotel room door, but eventually she was reasonably alert and presentable. She slogged her way through the conference's wrap-up breakfast feeling like she was merely impersonating a respectable academic. Ben wasn't helping; every time their eyes met, the corners of his mouth twitched in a small private smile, reminding her they were on the same wavelength. When the final speaker's comments included the word "engorge," Bea had the misfortune of making eye contact with Ben. The almost-imperceptible lift of his eyebrow had her reaching for her water to cover a fit of giggles.

Yet, all morning her mind was a jumble, gingerly prodding the question of how all this would be between them once they returned to their normal lives. After all, she was rather fond of her normal life the way it was. This was the worst possible time to upend it, with her final tenure dossier due in a couple of weeks, Heron's last year at Messiman, and that damned wedding. In ten days, she'd be spending Thanksgiving with her parents in Florida. She cringed, thinking about having to choose between truthfully saying, "No, mom, I'm not seeing anyone," and telling her parents about Ben.

Being with Ben felt good but Bea wasn't sure it felt right, whether they were on the same wavelength or not. Things had changed between them with breakneck speed, and it was too much for now. Maybe too much ever — how could it possibly result in anything other than catastrophe? She hoped he felt the same way, and they could walk themselves back from the brink.

⁓

As they drove east, the silence in the car was companionable this time rather than awkward. Bea hated to ruin it, but she didn't feel like she had a choice. They needed clarity and closure in place before they got back to Millet.

As if he anticipated her need, Ben gave her an opening. When they got to the stretch of highway skirting the river, he said, "At the risk of making a tremendous understatement, that was an unexpectedly nice weekend."

"It was…" she let her voice trail off.

"I'm sensing a 'but.'"

"*I'm* sensing a butt," she stalled, resorting to juvenilia. Ben laughed, but didn't say anything more, waiting for her to answer in earnest. "It's just that it was zero to sixty pretty fast. Maybe we should pump the brakes a little? Consider last night a gimme?" She felt his eyes on her and shot a glance in his direction to see how he was receiving this, but his expression — or at least the quick snapshot of it she'd been able to get without taking her eyes off the road for too long — was inscrutable.

"Like, what happens in Portland stays in Portland?"

"Exactly." After a mile of silence, she added, "Listen, I have a lot going on and I'm sure you do, too. I don't want you to feel like you have any sort of antiquated idea of, well, owing me something."

"Do you feel like you have to give me an out?" His voice was incredulous, with a barbed edge she couldn't place on the spectrum between teasing and genuine annoyance.

"No!" Yes.

"Well, I can assure you I would be delighted to repeat any aspect of this weekend, from sitting across from you over breakfast, to a dinner date, to spending the night, whenever you have the time and inclination."

"Oh." Bea drove on in silence for several miles, eventually switching her blinker on to turn into a rest stop. Without saying anything else, they separated into the restrooms.

When she came out, he was looking out at the bluff over the river, dry grass blowing at his feet in the cold wind. He turned around as she approached.

"Listen. I think maybe we both need an out," she said. "I had a great time too, but this all happened so fast, and I can't wrap my head around what it would look like going forward. For fuck's sake, Ben, two days ago we were barely civil colleagues. I need time to figure that out and frankly, I need time to decide whether it's something I even want."

His brow dropped into a scowl, and she couldn't tell whether he was putting it on for a joke or if he was truly hurt.

She continued, "Not you specifically — please don't take that personally. It's about me. Whether I want to add that element to my life."

He looked out over the gorge, then back at her, squinting. "I get it, I think. You're not sure you're ready to be somebody's girlfriend?"

"Right." Thank goodness he understood (also, "girlfriend?"). "So, when we get back to Millet, can we start over? Friends."

"Sure. Friends." He drew the word out as if he were giving her a chance to take it back.

And she did, a little, amending to, "Friends with potential? Maybe we could take things really, really slowly."

"I can do that," he said. "But," he stepped closer, and in the sunlight she could see the little flecks of gold in his hazel eyes, "we aren't back in Millet yet." Keeping his hands in his pockets, he bent down and brushed his lips across hers.

She didn't realize she was leaning toward him until he pulled away, causing her to stumble toward the guard rail.

"Yeah," he said, his voice low and gravelly, "potential."

Ben turned and marched back to the car, giving her an impenetrable look before he dropped into the seat.

Bea followed and took her place behind the wheel. They drove the rest of the way in silence pierced occasionally by excruciatingly polite chit-chat.

When she dropped him off an hour later in front of his apartment building, he said, "Thank you very much for driving. Enjoy the rest of your Sunday," as if they were merely colleagues between whom nothing noteworthy had ever occurred.

That was it? Taking this all quite literally then, was he? Fine. Great. If what she got out of this weekend was one night of definitely above-average sex and a cordial working relationship with Ben, she could live with that. In fact, it was probably the best possible outcome. At least she didn't have to devote so much of her mental energy to avoiding him anymore. Or...wait. Did she? Ben had agreed to put the brakes on pretty easily. Maybe too easily.

Was this post-fling version of Ben about to become an even bigger pain in her ass than he'd been before?

"You're welcome. I guess I'll be seeing you around campus. I mean, we're work friends now, right?"

"Sure we are," Ben said. As he closed the car door, he added, so quietly she wasn't completely sure she heard him correctly, "…potentially."

Chapter Eight

Bea

"Have you lost weight?" Bea's mother bustled out of the kitchen of her parents' Coral Springs bungalow, brushing her hands on her apron.

"Hi Mom," Bea returned the one-armed hug, set her suitcase down on the tile floor of the entryway, and promptly changed the subject. "This is fun." She inclined her head toward a seascape, children with their sandcastle silhouetted in front of a sherbet-colored sunset. "Is it new?"

"Oh, it is! I've been taking painting classes. Lots of the ladies are really only there for the wine, but I think I'm getting pretty good. I have a bunch of canvases in the guest room you can look through and take any you like home with you. I'm sure you could use something for the walls of that big empty house."

Bea's house was less than a thousand square feet, and the walls were already decorated, but she knew it would be futile to say so.

"Of course, I would love it if I had some actual grandchildren to paint. You know Sally Lombardi's daughter froze her eggs when she was twenty-six and now she has a toddler *and* a partnership in a law firm. She was a year ahead of you in school, remember?"

"I remember. Good for her." It actually sounded like Bea's worst nightmare, and Bettina Lombardi had been insufferable back then, as she almost certainly still was. Bea recalled a playdate shortly after Bettina had gotten an Easy Bake Oven for her birthday, when Bettina allowed Bea to help mix the tiny packet of cake batter, but after they'd watched the lightbulb slowly bake it, Bettina said she'd heard her mother say Bea "didn't need any more cake," and ate the whole thing by herself while Bea watched.

Why was her father taking so long to come in from the garage? He was probably out there tinkering with something, as he would be most of the weekend. In the car, she'd explained to him once again what was going on with Pluto lately, which seemed to be the extent of his curiosity about her work. That would be the longest conversation they'd have until he took her back to the airport on Sunday. Bea knew her dad loved her, but he didn't understand how to relate to her.

"Well, I suppose you still have a little time to do things the old-fashioned way, but you'd better hurry. Are you seeing anyone?"

"No, Mom."

Dialing things back with Ben had been the right choice; she could answer this question honestly. Otherwise, she could hardly fathom the interrogation she'd be in for, and somehow her mother always seemed to know when she was being blatantly dishonest. For a moment, Bea indulged the dark fantasy of telling her parents she'd reconnected with an old classmate. Her mother would have the entire wedding planned by the time they'd finished their pumpkin pie. No. As tiresome as it was to brush off all the passive-aggressive comments about her singlehood, dealing with their reaction to news of a boyfriend would be a thousand times worse, not least because she'd always been so firm about not wanting one. It was a shame, though, because she couldn't seem to stop thinking about Ben's wrists.

As her mother sashayed back to the kitchen, Bea inhaled and exhaled deliberately. Visiting her parents was an endurance event requiring expert-level agility in subject-changing, barb-ignoring, and careful selection of which bickering-related hill to make a stand upon. She took another cleansing breath and followed. This bright, white-on-white space was so different from the warm wood and earth tones of her childhood home, but some things, like the cow-shaped cookie jar that mooed when someone lifted the lid, had made the move to Florida with her parents.

"Well, you know, Mom, I'm up for tenure this year. Achieving that before forty is a pretty big deal, especially these days."

"Yes, I read an article online about how academic funding is drying up, and lots of people with doctorates are looking for jobs in private industry. Pharmaceutical companies and such. Of course, not much need to study space there. And you're certainly not in astronaut shape. I suppose these private space companies are not an option for you."

Len had sent Bea with wine for her parents, and he'd handed her an extra bottle of Merlot with a wink. "This one is for you. I know what a long weekend with my big sister can be like. Open in case of emergency."

She wondered whether it was too soon to retreat to the guest room and sneak a glass. Or a few gulps directly from the bottle.

Instead, she said, "Well, I worked hard to be where I am, and as I said, it's going very well, so you don't have to worry about whether I'm an astronaut candidate, I promise."

Bea washed her hands, rolled her sleeves up, and joined her mother at the counter. She reached into the bread bag to help, tearing bits into the enormous stainless-steel bowl they'd made stuffing in every Thanksgiving of Bea's life.

"Smaller, please," her mother said. Bea could never seem to tear them small enough. "I have a hard time believing you're happy in Millet, after all of the cosmopolitan experiences we worked so hard to give you in the city. I personally couldn't wait to get out of that little hick town as soon as I turned eighteen."

Her childhood home had been in the suburbs and Bea wasn't sure what cosmopolitan experiences her mother meant. The strip mall weight loss center she'd been dropped off at once a week in junior high? The once-yearly trips out of their suburb to look at downtown Seattle holiday decorations? "Well, it's changed a lot, Mom," she said, "now people aspire to retire there. Besides, I think it's a great little town and I love it. And it's nice for me to be near Uncle Len and Heron, too." There was nothing like visiting her parents to make Bea appreciate Len and Heron; at least she had some family who understood and loved her exactly as she was.

"That reminds me! You must tell me all about the wedding plans. This Charlie sounds like quite a catch. Good for Heron."

While Heron's impending nuptials were normally one of her least favorite subjects, talking about them prevented her mother from dissecting Bea's own life, so for once she was happy to discuss every tiny detail.

Heron

Heron's scissors hovered over the silk. She had already

whipped a muslin test garment together by the time the fabric arrived, tissue-wrapped in a white box tied with periwinkle ribbon. The pattern was right. Now, all the paper pieces were pinned to the material and the next step was to start cutting. Toni and her dad were enthusiastic about the muslin. So were Bea and Maggie when she texted them photos. But none of these people knew anything about garment construction. Before she cut, Heron wanted the opinion of an expert. She knew the department store where her mother was a seamstress would open for Black Friday sales later this evening but was closed now. Felicia usually called at some point on holidays, anyway. Having a dress to discuss would make the conversation less awkward.

Heron inhaled deeply and blew the breath out, set down the scissors, picked up her phone, and opened video chat.

"Honey!" Heron could never get used to the way Felicia's apartment looked on video calls. She'd never seen it in person. The time they had spent together since her mother's abrupt departure six years ago was limited to short vacations in places where they could avoid serious conversation; Disneyland, an Alaska cruise, Las Vegas. Felicia lived in a studio apartment in an old brick building on Capitol Hill in Seattle, a neighborhood more popular with young people than middle-aged mothers. It seemed like it must be half the size of Heron and Maggie's Millet apartment, and was furnished much the same way, with cobbled-together thrift store cast offs. But Felicia seemed happy, and over the years Heron had learned to be glad about that.

"Happy Thanksgiving, Mom," she said.

"Happy Thanksgiving. I was going to call you later."

"I figured. Can you talk now? I have some things to ask you about."

"I'm going to brunch with some of the people from work in about twenty minutes, but sure."

"Great." Heron turned the phone to show Felicia the pattern pieces laid across the fabric, which draped over her bed and floor. Felicia asked several questions about the fabric weight and weave.

"No train?" she asked.

"No, it'll be floor length. Hold on." Heron set the phone down and described the bridesmaid dresses to her mother as she changed into the muslin.

"Lovely," Felicia said. "I think that cut will work well for Bea's problem areas."

Heron bristled on Bea's behalf. "Okay," she said, propping the phone against her desk lamp and stepping back. "So, this is what I'm thinking, but in the silk it will be heavier. And of course, the whole thing will look better with tidier seams." For a moment, she thought the call had dropped, but when she picked up the phone to look more closely at the miniature version of her mother on the screen, she could see Felicia blinking back tears.

"It's perfect for you, Heron," Felicia said. "You've done a lovely job." With a tone Heron couldn't quite place but hoped was pride, she said, "You'll be a beautiful bride."

Heron felt tears well up and she tipped her head back to contain them. She should have realized sooner that the gown was the way to get Felicia to engage with her about the wedding. But she'd better not push it; this was enough. It would have to be.

Heron made her voice businesslike. "So do you think I'm ready to start cutting?"

"Yes," Felicia's tone turned brisk. "But remember, that's the point of no return. Go slowly, take your time pinning the pattern pieces down, and make sure your scissors are good and sharp. I'm working tomorrow, but text me if you have any questions."

"Okay, thanks Mom. Happy Thanksgiving."

"Happy Thanksgiving, sweetheart."

Heron was about to hang up when Felicia said, "Hey Birdie?"

Felicia hadn't used her childhood nickname in years. "Make sure you know what you're doing."

"Oh, I am," she said, "I'm taking my sweet time with this dress, don't worry."

"The dress." A frown flashed across Felicia's face, but it was replaced by a bright smile so quickly Heron wasn't sure she'd seen it at all. "Yes, I know you know what you're doing there. Enjoy your dinner. I've got to run."

"Bye, Mom. Love you."

"Me too."

After she hung up, Heron began cutting, stacking, and organizing the pieces of silk in the order in which they'd be sewn. Unable to resist, she ran two panels of the skirt together through her sewing machine. The material slid under the needle like water, and when the seam was finished, she held the beginnings of her wedding gown against her waist and did a test swish, back and forth, listening to the delicious rustle of the silk.

Bea

True to her word, Layla showed up promptly on the science building rooftop by eight every Saturday night. Bea's assignments for observation were flexible; the main point was simply to get the students to choose something they could watch in the sky over the course of the semester, to become used to tracking patterns and positions, learning the basics of operating the telescopes, and viewing celestial objects with an inquiring eye. Layla had chosen Jupiter and her excitement when she saw the red spot for the first time was worth Bea giving up a few hours of her Saturday nights.

Fall semester was always a little less enjoyable than spring because the nights started out warm but were bitingly cold by finals week. Bea was used to nights spent on windy mountaintops and had plenty of cold weather gear, but Layla had given up relying only on her coat and jeans. Tonight, she had a wool blanket tucked around her waist like a long Edwardian skirt. This would be their last night and Layla was sketching the storm patterns on the planet's surface—above and beyond the assignment, but she seemed to be enjoying it and Bea had some room in her rubric to give a little extra credit.

Bea huddled near the stairwell entrance, reading a planetary science journal on her tablet. There was a knock on the door, which was locked from the outside. Thinking it might be students looking for a place to hang out, or who had missed the last telescope lab time on Thursday, she cracked it open, careful not to let too much light spill over to where Layla was working and peeked through the gap. Ben stood on the landing, holding a drink carrier from The Beanery containing four tall cups.

"It's a cold night," he said, "I thought the stargazers could use a warmer."

She smiled and opened the door wider to let him out onto the roof.

"I got you a half-caff cappuccino," he said, remembering her evening coffee order from their dinner in Portland. "Layla, I didn't know what you liked so I have a peppermint hot chocolate, an almond milk latte, and a green tea."

"Ooh, can I have the latte?" she asked. "I need all the caffeine I can get."

"Sure thing," he handed her the cup. "Did you find the articles on *Beowulf* you were looking for?"

"I did, thanks. I'm gonna start my paper tonight."

"Great." In answer to Bea's raised eyebrow, he said, "I take a few Saturday reference desk shifts in the weeks before finals." He removed the hot chocolate from the drink carrier and took a sip. "Do you want this green tea, too? I think it tastes like grass clippings."

She wrinkled her nose. "Dishwater. Maybe Layla wants it."

"Yes, please," said Layla, accepting the cup with cheerful enthusiasm. She held one drink in each hand as she squinted into the eyepiece of the telescope.

Ben stepped deeper into the darkness to examine the lab space: four telescopes, tables, red-bulbed lanterns with downcast shades. The rooftop was six stories up, high enough to get above the safety lights illuminating the campus walkways.

"So, this is your ivory tower," he said.

"Yes, only it's not much of a tower and it's brutalist brick instead of ivory, but what really matters is up there." She swept her hand at the broad dome of sky, stars twinkling in the winter darkness, the faint reverse shadow of the Milky Way spanning the expanse.

Ben sat on one of the benches and craned his head back. After a few minutes, he straightened and rubbed his neck. "You must have one hell of a chiropractor bill."

She laughed. "You get used to it. Also, most of the time one uses a telescope to do any real observation. Looking up? That's just because I love it." She'd kept her eyes fixed on the sky, and when she looked back down, she found his gaze intent on her face, although in the dark it was hard to interpret his expression. "Anyway, it's better out of town a bit, where you can get away from the light. I take a blanket and lie down."

"I'd love to see that sometime." His voice was low, but she blushed and threw a glance toward Layla, who remained focused over her notebook.

Bea chuckled to cover the thrilled jolt of longing she felt at the idea of curling up with Ben on a blanket spread over the gentle swell of a starlit field.

"Maybe when the ground isn't frozen," she said with a louder laugh. It was a little too loud, a little too sharp, breaking the spell.

Layla turned her lamp up brighter and said, "I'm almost done, then you folks can get on with your date."

Fantastic. Rumors would be across campus by the time classes started on Monday. She knew protesting would only make the situation worse, but instinct kicked in. She laughed again and said, "We're only working on a project together."

Layla and Ben both rolled their eyes, in a way that would have made Bea giggle if she hadn't already put her complete lack of chill on display. Instead, she bit her lip.

Layla said, "Of course." Then the little twerp *winked* at her. "Don't worry, Dr. Hayes. I won't tell anyone. I think it's cute. Anyway, I'm all done. Thanks again. See you Monday." She bundled her papers into her backpack and bounced through the stairwell door.

"Did you hear that?" Ben playacted a swoon. "We're *cute.*"

"Shut up," she said.

"Geez. Some thanks."

"Oh yes, thank you very much for the warm beverage and irreparable damage to my professional reputation."

"A wee bit overboard on the self-importance, don't you think?"

He had a point. She was so unaccustomed to incorporating anything romantic into her life, she'd overreacted about the blending of personal and professional. Which, if she were going to date a colleague (*was* she going to date a colleague?), was something she would have to come to terms with.

"You're right. This was very thoughtful, and I do appreciate it."

"You're welcome. I was curious to see what it was like up here."

"You didn't take astronomy?"

He shook his head. "Two semesters of geology."

"Ah." She had an idea. "Then you haven't seen the planetarium either?"

"No."

Bea smiled. "Come with me."

Twenty minutes later, they were lying on the floor of the planetarium, southern hemisphere constellations whirling above them. It wasn't as cold as the wheat fields would be, but a chill radiated from the cement under the thin carpet. Bea barely noticed it through her sweater, jeans, and long underwear, but she felt Ben shiver and found herself inching closer in an attempt to pool their warmth, until their hands touched, and he laced their fingers together.

"Wow," he said.

"Yeah. I shouldn't run the projector for fun. The bulbs are expensive, and it uses a lot of electricity, but sometimes I can't resist."

"I don't blame you." Ben raised himself on one arm and leaned down to kiss her.

For a moment, she felt torn between laughing because they must look like they were trying to reenact a Disney movie, awe that she was finally getting a princess moment, and annoyance at herself for noticing or caring. Then she gave up and gave in to the realness of Ben, lifting her hands to his head, his back, feeling the way he balanced his torso above her so carefully, matched the pressure of his lips to her response. She was starting to wonder whether she'd remembered to lock the planetarium door behind them, whether she should check, when he pulled away and rose to a crouch. She fumbled around for the remote and turned the dim footlights on so they could see each other better.

"Thank you for showing this to me," he said. "It's getting a little late. I don't want to keep you out too long."

He stood and reached a hand down to help her up, but instead of taking it, she lifted herself on her elbows and said, "Are you serious?"

"Completely. You said you wanted to start over, taking things more slowly, and one kiss to end an impromptu first date seems about right."

"Oh." Turning the lights up brighter, she could see Ben's face bore a solemn expression, but there was laughter in the corners of his eyes.

"Yeah." Fair enough. Well played, Addison. She straightened her sweater and got to her feet. "I did say that. Thank you very much for respecting it."

"No problem," he said, and now there was laughter in his voice, too. "Can I walk you to your car?"

"Thank you, that would be nice. Can I give you a ride home? If I recall you usually walk to campus."

"Thank you, that would be nice." He offered her his arm, and, their exaggerated propriety forming the bubble of a joke between them, they walked to her car.

They settled into the car, and she said, "I have one more trick up my sleeve." She pushed the switches for both heated seats, knowing Ben's backside was likely as chilled as hers.

"Oh," he said, as the element warmed up, then he nestled into it with a little shimmy she had to admit was adorable. "Ooh, that's *nice.* You know how to live, Beatrice Hayes."

"You should see my electric blanket," she said.

"Is that a promise?"

"Maybe if you play your cards right." She pulled up in front of his building, and as she stopped the car, she turned to him and winked.

He pecked her on the cheek before he got out, and she could have sworn she detected a strut as he made his way up the walk.

Chapter Nine

Heron

Heron rushed out of her research seminar to meet Charlie at the library. They'd planned to go up to the Librotory to work on their final project, but when she found him at his favorite table near the back windows, he was slouched over his laptop and hadn't even begun to pack up.

"Ready, babe? We only have two hours on the press, and we can't get another slot before the project is due." She thought once he knew she was there, he would gather his things and follow her upstairs.

He tipped his head back to look at her, despondence written across his face. "I'll never be ready. I just took a practice test and got a 151. That's not good enough for any of the top schools, not with my GPA." Charlie's grades were fine, but he wasn't on the honor roll like Heron.

She squinted down at his laptop screen. "It looks like you need to spend more time on logical reasoning. Here, see—this is the chapter you should focus on. Why don't you reread it and see what concepts need more attention while I go print our stuff on the press, and then I'll help you? We can bind everything on Saturday."

She'd planned to spend Saturday working on her thesis; her outline was due at the end of the semester, but it could wait until Sunday. She'd figure it out. Other than the challenge of finding the time to fit everything in, she liked helping Charlie with his LSAT studies. It was satisfying to puzzle through the test questions, and she often found herself biting her lip to keep herself from blurting the answer before he got to it.

Charlie beamed up at her. "Really, babe? That would be so great. I know the Book Arts class is an easy credit, but I need to make a good grade in it for the sake of my GPA."

The art class wasn't easy, but since she'd been doing all the conceptual work and writing the artist statements while Charlie had been focused on the mechanical tasks like mixing ink, pressing paper, and setting type, she could see how he perceived it that way. It was fine though; she loved the class and for Charlie it was only a distribution credit.

"Sure." She smiled. "No problem. I'll swing by here when I'm done, and we can make flash cards." Dealing with material visually helped Charlie learn better. Heron found it fun to make flashcards and charts and bought a new box of markers every year for studying with Charlie.

"You're the best."

"I know." She waved as she made her way to the stairs, glad to find the Librotory empty. She'd rather Ben didn't know Charlie wasn't working on this with her.

Printing the pages took much longer on her own since she had to mix the colors, ink the roller, prepare the paper, and change all the blocks of type herself.

She consulted her detailed notes of how each page should be run. The assignment Ben had given them was to print ten copies of a twenty-four page book, text and images. Heron's concept was to print the Zodiac, with a list of words for each sign and an accompanying image. Some were literal interpretations of the signs. She had etched a simple line drawing of a lion onto a plexiglass plate for Leo, for instance. Others were representations of people she loved who were born under the sign. For Charlie, a Gemini, she'd found an anatomical drawing of a heart, then traced it as a mirror image of itself so they faced each other on the page, like butterfly wings. Heron and her dad were both born under Taurus and for that she'd traced a grape leaf onto a printing plate, planning to go in later to watercolor each page by hand.

She'd been surprised when Ben asked what sign Bea was, and then produced an old brass plate from the motley collection of antique printer's items, with labeled diagrams of the Scorpius, Hercules, Cygnus, and Sagittarius constellations marked on it.

"Don't feel obligated to use it," he'd said, "but I thought it might work. It caught my eye because I'm a Sagittarius, but Scorpio's there, too."

It was perfect, and Heron planned to give one of the copies to Bea even though astrology was very much not her cousin's thing. Using this image would make the whole gift even more special to Bea, she hoped. She'd caught a note of more-than-professional fondness in Ben's tone when he'd asked about her. Maybe her silly little plan was actually bearing fruit.

As she ran the prints, her mind wandered over what she needed to do in the next two weeks, before finals ended. She made a mental list:

1. *Finish Book Arts project — underway*
2. *Finish rough thesis draft — underway*
3. *Study for Social Justice final*

She knew the concepts, and some of them even overlapped with Charlie's law school application material. That would be fine, she was a good test-taker even though exams made her feel queasy.

4. *Write the final paper for Twentieth Century Art History*

Her stomach dropped. She planned to write about the collaboration between Jackson Pollock and Lee Krasner, but she hadn't even started. She'd been so focused on everything else, it had slipped down her to-do list, but it was due soonest — on Monday.

Heron's heart pounded as she mentally rearranged her outstanding tasks, trying to find room there somewhere for a day of research and a night of writing. Tomorrow? It would have to be tomorrow. She couldn't slide the thesis work any later; it was due Tuesday and she needed to have her advisor look it over before she officially turned it in. She blew a slow breath out through pursed lips. Tomorrow, then.

Done printing, Heron stacked the book pages with tissue between them to keep the ink from smudging, slid them into the cubby she and Charlie had been assigned, and went to meet him. She hoped he was feeling better.

Bea

Bea could polar align a Newtonian telescope without even thinking about it, but she went through six sets of printable dividers before she got the science division's photocopier to line up the section headings for her tenure portfolio properly. It was ridiculous that she had to submit a paper copy. Everyone reviewing it would have access to an electronic version with dynamic links and videos of her teaching and presenting, but according to Rick, reviewers liked to have a paper copy to leaf through "over a cup of tea." She'd spent the past hour swearing at the copier.

Finally done, she gave herself a moment to lean against the Formica counter in the copy room, paging through the summary of her professional accomplishments. It looked good. She was as ready as she would ever be. And the physical copy would be a nice memento to add to her bookshelf when she was awarded tenure. Or a good start on application materials for a new position. She winced at this last thought. She should try not to worry about it until she had reason to believe she needed to. It wouldn't help anything to torture herself for the months it would take to get the final determination.

It was drizzling, so Bea wrapped the binder in a plastic shopping bag. The sidewalk leading from the science building converged with the one leading from the library; Bea and Ben reached the intersection at the same time.

Ben fell into step next to her. "Hi."

Bea's face felt flushed. She'd been fussing with the hot photocopier, but she couldn't discount the warming effect of Ben's smile. "Oh, hey."

He nodded at her plastic-wrapped binder. "Is that the tenure tome?"

"Sure is. All my professional accomplishments plus all my hopes and dreams in one handy three-ring binder."

"I'll walk with you." It was raining harder now, and cold, but neither of them rushed.

After a moment, Bea said, "I didn't see you at the cafe today." Lately they'd been appearing in the coffee line together at roughly the same time. Surely only a coincidence, a vagary of their respective schedules, but she hadn't realized how much she'd been looking forward to it each day until she missed him this morning.

"No," he said, "I'm actually headed over to get a coffee now. I came in a little late today because I'll be on the reference desk until ten. Finals, you know how it is."

Bea nodded. She'd been holding expanded office hours all week.

"Incidentally, your cousin was huddled over a table near my office when I came in this morning and was still there when I left. I'm not sure she's even moved from her chair. I know these kids go pretty hard studying, but Heron looks monumentally stressed out. Would it be too weird if I took her a coffee?"

It was typical of Heron to be working so hard Ben would take notice. Bea admired how devoted she was to her studies, but it was beyond exasperating to see her knocking herself out to graduate with honors but totally complacent about figuring out what she was going to actually do with her degree once she got it.

"That's kind of you. I'm sure she'd appreciate it, but I'll go see if I can get her to take a break."

They'd reached the spot where their paths diverged again, hers up the steps to the administration offices, his toward the student union building. "Sounds like a plan. Good luck with that." He pointed at her binder.

"Thanks. Fingers crossed." Bea was struck with the urge for some small parting gesture, a quick, casual embrace. She must be losing her mind entirely. Instead, she said, "So, big plans for the holidays?"

"I'll fly to meet my oldest sister and her son in Chicago, then we'll drive to Peoria to spend Christmas with the rest of the family. I have three nieces and four nephews. It's all very Norman Rockwell," he said. "Every year, my mom drags everyone to church on Christmas Eve and then pretends to be annoyed when we have a snowball fight in the parking lot afterward."

"Sounds nice," said Bea, thinking of her Thanksgiving in Coral Springs, full of double-edged comments and awkward silences.

"It is, but it's also complete chaos. How about you?"

"No chaos for me. I'm staying here. I saw my folks over Thanksgiving and that dose will be adequate for a while. It'll be quiet."

"Ah, well, enjoy. I'll be back before New Year's, enjoying a little quiet, myself. Or, not so quiet, maybe, if I can drum up some plans."

"Nice. I bet you'll need a break from people after all the time with your family."

"Sure." He tipped his head to the side, as if waiting for something more.

Bea suspected there was some sort of standard, well-adjusted flirty girl response she was supposed to have made to his comment about New Year's Eve plans, a casual remark tossed off to let him know she'd be receptive to sipping champagne and sharing a midnight kiss. The problem was, she'd be damned if she knew what it was. Half the time she was around Ben, she felt comfortable and natural. The other half, she floundered, too unsure of her feelings — and his — to have any idea how to respond.

When she didn't come up with anything, Ben said, "You'd better turn that thing in before it starts raining harder."

"Right." She watched him walk away for a second before entering the building. Pausing in the vestibule, she removed the shopping bag and stuffed it in her coat pocket, pushed her shoulders away from her ears, and strode into the administrative offices. After giving the portfolio to President Phillips' assistant she felt a rush of adrenaline. Her future was quite literally in the hands of others now.

Professional anxiety mingled with the unfamiliar electricity of whatever the hell was going on with Ben, sending a current of nerves bubbling through Bea. Her step was brisk as she walked back toward the library, fueled by nervous energy from both sources. She was sorry Heron was having a rough go of finals week, but she couldn't help being a little glad her cousin's troubles would give her something else to focus on.

Heron

The library usually cleared out on Friday evenings, but finals week was different; it was still packed at six. Heron was in front of her laptop in one of the fourth-floor study carrels, a sliver of the library that had escaped renovation. Ancient carpet, which had possibly once been tan, was threadbare in patches where desks had been repeatedly dragged around by generations of students attempting to escape the insidious draft of cold air from the old casements. It was nearly always empty, which was why Heron liked it. She'd tried pulling one of the nubby pumpkin-colored armchairs up to her desk a few hours ago so she could curl her legs into it, but her feet kept falling asleep. Art books and highlighted copies of journal articles littered the table around her laptop, and she could scarcely keep her eyes open. She'd arrived at nine this morning to stake out her spot and gather her research materials. Now, her head ached and the last time she'd tried to stretch her neck her muscles had protested so severely, she'd decided it would be easier to remain tense. She kept catching her chin in a drift toward her chest. It took all her effort to keep her eyes open and focused on the page in front of her.

At a tap on her shoulder, she jolted and looked up into the concerned face of her cousin.

"I heard you've been here all day," Bea said. "Did you even eat lunch?" She picked up Heron's water bottle and shook it. Empty. "Honey, you're not even staying hydrated. Come on. I'm springing you."

"I can't just leave all this stuff. I'm so close to done."

Bea peered at her laptop screen and huffed. "Page four. You're halfway there. Maybe two-thirds if you half-ass it, which I know you won't. Come on, I'm taking you to my house for dinner and a nap. This will all be here when you get back."

"It will not," Heron complained. "The library assistants will come by and reshelve everything."

"No, they won't," Bea said. "I have an in with the librarian in charge of the reference desk tonight. He'll ask them to leave this corner alone."

Heron smiled at this. "But somebody else might take my spot."

Bea glanced around at the empty corridor. "I doubt it." She pulled a cardigan from her bag and draped it over the back of the chair. "There. It looks like you've only stepped away for a few minutes. Now, you're coming home with me, and I won't take no for an answer. The abstract expressionists can wait. I'll bring you back," she said, cutting off Heron's protest. "I promise. After a little food and some rest."

Heron did feel unsteady going down the stairs. Now that she was up, she felt hungrier and more exhausted than she'd realized. She let Bea usher her into the warm car and closed her eyes, opening them only when they pulled up in front of Gallo D'Oro. Bea dashed out minutes later with a bag of takeout cartons. She settled Heron on the couch with a plate of tacos, a blanket, and Herschel purring softly at her side.

An hour later, Heron was back in Bea's car rested, fed, and armed with a thermos of the Earl Grey tea Bea kept in her kitchen just for her. Bea tucked a bag of almond M&M's into her pocket. "For later. Don't tell Ben I encouraged you to take food into the library."

As they drove back to campus, Bea said, "Where's Charlie tonight? I thought you usually studied together." Heron could tell she was making an effort to keep her tone mild.

"He's super stressed. I mean, I only have finals and my thesis, Charlie has all that and the LSAT, which is way more important." This was technically true, Charlie *was* stressed, which was why he'd told Heron he needed to "blow off some steam" with the guys instead of joining her at the library.

"Mmm," was Bea's noncommittal answer.

Heron had to admit she felt much better, and the last pages of her paper flowed across the screen as she typed with renewed confidence in her assertion that Krasner's work had been far more innovative after Pollock's death.

She finished a few minutes after two. Heron wasn't keen on walking home alone at this hour, but she didn't want to call Charlie. She hoped he'd gone to bed so that he could make good on his promise to study hard the rest of the weekend.

Bork caught up with her in the vestibule. "Hey," he said. "Heading home?"

"Yes." They started across the quad together, chatting about how their senior year was going. Like Charlie, Bork was a politics major, but he was hoping to go to graduate school for public administration. "It's deeply uncool, I know, but I want to make a real impact. And I think maybe the best way to do that is to get into the rooms where policy decisions are being made."

"I didn't realize you had such a serious side."

He shrugged. "Well, I'm not that guy here. I'm Bork. Goofy nickname guy."

They were passing the amphitheater and Heron heard rustling and a giggle coming from behind the shrubs surrounding it. It had always been a popular spot for mischief, even on a frigid night during finals week.

She said, "Does it bother you? That everybody calls you Bork instead of Bryant?"

"At first, it did a bit. It started first year. The SOD house chef always has Friday nights off. When my mom and stepdad went out on weekends, I used to make pancakes for my little sisters. Most of the upperclassmen were out at the bars. So, I thought, hey, I'll make pancakes for the guys who are stuck here. But the flour was in this *giant* canister on the top shelf, and I dropped it and ended up completely coated. Half the kitchen, too. Like, absolutely everywhere, it looked like a blizzard."

Heron laughed at the mental image.

"We were all trying to grow mustaches that November. Mine came in fast. Apparently, with the flour all over my hair and face, I looked like the Swedish Chef, so when the guys came in and found me, they started chanting 'bork bork bork.' And there you have it. It stuck. Actually, it was Charlie who started the whole thing, now that I think about it."

She had to admit it did sound like Charlie to take a joke a touch too far. "Do you want me to talk to him? Ask him to knock it off?"

"Nah. Especially not now."

"I'm sure he would apologize if he knew it bothered you." They'd reached the sidewalk in front of her apartment building, and Heron stopped walking.

He shrugged. "Sure. But like I said, it's not something to make an issue of. I'd rather be goofy nickname guy than the guy who can't take a joke."

"Okay, well, thanks for the walk."

"Any time."

Heron let herself into the lobby, feeling the fatigue deep in her body as she mounted the stairs. Bork — Bryant — had such a clear ambition for after graduation. When she entered the apartment, she found Maggie asleep on their couch. Heron pulled a blanket over her friend. Maggie had her plans set, too; teaching middle school language arts. And Charlie had been planning to go to law school for as long as she'd known him. Maybe Bea was right that she hadn't thought enough about what to do after graduation.

Sophomore year, she'd decided on an art history major because those were the classes she enjoyed most. Then when Bea pressed her about the impracticality of art, she added sociology because those classes were interesting, too, and there were lots of ways they could be combined into a single thesis topic. She hadn't thought about what careers they might lead to, and if that was a mistake, it was too late to correct it now. Inspiring career paths had revealed themselves to everyone else Heron knew, past and present. Her dad had begun thinking about winemaking when he was her age, and Bea had already been applying to PhD programs. Was there something wrong with Heron that made her not want to think beyond graduation?

Heron definitely didn't want to apply to grad school just because she couldn't think of something else to do—especially not if she couldn't get into a program near Charlie. And what type of grad school exactly, she hadn't considered. So what if the only things she felt good at were making clothes and loving Charlie? Wasn't that enough for now?

Chapter Ten

Bea

Every year, on a Friday before Christmas (not necessarily in conjunction with the winter solstice, an inconsistency that drove Bea to distraction), Main Street closed to traffic so local businesses and crafters could set up booths for holiday shopping. This year, Toni had arranged for Heron Acres to have a mulled wine stall, where she ladled the spice-studded brew into paper cups. It was next to a food truck selling hot, fresh doughnuts and the aroma in their corner of the market was drawing the biggest crowd of the evening. Last week's rain had softened to snow in time to blanket the street and rooftops in a few inches of white. The whole scene resembled a real-world version of someone's mantle-top Christmas diorama. As they strolled through the booths, Bea filled Heron in on her most recent conversations with Ben.

"Bea," Heron was exasperated. "He was trying to ask you out for New Year's Eve." By now, Heron had heard a somewhat censored version of all the details of Bea and Ben's incipient romance. She had the grace not to gloat about her role in bringing them together, but she had given them a groan-worthy mashed up couple name. Heron saying she was on "Team Bean" was almost enough to make Bea throw the idea of dating Ben out the window completely.

"That's silly," Bea said. "If he wanted to take me out on New Year's he'd ask. Wouldn't he?"

Heron looked skeptical. "Not after you put the brakes on things. He might think it's too big a step. Or," — she scrunched up her face — "he thinks *you'll* think it's too big a step. It can be kind of a big deal, the kissing at midnight and everything."

"Oh." Bea sipped her wine. "I guess. This is exhausting. No wonder Herschel is my chosen life partner."

Heron giggled and shoved her on the arm with a mittened hand. "It's *fun*. Anyway, why don't you invite him to Dad and Toni's party?" Bea was considering this — she supposed she could text him — when Heron cupped her hands and called, "Ben!" Then she was waving him over.

Shit. Now? She quickly smoothed her hair as Ben dodged through the crowd, making his way toward them. He'd traded his Converse in for snow boots and his Cubs cap for a red and blue knit hat. Snowflakes gathered on the yarn and when he got closer Bea saw one clinging to his eyelashes. She suppressed the urge to reach up and brush it away. "I thought you'd gone to Illinois," she said.

"I leave tomorrow." His smile broke through the chill of the evening. "I was hoping I'd see you here."

"Here I am," she said, extending her hands in a ta-dah gesture and then immediately scolding herself. Dork. "Charlie went back to Connecticut right after his last final, but Heron doesn't leave until tomorrow, so we're having a girl's night out." She turned to include Heron in the conversation, but she was gone. Bea spotted her several yards away, disappearing into the crowd. "I guess I'll catch up with her later."

"Great. I have you all to myself."

Her cheeks grew warm as she slipped her arm through his extended elbow. They strolled through the warren of booths and stalls, stopping for a minute to listen to a group of carolers in Dickensian garb sing "Rockin' Around the Christmas Tree," a juxtaposition that struck both of them funny.

"You know," she said after they'd passed out of range and stopped snickering, "if you want to see me you could always just text me. Or call. Or email. I'm in the college directory, even."

"I know." His tone was glib. "But I kind of like the kismet."

"Kismet?"

"Yeah, you know, like, trusting we'll run into each other if we're fated to spend time together that day. Our paths do seem to cross pretty often."

When she'd been avoiding Ben, he'd seemed to pop up around every corner, although now that she was looking for him in the hopes of feeling the little zing she got when their eyes met, it didn't seem to happen as often as she would like. "Ha. You should talk to Heron about that."

"Oh, I know, she's very into celestial guidance, isn't she? Don't tell me she got it from you."

"No," Bea said emphatically. "While I have some interest in the overlap between myth and astronomy, I come down firmly on the side of science. I did my best to encourage Heron to be sensible, but she got interested in this stuff when she badly needed something to believe in and I guess there's no real harm done." She didn't think Heron would mind if she told Ben about her history, especially since, with classes over, he wasn't her professor anymore. Besides, there was enough town gossip, it was possible he'd already heard something. As they strolled through the market, she continued, "Her mom left the family when Heron was fifteen. 'Left,' as in, she was just gone one morning. Didn't tell anyone she was going, left her phone on the nightstand. The police had been involved for two days before Len found a note saying she'd be in touch once she was settled."

"Jesus," Ben said.

"And then, a position opened in the department here right as I was finishing my doctorate and I was able to move back here and help them through it. That seemed like fate to Heron. To me it only seemed like a wonderful coincidence. I would have been thrilled to work at Messiman under any circumstances, but it came at a time when they needed a little extra family around."

"Wow."

"It's nice for me to be near family, too. I'm an only child and I'm not especially close to my parents, so it's kind of like my extended family became my chosen nuclear family."

They were reaching the end of the market and the sounds of music and chatter were growing faint, the smell of popcorn and cinnamon fading, but neither of them suggested turning around.

"Yeah," Ben said, "I felt lucky to land back here too, actually. When the position opened up at the library, I felt like it was my shot to take, or my shot to blow."

"Well, you also make your own luck, don't you? I worked my ass off in grad school to make myself a good candidate for a position like this one. I had references on the faculty here and I rocked my interviews. I bet you did, too."

"Oh my," Ben clapped a hand to his heart. "Are you actually

acknowledging that I have some expertise in my field?"

"Stop it," she said, but she was laughing. "I did see an article recently, about how horoscopes and tarot are getting more popular. It's a mindfulness thing, a way of learning to see opportunities. That makes more sense to me," Bea said. Regarding Heron, it certainly did; Bea knew her therapist had encouraged her to explore mindfulness and meditation as a way to manage her anxiety. "Things are set up for you a certain way by fate or a deity or luck or whatever, but it's up to you to align everything and make it fall into place."

"We've both done a bit of that," Ben said.

They walked on in the crystal quiet of the evening. Bea listened to their feet crunching in the snow. She was trying to think of something else to say, something wry and breezy, but her wit failed her. Maybe it was just as well to leave the spell unbroken.

They passed a deserted block where a dentist's office and insurance agency sat closed for the evening, their storefronts lit by twinkling white lights. By unspoken mutual agreement, they stopped walking and Bea was sure one of them was going to suggest turning back to the market. Right as she was about to speak, snow began to drift from the sky in fat storybook flakes.

Okay universe, hint taken. Bea cupped Ben's face in her gloved hands and pulled it toward hers.

Heron

After Heron left Bea chatting with Ben, she indulged in a self-satisfied grin. She spotted her friends Luke and Jamie near the cider booth. They both went to school in Seattle, and she hadn't seen them since summer.

"Hey!" said Jamie, leaning in to hug her. "Let me see your ring!" Heron had posted engagement photos, but she wasn't going to turn down an opportunity to show the ring off in person.

She took off her mitten and held her hand out for Jamie to see.

Luke gave a low whistle, "Dang, Heron, congratulations."

"Thanks." She slid her mitten back on.

"Hey," Luke said, "I know Dave is happy for you, too."

"Oh." Awkward. Dave was Luke's best friend and they'd all hung out together in high school, when she'd been dating Dave. They'd broken up after graduation and expected to stay friends, but then she met Charlie and they fell out of touch. While she saw Luke occasionally because he could usually be found wherever Jamie was, she hadn't heard from Dave in a long time. "Thanks. How is he?"

"He's great. He graduated a semester early and is already starting at a gaming company." Luke laughed. "He's a total overachiever now."

"Good for him." In high school, Dave had been a bit of a slacker, but apparently game design had sparked his drive. Once again, Heron was reminded that everyone else seemed to have found careers to be passionate about and all she wanted to focus on was her wedding. Then again, so what? Her grades were fine and there was nothing wrong with putting love first. Maybe Bea was starting to figure that out.

Jamie checked the time. "Hey, we've got to run if we want to catch our movie," she told Luke, then said to Heron, "They're showing *Home Alone*. Do you want to join us? I can see if they still have tickets."

"Thanks, but I'm good. I have some errands to run." With Bea, Toni, and her dad otherwise occupied, this was a good opportunity to finish up her Christmas shopping. Jamie slipped her hand into Luke's as they walked away.

The couples all around made her miss Charlie. He was expecting his LSAT results back any time, and she was eager to hear how it went. She texted, "Thinking of you, Charlie Brewster, future esquire. I love you."

She expected him to reply as she wandered the market stalls, but her phone remained silent. It was late on the east coast though. And she would see him Sunday. She could hardly wait to meet Charlie's siblings and see his house and hometown, and be near him again.

She was thinking about last minute packing and considering whether a jar of sweet onion relish, a Millet specialty, would be a good hostess present for Charlie's mother when she heard a voice close behind her left ear. "Hi, Heron."

She started, and turning, saw Jason standing right next to her. Right, they were probably some of the only Messiman students who hadn't left for the holidays. "Oh. Hey."

"Stocking your little pantry?"

She put the jar down. "Well, um, just doing some Christmas shopping."

"Cool, cool. Where's Charlie? I thought you were making a big deal out of spending Christmas together this year since you're engaged and everything."

She frowned. They might have talked about it a little—it was exciting—but they weren't making a "big deal" out of it. As usual, Jason's demeanor made her uncomfortable. It was attentive but devoid of friendliness.

Frazzled, she made a conscious effort to keep her tone light. "Charlie went home to Connecticut a few days ago. I'll fly out to join him there tomorrow."

"A trip to the family estate, nice. Give you a chance to see how the other half lives. And with Charlie away, you'll have a chance to see Dave tonight. Nice for you."

What the heck was he talking about?

"No," she said evenly, "I haven't seen Dave since the summer before sophomore year, actually. I heard he's working now in

Seattle. Why would you think that?"

Jason winked at her, but there was no charm or playfulness in his expression. "You seemed so close when we were all in school together."

"We were, but that was a long time ago. You know how these things change." The hair rose on the back of her neck. Jason was standing too close, regarding her too intently. Her desire to put distance between them overcame her ingrained politeness and she took a step backward into the flow of foot traffic, muttering, "Excuse me," as a family group split up to move around her.

"I sure do, Heron," he said gravely, looking directly into her eyes over the heads of the children scurrying between them, brandishing candy canes. "I sure do. Have a Merry Christmas now." He disappeared into the crowd, leaving Heron confounded and unsettled among the lively shoppers.

Bea

Kissing Ben this time felt different to Bea than the others. Portland had been surprising, then frantic and desperate, as if she had to drink in as much of him as possible before the spell broke. The planetarium was illicit, then frustrating. This, this was just, *fun.* By unspoken agreement, they took turns guiding their kisses. First it was Bea using her gloved hand on the back of Ben's head to bring him where she wanted him, then it was Ben weaving his fingers into her hair, faces close and breath coming in sharp bursts between kisses. Mirth bubbled up from deep within her, and she broke the embrace with an undignified giggle.

Ben grimaced. "I'm so very glad I can amuse you." But then he laughed too. He took her hand and squeezed, their gloves padding the interlace of their fingers.

Bea looked up at him through the snowflakes gathering on her hair and in her eyes. "How early is your flight tomorrow?"

she asked in a tone she hoped sounded flirtatious rather than administrative.

His voice, when he replied, had a husky rumble that shot straight through her legs, putting her off balance. "Not until late morning. I have all the time in the world."

She grinned and said, "I think we've pumped the brakes for long enough and therefore it seems perfectly sensible to ask if you'd like to come home with me for a nightcap."

"A nightcap?" He quirked a brow. "How fancy. I didn't realize I was dating Grace Kelly."

"You should be so lucky," she said, flicking a little snow off his shoulder.

"Do you need to tell your cousin you're leaving?"

"She's getting a ride home with her dad. But I'll text her." She waited until they were in the car to take off her gloves and send a message to Heron, who responded with the thumbs up, flame, and grin emojis.

They made it through half a whisky each, an introduction of Ben to Herschel (who was not impressed but didn't hide under the bed — a pretty solid endorsement), and a tour of precisely half of Bea's tiny house before wandering hands caused them to drop the pretense.

"Come on, then," Bea said from the bottom stair, extending a hand toward him.

"Gosh," he said, "do all of your gentleman callers get ordered into your bedroom?"

She rolled her eyes. "What gentleman callers?" To his raised eyebrow, she said, "I don't get out much."

"Or in," he said, but his voice was gentle.

"Don't make a big deal of it, okay? It's just that I'm pretty busy, and I'm...an acquired taste." He looked like he was about to interrupt her, and she cut him off before he could get a word in. "I simply don't see much point in bothering unless someone is pretty special." Halfway through the sentence she regretted it. The whisky must have obliterated her filter. Surely Ben was not going to let that go without some teasing.

Indeed, Ben's brows shot up and his mouth opened, but she kissed him before he could respond, running her hands down his back and into the pockets of his jeans.

"Don't read too much into that," she said softly, her mouth directly at his ear.

His eyes, when he pulled back to look at her, burned into hers, but they had that little crinkle in the corner, which matched the one at the corners of his mouth and of which she'd grown so fond—funny how it used to annoy her so, making her think he was laughing at her rather than with her.

His voice was a whisper with a rough catch underneath when he answered. "I wouldn't dare."

It was more comfortable and familiar between them this time, trading the surprise of what they'd had in Portland for more certainty, and knowledge of each other's likes and dislikes and downright favorites.

Finally exhausted, Bea drifted to sleep with the expectation that she'd wake up in the middle of the night again, self-conscious, and fretful about sharing the bed—if it had been a problem for her in a hotel surely her own turf would be worse. But she slept through the night, waking in the morning to a nudge on her shoulder, and Ben's alarmed whisper.

"Bea."

"Hmm?"

"Bea." A little louder this time.

She opened her eyes completely and saw Herschel on the nightstand glaring daggers at Ben, who was clutching the covers over his chest like a scandalized Victorian lady.

"What does he want?"

"Breakfast. Don't worry, you're not it." She shrugged into her robe and made her way to the kitchen, where she shook some kibble into Herschel's bowl and started the coffee maker. The kitchen tile was cold under her feet. She finished her tasks and darted back up to the bedroom as quickly as possible, diving back into the warmth under the covers.

"Hello," Ben said huskily, rolling over to spoon her. Then, he shrieked like a teenaged girl when her icy feet made contact with his bed-warm shins. "Holy shit. That is something else."

"Well, my slippers are on your side of the bed. It's your own fault."

"Sure. Blame the victim." His hand, resting on her hip, traced a lazy circle, but then he sat up. "Much to my regret, I need to get my bags and be at the airport about an hour from now."

"I can drive you," she said, starting to rise.

He reached for his jeans. "Stay. It's only a couple of blocks to my apartment and I already have a car reserved to take me to the airport. I want to think about you exactly like this. Bedhead…" He tousled her hair. "Beard burn." He caressed a spot on her neck. "But I come back on New Year's Eve, and I'd like to take you out that night. And then, I'd like to take you out on a regular basis. Can we do that?"

She sat up so she could look at him more directly. The awkward sense of not knowing her lines was gone. "I suppose we could. Oh, except New Year's Eve. We can go out, but I've got Len and Toni's party at the winery. You want to come with me?"

Ben was dressed now, and he knelt in front of her, threading his fingers in her hair while his thumb brushed the side of her neck. "I would love to. If you wear that blue dress." He kissed her, lingering a long time, his hand winding more deeply and more insistently into the hair at the nape of her neck before he pulled away with a groan. "Dammit, I really do have to go."

"Can't disappoint all those nieces and nephews."

"No, ma'am." In the bedroom doorway, he turned and said, "Merry Christmas, Bea."

"Safe trip," she said, and then Ben was gone, leaving her to reckon with the aftermath of her own audacity. Did Ben truly want to start a full-fledged relationship? More importantly, did she?

Chapter Eleven

Heron

Heron ached to kiss Charlie the second she spotted him at baggage claim, looking handsome in an ivory cable-knit sweater and a black wool car coat she'd never seen before. Before she could, Charlie's parents swept toward her, each of them leaning forward in turn to give a dry kiss to the air near her cheek.

"Look at this pretty little bride," Charlie's mom ("call me Julia, dear") exclaimed as she hugged Heron while hardly touching her, before launching into a monologue about the schedule she'd made for the visit. "I can't wait to show you the reception space at the country club. They're squeezing us in for a menu tasting on Boxing Day. Of course, you'll see the church on Christmas Eve, and we have our photographer coming tonight to take a family portrait and so you can meet him. Don't worry, there'll be plenty of time for you to freshen up first."

Heron had flown into Westchester instead of one of the New York City airports. Charlie said they would take the train into the city to window shop and ice skate under the Rockefeller Center tree, but picking her up from JFK would be "a nightmare." The baggage claim area in Westchester was small and low-ceilinged; there didn't seem to be enough space between the clay-colored industrial carpet and the buzzing florescent lights for all these jostling holiday travelers to breathe.

Once Charlie found her bag and they were outside, Heron slowed her steps, using the moment it took to put on her coat to take three deep breaths: inhaling mindfully, exhaling slowly. When she'd packed her carry-on, she made sure to keep the anti-anxiety medication she was supposed to take as needed in an easy-to-access pocket. Flying wasn't usually a problem for her, but since it was just a few days before Christmas, she hadn't been sure about the extra crowds. As a matter of fact, she'd enjoyed her flights and the cheerful, busy atmosphere of instrumental holiday music playing over the sound systems between airport announcements, other travelers' bright sweaters and bits of wrapping paper poking out of bags. Now, all the noise and activity was starting to grate but she was probably just tired after her long day of travel.

Charlie turned back to check on her and extended his hand. Heron hurried to catch up, reaching for the solid grasp of his fingers. This was all fine. Charlie's family were nice people, it would be a busy time, but she could handle it. She could handle anything with him at her side. She still longed to kiss him, but he seemed aloof, which was understandable in front of his parents.

It was going to be so much fun filling Charlie in on how well their plan for Bea and Ben was working. Waiting for her connecting flight in Seattle, Heron had texted to get the scoop on her cousin's evening with Ben. The rundown included an admission that Heron seemed to have been right about Ben's New Year's hints. It seemed she'd been right about everything where Ben was concerned. Ha. It was too bad she'd miss seeing them together at the winery New Year's party, but the gala she'd be attending at Charlie's country club was going to be even more exciting.

In the backseat of Mr. Brewster's BMW, she laid her hand, palm up, on the seat between them for Charlie to take, but he didn't seem to notice, turning to look out the window instead as his mother chattered on about flowers and the Christmas Day cocktail party they held every year.

"It will be wonderful for you to meet all of these people, Heron, the timing is perfect. I am sorry we won't be able to come to the little shower your cousin is throwing, but it's such a slog to get all the way out there to Millet, and we'll be there soon afterward for graduation."

Bea was throwing her a shower in March, right before spring break. When she'd discussed this with Bea, they had both remarked on the oddity of Charlie's parents, extensive travelers, balking at two cross-country trips in a three-month period. But Heron hadn't wanted to think ill of her future in-laws. "This will be so much more fun," Bea'd said, "just your friends and family so we can keep it casual. I have a feeling Charlie's mother is the type to be scandalized by a co-ed shower." Taking in Julia's sleek, artfully highlighted bob, pearls, and cashmere twinset, Heron smiled a bit at the accuracy of Bea's assessment.

Charlie caught her and smiled back. "What are you grinning at over there?"

"Oh," she said, "I'm just so happy to be here."

"We're delighted to have you, my dear," said Charlie's dad, pulling into a circular drive in front of a sprawling Tudor home.

"Welcome to the Brewster family."

"Thank you so much, dear," Charlie's mother said, when Heron presented her with two bottles of her dad's best Pinot Noir, "but we're serving fish. I'll put these away for another time." The wine disappeared into the pantry. Should she have known to bring a white? How?

Charlie's siblings were both older and out of the house, but they came for dinner. His sister, Emma, was in medical school at NYU, and his brother Will was married and lived a few blocks away. Will's wife, Andrea, continually allowed her hands to drift toward her lower abdomen, cradling it. "I'll either be as big as a house at your wedding," she said when she gave Heron a brittle hello hug, "or nursing."

"Oh!" Heron said. "Congratulations."

"Thank you, you too. They're catches, these Brewster boys." Andrea flicked her eyes in Will's direction. "All this doesn't hurt, either." She let her gaze drift around the elegant living room, where they were having cocktails (cranberry juice and club soda for Andrea).

Heron hadn't ever given much thought to Charlie's family money other than to be intimidated by it, but since their engagement this sort of comment had cropped up from time to time, from Jason, Maggie, Bea. Even her mother had said not to let Charlie's money turn her head, as if anything could go to her head more than the simple fact of who Charlie was and how much she loved him. Now, she didn't know how to respond to Andrea, so she changed the subject. "When is your due date?"

"Sometime around the third week of June."

"Aw, the baby will be a Gemini, like their uncle Charlie," Heron said. "A social butterfly. Or possibly a Cancer. Very loyal."

Andrea let out a tinkly cascade of a laugh. "How wonderful," she said, "our own family astrologer. I'll have to ask you to do my chart later."

"I can try. Do you know what time you were born?"

Andrea laughed again. "You're too much!"

Heron wandered away to peruse the bookshelves full of leather-bound classics with uncreased spines. Emma came up beside her and whispered, "Don't pay any attention to her. None of us can stand her but Mother. I think even Will is sick of her half the time."

Oh. Andrea wasn't being sincere. "It's fine. I don't mind." Although, if she wasn't interested in astrology, she could have just said so.

"The bridesmaid dress you picked is very pretty," Emma said. "I'm sorry I can't stay to go to some of these appointments with you and Mother. I have a feeling you could use a buffer."

"That would be fun," Heron said, "but I'm sure I'll be fine." The idea of spending so much time alone with Julia Brewster was intimidating, though. Emma seemed to be the only member of the family, except of course for Charlie, who was easy to talk to.

Over dinner — a seared swordfish with broiled tomatoes that would have gone very nicely with a light red wine, in fact — Charlie's father said, "Heron, it's very nice to have you here."

"Thank you," she said.

"But," he raised a finger, "I hope you won't let Charlie get too distracted from his studies. He needs to buckle down if he's going to improve on a 160 next month."

She hadn't realized he intended to take the test again. He hadn't even told her he'd gotten his score back. A 160 was okay but much lower than they'd been hoping for. Softly, she asked Charlie, "When are you taking it?"

"I was going to talk to you about all this later. I can sit for the test again on January tenth. So, I'm going to do that here before we go back to school."

Her food turned to cement in her stomach as she processed this new information. They'd planned to fly back to Millet together on January twelfth, which meant Charlie would be studying nearly the entire time she was here. She'd just have to make the best of it. "Oh. Okay. I can help you study."

Charlie's dad chuckled. "I think you've helped him study quite enough, little lady, hence the mediocre score. I've got an empty office set aside at my firm for him. It'll be good practice, studying like it's his job. Which, it is."

Wow. Charlie would be in the city all day, while Heron was left to her own devices here. For nearly three weeks. They'd had so many plans; skiing in Vermont, sightseeing in Manhattan, drives up the coast. She supposed she could do some of it on her own; there was a midcentury fashion exhibit at the Met that was relevant to her thesis research, and she would love to study in the famous New York Public Library. There was also the public library in Darien. That was it; if Charlie was busy studying, she could, too, and at least make some headway on her own.

"Does one of you have a library card I can borrow?" she asked the group. "I can get some of my own schoolwork done."

Charlie's mother let out a peal of laughter. "Oh no, dear. While the boys are in the city, you and I will get this wedding all planned. We may even have time to take you to Tiffany's to register."

Across the table, Emma flashed Heron a sympathetic grimace.

"We really don't need very much," Heron said, "I thought we'd register at Target. I can do that in Millet."

Mrs. Brewster and Andrea both broke into laughter as if she'd told a very funny joke.

"Good one," chortled Andrea, delicately dabbing her eye with the corner of her napkin. "What are you going to register for, potato chips and toilet paper?"

Heron looked to Charlie for affirmation, but his eyes were focused firmly on his fish. "I only meant we don't need anything fancy."

"Don't be silly, dear. You'll be entertaining soon enough, and if Charlie gets into Columbia—"

"Charlie *will* get into Columbia," Mr. Brewster interrupted. "Having to settle for Messiman instead of an Ivy was a big enough disgrace."

"Be that as it may," Mrs. Brewster said, "if Charlie is in school in the city, you'll be staying in our apartment there, and you should start out with good quality things that last a lifetime. You want heirlooms, not…picnic-ware."

"City apartment?" She must be misunderstanding something. She'd always felt very fortunate the winery did well enough to keep her family comfortable, but the extent of the Brewster family's wealth seemed to keep unfolding before her eyes. She'd been imagining herself and Charlie in a tiny student apartment, the kind of romantically shabby place where her things from Millet would be at home. Doing things she'd seen in the movies, like finding antiques on the street, riding the subway, sitting on a fire escape on summer evenings.

"Yes," said Mr. Brewster, briskly, "it's mostly an investment property. We stay there from time to time if we go into town for a show. Will and Andrea lived there for the first few years of their marriage."

Wow. "But shouldn't Emma use it?"

Once again, it was as if Heron had made a joke. She blinked in confusion. Under the laughter, Emma said, "No free apartment for the single daughter. I have a studio near the hospital."

"Emma doesn't need to do the sort of hostessing Andrea did,

and you will do, dear." Mrs. Brewster said. "Even a first-year law student is making connections to last an entire career."

"I see." Heron said. Hostessing? She liked making people feel at home, but this was all starting to sound so different from what she'd pictured. She'd get Toni to show her some more recipes, she supposed.

"Don't let my mother freak you out with all the talk about entertaining," Charlie told her later as they were getting ready for bed. (At least his parents weren't old fashioned about having them sleep in separate bedrooms: "You're engaged, for heaven's sake. We may be a traditional family but we aren't sticks in the mud," his father had said.) "It's easier to let them think we'll be throwing cocktail soirees for my classmates, but if you can order pizza for a study group, that's all the help I need."

"Phew," she said, then went to sit next to him, laying her head against his shoulder. "Hey, I'm sorry about your test. I'm sure you'll do better next time."

"I'm sorry, too. I know you wanted to see the city and do fun tourist stuff, but we'll be able to do that next year, I promise. We'll do it all the time."

She wondered. If Charlie was starting school in the fall, he'd be studying next Christmas too. But there would be plenty of time, someday. "It's fine. I just wish I'd brought more of my notebooks so I could make progress on my thesis."

"Oh, my mom will keep you busy."

She laughed. "Yeah, I'm kind of afraid of that."

It was a strange feeling to be with someone else's family on Christmas morning. Over the years, Heron's childhood tradition of racing downstairs at the crack of dawn had turned into a slightly more sedate mid-morning affair with her dad, Toni, and Bea. They all enjoyed spending a relaxed morning in their pajamas, opening stockings over coffee and presents after breakfast.

Charlie's family all dressed before going downstairs, and they didn't have stockings. "Oh, we did them when the children were small, but they clutter up the mantle so," his mother said.

She hadn't had the foggiest idea what to get any of the Brewsters, and when she asked Charlie, he'd said not to worry about it, but she couldn't bring herself to show up empty handed. Heron sewed small cosmetic kits for each of them. Masculine stripes for Will and Mr. Brewster, tropical florals for Emma, Mrs. Brewster, and Andrea. She'd filled them with a few travel size toiletries.

"How darling," Charlie's mother exclaimed. "You made these? Imagine that."

"I know you all do a lot of traveling, so I thought they might come in handy."

"This is awesome," Emma said, "I've been needing something like this for my locker at the hospital."

"It's only something small," Heron said, "meant to be a stocking stuffer, but, you know, no stockings." She gave them a self-effacing shrug.

"My goodness," said Mrs. Brewster, "we'd better get the stockings back out next year. I didn't realize how attached some people could get to these childish traditions."

Would it be rude to point out that next year, there would actually be a small child in the family?

Andrea said, "Oh, this is so...sweet, Heron, but I'm afraid my skin is too sensitive for these products. The chemicals in drugstore cosmetics aren't the best for baby, you know."

"I'll take your shampoos and things," Emma said. "I can always use more of those."

Andrea handed the whole bag over to Emma as if it was dripping toxic waste.

"But you should keep your bag," said Emma. "It's so cute. You love orchids." Andrea's bag had been made using the last of a fabric Heron had particularly loved, printed with vanilla orchids in creamy shades of yellow and pale green.

"That's all right. Those harsh chemical scents tend to linger. But thank you, Heron, so much for the lovely thought."

Heron got a cashmere sweater in a gorgeous shade of sapphire blue from Charlie's parents; some nice loose-leaf tea and a Mary Oliver book from Emma, who followed her on social media and knew she liked tea and poetry; and a gift certificate for a facial at a local spa from Andrea and Will. "It's never too soon to start taking proper care of your skin," Andrea said. "We can go together on Friday."

Heron gave Charlie a vintage tie clip, and he gave her a Tiffany bracelet engraved with her future initials, HIB. The family clapped as he fastened it around her wrist.

"It's beautiful," she said. It felt rather heavy, but she supposed she'd get used to it. "I...had been thinking I would keep Hunter as my middle name, though. I never liked Irene."

Andrea snickered and Charlie's mother said, "No, dear, the women in this family don't do that. Once we are Brewsters, we are *only* Brewsters. Now" — she rose briskly — "let's straighten up; the caterers will be here soon, and we don't want expensive gifts sitting out while they're milling around."

Heron had never heard of such a big party on Christmas Day, but Charlie explained that his mother liked to give their housekeepers the days surrounding Christmas off, so it was a good time to bring outside caterers in. "My dad says it's nice to give them some business on the holiday," he said. "Since most people don't have parties right on Christmas." Heron wondered whether the caterers might prefer being home with their own families; her dad always closed the winery on December 23 and kept it closed through the holidays. Len and Toni did all the preparations for the New Year's Eve party themselves and invited the staff to attend as guests.

"Damn," said Andrea as she rose, clutching her skirt at the hip.

"What's the matter dear?" Charlie's mom was at Andrea's elbow in a flash.

"I popped the zipper. I suppose I need to buy my maternity wardrobe soon."

"Oh dear. Will, you'll have to run her home to change before the party."

"Can't you just safety pin it or something?" Will said. "We want to catch this game."

"Don't pin it!" Heron said. "That's shantung silk, a pin will pull and ruin it. Let me see." Andrea allowed Heron to bend down and examine the damage. "I can fix it. Come with me please, Andrea."

They went upstairs with Emma, who had a pair of scrub bottoms for Andrea to change into. "I feel ridiculous," she said, sliding them over her pantyhose. "And I look like a cow." She thumped the smooth curve of her stomach, which pushed against the drawstring waist of the scrubs.

"You look great," Heron said.

"Yeah," said Emma, "this is normal. You can't expect to stay a size four when there's another person in your pelvis."

Maybe the tense morning had made her loopy, or maybe she'd spent too much time around frat guys, but Heron couldn't contain her snort of laughter, and she arched a brow at Emma, who collapsed into giggles and said, "Gross, that's my *brother.*"

"Honestly," Andrea huffed. "I'm going to the kitchen to see if Julia needs any help directing the caterers. Thank you, Heron."

The Brewster family didn't seem to have a sewing box. Heron supposed they sent all their mending out. Fortunately, she found a good enough match for the thread color in the little kit she kept in her travel bag.

"You can bring that down to me when you're done." Andrea made an attempt to exit the room regally, but Emma's scrubs were a bit too long and she stumbled over the hem.

When she was gone, Emma wrinkled her nose and said, "Yeah, she's kind of a bitch. I'll spare you from having to be the one to say it."

Heron tried to give Andrea the benefit of the doubt. "She's pregnant."

"Please." Emma waved the excuse away. "She's been like this for years."

"I'm trying not to embarrass myself. Your family is very different from mine."

"Yours aren't the snobbersons?" Emma continued over Heron's laughter. "I'm sure they're lovely and I can't wait to meet them at the wedding. Look, I love my family, but they can be a bit much. Don't let them get to you, okay?"

"Thanks."

Emma stood up and dusted off her trousers. "I'm going to see what the boys are doing and raid the liquor cabinet. Can I bring you anything?"

"I'm good. Thanks. I'm almost done." She needed a breather, a little time alone with a needle and thread before facing the Brewster clan again.

After Heron finished mending the skirt, she made her way down the back stairs to the kitchen. She didn't mean to eavesdrop, but as she reached the landing, she heard Andrea say, "It's nice to have an on-call seamstress, at least."

Heron stopped cold three steps from the bottom when Mrs. Brewster said, in an exasperated tone, "Honestly. Did I tell you she's sewing her own dress for the wedding? I told Charlie we'd be happy to pay for a proper gown if her family can't afford one, but he said she wants to do it. She 'enjoys' it."

Heron felt like she'd been slapped. Of course, her father could and would have bought her wedding dress if she wanted him to. The fabric for hers cost almost as much as a gown from a traditional bridal shop, anyway. She only wanted the dress to be special, exactly as she envisioned it, with her love for Charlie in every stitch.

Heron heard the clink of ice cubes in a glass, then the sound of liquid being poured. "At least she isn't making Emma's dress, although apparently it's coming from some strange boutique. Look at the card." There was some rustling of paper from the small desk near the pantry.

Andrea let out a hoot of laughter as she read the card from Lucy's shop. "'Upcycled Occasionwear.' What does that even mean? Second hand? Goodness."

"Emma says the dress is lovely, but you know her taste. She'd wear pink scrubs to the wedding if she could. I can only hope it isn't too much of a spectacle, the homespun gown and the second-hand bridesmaids' dresses parading down the aisle of our family church and through the Maple Room at the club."

"Well," Andrea said, "she is a sweet girl." Andrea's tone was a clear indication of where she placed sweet in the hierarchy of virtues. "Unusual name. Did Charlie tell you where that came from?"

"It's very west coast hippie-dippy. Charlie said she's named after a song. About the birds, you know. Some local band her mother liked."

Heron heard the scorn in Andrea's voice when she said, "Good lord."

"Charlie told me her family calls her Birdie. That's kind of cute, don't you think? I had a friend in prep school, Birdie Douglas. Hers was a nickname for Elizabeth. I'm hoping we might be able to…work that in. Birdie Brewster has a nice ring, doesn't it?"

"Mmm, yes. It sort of suits her. A drab little magpie flitting about, bringing everyone sad little offerings."

"Andrea," Mrs. Brewster's laughter was a musical peal. She sounded delighted. "Stop it. You're terrible." She sighed. "Leave it to Charlie to go out to the wilderness and find a stray to bring home. Still" — Heron heard another clink of glass — "she is a nice girl, and God knows he needs a stabilizing influence to get him through law school. She'll be an adequate first wife."

Andrea said with a smug note, "I noticed she didn't get one of the grandmothers' rings."

"Well, it is the ring Charlie's father proposed to me with. I'm not sure Charlie knows I only wore it a month before it was replaced with this bigger one. I do think a modest stone is more becoming for someone like Heron, though, don't you think?"

As Andrea said, "Indeed," Heron looked down at her ring, sparkling against the deep blue luster of Andrea's skirt, clutched in her hands. She'd been enamored with the oblong stone and old-fashioned white gold setting since she found it in Charlie's things. When he slid it on her finger, it had made her feel cherished and special. His mother and sister-in-law made it sound like junk.

"Well," Charlie's mother said, "it will be time for an upgrade in a few years. Either for Heron, if she turns out to have staying power after all, or the next one. Charlie always did take a few tries to get things right."

Their laughter trailed them out of the kitchen. Heron stood, stunned, on the step for a few more moments, then crept back upstairs. It didn't matter. His family might be horrid, but Charlie was Charlie. The two of them were a team, they could do anything together. And, in a few years, if she was offered a different ring, she would proudly say this one was "more becoming for someone like me."

She draped the skirt over a chair in the guest room, then went down the grand front staircase to find the other women in the foyer, Mrs. Brewster directing caterers like an orchestra conductor while Andrea looked on.

"Your skirt is fixed," she told Andrea. "It's up in the blue guest room if you'd like to go change."

Andrea rushed forward and squeezed her arm. "Thank you so much, you're an absolute doll," she said, and bustled upstairs.

"Can I have someone get you a drink, dear?" asked Julia.

"Don't go to any trouble on my account," Heron replied. "I can get it myself."

In the kitchen, she found the bottles of wine her father had sent on a back shelf in the walk-in pantry. She opened one and poured a glass, letting the essence of fruit tended by her family and the oaky flavor of her father's cellar flood over her tongue. The taste of home was what she needed to wash away the snide words from Charlie's family.

Clearly, the visit with Lauren, the events coordinator at the country club, was merely a formality. Charlie's mother had already planned the menu: a filet mignon and lobster tail duet.

It sounded very nice, but, "What about vegetarians?" Heron asked.

"This isn't California, dear. Although...are your people vegetarians?"

Her people? "Not my family, no, but a few friends."

Charlie's mother pursed her lips for a moment. "We can ask the staff to bring them an extra salad to fill up on. Why don't you choose one?"

Half the salads on the club's catering menu had bacon or seafood on them, but there was one with spinach, strawberries and almonds that sounded nice.

Lauren smiled. "Good choice. It will be perfect in June. Unfortunately, we don't have in-season strawberries to make a sample for you now."

"That's fine," Heron said, "I'm sure it will be delicious."

"Surely, they have strawberries at the market, from a hot house or something. Why don't you send someone out to pick up a few?"

"Oh, but Mrs. Brewster, they won't taste anything like our own local strawberries when they're in season."

"Do you expect the girl to put something like this up to chance?"

"Really, I can tell from the description it will be lovely. I'm sure the chef wouldn't have it on the menu if it didn't taste wonderful." Heron hoped she sounded assertive enough but not too sharp.

Julia bristled. "If you say so. You're the one who made such a fuss about having a salad for the vegetarians. Now, about cake. Charlie's favorite has always been banana and they make his favorite here. It has a wonderful caramel filling. We should definitely go with that."

Heron knew how much Charlie liked bananas and sometimes baked banana bread for him, even though they were one of the only foods she couldn't stand. Still, if she agreed she'd be out of there faster. Brides didn't get a chance to eat much cake on their wedding day anyway, did they? She was sure she could suck it up for the one bite she'd take when they did the cake cutting.

It was tempting to suggest a cake with strawberries to see

what might happen, but she said, "That sounds fine."

It was like this for everything over the next three days as Julia carted her all around to the wedding vendors she'd already chosen: flowers, photographs, music, place settings. None of it was especially to Heron's taste, but it was easier to let Julia go with what she thought would make her son happy. Heron still had the reception her dad was throwing them at the winery. She knew he would encourage her to choose whatever she wanted.

Charlie was up and out of the house early each morning with his father; she never saw him until dinner. After dinner and after-dinner drinks, conversation with his parents during which Mrs. Brewster presented all the wedding planning decisions as Heron's, they retired to Charlie's room in time to maybe snuggle a little while watching a video on his laptop, during which he inevitably fell asleep. Then he was out the door the next day before she was fully awake.

It wasn't so much that Heron missed physical intimacy with Charlie. Honestly, she felt a bit uncomfortable about sex in his family home. She just missed *him*. She'd been here almost a week and it seemed like they'd barely had any time alone together. She felt like she was hanging on to the edge of a cliff by her fingernails. Charlie, usually the one to pull her back from the edge, wasn't there to help. She just needed to hold on a few more days, then she could fly back to the safety of school, the winery, and the kindness of her own family.

Chapter Twelve

Heron

Heron's eyes snapped open sometime in the early morning hours of New Year's Eve. Of all the nights not to sleep well. Although the household would rise early as always and Charlie and his dad would go into the city, they were coming home early to get ready for the gala at the country club. She needed to steel herself for a late evening hobnobbing with the Brewsters' social circle.

The gala had been all Andrea was able to talk about when they went for their facials. Quiet, relaxing time to herself at the spa would have been a welcome respite, but Andrea booked them into a two-table treatment room. "So we can have girl time," she'd said, but it was most likely an opportunity to keep track of any social blunders Heron might commit.

She didn't want to give Charlie's family any more ammunition. Heron would need to be bubbly and charming this evening, but the strain of the week was beginning to get to her and she was finding it difficult to remain unflappably pleasant. To keep her agreeable veneer from slipping away, she'd need sleep. Lying here staring at the wall wasn't helping.

Heron disengaged the arm Charlie was using to spoon her and turned over. Maybe she would be able to drift off if she were on her back. Before bed, she'd steamed the dress she brought to wear to the gala, a strapless column of emerald satin she'd been so pleased with when she packed it. Surely Andrea or Julia would ask where she got it, and she would have to tell them it was her prom dress, remade by removing the tulle overlay, leaving a straight, plain skirt which fell to the floor in an elegant line. She'd swapped the rhinestone belt for a wide black grosgrain ribbon, which she'd also used to trim the top of the bodice, raising and straightening the sweetheart neckline. A dark shape on the hanger, it hovered on the back of Charlie's closet door like a specter. She could almost imagine the dress spitting the derisive comments she expected from his family at her: *We see right through you. You aren't one of us.*

Heron's heart raced and sweat prickled along her back. Suddenly, the room was too hot, the plaid duvet on Charlie's bed too heavy. She couldn't find any cool, smooth relief in his flannel sheets. She looked over at him, in what she knew was a vain hope he'd be awake to talk through this with her, but in the traces of light seeping through the curtains she could see that he was sleeping peacefully.

To avoid waking him, Heron eased carefully out from under the covers. She threw Charlie's robe on over her pajama bottoms and the high school lacrosse t-shirt she'd stolen from Charlie's closet. The robe smelled like him: a mixture of his cologne, the fabric softener Mrs. Brewster's housekeeper used, and a little of the scotch he'd had with his father before coming upstairs. She pulled it around her more closely, drawing more comfort from it than she had from the actual man sleeping next to her. Barefoot, Heron eased out the door and into the hallway of the Brewster family home. As quietly as the polished hardwood floors would allow, she padded through the darkened house.

She wandered down the hallway, past the room where Charlie's parents slept, past Emma's empty room and the Dutch blue guest room where she'd left Andrea's mended skirt. Next she made her way down the front stairs, stopping short as one creaked, a sound she hadn't even noticed when the house had been awake. It seemed deafening now, and she froze for a moment, but she didn't hear any stirring from the household. It was irrational to feel like an intruder, afraid of being caught, but that was exactly how she felt.

Heron continued into the living room, where she sat for a long while watching the unlit Christmas tree loom gray and lifeless. Then into the dining room, where the family gathered for meals and conversation, no one saying anything of substance over the clink of fine silver against fine porcelain; into the family room, where the family didn't seem to spend any time; past Charlie's father's study; past the den where the men had gathered on Christmas day for Manhattans and football while the women tore Heron apart; the kitchen, where the marble tile was much colder on her feet than the hardwood had been, and where she filled and gulped down two glasses of icy water from the tap. And finally, up the back stairs and through the hallway to Charlie's room, where she softly shut the door behind her with the faintest of clicks.

He hadn't moved at all while she'd been gone. The worry

about waking him had dissipated while she'd been up, anyway. He could go back to sleep, she was sure. Charlie didn't seem to be having any trouble sleeping at all.

The solution had become clear to her while she'd been downstairs staring into the (coordinated, designer) ornaments on the tree. Heron's horoscope yesterday had warned about staying out in the rain too long. Now she knew what it meant. Her time was wasted here; the wedding planning was almost done and Charlie's mother clearly didn't need her for it anyway. All of her excitement about planning a perfect day had diminished, squashed under Julia Brewster's thumb. Now she just wanted to get the wedding over with so they could begin their marriage. She wasn't spending any quality time with Charlie. She could, and should, be using the two weeks before the new semester began to make headway on her thesis.

And she just couldn't face tonight's gala. It would be different, she hoped, when she could be on Charlie's arm as his wife, after she got a little more used to all of this. But Heron had learned that it was important for her to pay attention and avoid pushing herself into things that were truly too difficult. The country club gala, staying here another ten days? Heron had gotten good at knowing her limits, and that would be a push.

Telling Charlie she was leaving early would be a push, too, but it would be worth it when she was back home with her dad and Bea. Leaving abruptly was going to leave a poor impression with Charlie's people, but having a breakdown while she was here would be much worse. So, Heron set her resolve and reached for Charlie's laptop. By the time he opened his eyes and asked what time it was, she was packed and dressed.

"Hi babe," he said, the slow, lazy morning smile spreading across his face. "You're ready early. What's on your agenda for today?"

"Actually," she said, "I need to grab a ride into the city with you and your dad." She sat on the edge of his bed and took his hand. "Charlie, listen, I'm going home. You need to focus on your test, and I should be working on my thesis."

"What? But I thought you were excited about the party tonight."

"I was," she said, hoping it sounded true. "But I'll go next year. You don't need me there. I met a lot of these people at Christmas, and I'll see them again at the wedding. There's plenty of time."

"Heron. My parents are expecting us to go to this thing together. What am I supposed to tell them?"

"Tell them your future wife is thinking about your law school admission and I'm leaving so you can focus on your studies." Not that she was distracting Charlie, but she had a feeling the Brewsters wouldn't see it that way. "Or tell them I had a family emergency if you want."

"This is ridiculous, Heron. You have to stay. I know my mom can be a lot, but I'll tell her to give you a day off from wedding errands today. You can hole up here with a book, recharge."

It might have been enough two days ago, but Heron was past that point now. She shook her head. "I already changed my flight. It's at ten-thirty this morning, out of JFK. If I get a ride to the train with you, I can take a cab from Penn Station." (At least maybe she could drive past the Rockefeller Center tree before she went to the airport.)

"Charlie," she said, knowing her voice was breaking, "I just *can't*."

He knew her well enough to know when she'd hit her limit. "Okay." His lips pressed into a tight line. In a resigned voice, he said, "If you can't, you can't. I'll tell them something happened with your mom, and she needs you."

Heron finished packing her book and phone into her bag and said, "I'd rather you told them I need to get back to schoolwork, but you know what? Whatever."

"What? You *said* I could tell them it was a family emergency."

"You're right." She opened the door and stepped into the hall. "I did. It's fine, Charlie." She didn't like him scapegoating her mother, but just wanted to get home with as little fuss as possible. "Let's get going. I don't want to keep your dad waiting."

Breakfast was a tense affair, full of prying questions from Julia, thinly veiled as platitudes, which Heron dodged by repeating variations of "everything is fine, I just need to get back home" as many times as it took to get them through coffee and toast and into the car, where Charlie and his father seemed to forget her presence once she was buckled into the backseat of the BMW.

"Well, Heron," said Mr. Brewster as they stood on the train platform. She'd hoped to have a minute with Charlie alone to say goodbye, but his father lingered. "I'm sorry I couldn't take you all the way to the airport, but I have an early meeting and this one" — he jerked his head toward Charlie — "has studying to do. Have a safe trip home." Pleasantries sounded perfunctory and overly formal coming from him.

"Thank you for having me," she said. Then to Charlie, who laid a hand limply on her waist as he pecked her on the lips, "Bye."

"Bye," Charlie said. And then she was pulling away from the curb.

From the cab, she texted her dad to let him know she was coming home. He replied:

"I'm sorry to hear that, honey, I love you. Call me, or we can talk about it when you get here if you want."

It was a balm to her frayed nerves. She knew when she got home, she'd be safe. Her dad would listen, Toni would feed her, Bea would make catty commentary on her stories about Charlie's family. It would be so nice to be with people she could be completely herself around. Here, she hadn't even really felt entirely at ease with Charlie. The only person who'd made her feel welcome and comfortable was Emma.

Come to think of it, it was too bad she wouldn't have a chance to see Emma again before she left. She had a feeling if she explained what happened, Charlie's sister might understand. She sent a breezy direct message: "Hey! I had to go home a little early. Family stuff." Not technically a lie. Just not her own family. "I'm sorry to miss you at the gala, but I'll be in touch about bridesmaid details soon. XO."

Emma sent back an exclamation point and a frowning face emoji, but Heron didn't hear anything else from her before she got on the plane. She didn't hear anything more from Charlie either, but hoped he was busy studying. If so, good; the sooner he got this test over with and had a law school acceptance letter in hand, the sooner the pressure would be off and he'd be back to his true self — her fun, funny, sweet fiancé again.

Bea

Ben had been back in town for a day but between helping Toni with the party preparations and fetching Heron at the airport after her unexpected return home, Bea hadn't had a chance to see him. She'd barely had time to shower, dress (the blue velvet looking much more elegant with heels than it had with the riding boots she wore in Portland) and spoon some wet food into Herschel's dish, before Ben knocked.

She didn't have time to realize she was nervous, either, until the split second before she opened the door, when her stomach dropped. Seeing him there on her porch, that easy smile spread across his face, settled her nerves. It felt like they were picking up right where they left off; the kind of ease she'd felt with him wasn't something that went away after a week apart.

"Hi," he said, stepping forward to kiss her cheek in a

chaste greeting.

She raked her fingers through the short hair at the back of his neck, pulling him closer for a real kiss. "Hello." She'd never seen Ben in a suit before. He looked crisp and elegant, like a grown up. "Wow, a tie and everything."

"Uh, yeah, this is new, actually. From 'Santa.' My sister told my mom I was going to a party with a date, and she said she didn't raise me to wear jeans to formal events."

"Well, you look nice."

"You look fantastic," he said.

"This is a magic dress, I think." She smoothed it over her hips. "I should probably call the shop and ask them to make me a bunch more from the same pattern."

Ben's smile dimmed. "It's a nice dress, Bea, but it's not magic. You are lovely and the dress brings it out."

Bea's cheeks burned. She didn't know quite what to say. It was nice of Ben to go out of his way to flatter her; it pleased her that he would try so hard to make her feel attractive.

"I'll get my keys," she said, picking up her clutch and coat, too.

The Heron Acres tasting room was all evergreen swags and twinkly white lights. A jazz quartet was set up in one corner, playing softly enough to allow for conversation. The party, approaching full swing when they arrived, was reflected in the wall of windows facing the dark terrace and vineyard. Len and Toni had invited their friends, some fellow vintners, and the winery staff. Bea knew most of the guests, but they were new to Ben, and she stumbled over the introduction to the owner of the neighboring farm, "Ben is my, uh... date...type...person."

"Ben Addison, Bea's boyfriend," he finished for her, sliding his arm around her waist, and extending the other to shake hands with Len's neighbor. In her ear, he whispered, "Right?"

She answered by finding his hand where it rested at her hip

and covering it with hers. "Right."

Heron

Despite the whirlwind of plane-changes and explanations, followed by a ride home from the airport during which she filled Bea in on all of the highlights and some of the lowlights of the trip, Heron made it home in time to take a short nap before her dad's party. It only took half an hour of rest in her own quiet bed to wake up and see her world through refreshed eyes.

When she'd boarded the plane in New York, it had been with a dense pellet of dread in her stomach, the certainty that she'd ruined everything. Now things didn't seem nearly so dire. She had overreacted, but only because she pushed past her breaking point. Clearly, staying so long in Connecticut was a mistake. It would be wise to limit the duration of future visits with Charlie's parents. If everything went according to plan, they'd be living so close to the Brewsters that they could drop in for dinner or an occasional overnight stay. Like Emma. Yes. Staying for weeks with people she didn't know well had been the mistake, along with her unrealistic ideas of the recreational time Charlie would be able to spend with her. She should have managed her expectations better.

Heron shook the wrinkles out of the emerald gown she had intended to wear to the country club gala and put it on. Maybe it was overkill for this setting, but she felt festive and elegant in it as she entered the party. And confident—no one here would care that she'd worn it before or sewn it herself, that was for sure. No one would know how close she came to falling apart last night, either.

To reduce the need for catering staff, Toni prepared a buffet of things that didn't require a lot of attention or temperature control: a few hot appetizers in chafing dishes, salads, fruit. One entire table had been turned into a grazing board towering with cheeses, charcuterie, fruit, and other little tidbits. The colors and textures were visually pleasing as well as delicious; a Dionysian pile of bright grapes, thin breads arranged in vases towering over mesas of cheese, little pots of jam and honey placed everywhere like treasures.

Guests circulated, laughing and hugging as they filled their plates with their favorites. This was what she'd wanted for her wedding, not some stuffy plated dinner with no choices and too many forks, no one talking to anyone but the others at their own table (undoubtedly with a seating chart crafted by Julia Brewster to exile Heron's friends and family to back corners).

Bea, often found holding court at the center of an amused huddle at parties, appeared to be in particularly high spirits tonight. On Ben's arm, she was radiant, and if Bea was a charming conversationalist on her own, Heron could see even across the room that together they were captivating, each bouncing quips off the other, finishing each other's sentences. This was the potential she had seen between them, fulfilled. It was how she felt when she was with Charlie, and what she'd wanted Bea to experience.

"There she is," Bea said, as Heron approached. "My cousin," she told the group of vintners she was entertaining, "has recently returned from visiting her future in-laws in Connecticut." Bea pulled a face and the group laughed. She adopted a mid-Atlantic accent and said, "It was all very top drawah."

"They weren't so bad." Heron blushed. "But it's very different there. Kind of a culture shock."

"I'll bet," said Ben. "Now that I have had"—he squinted at his glass—"four glasses of wine, and turned in my grades, I can say you were my favorite student from last semester's class. I get a lot of kids thinking it's an easy credit, but you took it seriously and I appreciate that."

"Oh, but Charlie worked on every project with me," Heron protested. "He took it seriously, too."

Ben raised an eyebrow. "Right."

Heron was about to respond when Bea gently took her by the shoulder and spun her to face the archway between the entryway and the tasting room. Charlie stood there in a rumpled suit, scanning the party.

She moved toward him, and he moved toward her, and it was exactly like the movies; everything else faded away. The crowded party didn't matter, their tense morning seemed years away. She threw herself into his arms and kissed him, forgetting herself in the reality of him — her Charlie, solid, there, smelling a bit like an airplane, but whatever — pulling her into him. Applause, faint friendly laughter, and the tinkle of silverware tapping glasses brought her back to herself.

She pulled back and asked, "What are you doing here?"

Charlie gave her a half-smile and said, "After you left, Emma came to Dad's office and pretty much ripped my head off. She said you'd left because I abandoned you to Mom and Andrea, and I should realize how much that sucked for you."

As she listened, she pulled him out to the foyer, where she could hear better over the band and chatter. It was colder out here, and she shivered as they sat on one of the padded benches near the door. Charlie shrugged his jacket off and draped it around her shoulders. The silky lining radiated his heat and smelled like his cologne.

"I wasn't thinking, Heron, and I'm so sorry. I was only thinking about the test and studying for it the way Dad wanted me to. I should know better than anyone that my family is a little… overbearing."

She smiled at the understatement.

"So, I called the testing company and was able to talk them

into changing my registration to Spokane. Today was the last day to make any changes, so I won't tell my dad about it until tomorrow morning." He grinned.

"Charlie!"

"And then I changed my flights, and here I am."

She took his face between her hands and kissed him. "I'll help you study. Or leave you alone until you need a break. Whatever you want."

"I only want to be with you," he said. "I know I can get a better score if I'm not trying to do schoolwork at the same time. It doesn't matter where I am or whether I take an occasional break to go ice skating or whatever. I tried to explain that to Dad, but you know. My family"—the corners of his mouth twitched down—"listening skills are not their strong suit."

"They can be a bit much," she said, taking care to arrange her face into a neutral expression.

After a moment, Charlie's face became serious again. "That's the other thing, Heron. Right before I left, I told Mother we want to get married here." He dipped his head to catch her eyes. "If it's still okay with you."

"Charlie," she breathed, "that's all I really want." If a weight had lifted from her shoulders when she left the Brewster house, now she felt buoyant enough to fly. The joy about their wedding returned to her. There would be no country club. No hulking, musty stone church. No more wincing concessions to Mrs. Brewster's demands. Just her and Charlie making promises to each other in the sunlight.

"Great. Maybe we can talk to your folks tomorrow about turning the party they're throwing for us into a ceremony?"

"Let's go find them right now." She pulled him to his feet.

Bea

Shortly before midnight, Bea snagged a bottle of cabernet from the bar, saying, "I know champagne is traditional, but trust me, this is better." She led Ben out across the patio. After the warm press of the party, they drank in the chill and the stars. "See," she said, gesturing up once they'd gotten away from the building, "I told you the sky was amazing out here."

"Wow. Yeah."

They'd put on their coats but staving off the cold night was still a bigger task than their formalwear was equipped for. The icy air numbed Bea's exposed skin quickly, but the wine heated her from the inside out. They drank straight from the bottle, passing it back and forth as they huddled together for warmth. Ben pressed against Bea's back as he wrapped his arms around her from behind. They looked up together.

After a few minutes of silence, Bea disengaged one arm and lifted it to name the stars in Orion and point out Canis Major, Canis Minor, Auriga, Perseus. "To see the Pleiades, you have to relax. Fix your eyes here," she pointed, "and keep looking. The sisters are shy, but you can see them if you're patient."

His breath was warm in her ear while they watched. Their eyes adjusted to focus on the faint seven sister stars. And then, very slowly, his teeth closed on her earlobe and she yelped, breaking the silence and her skyward gaze.

"Sorry," Ben said. "I can only be so patient."

She spun in his arms as the shouted countdown, followed by celebratory cheers and the band's swingy version of "Auld Lang Syne" reached them across the darkened terrace.

Ben stopped laughing and looked into her eyes, "To you, Bea," he said, lifting the wine in a toast, "and our new beginning."

"To new years and new beginnings," she said, taking the bottle to drink after him.

He kissed her, long and lingering, full of nudges and wandering hands. Eventually he pulled away to say, "I mean, it's pretty out here, but holy shit it's cold."

"*You're* cold?" Bea gestured downward toward her bare legs and strappy heels. "At least you're wearing pants, buster."

As they scurried back to the shelter of the winery building, it occurred to Bea that she always seemed to find herself running somewhere, laughing, when she was with Ben.

Heron

Just after midnight, Heron led Charlie away from the party and back to the empty house. She felt every inch like Cinderella fleeing the ball, except her prince would be there in the morning. Once they reached her room, they fell into each other as if they'd been apart for weeks, and in a way that was true. Connecticut had been so full of stilted conversations, and they were so often pulled apart by circumstances, neither of them had been themselves.

Lying in bed, Heron mapped out the next two weeks in her mind. Charlie could move into her room in the apartment to study — Maggie wouldn't be back before the start of the semester, and it was quiet there. She'd alternate between joining Charlie to help him get ready for his test, the campus library to do her own studying, and her dad's house.

At least every other day they should take time to do something fun. It was no Rockefeller Center, but Millet had a temporary outdoor ice rink set up not far from campus. Or they could cuddle up and watch a movie. Whatever they did, they would be together. Forever, she thought, as she drifted off to sleep in her future husband's arms.

Chapter Thirteen

Bea

Moving Ben's poker night to Bea's house had been a practical decision. She had a larger, more comfortable space and as it turned out, Ben's friend Marcus lived around the corner from Bea, which meant he could sit one hand out to run home and read a bedtime story to his kids. A person would have to be completely dead inside not to find that endearing.

Bea was always at the Venerable Grape's live music night with Sarah on Thursdays, so it worked out nicely. She felt a little sheepish about how fond she'd grown of coming home while Ben was cleaning up the card table, sharing a few stories about their respective evenings, and going to bed together. According to Ben, Herschel seemed to like the activity around the table so much —

the slap of the cards and the occasional fallen potato chip—they'd started pulling up a chair just for him.

Tomorrow, however, Sarah had a mandatory all-hands meeting at work. Bea wouldn't have minded going to the Grape by herself, but this week's performer wasn't one she cared for; a guy from Spokane whose set was eighty percent yacht rock covers.

"We're not going to kick you out of your own house, Bea." They were on their morning coffee run. Ben rummaged in his backpack until he found his reusable mug. "We'll just do it at my place. Kevin prefers it. He says it reminds him of when he was 'single and free.'"

"Don't worry about it. I'll see if Toni wants to go to a movie or something," Bea said. She craned her neck toward the front of the line. She had twenty minutes to get to the science building and tee up her slides before her nine o'clock class and at the rate this morning's baristas were going it was going to be a close call.

Finally, they reached the front of the line. Bea ordered her latte and Ben's mocha and bagel. They'd fallen into a steady rhythm of taking turns paying for things. Bea always got the morning coffee and pastries, Ben got lunches, which they usually managed every other day.

Ben re-shouldered his bag. "Why don't you join us?"

Bea responded with only a laugh.

"No, really," Ben said, "we'll be down to three because John's going to be at the Sunset Home meeting with Sarah, Marcus thinks you're great, and we all put up with Kevin, so Kevin can suck it up and have a lady in his game."

"Oh my, what an irresistible offer," Bea said, but she thought about it. She should have realized John, Sarah's coworker at the nursing home, would be busy. Bea liked Marcus. It turned out they'd been neighbors for years, but she hadn't gotten to know him until she started seeing Ben. She'd had his kids over to peer through her backyard telescope, and his wife Nicole, bless her heart, kept giving Bea pothos cuttings which she promptly killed.

"Come on, please? To be honest it'll be more fun for me if you're there. I miss you when we're not together, you know."

Bea rolled her eyes. But hadn't this been what she wanted? Ben, enthusiastic about spending time with her in front of other people. Maybe even wanting to show her off a little bit to his friends? She used the moment it took to pick their order up from the end of the bar to deliberate.

"Fine," she said, handing Ben his mug and the hot paper bag containing his bagel. "But I'm not letting anyone win."

"I'd be disappointed if you did."

Heron

Heron changed from her jeans and sweatshirt into dress pants and a blazer—one of Toni's from the nineties that had come back into style—and made her way across the street to the SOD house. Tonight's chapter meeting had been replaced with an open session, a guest speaker on resumes and cover letters. It was meant to be a low-key member recruitment event, something serious to balance out the party image of the fraternity. Women were allowed to attend, too, and Charlie had asked Heron to come. "You make me look good," he'd said, and how could she turn that down?

Bryant, Jason, and a few other guys were in the living room when she entered the house. "Ah, the first lady of SOD has arrived," Jason said with a smirk.

Bryant told her Charlie was on a video call with his parents. Not eager to speak to the Brewsters, she took her time on the stairs, easing Charlie's door open when she got to his room. Sure enough, he sat in front of his laptop. On the screen, Charlie's parents sat in front of the bookcases in their study, formally positioned as if they were being interviewed on TV.

Charlie turned around and beamed at her, giving her the gumption she needed to fully enter, saying, "Hi, Mr. and Mrs. Brewster. It's nice to see you." She pulled a chair over so she could squeeze into the frame behind Charlie.

"Nice to see you, too, dear," Mrs. Brewster said. She had long since stopped asking Heron to call her Julia. "Thank you again for the flowers. I hope your mother is faring better."

Heron still didn't know exactly what Charlie had told his parents at New Year's. She'd sent flowers and a vague but gracious note thanking them for the visit and apologizing for her hasty departure. She'd hoped when Charlie changed his ticket and LSAT testing location, and insisted on holding the wedding in Millet he had come totally clean about why she'd gone home so early, but apparently he hadn't.

"She's fine, thank you." Technically true, Felicia had been fine all year.

"So, I have some news," Charlie said, cockiness tugging the corners of his mouth up, "and I wanted to tell you all at the same time. Although it may not be much of a surprise. I got my Columbia Law acceptance letter this morning."

"Charlie!" Heron forgot his parents for a moment and threw her arms around him. "I knew you could do it. You worked so hard on your last LSAT." After all the studying they'd done over winter break, Charlie had gotten a 166 on his second test.

"Good work, son. It was touch-and-go for a bit there, but you are a legacy, after all."

"We'll start getting the apartment ready for you. Heron, I assume you don't have any color preferences?" Mrs. Brewster peered down her nose into the camera.

"Gosh, don't change on our account. I'm sure whatever is there will be fine." What was the point of asking for blue drapes instead of green if she wasn't really going to be able to make the space her own?

"Nonsense. We haven't redecorated since Will started law school and it's past time for a change." She pursed her lips. "On second thought I should wait for you to get here. I can introduce you to some of the decorators I've worked with and you can start getting a feel for putting an elegant space together."

A space designed by a professional decorator could never feel like home to Heron. "I think I will probably be pretty busy with work or school. Maybe both." Now that she knew she'd be in New York, she wanted to start looking for entry-level job openings and graduate school options. She'd considered Parsons but wasn't sure she wanted to do something creative professionally. Somewhat to her surprise, the research and construction of intellectual arguments for her thesis had turned out to be much more satisfying than her creative projects, as much as she loved them, and that had led her to think maybe she'd prefer to keep art as a hobby and pursue a more cerebral career path.

"Darling, you don't have to work." Mrs. Brewster laughed, a titter that brought Heron right back to feeling frozen on the back stairs of the house in Darien, listening to Charlie's mother and sister-in-law verbally eviscerate her on Christmas.

"Our deal with Charlie, my dear," explained Mr. Brewster, "is that we will cover his expenses while he is in school. And of course, that extends to expenses for his wife. You'll be part of the household."

"And your family has already been so sweet to save us so much money on the wedding," Mrs. Brewster added, "with the charming little backyard party."

Heron glanced sideways at Charlie for guidance, but he seemed blasé. If anything, he was a little surprised at her surprise, furrowing his brow at her before returning his attention to his parents.

"Oh," she said to the screen, "thank you, but I'll want to keep busy."

"You'll be busy, darling. There are several philanthropic organizations I've been involved with for many years, and Andrea has graciously offered to take you under her wing. Brewster women give back, dear, instead of working for compensation." She said "compensation" like it was a dirty word. How did Emma's medical studies fit into the Brewsters' idea of appropriate work for women? "There are lots of options. Would you like to volunteer at a museum or an arts program for underprivileged children?"

The whole socialite philanthropist thing wasn't for her, but it might be nice to do a little volunteer work. Something she could do in addition to a job. Maybe something that could eventually lead to a career path. Maggie was planning to teach; maybe working with kids a bit would help Heron figure out if that was something she should pursue as well.

She was about to say as much when Mr. Brewster added, "The main thing, of course, my dear, is that you be a help to Charlie and not a hindrance. I don't want to see any more flops like his first LSAT score."

He said this more to Charlie than to her, she thought — it was hard to tell through the screen — but Heron flushed with indignation. She hadn't done anything different to help Charlie study for the LSAT the second time around. If anything, the difference was Charlie taking it more seriously. But one look at Mr. Brewster's stern face told her a contradiction would be pointless.

Charlie answered before she had a chance. "Yes, sir." He put his hand on her knee and squeezed, a gesture Heron imagined to be saying: *Don't worry, I'm only telling them what I must to get them off our backs.*

Bryant tapped on the door and popped his head into the room.

"The guy from the career center is here."

Heron glanced at the clock. It was ten minutes until meeting's scheduled start time. She saw her escape. "I'll go make sure he has what he needs to get his slides set up," she said, kissing Charlie on the cheek before she stood. "You finish your call."

As she exited the room, she heard Mr. Brewster say, "Already doing her job so well."

And from Mrs. Brewster, a derisive sniff.

She was never going to win that woman over or to live up to their expectations. But it didn't matter. She and Charlie were a great team, no matter what, and as long as they both knew that everything was going to be great.

Bea

Bea focused on keeping her hand steady as she looked down at her cards, then back up to meet Kevin's eye. It was down to the two of them; Ben had folded early in this hand and Marcus was down the street, putting his kids to bed. She'd been dealt the queen of clubs and ten of diamonds. There was some potential, but it wasn't great. Kevin was a good player. His expression was unreadable, but he slid a tall stack of chips into the pot, making her think either he had something, or he thought he could play her. Maybe she should cut her losses and wait for Marcus to come back, for the others to be dealt into the next hand.

She hated to admit to feeling a little off balance at her own dining room table. Kevin had claimed the chair nearest the kitchen, her habitual spot. She was at the other end of the table, in a chair she never used. Behind Kevin's head she could see that the landscape print on the kitchen wall behind him was hung slightly off center. Why hadn't Heron or Ben ever mentioned that to her? Kevin caught her staring past his head and glanced over his shoulder; maybe she was keeping the home-court advantage after all.

Ben sat to her left, inscrutable. They both avoided eye contact. She didn't want his help and he was trying to avoid any appearance of unfairness. He played the role of impartial dealer well.

When the flop revealed the nine of spades, Bea decided to stay in. It was a long shot, but she might have something. She had a hard time keeping her cool when the turn was a jack—clubs again, but she pushed another stack of chips toward the pot, smiling politely at Kevin. "Might as well see what we've got, don't you think?"

Ben turned the final card. "Ah, the king of hearts."

Kevin pushed the rest of his chips into the pot. He said, "It's cute how you've been bluffing me, but really, honey, I don't need to take any more of your money tonight."

Bea matched his bet. "I think I'll stay in. Honey."

Kevin hummed the first bar of "We Three Kings" and laid his cards on the table. "Two kings in the hole. Sorry, sweetheart. You did a good job for a novice, though."

Bea turned her cards over, widening her eyes into her best ingenue impression. "I know I'm only a novice, but…doesn't a straight beat three of a kind?"

Kevin flung his kings down on the table and Bea tried not to smirk as she pulled the pot toward herself. This wasn't a high stakes game, but she'd end the night up forty dollars, a good amount to replenish the stash of snacks she kept in her office for students.

Kevin turned to Ben. "I thought you said she didn't play."

"She doesn't. Or, at least, she said she doesn't." He clapped a hand to his heart in a parody of shock. "My god, Beatrice, have you been hustling us? Is that what I've been to you this whole time? A mark?"

Bea looked up from counting her chips and winked at him.

"I guess the jig is up." She straightened her face before telling Kevin, "I read the Wikipedia page. Knowing to bet aggressively on a possible straight isn't exactly rocket science."

"Research is one of her hidden talents," Ben said, leaning over to kiss her on the cheek.

"Yeah, I guess she probably has a lot of hidden talents," Kevin grumbled. "Well hidden."

Hot, embarrassed anger flooded Bea's veins. "I beg your pardon?" she said, taking care to keep her tone cool and even.

Ben stood, his chair making a horrible scraping sound on Bea's hardwood. "Dude," he said. A casual word, but this time it contained a bundle of warnings and no friendliness.

"Come on, Ben," Kevin said, "this is what you're settling for? If I wanted to be emasculated by a dumpy chick I would stay home with my wife."

Frankly, Bea was shocked he knew the word "emasculated" and had used it correctly, which threw her off for a second and gave Ben time to respond before she could begin unleashing a tirade that would leave Kevin with little doubt about what being emasculated felt like.

"You should do that from now on, then," Ben walked to the door and pulled Kevin's jacket off the coat rack, tossing it to him. "You need to go."

"Bitch wiped me out anyway," Kevin muttered, gathering his things.

Ben yanked the door open. "Out. Now."

Before he walked away from the table, Kevin gave Bea an up and down look that made her feel like she was sitting there naked. He whispered, so quietly she would never know whether Ben heard, "Fat bitch."

Oh, very creative. She didn't respond, but she held his eye contact, unwilling to let him think he'd gotten the better of her.

Kevin's desire to slam the door behind him was palpable, but Ben retained a firm grasp on the knob, closing it behind him with a soft click. They could hear him taking his frustrations out on his truck door, then peeling away down the quiet neighborhood block.

Ben said, "I'm sorry—"

Bea held a palm up to cut him off. She was determined not to cry, and if they talked about this right now, she would. She forced a smile. "At least I got forty bucks out of it."

Ben's expression remained fretful.

"Leave it alone, Ben. Please."

The kicker of the whole thing was…she'd been having fun. She was nervous about this, after what Ben had said about his poker buddies and that night at the Grape last fall, but once they started playing, she'd been laughing along with them as they ribbed each other about their bad bluffs.

When Marcus came back, Bea and Ben were sitting silently at either end of the couch, Bea's fingers buried in Herschel's fur.

"Ah, man, did Kev go home? Sorry guys, I got sucked into a repeat performance of *Stellaluna*."

"I cleaned him out and he went crying home to his wife," she said, hoping she was hitting the brassy, casual tone she was going for. "Want to be next?"

"Do your worst," Marcus said, his hearty laugh filling the room.

They played a few more hands, but Bea's head wasn't in it for bluffing, and she kept folding early. It wasn't very late when Marcus went home, but by the time he did all she wanted was sleep. She should feel glad Ben had stood up for her so immediately and without being asked to, but she only felt sad and empty.

On the nights Ben played poker while Bea was out, they usually couldn't wait for the guys to be out the door before they both got handsy and scampered up to the bedroom. Tonight, by mutual, unspoken agreement, they were reserved as they got ready for bed, brushing their teeth without any of the usual bedtime banter.

Bea was beyond grateful to Ben for not saying anything else about Kevin. She could not have handled a conversation where he apologized or made excuses for his friend. She hated that she was embarrassed, she should be long past letting things like this get to her. When they slid into bed, Ben settled his hand over her hip and she placed her fingers over his, holding on until they both fell asleep.

Heron

Charlie called as Heron was on her way out the door to meet him. Ever since he and Ben had both become regular Sunday dinner attendees, they'd been driving separately. Charlie said riding in the backseat of Bea's car made him feel like a kid being driven around by a carpool mom.

"Hey," Charlie said, "is it too late for you to catch a ride with Bea?"

She paused on the entryway stairs, checking the time. "Probably not." Bea and Ben usually left a little later than they did, since Heron and Charlie often had a wedding detail or two to discuss with Toni and Len.

"Why, is everything okay?" She was careful to keep disappointment out of her voice, giving Charlie a fair chance to explain his reason for the last-minute change of plans.

"Oh, yeah, sure." Now she could detect a beery blur in his voice. "It's Jason's birthday and we're still" — he was drowned out by a burst of laughter and shouting — "from last night."

"Okay." She tried hard to keep her tone patient. Charlie had been so good to her ever since winter break. "We were supposed to finalize the menu with Toni tonight."

"Pick whatever you want, babe, I'm sure it'll be great."

She'd been looking forward to making the decision together, but she could probably guess what Charlie would want. "Okay."

"See you later." He hung up before she could say goodbye.

Heron called Bea. Normally, she would have texted, but she wanted to be sure she caught her before she left.

Ben picked up. "Hi, Heron, Bea's driving. What's up?"

"Darn, did you guys already leave? Charlie can't make it and I was hoping I could catch a ride."

"No worries. We're still close. See you soon."

Heron waited for them on the porch of her apartment building so she could hop into the car quickly and wouldn't be inconveniencing them any more than she already was. Across the street, thudding bass and the occasional shout came from the SOD house.

Bea's car glided to the curb in front of her and as soon as she got in, Bea tilted her head toward the frat house. "Obviously Charlie's very busy."

Heron felt a flash of irritation. Now she had to defend Charlie, even though she was annoyed with him, too. "He's just blowing off some steam. He's been under a lot of pressure lately."

"Uh huh," Bea said. The car seemed filled with the static of tension. Maybe she was imagining it, but Heron thought it had been there before she got in, a rigid set to Bea's shoulders, the way they both had been looking straight ahead when they arrived.

It was Ben who broke it, saying, "So I hear you'll definitely be in New York next year. You must be excited."

"Yes." Heron waited for Bea to say something about applying to grad school or looking for a job, but her cousin remained silent.

Ben said, "I have a friend who runs a gallery in Greenpoint; you should look her up. Her operation is small, but she might know someone looking for an assistant."

"Really? Thanks." She knew Bea thought she should continue school, but it seemed sensible to spend some time gathering her thoughts. She definitely needed to do something, though. Surely there was a happy medium between immediately starting graduate school and Mrs. Brewster's life of philanthropic leisure.

Going over the sample menus with Toni was fine, despite her disappointment that Charlie wasn't there to help, but there was an awkwardness around the dinner table. Heron felt like the odd one out, sitting next to the empty chair where Charlie would have been across from Bea and Ben. To make matters worse, Toni had prepared individual shepherd's pies, so there was an entire entree intended for Charlie, sitting lonely in its ramekin.

Toni insisted on sending it home with Heron. "He can eat it as a late-night snack," she said.

Toni's pies were always delicious, but the mashed potatoes clumped like paste in Heron's mouth. She noticed Bea also pushing more food around with her fork than she was eating.

As Heron's dad refilled Bea's wine glass, he said to her, "So, I heard you crashed Ben's poker night. How'd you do?"

Bea took a long drink, bringing the level of her glass back down to half empty. "Not bad," she said, "but I think my card shark career is going to be short."

"Ah, that's too bad. I used to like playing but got out of the habit when Heron was born. Maybe we should start playing a hand or two on Sundays."

Toni laughed. "I'd be terrible. My face is an open book."

"Mine, too," said Heron.

"I know, sweetie. I've played Uno with you. And you"—he leaned over to kiss Toni on the cheek—"never could keep a secret."

Ben said, "Actually, Len, if you want to join my game, you're more than welcome. We're down a player."

Bea looked at him sharply. "You are?"

Ben's look back at her was level, serious, and a little confused, his brows drawn together. There was definitely something weird between them. Heron felt panic flare, an adrenaline surge that heated her cheeks and sent a quick flush of sweat down her spine. Bea and Ben had been so happy together these past two months. If it ended, Bea would feel more alone than she had before, and it would be Heron's fault.

"Yeah." Ben's tone was clipped. "You know that."

He said it quietly, but he sounded frustrated. There was a blink-and-you'll-miss-it flash of consternation across Bea's face.

Toni must have picked up on the strangeness between them, too, because she changed the subject to bright chatter about preparing the vineyard for spring and the upcoming seasonal changes to the tasting room menu. Despite her efforts, the meal continued to lack the usual cheery mood.

Bea

It had become Bea and Ben's habit to take a stroll through the vineyard on Sunday nights. Next week, after daylight savings time kicked in, they'd be taking this walk at sunset. It was dark now, but only the brightest stars were visible; Sirius and Procyon twinkled near the horizon as they walked south, Capella was over their heads. In her mind's eye, Bea filled in the gaps of the constellations. If it were darker, the positions of the stars wouldn't look so very different now than they had at midnight on New Year's Eve. Months passing brought this configuration closer to daylight and made the fainter stars more difficult to see, but it was a comfort to know they were always there, a constant, even when they were invisible.

She and Ben had been mostly normal with each other since Friday morning, falling back into what had become their routine over the past two months: Friday morning coffee at the cafe; a movie and dinner date yesterday; a lazy Sunday spent reading and catching up on work before going to the vineyard for dinner.

They hadn't talked about what happened with Kevin and Bea wished they could forget it, but the incident chafed between them like a grain of sand. The last time some jerk's potshot at Bea had caught Ben in the crossfire, the wound festered and she'd ended up hating Ben for fifteen years. They were both edgy and needed to clear the air of the undercurrent of tension between them. She wondered if he had asked Len about joining the poker game tonight as a way of sending up a flare, opening the issue. Until he had, she hadn't been certain he truly meant to permanently kick Kevin out of the standing game.

She told the flutter of butterflies in her stomach to cool it and started the conversation. "So, you are totally done with Kevin, then?"

Ben stopped walking. "You know I am. You were there."

"I didn't know that was for good."

"Bea," Ben's tone was patient but there was an edge to it. "Of course."

"You're telling me you got Marcus and John to agree to booting Kevin from your longstanding poker game." She was agitated now and heard the tone of skeptical accusation in her voice but couldn't filter it out. "Permanently?"

"Yeah. Marcus could tell something was up when he got back and all I needed to say was that he'd been shitty to you. John was a little annoyed—he brought Kevin in—they were high school friends—but he'll come around if we can fill out the game with a fourth player."

"So, you told them what he said." To her. About her. Bea's cheeks flushed hot.

"I told them he was disrespectful to you, and either Kevin was out, or I was." Ben's voice grew a little louder.

Bea could tell he was getting defensive, frustrated, but she wasn't ready to let it go. They kept walking and she said more to the naked winter grapevines than to him, "So much for bros before hoes, am I right?"

"Is that what you think, Bea? Really? Grown men can't wait to get time alone together so they can talk shit about women? We think stuff like that is okay as long as we don't get caught?"

A few steps ahead of him, she turned and threw her arms up. "I'm a scientist, Ben, I make evidence-based determinations, and to be totally frank with you, that's the logical conclusion of what I've seen. You've practically said as much yourself."

Ben stopped short and opened his mouth to speak but she cut him off, continuing, "This is the thing—I don't know where I stand when it comes down to you choosing me over other things. Other people." This was humiliating. She didn't know whether to feel worse that she was such an insecure mess, or that she had a valid reason not to be completely sure Ben would stand up for her.

"I'm always going to pick you, Bea," he said, quietly now, as if her tirade had exhausted him, too.

"Oh." Bea turned around and kept moving down the row. Behind her, she heard Ben take a few quick steps to catch up, grabbing her hand and squeezing it. It was cold, but neither of them wore gloves and the skin-to-skin contact was an immediate balm to her chilled fingers.

"Bea." Ben stopped again, using his grasp on her hand to stop her and pull her around to face him. He wrapped his arms around her waist. The fabric of their winter jackets rustled as their bodies drew together, releasing a little puff of Ben's warm evergreen scent. "You win, every time. Got it?"

"Okay," she answered.

He was staring hard into her eyes as if willing her to believe him. To temper the intensity of the moment, Bea tipped her head back and found Polaris, fainter than the other early stars but always there, orienting travelers for millennia.

Gently, Ben touched the side of her face and moved her gaze back to him. From the intensity in his expression, she expected a kiss, but instead he pulled her head toward his shoulder and then closed his arms around her in a hug. He held her like that for a long time, and she believed Ben meant what he said. She wanted to believe it was true, too, but at the back of her mind she held a fear she could barely admit, even to herself. *What if he decided she wasn't worth it?*

Heron

Through the window of the family room, where she sipped peppermint tea with her dad, Heron was just able to make out Bea and Ben in the vineyard, shadows moving through the darkness in fits and starts. Even under those conditions, she could tell her cousin was agitated from the way she was waving her arms.

The cloud that had been hovering over them seemed to have lifted by the time they said goodnight to Len and Toni. Walking to the car behind them, Heron saw Bea reach for Ben's hand and lace her fingers through his. Ben caressed Bea's shoulder as she settled into the driver's seat. Heron felt like she was intruding on them as she slipped into the backseat behind Bea. She looked out the window, the darkness broken by the occasional pair of headlights headed out of town.

The silence was comfortable, companionable, but a few miles down the road Ben twisted around to ask, "So Heron, how's the thesis going? I haven't seen you in your writing spot for a while."

"I'm all done with my rough draft and pretty happy with it. Now I have to polish it up and prepare for my defense."

"You'll do fine." Ben gave her a reassuring smile before

turning back.

"I hope so." She needed to make sure she had defenses prepared for any of her statements that might be challenged, but there always seemed to be something else to do. Ever since Charlie had blown her away by choosing to spend the rest of winter break with her, she hadn't felt right about saying no to spending time with him.

Her relief that Bea and Ben seemed to be back on track didn't last long. Thinking about the work ahead made her heart pound, and her palms sweaty. She should be preparing more. Maybe she could make some headway tonight. It was still early and her reading for tomorrow's classes was already done. Then she would feel more relaxed.

When they dropped Heron off in front of her building, the SOD house had quieted down, although the strains of someone picking through "Wonderwall" on an out-of-tune guitar drifted over the lawn. As soon as the car pulled away, Heron saw Charlie jogging across the street toward her. He caught her around the waist from behind and buried his face in the back of her hair, his lips finding the juncture of her neck and shoulder.

"Hey," he mumbled. There was beer on his breath and he had the sharp, sweaty smell of someone who'd spent a lot of the past twenty-four hours drinking and none of them showering.

With a pang of guilt, she shrugged out of his embrace and unlocked the door of the building.

"I've got to get some studying done, Charlie."

He followed her inside, shoulders set in a petulant slump. "Aw, but I missed you." He reached for her again, but she was headed up the stairs and his fingers only grazed her hips.

"Okay, then come in and drink some water. I have leftovers

for you, too. But you have to be quiet and let me work."

He traipsed up the stairs behind her. Maggie wasn't home yet. Good — at least Charlie wouldn't be disrupting her studies, too.

Charlie dutifully drank the glass of water Heron gave him. She microwaved the shepherd's pie and handed it to him, along with a fork and a napkin. He set it on the counter and followed her into her room, where she sat in front of her laptop to pull up her thesis. Leaning heavily on the back of the chair behind her, Charlie flipped the computer closed and put his mouth on her neck again. Pushing him off, Heron stood.

"Really, babe. I need to study. Let me get an hour or two, okay?"

"I'm sleepy, though. Just come to bed for a little bit. Then you can do your homework."

If she did that, she'd be up far too late to be rested enough for her Monday morning class.

"Charlie, no."

He flung himself down on her pillows, releasing a puff of beery body odor. Heron wrinkled her nose.

"Why don't you head home and I'll see you tomorrow? We'll do something nice tomorrow night, okay?"

He made a dismissive grunt and nestled into her pillows. "I've been there all weekend. I want to spend time with you now."

"And I need to spend time on my thesis. I haven't been doing enough and it's kind of freaking me out." Charlie would understand. He knew how she got when she was stressed about school.

He burrowed more deeply into her bed. "But I haven't seen you since Friday."

Heron's temper flared hot enough for her to forget herself. She snapped, "Whose choice was that? I was supposed to see you hours ago, remember? And then you blew off dinner with my family."

He snorted. "You literally ran away from *my* family, baby. I think I'm entitled to skip one round of good old Len going on about pruning his vines."

Did he have a point? Charlie had always said he liked her family but maybe all the Sunday dinners and wedding planning had been too much to ask. But no, Heron escaping his mother's unrelenting barbs was totally different from Charlie deciding to party with his boys instead of spending a few hours with her family.

"That was different, and you know it."

Charlie sat up, and when he spoke, his tone was more sober and pointed. "Yeah, it was different, Heron. I bet Len and Toni didn't mind me being gone at all. Meanwhile I've spent the past two months defending you to my parents and I'm sick of it."

"I never asked you to defend me." How could he fling that back in her face? He had promised that he understood.

"But you expected me to."

She supposed she had. Wasn't that part of loving someone? She'd been so happy when Charlie had chosen her at New Year's, but now she wondered if the cost had been too high. Heron's head swam with the pressure of figuring out how to make this right, on top of the ripples of anxiety about her thesis. She needed time alone to think, to do something concrete. Continuing this conversation wasn't going to do either of them any good.

"You should go home, Charlie. We'll talk about this tomorrow."

"Fine."

He slammed the door to her bedroom as he left, and she heard the apartment door slam, too. Heron flinched. It was unlikely that any of the other building residents, all fellow students, would be sleeping yet, but she tried to be a considerate neighbor. From her window, she watched him stride across the street and considered going after him, but they weren't likely to get anywhere constructive tonight. She'd leave it for a better time.

A light came on in the window below Charlie's. Jason's room. Heron could see him standing at the window and could have sworn he was looking straight at her. He was statue-still, and his hand rested on the neck of the lamp as if he'd been there a long time, watching, and only revealed himself with a flick of the switch when he wanted her to know he was there. Her upper arms erupted in goosebumps. She reached over to close her blinds, pulling the cord with such force that they came loose from the window frame and crashed onto her bed. She hardly dared to sneak a glance at Jason's window, hoping he hadn't seen her be so rattled. The light was off, as if she'd imagined the whole thing.

Leaving the mess for another time, Heron pulled her fluffy cardigan off the back of her chair and shrugged into it, grabbed her laptop, and went out to the living room table get some work done.

The words of Heron's thesis jumbled in front of her eyes. It seemed like a document she'd never seen before, rather than one she'd been painstakingly crafting for months. She gave up and took a blanket to the couch, where she failed at sleep, too, tossing and turning until dawn.

Chapter Fourteen

Heron

Before bridal shower guests began to arrive, Heron's mother brought her a pink paper plate piled with food. "Trust me," she said, "eat now. You might not get a chance later." The setup was finished, but Felicia continued to hover, adjusting a decoration here and there, smoothing her dress. Although Heron had assured her it wasn't a formal event, Felicia's dark hair was in polished, beauty-contestant curls and she wore a pink silk sheath and matching heels — a contrast to Toni's denim shirtdress and Bea's red t-shirt dress. Even Heron's floral sundress was far more casual.

Heron took a bite of a cucumber sandwich. She'd skipped breakfast and should have been hungry, but she was too excited to eat and abandoned the plate on the kitchen counter. Today felt like the start of everything, her worlds coming together. She couldn't wait for her mom to finally meet Charlie and see what a wonderful husband Heron was going to have.

In March in Millet, the weather could go either way. Fortunately, today was warm because Bea's cute little house wasn't built for large parties. Bea had propped open the front and back doors, expanding the mingling space onto the porch and into the backyard, and moved some of her living room furniture (along with a protesting Herschel, upset to be excluded) into the bedrooms to create more space. They pushed Bea's dining table up against one wall. Now it was piled with finger foods courtesy of Toni.

Although Bea and Heron had shot ideas back and forth about polite wording and settled on "Heron and Charlie ask only for your presence to celebrate with them," Toni and Felicia both said people would bring gifts anyway, and Toni had placed a discreet table at the bottom of the stairs, right next to the front door.

Heron hoped she could open any gifts later; she would be happy to write thank-you notes if it meant not sitting as the center of attention while all the eyes in the room focused on her. Thank goodness Bea said she'd do anything to avoid making bridal gowns out of toilet paper. Shower games might have been fun in a group of a dozen girlfriends, but not with a mixed crowd like the one they were expecting.

A few early guests arrived. Charlie wasn't there yet, but he wasn't technically late. Bea lived on the opposite side of campus from the SOD house. Most of the fraternity was going to walk over together, the way they did when they serenaded a girl who was getting pinned. It could take a while to make the walk. More guests trickled in, and soon Heron was wrapped up in a flurry of congratulations and questions, talk of their plans for the coming year.

"Yes, I'm so excited about New York," she must have said a dozen times, craning her neck around the room to see if Charlie was there.

Charlie strode up the front walk twenty minutes after the party had been scheduled to start, with a phalanx of SODs at his back and a stormy look on his face. Heron saw Jason toss a beer can into Bea's hydrangea bushes and rolled her eyes. They'd pre-partied. Fantastic. This must be why Charlie looked so irritable; she imagined him trying to round the group up, get them moving. Of course.

She started to make her way toward him, but every time she got closer it seemed either she or Charlie was pulled away by the attention of a well-meaning guest. It was touching that so many of their professors were here, along with the girlfriends from her first year dorm she hadn't seen as much of as she could, often choosing to spend time with Charlie instead. It was so sweet of the fraternity boys to come. They really loved Charlie. She was proud of his leadership skills. Even Jason seemed to have come around; he had been at Charlie's side all day.

Finally, Bea clinked her fork on a glass and said, "I want to thank you all for coming today to celebrate my dear cousin. Cousins," she corrected herself, with a warm look toward Charlie.

Suddenly, the crowd that seemed to have been conspiring to keep them apart all day was gently pushing Heron toward the front of the room, and she saw Charlie being ushered forward in a similar manner. Then they were standing together before their guests. She reached for his hand and it was cold, rigid, but his fingers eventually closed around hers and squeezed with a pressure that felt almost desperate. It wasn't like Charlie at all.

"I don't know what to say," she said. "Thank you so much for coming. It means a lot to us for you to be here with us today to celebrate." She looked up at Charlie, certain he would have more to add.

"Yes." Charlie's voice sounded strangled. Was he okay? Heron wanted to get him a cup of water, but she felt pinned in place by the attention of the room. "Thank you so much for being here. If you'll indulge me, I'd like to show you all exactly how special Heron is, and exactly what she means to me."

As the room broke into a collective "aww," Jason turned on Bea's TV and plugged a flash drive into the USB port. Charlie flicked a button on a remote Heron hadn't realized he'd been holding. The screen filled with images of her and images of them together, as the strains of the song he'd played when he proposed drifted through the room.

Tears sprung to her eyes as the warmth of his love washed over her. She could see it clearly in the pictures he'd taken. She was on the quad, walking toward him. She was bent over her desk, a pencil tapping absentmindedly against her ear. She was laughing in the sun, the fields of her father's vineyard behind her. And the pictures of them together were a catalog of their relationship: an awkwardly posed photo on their first official date, Charlie's freshman year fraternity formal; at a Halloween party, dressed as Superman and Lois Lane; sitting together on the grass watching an Ultimate Frisbee game, arms and legs casually overlapping; the night they got engaged, fairy lights of the terrace behind them, Heron gazing adoringly up at Charlie in her moon-colored dress, Charlie grinning proudly for the camera.

Heron felt her upper lip quiver and tears brim. She tipped her head back so they wouldn't spill down her cheeks. She'd known she'd get emotional today, but she didn't want to cry with all of these people looking at her.

Abruptly, the music stopped, and the slideshow of photos switched to video. It was grainy at first, shaky, but as the picture focused, she could make out two people, kissing fervently and groping each other, their embrace growing more passionate as the female figure tumbled to the ground, followed by the male. The camera zoomed in on their bodies moving together. Her pale dress had dark tendrils of vines embroidered on it. Charlie hit pause. In the blurry image, the footbridge and grassy hill in the background were unmistakably the Messiman amphitheater. The girl was unmistakably Heron.

As the nature of the video became apparent to the partygoers, the sentimental mood turned to shock and discomfort. Some of the faculty members gathered their things and discreetly slipped out the door.

How could this possibly be real? It felt exactly like a nightmare, her limbs stuck in place, her perception untrustworthy. Heron looked around, frantic, finally fixing her gaze on Charlie's stony face. She was desperate for him to meet her eyes to explain, but he refused to move his head toward her. She caught a glimpse of Bea, saying something rapidly, urgently, to Ben, before her eyes landed on her father, whose face was deep red.

"Son," he said, a bite in his words, "Explain yourself. I've been happy to be modern about your relationship with my daughter; you love each other, she's an adult who can make her own choices about intimacy. But this is not the time or place for you to" — he sputtered, searching for the right words — "prove it."

"That's not *me*." Charlie exploded, waving a furious arm at the images on the screen. "Look how dark his hair is. This is your whore of a daughter, Len, showing how very much our relationship means to her. Look at her dress! This is the night we got engaged."

The room seemed like it was spinning around Heron, but she could fix this, and she had to try. "Charlie," she said, putting her will into keeping her voice calm, "you're right, that is me. It's me and Dave, the night of our homecoming dance, a year before I ever even met you. I wore the same dress both nights. I don't know who took this video." She had a pretty good idea, actually, looking across the room at Jason, who stood next to the screen, arms crossed, unable to keep the satisfied smirk off his face. "But it doesn't have anything to do with us. You knew I'd been with Dave. You had girlfriends before you met me."

The reaction from the party attendees who remained in the room ranged from shocked silence to uncomfortable laughter. Toni laid a hand on Len's arm and leaned into his ear to say something.

"Okay," Bea said, in her best teacher-getting-the-class-under-control voice. "I think we've all seen enough. More than enough." She stepped forward to take the remote away from Charlie, who jerked it out of her reach.

"Even if I believed you," he spat, "that tidy little explanation doesn't work on this." He restarted the video, mercifully fast-forwarding to a new clip. The window of Heron's apartment appeared on screen. Her bed was centered in the shot, dimly lit by the string of filament light bulbs they'd installed when she moved in. Two nude bodies moved together in the soft light.

"This is *last night*, Heron. Last. Night. I saw it with my own eyes. How could you? How *dare* you?"

Heron could see Jason across the room, laughing, and the stricken faces of her family and friends. But all she could hear was her blood in her ears. She tried to slow down her racing thoughts, reminding herself to slowly inhale and exhale, but there didn't seem to be any air in her lungs. Then she plummeted away from the scene into darkness.

Bea

Bea wasn't close enough to catch Heron. Charlie was, but he

didn't. That was more shocking than anything else, the way he let her fall. Bea knelt to cradle her head, feeling her pulse, which was slow and faint, but steady. Len was right there with her, thankfully, otherwise she was pretty sure he'd have strangled Charlie where he stood.

She shot a sharp look to Ben, who took the remote from Charlie. "*Enough,*" he said, snapping the video off.

Throwing up his hands, Charlie strode out the door, muttering, "I'm done here." The SOD brothers followed. Jason, that smirking little shit, was right behind Charlie.

Bea stood up and began to issue orders. "Toni, get a cold cloth from the kitchen. Maggie, go back to your apartment and find Heron's emergency meds and some warm, comfortable clothes. Take my car, the keys are on the hook by the door."

Maggie's face was drained of color and her eyes were glassy. Was she okay to drive? She seemed to snap to her senses quickly enough, finding Bea's keys and hurrying out the door.

"Everybody else, um, thank you for coming, but the best thing you can do now is give us some space."

The room emptied. A couple of people, Bea noticed bitterly, picked up their gifts on the way out. Then, only Len, Felicia, and Toni were left.

And Ben. "You too," she told him. "This is a family matter."

She saw a hurt look cross Ben's face, and knew he wanted to be considered part of the family, but she had too many things to worry about right now and his feelings would have to wait.

"Go on," she said, more gently, "please. There's nothing for you to do here. I'll call you later."

Ben gave her one short, sharp nod, then shuffled out the door.

"Shouldn't we call an ambulance or something?" Felicia was twisting her fingers together.

"No." Len's voice was tight. "She's coming around. We will if she's not all right in a minute or two, but a fuss will make it worse."

Because Felicia was the only one who had never seen Heron panic so badly she fainted, Bea explained, "This has happened before. A couple of times."

"Oh." Felicia's face was pale, making her carefully applied makeup look clownish. She was standing behind one of Bea's armchairs, and she rested her hands on the back, leaning forward.

"Felicia," said Toni, emerging from the kitchen with a cold washcloth and a glass of water, "maybe you should sit down. You don't look so great yourself."

"Yes." Bea tried to keep her tone brisk. "We certainly don't need two patients."

Heron stirred. Bea and Len helped her into a sitting position against the wall, and Toni gave her the water. "Small sips, honey."

"Is he gone?" Heron asked.

"Yes," said Bea, "everyone's gone but us."

Bea went to the kitchen to put the tea kettle on, pulling one of Heron's favorite herbal blends from the cabinet, while Toni got her settled on the couch.

"What can I do?" Felicia asked.

"We've got it, Leece," Len said.

She sat limply for a second, then said, "I'll finish the tea," and disappeared into the kitchen. Good. They had enough on their hands without managing Felicia's reaction to all of this.

They sat silently with their mugs. Bea watched Heron, making concerned eye contact with Toni every so often. Len's eyes were fixed on the floor.

Maggie's return broke the silence. She was accompanied by Charlie's friend Bryant, still in his uniform from the day's baseball game. Annoyance flashed through Bea, that Maggie would bring someone else here, especially one of Charlie's frat brothers, but she pushed it back, not wanting to add more tension to an already fraught situation.

Maggie handed the bottle of pills to Len, who removed one and gave it to Heron. "Bird," Len said, "you don't have to talk about this yet if you're not ready, but I'm here to listen to anything you have to say."

"Actually," Maggie said, "we have something to say first if you don't mind, Mr. Hunter."

Heads swiveled toward Maggie, who perched on a straight-backed chair near the door. Bryant stood behind her with a hand on her shoulder. Bea realized they were together. And then the pieces clicked fully into place.

Heron

With the crowd gone, Heron was starting to feel better. The medication was helping, although the adrenaline flooding through her body had mostly receded by the time she took the pill. Now she felt exhausted and confused. None of this made any sense. She'd had a sleepover here with Bea last night. Charlie couldn't have seen her in her own bed alone, much less with another man. She had some idea where the video from homecoming night had come from, a vague memory that she and Dave had heard noises as they walked through campus after the dance, stopping in the amphitheater with a blanket and a bottle of wine she'd snuck out of the tasting room. At the time, they'd thought they were going to be caught by a campus security patrol or maybe someone out walking their dog, but when nothing came of it, they promptly forgot all about it. But she knew Jason had been angry when she turned him down for the dance, and she'd seen him there, alone, leaning against the wall of the gym. He must have followed her and Dave when they left.

"Heron," Maggie said, leaning forward to make eye contact with her friend, her expression grim, "it was us in the second video, me and Bryant." She looked up at him. "We've been hooking up all year, actually," she said with a small, sheepish smile.

"Oh." Heron could barely sort through the pain and confusion of the day, but she felt a nudge of happiness for her friend. Maggie and Bryant made sense together. This was wonderful. Maggie should bring Bryant as her date to the wedding. Wait, would there still even be a wedding? Of course there would. Things couldn't possibly end this way. They'd work it out.

Bryant, looking like he'd rather be anywhere else, squeezed Maggie's shoulder and took over the explanation. "I was talking with the guys in the house," he said, looking pained, "and I said something about that rickety little futon Maggie has—"

"Go on," Bea said, in the stern voice Heron had heard her use on students who hadn't done their reading.

"Jason said, if you're sleeping somewhere else and you have such a nice big bed, I should ask Maggie if we could use it. We washed your sheets. I'm so sorry, Heron."

Heron sat up. The pieces were clicking together to form a horrible picture. "And Jason showed that homecoming night video to Charlie, and then told him to watch the window."

Bea's tone moved from stern to enraged. "That absolute little fucker. I'd like to rip his smug head right off."

"I intend to do that myself, Dr. Hayes," Bryant said. "Or at least, give him a real good piece of my mind." One hand was clenched into a fist at his side, the other hadn't left Maggie's shoulder.

"We're going to tell Charlie everything," Maggie said. "I promise."

For the first time since the music on Charlie's video had stopped, Heron felt hopeful. All they had to do was explain everything to Charlie. It was all a big misunderstanding. She couldn't believe he had jumped to conclusions and humiliated her like this, but life without him was unimaginable. Once he understood, he'd apologize and she would forgive him.

Bea

Bea fumed. A profanity-laced rant formed in her head, but she knew it wouldn't help Heron to see exactly how angry she was, so she kept it inside. "Thanks," she said to Maggie and Bryant. "But I think it's better if you let the family sort this out. Do you need a ride home?"

"It's not far," Maggie said. "We can walk."

"Feel better, Heron. Sorry." Bryant exited with a shrug, looking like he wanted to say more but really, what could one possibly say in this situation?

Heron was gathering herself up from the couch. "Wait. I'll come and talk to Charlie with you."

Toni laid a hand on her knee. "Give it some time, sweetheart," she said. "You can talk to him tomorrow. You should rest now."

Bea walked the kids out. On the porch, Maggie grimaced and said under her breath, "We already tried to catch Charlie before we came over here, but he's gone off somewhere with Jason. I'm so embarrassed, Bea, and I feel terrible."

"It's not your fault. Or yours, Bryant." Bea was frankly a little annoyed with both of them. Who borrows someone's bed without asking? But they'd been wronged here, too.

"I know," he said, "but I feel awful. I keep trying to call Charlie, but he's not answering and it doesn't look like he's reading his texts. I'll do what I can to make it right as soon as he comes back to the house."

"Good." She watched Bryant put his arm around Maggie as they made their way down the sidewalk.

Back inside, Heron had nodded off to sleep, her head on Toni's shoulder. Len and Felicia were glaring at each other and seemed to be in the middle of a hushed argument.

Felicia hissed, "I thought I was leaving her in better hands than this. Out in plain sight where some creep could take a video, honestly, Len, if I'd been there—"

"Yeah, well, you weren't here, were you? You left me alone with a terrified fifteen-year-old. You have no idea what it was like for her after you left, how scared she was something else terrible would happen." Oh, god, and something terrible had just happened, hadn't it? She looked at Heron asleep, peaceful now because she was exhausted. Bea knew a tempest raged under the surface. The damage Charlie had done to Heron's confidence today might take years to repair. "Thank goodness for Bea," Len said, turning a grateful smile her direction.

"Oh, yeah," Felicia snapped. "Clearly Bea has been a fantastic influence."

"Hey," Bea said, "that's not fair and you know it." She reached for her phone and pulled up a rideshare app. "I'm calling you a car, Felicia. I think it's time for you to go back to your hotel."

"No need," said Felicia. "My hotel's a few blocks away. I can see myself out."

"Fine."

"Fine."

"Fine."

Toni rolled her eyes at all of them. She gently caught Felicia's wrist as she passed the sofa on her way out. "We'll call you in the morning. I'm sure Heron will want to see you before you head back to Seattle."

Felicia sent a regretful glance toward her daughter but didn't say anything more.

Now that she had her phone in hand, Bea could see several text messages and two missed calls from Ben, but she didn't have it in her to deal with him yet.

Heron shifted and opened her eyes. Bea said, "Bird, do you want to go home with your dad? Or do you want to stay here?" Her own apartment was not an option for a number of reasons, and Bea hoped she wouldn't ask to go back there.

"Here," Heron mumbled. "But can I just call Charlie and tell him where I am? I want him to know I'm okay."

Heron's phone was on the end table next to Toni. Bea caught Toni's eye and gave a tiny shake of her head. "Why don't you give him some time to cool off, honey?" Toni said. "Maybe in the morning."

Bea winced, but Heron would have to face him sooner or later. It might be better for her to get it over with.

"I'll put your stuff in the guest room." Bea picked up the backpack Maggie had brought. Toni handed her Heron's phone, which she slipped into her own pocket.

She paused at the bottom of the stairs as Len took her place on the ottoman across from his daughter. Putting a gentle hand on her knee, he said, "Love you, sweetheart. So much. Nothing could ever change that. We'll sort everything out." He leaned down and kissed her on the forehead. "Call us if she needs anything," he said to Bea, "and we'll talk in the morning."

"She'll be okay, Len," Bea said. "We'll get her through this."

Bea's phone buzzed again. Ben. The text was simply "???!" She turned the notifications off and left it face down on the entryway table. He could wait.

As she was walking into the kitchen, she heard a chime in her other pocket. Heron's phone. Charlie, asking, "Are you ok?" So the kid had some decency after all. But it wouldn't hurt him to stew in the consequences of his actions. Bea had always known the passcode for Heron's phone—Len's birthday—so it was easy to punch it in and type a reply.

"This is Beatrice. Of course Heron isn't okay. You'll have

further updates when or if she's in a position to decide that's something she wants. For now, it's family only, and that certainly doesn't include you after what you did."

And then she turned the phone off.

Chapter Fifteen

Heron

Heron didn't think she could possibly sleep, but emotional exhaustion, extra drowsiness from the meds, and the safe quiet of Bea's guest room conspired to send her into bleary oblivion. She woke up filmed with sweat and vaguely aware of a dream in which she searched for someone in an airport, the crowd always keeping her away just as she spotted them. At least she rested until morning. She had a strange sense of deja vu from having slept in this room the night before the shower, but this was the nightmare version of the previous day: her pretty floral dress thrown carelessly across the chair instead of hung fresh on the closet door, her head pounding with tension instead of lightly fuzzy from the cocktails she'd had with Bea during their pre-shower movie night, an overwhelming sense of dread and doubt instead of joyful anticipation. The details of what had transpired came back gradually as she showered and dressed, along with her plan for what she would do.

By the time she was ready to go, resolutely descending the stairs with her backpack, Bea was in the kitchen.

"Hold it right there, missy. You're not going anywhere until you eat a little something."

She felt like her stomach was full of wet, rotten leaves. But she was also a little lightheaded and shaky, and the eggs and toast Bea was setting on the table looked good. The smell woke up her appetite and she felt like she could probably manage a little. She sat and took a small bite.

"Thank you, Bea. For this, and for everything yesterday. It's just a big misunderstanding, but I'm sorry it ruined the nice party you threw for me."

Bea ripped her own bread crust into tiny pieces before she said, "Heron, have you...thought about how *you* feel about what Charlie did yesterday?"

"What do you mean? Charlie is as much a victim here as I am. I'm sure Jason tricked him, just like he manipulated Bryant."

"I think so too, but Charlie could have talked to you privately. That boy put a lot of effort into that video."

Heron put her fork down. The ball of rotten vegetation was creeping out of her stomach, up her throat and out into her limbs, making them feel numb and heavy.

"He was hurt, Bea. Anyone would be. You have to think about how all that would have looked to Charlie."

"So, you're just going to smooth everything over?"

"Yes." Heron was baffled. What else would she do? "Obviously."

Her phone sat on Bea's kitchen table, and she picked it up.

The screen was black and she thought she'd have to ask Bea for a charger, but when she pushed the button, it lit up. When the screen came to life, a message from Charlie appeared on the home screen. It said only, "Okay."

Confused, Heron clicked through to see the conversation. Blood rushed into her face, warming her cheeks. She held the screen towards Bea, "Why would you do this?"

Guilt washed over Bea's face. "Well, you weren't okay, were you? I thought he should know that."

"What the hell, Bea?"

Bea sat. "I'm sorry, Bird. That was rash but it's better than he deserves." She squinted at the screen, still open to their conversation.

Heron stood up, putting the phone in her pocket. "I'm going over there now. He must be worried sick."

"Finish your breakfast first. You need to eat something."

Heron pushed her chair in too hard, rattling the breakfast dishes. "Why don't you let me decide what I need, Bea, okay? I need to see my fiancé and make sure you didn't make this mess bigger."

"Let me at least give you a ride."

"No thanks. I need the walk." Anticipation thrummed through her body. She wished she could skip ahead to the part where she and Charlie had already made up, put the awkwardness behind them.

Bea sighed. "Okay. Call me if you need anything."

At first, the walk across campus felt good. Crisp spring air filling her lungs, the exercise burning away the energy from her nerves and anger at Bea. Heron looked around, steadying her nerves by taking note of the springtime campus: ducks playing in the pond; daffodils blooming in sunny bunches near the benches and sculptures dotting the quad; some of her fellow students already outside enjoying the warm weather. But she also noticed a few long glances from a group of students standing in a cluster near the library. One of the girls walking toward her swiveled her head Heron's direction as they passed on the path. She saw a trio of students clustered in a window of the first-year dorm, staring at her.

Heron's brisk walking pace wasn't enough to outrun the adrenaline running through her limbs. Maybe it was paranoia, her fight-or-flight heightened from yesterday's shock and alert to every potential threat, but she felt certain people were paying more attention to her than they normally would. The Messiman rumor mill had likely churned away overnight, descriptions of the scene at the shower making the rounds at the Saturday night parties. Her heart pounded and she was dizzy, but she forced herself to slow, focus on her breathing. Word got around campus fast, but that could work in their favor. Wouldn't the truth spread just as quickly?

The SOD house was quiet when she arrived, but the back door was unlocked. She let herself in and tiptoed up the back stairs, crossing her fingers she wouldn't run into anyone before she got to Charlie's room.

Her luck held, and she eased the door open, closing it behind her with a dull thump. Charlie was still in bed. She bet he was up late worrying about her. Beer cans and a tequila bottle littered the floor. The room smelled sour. A stubby tripod was still set up on Charlie's desk in front of the window, though the camera was gone. Charlie didn't own a tripod, Heron knew. This one must be Jason's. How helpful.

She sat on the edge of the bed and placed a hand lightly on Charlie's bicep. He cracked his eyes open, then shook her off and sat up.

"Hi," she said.

"Hey. What do you want?"

"I wanted to let you know I'm okay. A little tired and shaken up, but I'm fine."

"Yeah. I can see that." He rolled over to face the wall.

She didn't know what she expected, but it wasn't this. Maybe he didn't understand.

"I was really okay, I just needed some rest and to see you. Bea just wanted to make you worry. You were worried, weren't you?"

Heron gently touched Charlie in the way she knew he liked, his shoulder, his hip, trying to reestablish their connection, but he moved away. He wasn't acting like someone who'd been worried.

She'd woken him up—she should give him some space to stretch, rise, maybe brush his teeth. She stood and was about to sit in his desk chair, but the tripod stopped her short. Maybe it wasn't rational, but she didn't want to be anywhere near that thing. She sat at one of the chairs at the table instead, pulling her feet up to hug her knees. Once she was away from the bed, Charlie sat up and swung his feet to the floor, bracing his elbows on his knees, but he didn't move any closer to her.

"Don't you think we should talk?" she said.

Charlie dipped his head, running a hand over the back of his skull. "I guess. There's a lot to sort out."

"I was thinking about it on the way here, and I think this will all blow over if we get the word out quickly that it was a misunderstanding."

"Blow over?" Charlie's eyes bored into her, and his tone was sharp.

Heron stammered, "Well, yeah, didn't Maggie and Bryant talk to you?"

"They did. Maggie's a good friend to you, Heron, better than you deserve."

"What?" Maggie was a good friend, but why was Charlie

saying so now? "Wait. Do you not believe her?"

"You know what I realized," he said, "is that it doesn't really matter."

"What?"

"It doesn't matter, Heron. Whether what I saw Friday night is Maggie and Bork or you and some other guy, whether the video Jason showed me is from four years ago. It doesn't matter."

"How can that possibly not matter?" Heron's panic swelled. "Charlie, I haven't even looked at anyone else since our first date. I've never been anything but faithful to you. I don't know what I'd do without you. I love you."

She unwound her arms from around her knees, wanting to go to him, but his demeanor, cold, unyielding, had her frozen in the chair. There wasn't a trace of her Charlie in the angry man across the room from her.

"I think I fundamentally misunderstood who you really were, Heron. I thought you were sweet. It was so easy to picture you mothering our children. But now, I've seen this different side of you and so has half of campus."

What? She'd told him all about Dave years ago. Had he just brushed that detail aside until seeing the video made it impossible to ignore?

"You're the one who showed half of campus."

"That's what this did to me, Heron. I won't be blamed for it."

Who else was to blame? Jason, but...Jason had only shown Charlie this path. He didn't have to go down it.

She didn't want to say it, didn't want to ask. But she reached a point where the uncertainty and the silence in that sour-smelling room was worse than the answer she knew was coming.

"So, that's it for us, then? We're over?"

Charlie's eyes met hers, glittering and impervious. "What do you think?" But he didn't give her a chance to answer, continuing, "I can't be this, Heron. I can't be some...cuck."

Her mouth fell open. Who *was* this person?

He continued his rant. "Like I said, it doesn't matter if it's true or not. It only matters that it was believable, to me and others. I'm so glad my eyes are open now, and I'm glad, honestly, this all happened before we got married. Christ, can you imagine?"

This whole thing was unimaginable, actually. Heron didn't trust her voice to respond. Maybe she was still dreaming. Maybe if she didn't say anything and waited to wake up, it would all go away. A nightmare was the only possible explanation for any of this. But she also couldn't be in this room anymore, couldn't stand one more second under the steel of his furious gaze.

She stood to leave.

"Heron?" Charlie said, his voice strained, when her hand was on the knob.

Hope welled in her chest, and she turned, prepared to rush him with kisses and forgiveness, if he would only be her Charlie again.

"My ring?"

"Oh." She twisted it off her finger and was so tempted to hurl it at his face, the face she still loved in spite of herself.

Instead, she set it on the table with a soft click.

Bea

After Heron left, Bea surveyed her living room. She'd shoved most of the food into the fridge yesterday to keep it away from Herschel, but the cupcake tower still stood on top of her corner credenza, every surface was littered with crumpled pink napkins and half-empty cups of punch, the bags of party favors still waited by the door. She willfully ignored it all—she'd deal with it later—and climbed the stairs to shower and dress. She took her time there, letting the hot water and steam ease some of the tension from her neck and shoulders.

When she was toweling off, she heard a key in the front door, and Ben calling, "Bea? You here?" up the stairs.

She tamped down a bristle of irritation (unfair, but whatever), and yelled, "Hang on, be right down. There's coffee." She threw on jeans and a sweatshirt and went down to find Ben in the kitchen, rinsing the breakfast dishes and loading them into the dishwasher. "You don't have to do that," she said.

Ben's mouth was tight when he answered. "Just trying to help." When she didn't say anything further, he turned and leaned against the sink. "Did you get my texts?"

"I've been busy, Ben."

"I realize that. And I wanted to help take some of the burden off."

She looked at her phone. The messages from Ben read:

"Call me if you need anything."

"Is Heron ok?"

"Can I do anything?"

"Want me to swing by with dinner for you?"

"Please just let me know if Heron is ok."

"Are YOU ok?"

"Please answer something, Bea. I'm worried."

"???!"

Then one from this morning:

"I'm coming over."

She met his eyes. She could tell Ben was upset and also that he was trying not to show it. His lips were pressed together in a tight line, but his brow was raised, eyes searching hers, asking for an explanation.

She didn't have one, at least not for ignoring his calls and texts. If he didn't understand why she needed space right now, he wasn't ever going to get it.

She looked away and said, "Heron's as okay as can be expected. She came around pretty fast but we tried to keep it a quiet evening for her. And we figured out what happened, mostly." She explained what Maggie and Bryant had told them while she finished clearing the counter.

Ben pulled out a chair and dropped into it. "That does makes sense," he said. "I didn't see Charlie getting there on his own."

"It didn't seem like it was too hard to get him to go along for the ride." Bea put the sugar back in the cabinet and closed the door with a satisfying slam.

"I'm not sure what I would have thought in his shoes."

"You're not?" Was he fucking joking? "Ben, are you telling me if someone made you think I'd been with somebody else, you would show a fucking video of it to my friends and family?"

"No. I'm sure I would talk to you about it first. But I'd be pretty upset."

Out of things to tidy, Bea joined Ben at the kitchen table. "Yeah well, Heron's pretty upset, too."

"As she should be. Poor kid."

"She's over there now, trying to work things out with Charlie."

Ben grimaced.

"You could give him a talking to about how unacceptable his behavior was."

"Sure," he said, but he didn't sound firm.

"Don't you agree that what he did was wrong?"

He set his mug down with a clank. "Of course I do, but this is between the kids. I'm not sure lecturing Charlie on how to treat his girlfriend is my place."

"Oh really?" She waved her phone at him. "What is all this, then? All this, 'let me know if there's anything I can do to help?' Are you on our side in this or Charlie's?"

"I wasn't aware there were sides."

"You saw how devastated she was."

"Beatrice, I saw two devastated people."

"Oh. How *egalitarian*."

Ben stared out the kitchen window for a long time, before saying, "I'm only trying to be fair."

"And if 'fair' means repercussions for the SOD house, are you going to get behind that? Or are you going to have Charlie read an apology letter and call it bygones?"

His head snapped in her direction. Bea knew she was playing dirty and all her anger at Charlie and worry about Heron was pouring out onto Ben, but she couldn't seem to tamp it down. The dam had burst, and she couldn't stop it.

Ben said, "I think you know I'll do what's necessary to ensure they make things right. It's pretty clear that Jason orchestrated this whole thing and if anyone should face consequences, it's him."

"Yes," she replied, "I looked into how to file a code of conduct complaint last night after Heron went to sleep. Both Jason and Charlie can be named, and the penalties range up to expulsion. Unfortunately, faculty can't register a complaint unless they themselves are the wronged party. Heron would have to do it. Maybe Maggie or Bryant."

"Isn't that as it should be? I know she's family, Bea, but you can't fight this battle for Heron."

"If I don't, I'm afraid no one will." Everything was catching up with her, and these words caught in her throat. She knew Heron well enough to know she only wanted her stability back, wouldn't want to hurt Charlie, even if it meant letting what he and Jason had done to her slide.

"I know," Ben said. He patted her hand, got up to refresh their coffee. He waited until he sat back down to speak again, and his voice, when he did, was gentle. "But that's Heron's decision to make, isn't it?"

"Not if she won't make it."

"Bea." His voice had a stern edge. Was he actually scolding her?

"Well." She flailed her hands. She needed Ben to see how extreme this situation was, understand the sensible approach he was advocating for wasn't necessarily going to work.

"I think Heron's stronger than you give her credit for," he said. "You have to let her figure this stuff out on her own. You can't expect her to get her future husband expelled from undergrad, can you?"

She snorted. "You can't still expect her to marry him, can you?"

"It's not up to me," he said, and she wanted to throw her coffee spoon right at his smug face. "But if it's what Heron wants, trying to talk her out of it isn't going to work, Bea."

"What kind of relationship can they possibly have, if every time she looks at him, she remembers how humiliated she was? She'd always wonder if he were going to do it again."

"Maybe it's easier for Heron to forgive than—"

"Than who? Me?"

He raised his palms in a surrendering gesture. "I didn't say it."

"Yeah, well, you were about to. This is completely different, Ben, this isn't some dumb frat guy joke. This is Charlie showing… *revenge porn* in front of Heron's parents, for fuck's sake."

"I know. I didn't say it was about us."

"But you were thinking it, weren't you?"

Ben bowed his head, rubbing the back of his neck. "Okay. So, now that the can of worms is open then, do you?" He looked up at her, catching her eyes.

"Do I what?"

"Do you trust me not to hurt you again?"

How did this conversation become about them? And, did she?

"I'm not sure."

"Wow."

"I mean, for god's sake, Ben, not exactly the best day to ask me a question like that."

"I think it's the perfect day for it, actually. I've been trying to help you during a time when most women would be grateful to have a supportive partner to lean on and you're totally shutting me out."

"Well," she huffed, "I'm so sorry I'm not most women." And who said dating for three months made them *partners?*

"I love you for that, but I need a little help here." Sighing, he pinched the bridge of his nose. "I can't keep waiting for you to give me the benefit of the doubt."

The warmth of her kitchen, formerly cozy, suddenly felt oppressive, stifling. She stood to open the window and said, "But you can't expect me to be a completely different person."

"Evidently."

She glared at him; he looked back. It was a look she was familiar with by now, calm but not willing to let her off the hook. She hated being familiar with that look, hated being known and held accountable by someone, hated the way Ben was pushing harder and harder for them to be more of a thing than she was ready for. It hadn't escaped her notice that he'd just said he loved her. She was pretty sure she loved him too, but that wasn't an idea she could confront right now.

Bea was trying to decide what to say when her phone buzzed, Heron's name flashing across the screen. She took a deep breath, pulling herself together before she answered. "Hi, Birdie," she said as cheerfully as possible.

Bea could hardly make out the words on the other end. It was mostly sobbing, but she heard, "Come get me," and that was all she needed to be out of her seat.

"I can't have this conversation right now. I have to go."

"Okay." Ben stood up. "Can we talk more later?"

"I don't know, Ben." She was exasperated. "I need to handle what's going on with Heron before I can deal with your feelings, okay? Just...let yourself out, I guess."

"Sure." His answer was clipped, but she was halfway to the car before he even gave it.

Heron

Heron walked into her dad's house to find her mother sitting on the couch. The last time she'd seen her mom in this spot, where she had usually settled each evening to watch TV, was two nights before Felicia left them. It was jarring, but after everything that had happened over the past day, she was emotionally numb and all she felt was a mild jolt of dissonance.

"Oh. Hi, Mom."

"Hi, sweetie."

"Hello, Felicia," Bea said, entering behind Heron.

Her dad came through from the kitchen, saying, "Why don't you come stay here for a while? Toni or I can drive you in for your classes, and you'll get a little break from campus life."

"And from having to see that boy," Felicia added.

She turned toward Bea, looking to see what her cousin thought of all this.

Bea added, "Or you can stay with me. Whatever you want."

Felicia cleared her throat. "It's probably not your first choice, but you could spend spring break with me in Seattle. I'll be at work during the day, but you can study or see movies or just hang out."

Heron was stunned. They'd made all of these plans for her, coddling her as they had when she was in high school. Everyone seemed to know what was best for her, which was funny because Heron didn't have any idea herself. "I don't know," she said, looking at each one of their concerned faces. "Can I think about it?"

"Of course, Birdie."

She drifted to her room with the intention of crawling into her childhood bed — she'd slept so much over the past day but still felt exhausted. When she reached the doorway, her wedding gown loomed like a ghost in the corner of the room. It was almost finished; she only had the hem and some detailing left.

Heron opened her closet and shoved the whole thing inside, dress form and all, the gown toppling down over a box of old school papers. Then, she slipped under the covers and sobbed. The past two days had been an onslaught her body had, until now, protected her from: Charlie's loving gesture turning into a humiliating spectacle; the coldness in his voice as he told her he was finished; the realization that all of this had been because Jason set out deliberately to hurt her. Heron cried until she was completely spent, vaguely aware of the murmurs in the living room, footsteps passing her door.

She must have fallen asleep because when she opened her eyes again, the light in the room had shifted. Late afternoon sun was coming in through the window now. At some point, someone had come in and put a glass of water on her nightstand. She sipped it, and when the liquid hit her stomach, she realized she was hungry.

Heron went into the bathroom, splashed water on her face and looked into her own eyes, red-rimmed and bright. She thought about tomorrow, about going back to class and she realized...she certainly could. She was stronger than everyone realized. And yes, it would be humiliating, she'd hear the whispers and notice the stares as she had on her trip across campus this morning, but she could handle it.

She didn't want to handle it, though. It would be exactly what Jason had wanted, and it must on some level be what Charlie wanted, too, to hurt her in retribution for not being the perfect sweet girl he thought he was getting. To see her broken. She didn't want to stay with her dad or Bea, either. They'd coddle her and Heron couldn't stand the thought of that.

Then she thought about her mother's offer. Her mother had never invited her to Seattle before. She'd always been curious about what Felicia's life was like there. She certainly wouldn't be coddled. Maybe some time away from Millet would help her gain perspective, to figure out why Charlie found it so easy to leave her.

Heron showered and put on fresh clothes before she returned to the living room. This was a step that would have seemed insurmountable under any other circumstances, but her world had already been turned upside down. Maybe something drastic was just what she needed. "Mom, I'd like to stay with you for a few weeks, starting now."

Her dad set his drink down. "Are you sure that's a good idea, Birdie?"

"Why not, Dad? She's my mother. And I could use a change of scenery. Just through spring break. Then I'll decide if I want to stay here or at Bea's or go back to the apartment." There was still a tiny flame of hope that she'd be back with Charlie by then, but it was getting weaker every second. After what he'd said to her in his room, she couldn't see a future for them.

"Don't you have a week of classes left before spring break?"

"Yes, but I don't have any tests. I have one paper due on Tuesday but it's nearly done, and I can submit it by email. After four years of perfect attendance and good grades, I think it's probably okay to miss a couple of classes. Right, Bea?"

"Honestly?" Bea said. "Probably. Half the seniors on campus will skip their classes next week."

"See?" Heron said. "Look, I've thought this through. I'm caught up in my current courses. The main thing I need to work on is finishing my thesis, and I can do that anywhere. What do you say, Mom?"

Felicia straightened her cardigan, "My apartment is small, but I think we girls can make do for a little while. It'll be fun, like a slumber party."

"See?" Heron said, "It's a great plan."

"Well, all right. I can always come pick you up if you decide you're ready to come home."

"I can drive her back at the end of spring break, Len."

Before Heron had a chance to say she couldn't bear to go back to the apartment, Bea called Maggie, who agreed to pack for her, so Heron and Felicia could get it on their way out of town. Bea handed her phone over so Heron could tell Maggie what she needed.

"Hey," Heron said into the phone.

"Hi. Are you okay?"

"I mean...kind of. I think I will be. Are you? I'm so sorry you got dragged into this."

"It's fine. Honestly, I'm not that bothered about it, except about being manipulated into doing something that hurt you. None of us has anything to be ashamed of. Bryant is furious too, by the way. We are both so, so sorry."

"Tell him it's not his fault. If you guys had asked me to use my room, I would have said yes."

"About that...If you're not going to be here next week, do you mind if Bryant stays at our place? He's not getting along so great with the other guys in his house right now."

Yikes. She could only imagine what it would be like for him there now. "Oh my gosh, yes, of course he can."

"You're the best, Heron. Now tell me what you need."

Bea

The exhaustion of the weekend finally sunk in for Bea as she drove home. She'd been on alert for a day and a half; setting up and hosting the party, taking care of her cousin, half-sleeping in case Heron needed something in the night, the strained conversation with Ben, navigating the tension between Len, Felicia, and Toni in the context of their joint concern for Heron. All she wanted to do was crawl into bed and sleep until her Monday morning class. Thank heavens she was finally home and could be alone.

Her tires crunched on the gravel of the driveway. A figure rose from her porch swing and stepped into the light, giving a tentative wave. Ben. Shit. She needed to talk to him, but right now she couldn't bear the thought of another heavy discussion. Or any further human interaction at all.

"Sorry to miss Sunday dinner," he said. "I wasn't sure what the plan was, so I came by at five."

It was after nine. "Sorry," she said. But she was annoyed, too. Could he not have inferred when she rushed off to get Heron that this evening wouldn't be business as usual? They hadn't finished their conversation, but she'd been pretty clear about the space she needed. "I took Heron straight out to her dad's after I left here." As she opened the door, she shot him a sidelong glance. "Have you just been lurking on my porch this whole time then?"

"No." Ben sounded annoyed, and as she swung her door open, she could see why. All the party debris was gone. No more tissue paper flowers, party favors, gifts, cupcakes. The living room had been cleaned.

"I took the leftover food to the library. There are a lot of students getting ready for midterms today. The gifts are in a box in your hall closet. I put the party favors in the closet, too, in case you want to give them to Sarah. Everything else is gone."

"Thanks," she said. "You didn't have to do that."

"I wanted to help. I told you. There's also this." He handed her a flash drive.

"This is the—"

"The video." His voice was tight. "Yeah."

She had a ridiculous urge to throw it into the street. How could something so tiny cause so much trouble? Instead, she put it carefully in the glass dish on her coffee table. It might be needed later if there were going to be consequences for Charlie and Jason.

"Thanks." Bea sank onto the couch, leaning back and closing her eyes. Ben still stood in the doorway. She could tell he was waiting for a cue from her. An invitation to come sit down, to hold her, to do whatever other supportive boyfriend bullshit he thought would help. All she wanted was to be left alone. "What an exhausting day."

She opened her eyes and tipped her head back up to look at him. "Do you…need something else from me?" she asked. She knew she was being unfair, but this was unbearable. For the first time since the rush of her feelings for Ben, Bea deeply missed her solitary life. She would have gladly cleaned up the party debris herself if it meant not having to have one more goddamn conversation.

"I guess not."

"Good." She pulled the afghan down and curled her legs onto the couch. To lie down for a little while before changing her clothes and brushing her teeth. That was all she needed. Ten minutes of quiet.

She felt the sofa cushions sink next to her feet, a hand light on her calf. Bea swung her legs back down and sat up to glare at Ben. "Seriously?"

Ben's hand drew back as if her leg were a hot iron. "I'm not trying to start anything, Bea. It's been a rough couple of days, and I wanted us to spend some time together. This is a thing people do."

"Oh no," she knew her voice dripped with sarcasm now, but she didn't care. "Has it been rough for you? Hard to see your protégé wronged by his girl?"

"That's not fair, Bea."

"*That's* not fair."

"You seem to think this is a thing that happened to you. It's not. This is Heron's issue to deal with."

"I know that."

"Do you? Because it seems like you're more invested in her love life than your own."

She sat up straight. So, they'd be arguing after all, then. Fine. "That's ridiculous."

"Is it? Because all weekend I've been trying to be a good partner to you and all weekend you've been slamming doors in my face."

"You asked me what I need. I need space. I don't understand why you won't give that to me."

"And I don't understand why you think you have to do everything difficult alone."

Her voice broke as she blurted, "Because that's the only way I know how to do it." She was so tired. "Can't teach an old dog new tricks, y'know."

It wasn't only that. The way Charlie had hurt Heron reminded Bea she'd given Ben the power to hurt her, too. She had to claw some of it back.

"It doesn't seem to me like you're even willing to try." Ben straightened his posture on the couch, too, so now they were staring each other down from their positions against the opposite arms.

"You don't think I'm trying? If you can't see how I've twisted my life around to bring you into it, I don't know what to tell you."

"I don't know, either." Ben slumped into the cushions. "Because from where I've sitting, you've made precisely one drawer's worth of room in your life for me. Is that twisting your life around? Because it shouldn't be so difficult."

"No. It shouldn't." Bea stood, moving toward the entry. "So, I guess that's it, then. You should go."

"Okay. Yeah. We can talk about this more tomorrow." Ben rose, too.

"No. You should *go*. If we're done, we're done. In fact, let's go empty your drawer now, it'll save us some awkwardness later."

She was energized. Maybe this was all just too much for her, she wasn't built for it. She wasn't a person who could handle interpersonal situations this intense, nurturing another person's feelings when she was so upset herself. Bea simply didn't know what to do with all the emotion roiling inside her, so she turned it into action.

She strode up the stairs, stopping halfway to the second floor when she sensed him still standing in the middle of the living room. "Let's go."

"Bea." Standing at the bottom of the steps, he looked up at her, shaking his head.

"What? I guess I can pack it up for you." She turned to continue up.

He took a few steps up to join her, putting a hand on her shoulder, which stiffened. "Bea. Come on. This is a fight. People fight."

She turned around. Ahead of him on the staircase, she was taller and looked down into his face. "I don't. This is either working or it isn't, Ben. I'm tired. I don't want to do this with you if it means being at odds like this all the time. Maybe we were just fun until something tested us, and now we know we can't withstand something like this. It's better that it happened sooner rather than later."

"Bea." She couldn't bear the way he kept saying her name. It was like a plea, a prayer, an appeal to reason. Ben was a weak spot in her rationality. She turned her back on him and marched up to her bedroom. Don't look at him, she told herself. You can get through this if you don't look at him.

She pulled a conference-freebie tote bag out of the pile in her closet. She could feel Ben's eyes on her from the bedroom doorway, trying silently to catch her gaze. She wasn't going to take the bait. Carefully, she packed his socks, his underwear, his flannel pajama bottoms, his shaving kit into the tote, giving herself points for each item she didn't fling at his face.

When she was done, she marched down to the front door, and stood with it open until he came down the stairs.

Gently, he took the bag from her hand and said, "I love you, Bea."

She couldn't speak for a long moment. None of this felt right. It felt like taking the wrong exit on the freeway because the sign has your destination on it, even though none of the scenery looks like a place you want to go. But asking Ben to stay wouldn't feel right, either. She needed everything to stop, so she could get her bearings.

Bea swallowed hard and said, "Maybe I loved you, too. But I can't do this. I just can't. I am sorry."

She went back inside before Ben reached the sidewalk. Her empty house was as she wanted it. Everything in its place, no one there to demand her attention but Herschel. This was better. This was easy. She would have to get used to it; the same way she had gotten used to being with him. It might be rough for a while, but she'd eventually be back to her old self.

Chapter Sixteen

Heron

Despite her eagerness to get out of Millet, Heron hadn't been sure what to expect in Seattle. She'd spent some time in the city for short visits, but not since Felicia moved there. She'd surprised even herself with wanting to go, and by the time they'd been in the car an hour, she was second-guessing herself. After Charlie's cruelty, maybe it was foolish to leave the people she could rely on to treat her kindly, even if their kindness sometimes felt stifling. The drive was tense and mostly silent. She and her mom had so little to talk about under normal circumstances. Since October, wedding planning had been monopolizing most of Heron's conversations and its absence as a viable topic was a gaping void. Deep down, Heron knew they needed to have a real conversation about their relationship, but she couldn't face that yet and sensed Felicia wasn't interested in doing so, either.

The discomfort subsided once they had the distractions of the city. During her first week staying with her mother, Heron discovered she liked the bustle and anonymity of the city neighborhood. Felicia worked days doing alterations at Nordstrom. She was usually up from the sofa where she insisted on sleeping (leaving the Murphy bed to Heron) and out of the apartment by eight. Heron would rise, shower in the doll-sized bathroom, and take her laptop to one of the seemingly countless coffee shops nearby. She was fine-tuning her thesis, but it was pretty much done. She liked the idea of being a student hard at work in a cafe so much, she went over the prose again and again just so she could continue to play the role.

On the first day, her latte, an elaborate cluster of foamed leaves in a big cerulean bowl of a mug was so pretty, she took a photo of it next to her laptop for social media. Then she decided to do that every day, a photo of wherever she was working with hashtags like #citygirl and #studylife. Soon, she had to scroll far down her grid to find any pictures of Charlie. Charlie's own social media accounts were silent. She wondered what he was doing. She shouldn't care what he was doing. She hoped he was okay.

The other thing Heron discovered, well, rediscovered, was that her mom was *fun*. She'd forgotten the nights they used to play dress-up or go out to dinner, just the two of them, before Felicia left. Once or twice, they cooked together in the corner of Felicia's apartment that served as the kitchen, bumping into each other, sitting at the table to chop vegetables, washing the dishes afterward in a kitchen sink so tiny it barely fit one plate. Most of the time, they went out. Happy hours in the spots near the apartment full of students and young professionals, or the restaurants near Felicia's work, full of office workers waiting for

HOW TO ALIGN THE STARS

the commuter traffic to clear.

One night, they dressed up and Felicia took Heron to the Space Needle. They ate seafood and drank swanky cocktails as they watched the sun set over the bay and the lights of the city twinkle beneath them.

Over dessert, Felicia leaned forward and said, "I'm proud of you, honey."

Heron didn't know quite how to react. "Thanks, Mom," she said, ducking her head.

"I mean it, Heron. You've picked yourself up, you're not letting your schoolwork slip, you're not letting what happened get in your way."

"I don't really know what else to do, you know? I'm just… trying to keep going."

"Atta girl. Pretend it never happened. Who needs 'em?"

Heron tossed and turned all night, thinking about what her mother said. She would never forget what happened or forget Charlie, but she was on her way to pretending she had, which was at least something. Here, away from Millet, it was easy. She spent whole hours without thinking about how much she missed Charlie or how much his rejection hurt.

But letting it slide to the back of her mind wasn't quite the right thing to do, as much as she wanted to let the whole thing go and move on. After Felicia went to work one day, Heron pulled out the little packet of papers Bea had tucked into her backpack, right on top. Non-consensual nude photography was listed and the consequences for code violations ranged from censure to expulsion. To file a complaint, one needed only to fill out the form and email it to the review board's inbox. It seemed far too easy and also insurmountable.

The packet sat next to Heron all day, as she polished the chapter of her thesis that detailed second-wave feminism's impact on professional dress. Every time she thought about it, she got a shaky, heart-pounding feeling. Heron checked her horoscope app, reading:

TAURUS: Doing the right thing isn't easy but living with the wrong thing is always more difficult. Buck up, little bull.

She knew what she ought to do, but she closed the app and stuffed the papers back into her bag.

Bea

Bea had been sleeping in her guest room for ten days. It all started innocently enough. With her dresser drawer reclaimed from Ben, she was able to sort her bras and underwear into different drawers again instead of having them all jumbled together. But then she decided to go through it all, getting rid of the lace bras that itched, but she kept because Ben seemed to like them, the underwear that was pretty but rode up every time she wore it. She didn't need that stuff anymore and didn't expect to need it ever again. Ridiculous to have it in the first place. The same went for the satin shortie pajamas with the slit on the leg Ben liked to slip his hand into as they were falling asleep, to rest on her bare hip. Soon, the entire contents of her dresser had been dumped onto the middle of her bed. And then she started emptying the closet, because, why not?

She'd heard you were supposed to hold each thing, ask yourself if it brought you joy, and let that feeling help you decide whether to keep it. The Messiman sweatshirt from her freshman year, perfectly faded and soft? So much joy. Keep. Her flannel *I Love Lucy* pajamas? Joy. Her industrial strength, practical underwire bras? Absolutely no joy but they cost $125 each and although teaching braless would be a baller move in the fight against the patriarchy, she couldn't bring herself to do it. Reluctantly, keep. A drab brown blouse she'd bought only because it was appropriate for teaching, and it fit? Toss.

Herschel climbed to the top of the pile and enthroned himself on a stack of Bea's sweaters. Bea reached over to stroke his back, and her eyes fell on a midnight shimmer. Her velvet dress. She pulled it from the pile and held it, letting the cool fabric slip through her fingers. Wearing this dress, she'd felt beautiful for the first time in her life. She'd been satisfied with her appearance before: thought she looked sharp in her suits; cool in a pair of skinny jeans and a flannel shirt; cute in the retro dress she'd worn to the reunion. But she had never before felt powerfully beautiful — sexy — the way she had in the blue dress. Some of it was Ben, the way he'd looked at her when she wore it, the way it seemed to invite him to touch her, but it wasn't all him. She'd felt it before he ever saw her in it. The velvet crumpled in her clutching fingers, and she spread it over the pile on the bed, backing up to look at it. Did she even want to feel that way again? Because right now, she felt like she'd been dropped off a building. Like she'd gotten used to the feeling of being supported by wings, only to find herself looking at her own pudgy, useless arms again, plummeting. But knowing she could feel it was something, at least. What would one call that emotion?

Unable to answer, or decide what to do with the dress (Pass it on so some other woman could have a similar magical experience, like the jeans in the books Heron read in junior high? Bury it? Burn it in a ritual?) and overwhelmed by the pile of clothes — half of which she knew she hated and had only bought because they fit on her body — Bea had simply closed the bedroom door and gone to sleep in the guest room. Why not? She'd decorated the room in a whimsical patchwork of bright jewel tones, and it held the shelves where she kept her novels. The bed was comfortable, and none of the pillows smelled like Ben. He'd never slept in it or held her in it, the empty expanse next to her didn't make her think about him. She'd never learned to sleep on "her" side of this bed. She spent a week holed up in there, reading. Thank goodness for spring break.

Frozen with indecision about the pile of clothes on her bed, she'd been wearing a wild hodgepodge of outfits pulled off the top of the pile or things from the guest room closet, which held various special occasion clothes. That was why, when Sarah dropped by to pick up the serving platter Bea had borrowed for Heron's shower, she found Bea dressed in her Rosie the Riveter Halloween costume. Bea was finding it practical and comfortable — the coveralls had oodles of pockets and no waistband, and the polka-dot headscarf was keeping her overgrown bangs out of her eyes.

"So," Sarah said, "this is an interesting look."

"I'm cleaning out my closet. The life-altering magic of getting rid of shit you don't want."

"I see. And...doing your part for the war effort?"

"Well, I have to wear something."

Sarah squinted at her. "Mmm hmm. How long has this project been going on?"

"I started on Saturday."

"I've heard that Kondo thing takes a few days."

"Last Saturday."

Sarah blew out a resigned sigh. "Take me to your pile." Bea sheepishly led her upstairs, and when Sarah surveyed the bedroom she said, "Oh, honey."

"I tried to do the hold-each-object-and-see-how-it-makes-me-feel thing, but it turns out there are more complicated emotions than 'joy' and 'not-joy,' and I kind of got stuck."

"Okay. Well, let's simplify it a little bit, then." Sarah held up a forest green sweater. "Do you like this?"

"It's one of my favorites."

"Keep." Sarah folded it and placed it on the top shelf of Bea's closet. "This?" It was a black blazer.

"I don't love it, but it was expensive, and I need a dark jacket for conferences and important meetings."

"Keep." They went on like this for some time, folding together. "So," Sarah said, in what Bea recognized as a trying-to-be-casual voice. "I ran into Ben at Mostarda. He asked how you were doing, and I said I thought he ought to know better than me, since he sees you much more often these days. He said you broke up. Were you ever going tell me about it?"

Bea sank back into her pillows, visible now thanks to Sarah's capable handiwork. "I didn't want to be, like, heartbreak girl, you know? I'm sorry," she added in response to Sarah's hurt expression—she'd Ben & Jerry'd Sarah through more than one ugly breakup. "It was just a lot. I don't have the easiest time dealing with emotional stuff."

"Oh?" Sarah's voice was full of gentle sarcasm. "I hadn't noticed."

"I knew I would have to tell people about it eventually, but I couldn't quite cope yet."

"So, you decided to be Little Edie for a while?"

"I can think of worse things to be. I always have been staunch."

Sarah laughed. "True enough." She folded a few more t-shirts, then said, "Bea, what *happened*? Obviously, I'm on your side no matter what, ovaries over brovaries and all that, but Ben seemed pretty great."

"You saw everything that happened at the shower—"

"Shitshow."

"Shitshow, yes. But I had things under control, and Ben wanted to help, but he was in my face so much and I really needed, like, a second to think things through. I felt smothered." Answering

Sarah's wince, she continued, "He was upset that I wanted space and I just…couldn't deal." Bea stood and began slamming sock balls back into her drawer. She didn't need this mess, either. She was a thirty-eight-year-old, fully capable grown woman and not sleeping in her own bed because of a breakup was ridiculous.

"Wow, Bea." Sarah's tone was gentle. "It sounds like you had a stupid fight, not a relationship-ender."

Sarah made a good point, so Bea handled her friend's insight the only way she was equipped to. By ignoring it. "Anyway, I think the whole Ben thing was just…an experiment. To see if I could be a couple person after all. I am not a couple person. Being with someone must improve upon being alone. That's a pretty high bar for me. I'm great alone."

Sarah gave Bea's costume and the disarray of her bedroom a pointed once-over. "Yeah. You seem super great."

"I'm a little upset about the transition, that's all. Being with Ben is over for me and it's fine. This thing isn't over for Heron, and I need to be able to be there for her without also having to mollycoddle some man into feeling helpful."

"How is Heron?"

"She seems okay. She's been texting and tells me the final draft of her thesis is almost done. She says she's enjoying spending time with her mom. She said she's still thinking about registering a code of conduct complaint against Charlie and Jason. I think she's coming around to the idea that she needs to stick up for herself."

"And you're sure you're okay with this breakup? Because I got the feeling Ben was hoping you'd change your mind."

"Yes." It came out sharper than Bea intended, and she added, "Sure, I'm sad, but I'll be fine. With a little help from my personal closet organizer." She threw a sock ball at Sarah, who caught it and tossed it into the drawer. More solemnly, Bea added, "Ben's better off without me, too. We had some fun but neither of us needs the drama."

"Hmm," Sarah was using her thoughtful tone again, the one that was slightly infuriating when you were trying to talk yourself out of dealing with your feelings. "Well, you wouldn't want to keep anything you don't need around." The blue velvet dress was the only thing left on the bed. Without asking Bea how the item made her feel, Sarah picked it up and hung it at the back of Bea's closet.

Heron

The email came while Heron and her mother were eating breakfast. Felicia grabbed bites while doing her hair and makeup for work. Heron was perched at the tiny kitchen table with her laptop. It was Charlie's mother, demanding repayment of a deposit the Brewsters had made for a wedding reception they'd planned to hold in Darien in the fall.

Black spots swam in front of Heron's eyes. Now she could be sure Charlie had told his parents about the breakup. It was stupid, but she'd been holding onto a tiny little piece of hope that they'd get back from spring break, he'd apologize, and they'd move on as if nothing had happened. This message thoroughly deflated that balloon. What had he said about her? How was she going to get thousands of dollars for Mrs. Brewster's deposit? And that was on top of all the money her dad and Toni had spent on a wedding which wasn't going to happen.

Heron's pulse rose and her head went light. The image of her laptop sitting on the table blurred.

"Mom," she called, but she could barely hear her own voice over the roar of blood in her ears. Then she slid off her chair onto the floor, pulling her knees up to her chin to hug them. "I think I need help," she said. Or, thought she said. It felt like there wasn't any air in her lungs to push the words out.

Felicia came to her side, finally. "What's wrong?"

Heron gestured at her computer, but it had gone to sleep, the blank screen temporarily replacing the messages with her screensaver.

"It's too much, Mom. I can't do it."

"Yes, you can. Pull yourself up, dust yourself off. Keep trucking."

"I can't."

"For chrissakes, Heron, you can too. You're stronger than you think you are."

Felicia filled a glass at the tap, handed it to Heron, then came back with a cold washcloth. "Lean forward," she said, putting the cloth over the back of Heron's neck. With the cold and the change of position, her head began to clear.

"I have to go to work. Take a warm shower, get dressed, drink some juice, and pull yourself together. I promise you'll feel better."

And then Felicia just…left. She didn't slam the door behind her, but when she closed it, Heron jumped as if she had.

Right before she turned fifteen, Heron saved up to buy a pair of knee-high boots she'd fallen in love with. They were perfect, just the right shade of deep, chocolate brown, knee high, with a low chunky heel. She'd kept them in the box and was saving them to wear to school on her birthday, wanting to mark the occasion with a sophisticated outfit.

The day before her birthday, Heron came home from school to find her mom on her way out to the book club she attended at one of the wine bars in town. Felicia was wearing a body-hugging, cream-colored dress with boots that looked…suspiciously familiar.

"Are those my boots?" Heron asked.

Felicia looked down. "Oh, yeah, you don't mind, do you? I love that we're the same shoe size now. Hopefully your feet won't grow much more."

"I kind of do mind. Can you change? You're stretching them out." Their feet were the same size, but Felicia's calves were fuller.

"Oh, they're fine. You'll thank me when you don't have to stuff your jeans into them." Felicia looked at her watch. "Besides, I don't have time to change and my black boots don't look right with this dress."

She moved to go, and Heron's anger flared. This was so unfair. She got between her mother and the door. "Mom. Give them back. Please. I bought them with my own money."

Felicia tried to step around, but Heron moved with her. "Don't be ridiculous, honey," she said. "They'll be fine, and I look great, don't I?"

"You look like mutton dressed as lamb." She had heard Felicia use this phrase herself when she was being catty about her friends. Heron knew it was too far—Felicia took a lot of pride in looking young and staying up on trends—but her mother wasn't listening, and she needed to command her attention. It worked.

"You ungrateful little bitch." As soon as the words were out of her mouth, Felicia recoiled, pressing a hand to her mouth. And then, she reached down, unzipped the boots and stepped out of them, jammed her feet into a pair of garden clogs she kept by the door, and slammed out of the house.

Heron presumed she'd gone to book club. She shoved the boots under her bed, and when her father came in from the cellars to eat dinner with her, she didn't say anything about the argument. She heard her mother's car pull into the driveway late that evening and assumed they would make up in the morning, but when she woke, Felicia was gone. Later that day, Len got worried enough to call the police. Heron had been working up the courage to tell them about the fight when he found Felicia's note. At that point she figured it didn't matter. It was her fault her mother left them, but she couldn't bear for him to know. He was all she had left.

In the seven years since, she'd buried the incident deep in the back of her mind, just as the boots were buried under the bed. But now that she took the memory out and looked at it in the light of day, she felt a new surge of outrage. Heron always believed the fight about the boots had been the last straw for Felicia, pulling the disappointment of having a daughter she didn't like into sharp focus. All these years, she'd been so wrong. She hadn't been out of line, not really. Even if she had, who left their child over something like that? It wasn't her fault at all, it was something within Felicia that made her leave. Just as what happened with Charlie was more about him than it was about her. She hadn't failed to be good enough for him. He had failed to love her as she was. More than that, he had failed to treat her with decency.

Using the seat of the chair, Heron pulled herself up from the kitchen floor. She felt a little wobbly, but stable enough. Her meds were in her toiletry kit, and she considered taking a pill, but there wasn't any point. If she'd had one before she read the message, maybe she could have staved off the reaction, but the reaction was over and she felt...like she'd been run over by a truck, actually. But also like she would be okay.

Heron took a shower. She made a pot of tea, adding a big spoonful of honey to her cup. She read the messages again. Okay. She could handle this. A short internet search told her Charlie's mother probably didn't have legal standing to demand reimbursement. The Brewsters were trying to scare her. By freaking out after reading the message she'd done exactly what they wanted, but they would never have to know it. She did feel bad about them being out money, even though they could obviously afford it, but maybe she could fix this another way.

Heron's heart thudded again, but this time the adrenaline signified her determination to get things done. The first call she made was to the country club in Darien. Lauren remembered her from their planning session, and when Heron said the wedding had been called off, her reply was "I'm so sorry to hear that." But then she added under her breath, "To be honest, you're dodging a mother-in-law bullet."

"That's actually why I'm calling." Heron explained about the deposit. "Would it be possible for you to refund it?"

"Let me check…Yes, we can do that. Honestly, the Brewsters are such longstanding members we probably would have waived it anyway."

"Great. Lauren, would you please issue the refund, email a copy of the confirmation to me, and cc Julia Brewster?"

Heron could hear the grin in Lauren's voice over the phone. "I'd be delighted to. Take care, Ms. Hunter."

Next, Heron called Lucy at Old, New, Borrowed, Blue.

"Heron!" Lucy said. "I was just about to ship your bridesmaid dresses."

Heron surprised herself with a self-effacing chuckle. "Don't bother."

"Oh, honey. What happened?"

"It's a long story." She'd have to figure out a way to make it shorter though, wouldn't she? She'd be telling it a lot. "Charlie wasn't who I thought he was. Or I'm not who he thought I was. Both, I guess."

"I'm so sorry. I'll tell you what. I haven't charged your card for the second payment on the dresses yet. I'll put them on consignment. There are a lot of brides realizing summer wedding season is sneaking up on them and these are a popular design. I bet they'll go like hotcakes, and if they sell, I'll refund your deposit. Sound good?"

"That's great. Thank you so much."

"And if you haven't started on your gown yet, I'm happy to take the silk back."

Heron laughed bitterly this time. "It's almost done."

"Oh, honey."

"I know. It was really beautiful, too." She sniffled. "Is really beautiful."

"I'm sure it is. And I bet you'll wear it in the future with someone better than Charlie."

Heron considered it. She couldn't stand the idea of putting that dress on again. "I don't think so. If I get married someday, maybe I'll wear red."

"Send me some photos, then. I'm not making any promises, but if the construction and design are good, I might be able to sell that on consignment, too."

"Thanks, Lucy."

Then she called her dad.

"Hi, Birdie, how are things going over there?"

"Fine," she said. And then, she did the hardest thing. She told him about the fight over the boots, and how she'd kept it from him.

Her dad was silent for a long time. Finally, she heard a shuddering exhale. "Birdie. Sweetheart. It wasn't your fault. I wish you had told me."

"I know I should have. I'm so sorry."

"You don't have a thing to be sorry about."

"Dad?"

"What, Birdie?"

"I'm also sorry about all the money. For the wedding."

"We aren't out a dime, sweetie. Toni was going to handle all the catering, we hadn't made any deposits yet for the photographer, we were going to use our usual DJ. In fact" — he switched over to video — "we redirected part of the budget to your graduation gift."

He turned the phone to show a cherry red electric car sitting in the driveway of the winery.

"Dad! Are you serious?"

"Totally serious. It's yours. I'd been planning to do this for ages, but when it looked like you might be in Manhattan next year I held off. I thought, well, if you're more comfortable staying in your old room when you come back to school, you'll need wheels to go back and forth."

Heron felt like she'd been wrapped in a warm blanket. She'd spent so long absorbed by Charlie, then despondent when she lost him, she'd forgotten how many other people loved her. It wasn't only the car, although the car was wonderful. It was the way her dad had anticipated her needs.

She reached into her bag and dug out the conduct complaint information. It was time. She deserved an acknowledgment that what happened to her had been wrong. Maggie and Bryant did, too. Heron wrote up her account of the incident, keeping her tone as dispassionate as possible. Her finger hovered over the "send" button for several minutes before she squeezed her eyes shut, took a deep breath, exhaled, and clicked.

The hardest part came after Felicia got home from work. Heron suggested they go to the diner down the block to have breakfast for dinner, a mother-daughter tradition from when she was little.

"I have an anxiety disorder, Mom," Heron said evenly. "It's

a real thing. It's just how my brain works. My fight or flight response is disproportional sometimes."

Heron had been in the middle of telling her mother about filing the complaint and how difficult it had been to work up the courage, when Felicia broke in to say she didn't understand the problem with Heron's "nerves."

"But you were never like that as a young girl. Totally fearless on the playground. Not a bit of stage fright when you were in *Annie*..."

Heron took a deep breath. "It's different for everyone. Both the things that trigger it, and when and why it starts." She hesitated to say the rest, but maybe it was time to stop protecting Felicia from the truth about the impact of her departure. "For me, it started after you left. Dad and I were so scared before he found your note, there were police in the house. You and Dad never even fought, but you and I had been arguing a lot, so I thought it was my fault."

Felicia set her fork down. "Don't be ridiculous, Heron, of course it wasn't."

"I know that now."

"You're saying this...disorder...is because of me."

"I'm not blaming you, Mom. I'm just explaining. For all I know I would have had these issues anyway. But, when you disappeared, I felt like the bottom dropped out of everything all of a sudden. It took me a long time to recover. And I guess I just wanted you to know I'm doing okay. Because it dropped out again, with Charlie—"

"I'll say."

"And it was awful, but I am recovering. It still hurts, but I'm okay. And I'm proud of myself and I guess"—the words rose like a lump in her throat—"I want you to be proud of me, too."

"Oh, sweet girl. I am proud of you. So proud. I always have

been. You have such a bright future and you can do anything you want with it. I envy that."

Heron felt a fat tear spill down her cheek. She hadn't noticed it form and wasn't sure which emotion had created it. "You could still do something else if you wanted to, Mom. Even go back to school."

Felicia shrugged. "I could. But I like my job now and I don't need a degree for it. If I'd stayed in Millet, I'd be so miserable. I *was* miserable and I tried to push it down and hide it for as long as I could, until I couldn't stand it anymore. It might have been our arguments that made me realize that, but you didn't do anything wrong, honey. The way I reacted to you made me feel like I didn't have any business being your mother, like I was going to do more harm than good. I'm so sorry the way I left hurt you and your dad, but I'm not sorry I left, love. I'm sorry I didn't go sooner. If I had, I think I would have still had it in me to make it a little easier on you."

"I wouldn't have wanted you to be unhappy, Mom."

"I know."

"I'm glad you're happy now."

"Me too. And I want you to be happy, too. I'm so sorry what happened with Charlie this year hurt you, but to me, your future looks brighter than it would have if you were getting married next month."

"Well. It certainly looks different."

For the first time, a future without Charlie felt like a kaleidoscope of possibility instead of a minefield of uncertainty.

Chapter Seventeen

Bea

Bea was already in a bad mood when she got to the campus cafe. The students in her Monday morning class had been scattered and disengaged; understandable the Monday after spring break, but at this point in the semester they needed to pay attention in order to be ready for the final. Heron had texted she wouldn't be on campus today, which was worrisome — Bea knew the return to campus would be difficult, but she had to come back sometime. Heron was nervous about bumping into Charlie of course; Bea understood the feeling all too well.

The barista, a sophomore who'd been in Bea's class the previous semester, over-poured the foam on her latte, but in a hurry to get out of the student union, she put the lid on anyway, causing a tiny volcano of steamed milk to erupt from the hole in the lid. She was turning back to get a napkin when she heard "Hello," in Ben's voice. Fantastic. But there was no reason she couldn't be cool. Breezy. No-nonsense.

"Yes?" It came out waspish.

"I just thought I should say hi."

"Why?"

"Pardon me?"

"Why?" She said it slowly, as if he had misunderstood the simple word. She knew she was being horrid; it would be easier to politely say hello and then beat a hasty retreat. But the venom came out before she could stop it. Maybe it was for the best anyway, the sooner they were back to thinly veiled hostility, the sooner she would feel normal again.

"Uh, to be civil adults? And because I wondered how you were doing."

"Well," she moved away from the coffee bar, aware they had already attracted curious glances from a few students. "First of all, we don't need to go out of our way to exchange pleasantries. We managed to avoid each other before, we can certainly do it again. In fact, it'll be easier this time since we know each other's habits thoroughly. Secondly, I am fine. You ought to know me well enough to know there's no reason I wouldn't be. Did you expect me to be pining away for you?"

"No." His voice was tight. "I definitely didn't expect that."

"Good. Great. Take care." She turned and moved toward the door with as much dignity as someone with steamed milk dripping down their forearm could muster. She loosened her grip on the paper cup.

"Bea."

"What?" This time she knew her voice held a note of anguish. Ready tears sprang up, hot behind her eyes. She hated herself for it. She hated Ben more. She'd been fine before him. Now, missing him hurt, and the pain pissed her off because it was so unnecessary; they were right back where they'd started. If Ben had only stayed in his own damn lane as an annoying sometime-nemesis and hadn't turned out to be well, rather wonderful, really, she wouldn't be feeling all of this right now.

She calmed her tone and said, "What, Ben. What else could you possibly want? Can't you let it be? Please." She looked hard at his face for the first time in this encounter. Bea wanted to see the blithe smugness she'd avidly loathed in the past. Instead, he looked drawn, as if someone had opened a tap and drained out a little of his vibrance. His eyes drooped at the corners. She knew this hurt for him, too, but she had too much on her emotional plate to worry about whether she was being unfair to him.

He swallowed. "Okay. Yes. Easier for me, too. Take care, Bea."

"I intend to." She started to walk away, then added, "you too," as an afterthought.

Bea made it to her office before she cried, grateful for a few minutes to compose herself before her next class. Afterward, her office hours were full of kids with questions about their midterm grades and preparing for finals. She didn't think about Ben again until she was walking home in the late afternoon. What the fuck was wrong with her? This breakup was her idea, she should be fine, but the first time she saw Ben again she fell apart? She needed to pull her shit together and dust herself off. This was the worst it would ever hurt, because it was over. Ben couldn't hurt her now any more than she'd already hurt both of them. And every day the pain would recede, until she was back to normal.

Heron

The code of conduct hearing was held in the administrative building. Heron had only been here once before, to file an appeal for admission to a class that was technically at capacity. She climbed the steep stone steps, glad she was wearing the jet-black suit she'd bought for job and grad school interviews. It felt like armor. She checked in with the receptionist and was led to a conference room. Despite rushing from her nine o'clock class, she was the last to arrive.

The conference room was windowless and gray, containing only a long laminate table. There was nothing on the walls except for a clock and a whiteboard bearing the smudged remains of notes from a prior meeting. The review board sat on one side of the table and consisted of a sophomore Heron vaguely recognized, Dean Lucas, and Professor Fielding, who Heron had taken a political science class from junior year at Charlie's recommendation. The professors nodded cordially as she made eye contact, the sophomore didn't look up from her paper. Was this all? She'd read about the reviews having representation from administration, faculty, and the student body, but had expected…well, more people. Or people who were more qualified.

Bea, who was already seated at one end of the table, gave her a buck-up smile. Next to her, Maggie and Bryant had scooted their chairs close together, signaling they were a unit. Bryant looked straight ahead with a stony expression, but Maggie was glaring openly at Charlie and Jason, who were seated at the other end with Jason's mother. Heron recognized her; as the wife of the college president, she attended events occasionally, but she'd never seen her with her son before. They leaned slightly away from each other with barely disguised hostility.

Ben sat in the middle, leaving a seat empty between himself and Charlie. Heron cringed inwardly for Bea, but Ben gave her a kind smile as she sat down.

Dean Lucas began the hearing by asking Heron to state her complaint.

She explained about the videos, where they were taken and when. Maggie and Bryant confirmed they were the subjects of the second video and hadn't known they were being recorded.

"It wasn't only the violation of having the videos taken," Heron said, using all of her effort to control the waver in her voice, "but to have them shown in such a surprising, public way made it so much worse. At first, I was upset because of the breakup of course. I think anyone would have been. But that pales in comparison to the violation of learning that this video of me existed in the first place, and was shown at a time clearly chosen to be as hurtful as possible."

Charlie spoke for his side, explaining about how Jason had come to him with the first video, then suggested watching Heron's apartment to see if she was really spending the night at her cousin's. "Then," he said, "when…activity…began in the room, Jason got his camera and said we should 'collect further evidence.'"

Bryant's fist clenched, and Heron saw Maggie lay her hand over his and squeeze. He relaxed. As glad as she was her friends were together, Heron missed being part of a team like that.

Charlie continued, "To be honest, I don't remember much about the rest of the night or the next day, except for being very hurt and very angry. I will admit that if I had it to do over again, I would have spoken to Heron privately." He glanced in Heron's direction and for a moment he was her old caring Charlie, then his face closed off again as he finished his statement. "But what's done is done and I think overall the incident has stopped me from making a bigger mistake."

The air left Heron's lungs and she pressed her soles against the floor to stop her legs from trembling. Had Charlie just referred to their engagement as a mistake? She would not cry here. She wouldn't. She bit the inside of her cheek to keep her face still.

Jason spoke next, confirming Charlie's story. "I had the footage in the amphitheater leftover from a short film project," he said, and it took great effort for Heron to suppress an indignant remark. What kind of short film might that have been? But at least he'd admitted to taking it. "The second video was taken merely for evidentiary purposes. It may not have been polite to play them publicly, but we had reason to believe it was necessary, as Ms. Hunter is clearly a very deceptive person."

Maggie muttered "bullshit" under her breath. Heron used her shoe to tap Maggie's ankle under the table. Being combative wouldn't help.

"First," said Dean Lucas, "I would like to ask if anyone disputes the content of the videos. If not, I think we can forgo reviewing this sensitive evidence at this proceeding. The committee has reviewed them privately."

Heron's skin flushed with embarrassment at the idea of anyone else seeing the videos, but at least they wouldn't all be watching them here, together.

"No dispute," Charlie said.

"Me neither," said Heron.

Jason said, "I do not believe Miss McIntyre is in the second video. I still say it is Heron and her friend is covering for her. Bryant" — he enunciated the given name crisply and a bit of spittle flew out of his mouth — "has been living in the apartment rented by Miss Hunter and Miss McIntyre since before spring break and I believe this is the reason he has agreed to lie for her."

Everyone on Heron's side of the table knew this was a blatant lie, but they'd agreed not to bring up Jason's scheming at this hearing because they thought it would sound too implausible. Bryant's response was icy and restrained, "I found myself in need of a new living situation, and Ms. Hunter was kind enough to let me take over her share of the rent."

"That's right," said Heron. "After this incident, I found it difficult to live in such close proximity to Mr. Brewster and Mr. Shultz, so I sublet my room to Mr. Hardy and have been staying elsewhere."

The committee scribbled notes on their legal pads. So far, neither Professor Fielding nor the student had said anything. This was Dean Lucas's show, she realized. The others were there only to provide the illusion of balance.

"And the date the first video was taken is?"

Heron answered. She knew the exact date because the date of the homecoming dance was printed in her yearbook. She'd looked it up during her preparations.

"And the apartment in which the second video was filmed is not campus property?"

"Correct," said Heron. "All the tenants are Messiman students, but it's a privately owned building."

With these questions, the stone that had been sitting in Heron's stomach all morning grew heavier. She could see the lines he was trying to draw, and the picture didn't look good for her.

"I see," said the dean. "We will adjourn to deliberate. Please remain in the vicinity and we will call you back in when we have our decision."

That was it? The whole thing had taken less than fifteen minutes.

They filed out of the room. Bea, Heron, Maggie, and Bryant clustered on one side of the lawn in front of the building, Jason, Dr. Shultz, and Charlie on the other. Ben drifted off on his own to lean on the railing running down the middle of the steps.

Bea gave him one of her trademark disdainful looks. "Literally on the fence, I see."

"Don't be too hard on him, Professor Hayes," said Bryant. "He's supposed to be here as our advisor. I don't think he wants to support Charlie or Jason."

"Could've fooled me," Bea said. It was true, Ben had been silent through the proceedings although Heron wanted to believe he was on her side, for Bea's sake as well as her own.

When they were called back twenty minutes later, no one on the committee would look at Heron, but Professor Fielding smiled at Charlie and so she knew exactly what was going to happen.

"Ms. Hunter," Dean Lucas began, "while we can't deny what happened to you, as well as to Mr. Hardy and Ms. McIntyre, is not polite conduct, we have found no violation of the student code. The first video was taken on Messiman property, but neither you nor Mr. Shultz had matriculated at the time it was filmed. We can't hold either of you responsible for abiding by a code you hadn't signed yet. While the camera for the second video was on Messiman-associated property, although Sigma Omicron Delta owns the house"—he cleared his throat—"the featured act was on private property in front of an uncovered window, in clear public view. The display of the videos was in very poor taste. However, so were the acts depicted therein. Furthermore, while they were shown at an event attended by many people associated with the college, it was nevertheless a private event on private property. This board finds no violation of the code of student conduct." The dean closed his folder with a slap as definitive as the rap of a gavel, and the three board members stood as if they'd choreographed the motion, leaving the room before anyone had an opportunity to comment.

Heron felt like she'd been punched in the stomach. She was prepared for this but had still held out hope of getting some sort of vindication. Bea put her arm around her.

Jason's mother set her mouth into a grim line, muttered, "Okay," in a businesslike tone, and was the first to leave the room. Charlie left next, eyes on the floor. Jason had the gall to smile at them as he left. Ben cast a regretful glance toward Bea before filing out behind them.

"I'm so sorry, Heron," said Maggie, as she and Bryant stood up from the table.

"Me too," Bryant added. "I'm sorry for my role in this, especially, Heron."

"It's not your fault," Heron told him.

"This is bullshit," Bea spat. "And it's not over, Birdie, I'll find out what other recourses are available to us."

"Bea, don't. It's pretty clear they wanted to use very black and white criteria, and the technicalities weren't on our side." She didn't regret filing the complaint, it seemed important that she had stood up for herself even if the decision didn't go her way. "I don't want you to jeopardize your tenure or make things awkward with your coworkers."

Bea reacted with a choked-sounding snort. "Oh, sweetie, making things awkward with coworkers is my specialty these days."

Ouch. That was Heron's fault. It was Bea's nature to make light of things, but she wasn't herself these days. If Heron's ridiculous plan hadn't thrown her and Ben together, she wouldn't be hurting now. "Still. Let's please leave it alone now, okay?"

"If that's what you want."

It wasn't, actually. Heron was still angry. None of this sat right with her, she just didn't know what else she could do about it.

Bea

Bea hadn't wanted Heron to know her meeting with President Phillips to hear the results of her tenure review was this morning. The timing couldn't have been more awkward, in fact. After the hearing concluded, she had fifteen minutes before she was scheduled to meet with the president. Not enough time to comfort Heron, too much to wait in the lobby. Maggie and Bryant shepherded Heron away, so at least she wasn't going to be alone. Bea took a lap around the library to quell her nerves and clear some of the frustration lingering from Heron's hearing. The whole thing was asinine.

Rounding the corner, she saw Ben on the library stairs with Charlie. Ben was gesticulating, and she couldn't catch all of what he was saying but she made out the words "dumbass" and "consequences." Charlie looked miserable. Good.

Three minutes before her meeting, Bea mounted the stairs of the administration building for the second time that day. The door to President Phillips' inner office was closed when she arrived, so she perched on one of the chairs in the reception area and waited. A moment later, Dr. Shultz emerged, looking pained. The president walked her wife down the hall. Bea could hear them speaking in low tones but wasn't able to make out any of the words. To be a fly on the wall in that household tonight…

President Phillips returned to her office suite. "Dr. Hayes, please come on back." Her voice was full of its customary warmth, but there was a waver behind it.

Bea stood, followed her in, and settled into one of the chairs across from the stately oak desk, trying to look confident and casual.

"I'm sorry about the awkward timing of this meeting. I was aware, of course, you also had a family connection to these conduct proceedings, but I didn't realize the hearing was scheduled for today. That was probably rather stressful, and I apologize."

"It's fine." Even though the tenure decision was presumably made and her behavior in this meeting shouldn't impact it, she didn't want to appear as if she couldn't handle pressure well or wasn't able to separate personal matters from professional ones.

"I won't keep you in suspense. Everything in your portfolio looks good: the entire science division speaks very highly of you, your student evaluation scores are some of our highest, and your letters of recommendation are glowing. It is my pleasure to approve the faculty personnel committee's recommendation that you receive tenure."

This was it for Bea. The moment she'd been working toward for fifteen years, everything she had ever wanted had been handed to her. And it wasn't that she wasn't thrilled. She was. But shouldn't she be happier? When she'd pictured this moment, she imagined herself jumping for joy.

She smiled, but she had a feeling her reaction appeared more subdued than President Phillips was expecting, too. "Thank you so much."

The other woman leaned across the desk. "On a personal note, Beatrice, I want to say it's a pleasure to have you as part of the Messiman community. It's wonderful to have someone on staff who has been through the student experience here and opted to make it her professional home. Your dedication is an asset to Messiman."

Bea nodded and smiled mildly.

President Phillips continued, "In the interest of impartiality, I recused myself from anything related to these misconduct allegations against my stepson, but I know the proceedings were awkward and difficult. Part of fostering a close community here is fallout when there are conflicts, of course."

"Of course." Bea could feel her smile starting to slide off her face.

"If I can speak off the record, I think it would have been wise if my stepson had attended school in California as he wanted."

Where was this going?

"Kelly felt she'd missed out on too much of his teen years. And here we are. But I want you to know, again, strictly off the record,

I deeply regret what happened."

Bea felt it best to maintain a cool, professional demeanor. She would have loved to get a glass of wine with Jane Phillips and hear more about what she honestly thought about all of this, but tenure or not, it was a professional line she shouldn't cross. "I think Heron would probably just like to move on. But she doesn't want something similar to happen to someone else. And she wasn't the only student impacted by this."

"No, of course not. And I am going to call for a review and revision of our conduct policies."

"I'm happy to hear that," Bea said. "Please let me know if I can be of any assistance. I have some ideas."

"I'm sure you do." President Phillips rose, a clear indication for Bea to do the same. "I'll be in touch."

Bea stood and took a step toward the door. In the interest of getting out of the president's office before things became more awkward, she returned to the mental script of what she'd imagined she would say at the conclusion of this meeting. "Thank you so much for the wonderful news. I am truly looking forward to continuing my career at Messiman."

President Phillips stood to walk her out. "It's well deserved. Congratulations, Dr. Hayes."

It was customary for the college administration to send an email announcement to a faculty member's division upon tenure approval, and it must have gone out while Bea was walking to the science building, because all the way down the hall to her office, she fielded congratulatory exclamations from her science division colleagues.

Rick was perched on the edge of her desk when she got to her office, waiting to give her an angular hug. "I didn't doubt it for a minute, kiddo," he said. "Can I take you to a celebratory lunch? Or do you have plans with Ben? I don't want to usurp the boyfriend."

"Thanks. No, um, Ben and I broke up." Perhaps it was Rick's lofty height keeping him above the gossip that circulated among Messiman faculty. Despite Bea and Ben being seen together all over campus this winter, Rick had been surprised to learn they were dating when she'd finally mentioned something to him. Nonetheless, she'd hoped he would hear about the breakup through the grapevine so she could avoid being the one to tell him about it.

Rick looked so distressed, for a fleeting moment Bea felt guilty for telling him. "I'm sorry to hear that. Too good for him, huh?"

"Something like that." She felt a wistful tug at the corners of her mouth.

"Well, kiddo"—Rick clapped a hand on her back—"get your coat. I'm taking you to brunch. How do Bloody Marys and burgers sound?"

"Great." The grin spreading across her face was her first genuine smile of the day. She still had amazing people in her life who appreciated her no matter what.

Heron

Heron had been dividing her time between Bea's guest room and her old room at the vineyard house. It was nice to get to see her dad a little more. Toni had come into the picture too late to truly act as a maternal figure, but Heron was glad to have her as part of the family. Staying with them gave her the opportunity to understand how happy Toni made her dad.

After the hearing, she retreated to her childhood bedroom, burrowing under her mother's quilt. She wasn't all that surprised by the conduct hearing results. Bea had told her, as far as she knew, this type of proceeding hadn't ever resulted in a serious sanction, which made it obvious the policies were designed to get the college off the hook. And with Jason being the president's stepson, she'd known the other administrators would be reluctant to take action against him.

She was profoundly disappointed, but just wanted to move on with her life. Close the Messiman chapter. There was a lot of good to outweigh the bad, and she knew she'd look back on positive memories from her time here. Four years of her life. Five, if she counted the college-prep program, whose high school-aged participants were treated like matriculated students, at least for one class a semester.

Something clicked in her mind, like a puzzle piece finally snapping into place after being turned every which way. She went to her closet, pulling aside the dress form, still stashed there from the awful day after the shower. Heron made a promise to herself to unpin and fold the wedding gown, putting it away nicely until she could decide what to do with it, but right now she had something more pressing to deal with.

Under the dress, she found a box of mementos from high school. She dug through corsages, student theater programs and papers, until she found the paperwork from the Messiman college prep program. She flipped through the folder and found her copy of the student code of conduct, signed at the beginning of her senior year of high school, during program orientation.

Using her best professional voice, she called the administrative offices and made an appointment with Dean Lucas for the following day. Any of the students who participated in the program and subsequently enrolled as full time Messiman students should have a copy of that original signed code in their student file. She had to bite her tongue to keep herself from telling her dad and Toni and hold herself back from texting Bea. She didn't want to raise their hopes or rile them up.

"Ms. Hunter," the dean said, as he showed her into one of the plush leather guest chairs, "I'm always happy to make time to meet with a student, but if you're here to discuss the outcome of yesterday's hearing, I'm afraid there isn't much I can do for you."

Heron began. "I was hoping you could help me understand a bit more clearly. If the videos had been shown at a student event, that would have been a violation of the code?"

"That's right."

"And if Maggie and Bryant had been on school-owned property when they were recorded, that would have been a violation of the code?"

"Correct."

"And"—Heron folded her hands in her lap to keep them from shaking—"if Jason Shultz had been a student when he took the video of me and my date in the campus amphitheater, that would have been a violation of the code?"

"Indeed, Ms. Hunter, but the fact of the matter is, he was not. We can't hold students accountable for abiding by the code of conduct before they've signed it. And, young lady, I must remind you that you yourself were engaged in a lewd act in a public place, which, while not technically a code violation, was certainly not an example of exercising good judgement."

Heron's cheeks flushed, but she wasn't going to let him get to her. Her behavior was beside the point. If Bea were here, she would have something to say about it.

Well, she should have something to say about it, too. "That's true, Dean Lucas. I was seventeen, on a date with my boyfriend. Surely you aren't saying I deserved to be filmed, or to have that film shown at a very public event five years later?"

"Of course not." The dean's tone was icy. "I'm simply saying I can't help you with whatever retribution you seem to be seeking."

"Because the person who has admitted to taking the film had

not signed the code at the time?"

"Correct." It was clipped. He was clearly losing patience with her questions.

Heron pulled the paper she'd found yesterday out of her backpack and pushed it across the desk blotter. "This is my own code of conduct, Dean Lucas. I believe a copy will also be in my student file. You'll notice that I signed it five years ago, when I was a senior in high school, one month before the video in question was taken. Students who participate in the college prep program are required to sign it."

"That's true. I suppose you were subject to the code at this time, but no one has made a complaint against you for violating it, so I—"

"Jason Shultz was also in the prep program that year."

The dean sputtered, "Well, I... Oh. I see."

"Why don't you check his file? I'm happy to wait." She sat back in her chair.

He picked up his desk phone and called to have the administrative assistant bring in the file. While they waited, Heron fixed her gaze on the diplomas on the wall behind him and focused on keeping her breathing steady. She hoped she looked calmer than she felt.

As soon as the folder was in the dean's hands, he shuffled madly through the papers until he reached one at the very bottom. Heron leaned forward to peer over the desk, reading upside down, a code of conduct signed the same date as hers.

"Can I trust you'll take appropriate action in light of this new information? I'm happy to discuss the matter directly with President Phillips if necessary." Heron's legs trembled, but she managed to keep her voice steady. "I understand you may feel it's sensitive because of her personal relationship to Mr. Shultz."

Dean Lucas had turned an alarming shade of white. He could

certainly use some deep breathing techniques.

He said, "That won't be necessary. I will contact the other review board members about reevaluating our decision regarding Mr. Shultz. I'm afraid the conclusion regarding your allegations against Mr. Brewster will remain unchanged, as he was not involved in the creation of this video."

"I understand," she said.

Heron's mind was on Charlie as she descended the administrative building's steps. She would have liked to see him face a consequence for hurting her so deeply and so deliberately. She would have to hope the shame of how far he'd gone to hurt her and how badly he'd been duped by Jason would catch up with him someday.

Her next class wasn't for another hour, so she dropped into Bea's office to tell her the news. When she got to her door, she had to push through a curtain of streamers to get into the office. A "Congratulations!" banner was draped across the top of the doorway, and a vase of stargazer lilies sat on Bea's desk.

As Heron stepped into Bea's office, her eyes fell on the flowers, then on Bea, who was peering at her computer screen. She looked up with a sheepish expression, like she'd been caught out at something.

"Hi, Bird."

"Bea! Your tenure? Why didn't you tell me?"

"Yep." Bea grinned. "My last meeting was yesterday but I didn't want to stress you out before your hearing, and then it would have been shitty to dump all over your disappointment with my good news, so I figured I'd tell you later."

"This is amazing. I'm so happy for you!"

"Thanks."

"I have some news, too." Heron told Bea the story of her meeting with the dean. "I still don't have my hopes up too high," she said, although the bubbly feeling in her stomach belied the statement, "but there should at least be some consequences, and now I feel like I've done all I can."

"I'm so proud of you, Birdie. I can't believe how you handled that meeting all by yourself."

Heron bristled. She was a grown woman. She could handle things. In fact, she'd done a pretty great job at it. She'd been nervous, but not unmanageably so because she'd been well-prepared and confident she was right. She'd spent far too much time letting others handle her with kid gloves. But it wasn't Bea's fault, or her dad's, that she'd allowed them to treat her this way, so she resisted the urge to snap at Bea that she wasn't a baby.

"It was fine," she said. "It was actually a little bit fun. You should have seen the look on his face."

Bea chuckled. "I can only imagine."

Chapter Eighteen

Bea

Bea wished she were the kind of person who always had limes on hand for cocktails. She ran a damp paper towel around the rims of the glasses before dipping them in salt for margaritas. Ben had always been good about keeping this kind of thing in the fridge; last time she and Heron had a girls night, she'd made an offhand comment about wanting to make old-fashioneds and Ben had left a container of beautifully curled orange peel in the fridge and a new bottle of fancy bitters on the counter before retiring to his own apartment for the night.

That had been the night before Heron's shower, the night before everything changed. Well, it had changed again. Friday movie night was going to be a celebration this week because things were finally looking up. They'd drink to Heron's code of conduct triumph and Bea's tenure. Maggie and Sarah were coming, too, to make it even more festive.

"Come on in," she called when she heard a thump at the door. "I'm back here."

Maggie appeared, carrying a grocery sack, and followed, as she usually was these days, by Bryant, who held a foil-covered casserole dish.

Before the words "girls' night" could escape Bea's lips, Bryant said, "I'm not staying. I'm only here to carry things." Maggie looked at him with moony eyes. At least someone's relationship had survived the spring. Was thriving, in fact — these two clearly adored each other. "Actually," he continued, "I made you ladies something. My parents work a lot so I'm in charge of family dinners when I'm home. My sisters love this. We call it nacho-tacos. They should go in the oven for about half an hour. And there are toppings." Bea peeked under the foil and saw rows of taco shells, already filled with meat and cheese.

"That is…not something I would expect of a frat guy," Bea said, taking out a cutting board to slice the lettuce and tomatoes Maggie set on the counter. "But I'll take it."

"Not a frat guy anymore, actually," Bryant said. "I resigned my SOD membership."

"I'm sorry to hear that."

"I'm not sorry. I ignored a lot of stuff and I'm done ignoring it. How they treated me, what they did to Heron, what they did to Maggie. I don't want to be part of that anymore."

"Good for you."

"Hello," Heron called from the front room.

"We're in the kitchen."

"Hey guys," Heron said to Maggie and Bryant. "Did you tell her?" Maggie shook her head, and Heron said, "I'm moving back into the apartment. I so appreciate being able to stay here, and at Dad's, when things were tough. But I feel better, and I can't hide from Charlie forever. There's only a month left of school, but…I don't want to miss out on any more. My last semester of college is supposed to be fun, and I intend to enjoy the rest of it."

If Heron believed she was up for this, Bea would have to trust she was. She knew Maggie was good support and it sounded like Bryant was, too.

"So, anyway," Heron continued, "I have some stuff here I need to pack up."

"If you do it now, I can take some things back to the apartment with me," said Bryant.

"Really? That would be great."

"I'll help you," Maggie said. She and Heron disappeared upstairs.

"So, leaving SOD," Bea said. "Quite a big deal when you only have a month left."

Bryant took the knife she handed him and started chopping tomatoes while she washed the lettuce. "Ben called our national office for me. I'll get to keep my alumni status. I'm only resigning from this chapter. I'm not really sure it matters, but it might be helpful for networking."

Bea felt a tug at Ben's name. "That's nice." She shook the extra water off the lettuce, and began tearing the leaves off, laying them on a paper towel.

"Yeah, so, um, Ben has been pretty great in general, actually. He told me he considered resigning as alumni advisor but didn't want us to end up with someone who would look the other way regarding bad behavior."

"I see."

"He also made Charlie resign as president. Austin Chafee was elected for next year and he's already stepped up. Charlie moved out of the big room and into Austin's, which is in the basement."

Bea snorted with satisfied amusement.

"I know. He's not getting expelled like Jason, but at least it is something."

"Jason is getting *expelled*?" Wow.

"Yeah. Austin told me. He found out this morning. Jason has to be out of the house by Sunday night."

"Heron!" Bea yelled up the stairs, "Get down here. We have some news."

Heron

Heron already knew about Jason's expulsion. The thing about the Messiman rumor mill was that sometimes it worked in your favor as well as against you. She hadn't gotten the official email from Dean Lucas until mid-afternoon, but she'd been catching knowing grins across campus all day. The administrative office's work-study students must have gotten wind, and from there the rumor would likely have propagated quickly.

Bryant excused himself when Sarah arrived, saying, "I've got studying to do and I'd better enjoy the empty apartment while I can." Then he said to Maggie, "I'll come back to walk you and Heron home. Text me when you're ready."

"That," said Sarah after the door closed behind him, "is a nice boy."

"I know," sighed Maggie.

Heron wondered what things would be like for her if Bryant had asked her to fall formal freshman year instead of Charlie. But that might mean he wouldn't be with Maggie now, and they seemed like they might be in it for the long haul.

They'd decided on a Reese Witherspoon marathon. Heron picked *Pleasantville* to watch while they ate tacos because she loved the costumes and production. Maggie thought the manipulation in *Cruel Intentions* would hit a little too close to home and Bea vetoed *Just Like Heaven* with a margarita-fueled cry of "This is a now a Ruffalo-free household!" So next they watched *Legally Blonde*.

"A classic," Maggie said, selecting it from the streaming menu.

During the first scenes, when Warner dumped Elle, Heron caught Bea shooting little concerned glances her way. She couldn't blame Bea for seeing some parallels. And then, as Elle began to study for the LSAT, she saw parallels herself.

After all the time she'd spent — wasted — studying with Charlie, what score might she be able to get? She'd sometimes suspected she had a firmer grasp on the topics than Charlie. She hadn't wanted to steal his thunder, but that wasn't something she needed to worry about anymore. A plan began to take shape.

Bea

Bryant came back at one in the morning to walk Heron and Maggie home, and then it was just Bea and Sarah with the dregs of the margaritas and the last half of *Sweet Home Alabama*.

"She seems better," Sarah said, her words slowed by tequila.

"Yeah. I think she's going to be okay. Thank heavens."

Sarah switched the TV off. "And how are you?"

"Me? I'm fine as long as Heron's fine."

"So, no more swanning about in Halloween costumes for you?"

"Honestly, I answer the door dressed unconventionally *one time*."

Sarah's face grew serious. "Bea, I know you've been worried about Heron, but you ended a relationship this spring, too, and you can't fool me into believing that's not a big deal for you."

"Oh." Bea shrugged, standing to fold an afghan. "It's fine, I'm fine. Really, it's better. I think I was right all along, you know. Some people are better suited to being alone, and I'm one of them. I miss a few things I can't do by myself — *not* sex," she said, catching Sarah's raised eyebrow. "I mean yes, I do miss the sex but I'm perfectly competent with...self-care. But kissing? I miss kissing. I miss having someone to hug me when I've had a shitty day. I miss...having someone around who would remember to buy limes."

"Oh, honey, I'll buy you limes."

"I know you will. I guess I'm just saying, some of those companionship things. You know?"

"I do know."

"But I guess I am a little more open to dating now. I think my problem was that I got too attached to Ben, too quickly. I got used to the idea of having him as a partner and then when it didn't work out, I felt lost. I wouldn't mind being like one of those great old-timey dames who has a fabulous life all on her own, but also a devoted man friend for occasional dinners or traveling."

"Well...we do have a new physical therapist at work. Early forties, I think. Divorced, kids in high school. Super nice guy, he's been bringing tulips from his yard in for the residents. He asked me to dinner, so we know his taste is good even if he isn't the most perceptive. When I turned him down, he asked if I had any friends who might be interested. He's new in town and I think he's lonely."

It was probably the lingering effects of the tequila that made Bea say, "Why not?" She was sober enough to add, "But just a casual lunch." How much harm could a lunch do?

Heron

It didn't take Heron and Maggie very long to switch their things from room to room. Maggie's futon turned out to be pretty comfortable for sleeping. She liked how she could drop her book and phone on the floor and still be able to reach them, how through the down-slanted blinds she could see trees and sky outside the window. And she liked how it felt more slapdash and less grown-up than her big bed. The futon only had room for her.

Taking a bag of recycling to the dumpster in back, she rounded the corner and bumped into Jason. He was pale, his hair greasy, almost like a person who'd been ill. He smiled when he saw her in a way that flooded her with the urge to turn, run, or shove him.

"What are you doing here?" she asked, speaking carefully to keep the tremble out of her voice.

"Jesus, relax," Jason said. "The trash is full at the SOD house and I'm cleaning out my room there. I thought it would be okay if I put some of the extra in here. You're not going to report me, are you?"

"No." She tried to step around him, but he moved to the middle of the path. To get by, she would need to squeeze herself between him and the brick wall of the building.

"And actually," he said, stepping forward a bit to put a hand on her arm, "I wanted to thank you."

It was only a couple of fingertips on her forearm, but she jerked away, causing the cans and bottles in her bag to clink. He smiled, and her skin crawled.

"Thank me?" She kept her tone flat, not letting her pitch rise at the end of the question.

"Yeah." His grin widened. "My expulsion means I won't graduate this year, sure, but that's no big deal. It was worth it to show everybody you're not such an angel after all, and to knock golden boy Charlie Brewster down a few pegs." He laughed, an unappealing cackle. "High school seniors are deciding where to go right now, and what do they see when they google Messiman College? Articles about the growing phenomena of 'Revenge Porn.' My name's not in them, but my stepmother's is. It doesn't look so great for her. And what do I get? A do-over senior year at USC, living with my dad who lets me do whatever I want. So, anyway, thanks. A whole year of California girls, who I bet aren't cock-teasing little bitches like you."

He stepped around her. Heron shrunk into the hedge and a sharp branch poked at her back. At least she wasn't trapped against the unyielding wall of the building, but he still passed closely enough for her to smell the sour beer odor of his breath. He paused in front of her and made eye contact.

Heron rolled her shoulders back, planted her feet, and held his gaze. She was prepared to hit him if she needed to, but he didn't move any closer.

She said, "Okay. Best wishes for your future. I hope you get everything you deserve."

Jason looked at her a beat longer as if trying to gauge her sincerity. She did mean what she said — she truly hoped Jason's future was full of people seeing him for the devious jerk he was — precisely what he deserved. It took all her willpower, but she continued to hold eye contact until he turned around and walked out to the street.

Shaking, she stood for a moment catching her breath and staving off a flood of guilt. She hadn't meant for any of this to hurt President Phillips, she felt awful that she'd been a pawn for Jason to use to hurt Charlie.

Then, outrage swept over her like a tide, replacing the fear and guilt. Charlie had only been hurt because he didn't trust her, didn't believe in her, didn't see her for who she really was. Maggie was right, when she'd made that crack about Heron's caretaking tendencies. Charlie had only thought of Heron in terms of what she could offer him. And if the college president's family matters were impacting her professionally, Heron couldn't be held responsible for that, either. As for Jason, he could think whatever he wanted about a twisted bright side for himself, but she had a hard time picturing him getting the carefree California life he'd described.

Bea

Sarah's coworker, Owen, called Bea promptly to politely invite her to lunch. When he suggested Mostarda, she thought it would be better to seem easygoing and agreeable than explain why she preferred a place with fewer ex-boyfriend associations. And so, she found herself walking there after her eleven o'clock class.

She saw Ben come out of the art supply store down the block, but it would have been awkward to cross the street to avoid him, then cross again to go into the restaurant. It was even more awkward when they both turned in under the Mostarda awning. He flushed pink and said, "Whoops. Uh…I'll go to the cafe on campus."

"Don't be silly," she said.

"Me, silly? Wouldn't dream of it. I don't want to seem like I'm invading your space." His expression was friendly and neutral but there was an edge to the tone of the last sentence.

She couldn't blame him. She'd been childish that day in the cafe when she lashed out. It had all still been so fresh. "Look, I'm sorry about that. I was still feeling a little raw. We can probably be in the same room without either of us spontaneously combusting."

"I'm glad to hear it. I've missed you, Bea." Oh, there were the eye crinkles, there was his wry, slow smile.

"Don't get carried away." She wasn't sure if she was saying it to Ben or to herself. "But I missed you, too. I hate having to choose between the turkey sandwich and the spinach salad." Mostarda's two best lunch entrees — they'd regularly ordered one of each and split them.

"Do you want to join me for lunch, then? We can get the indecisive person's special."

"I would, but I'm meeting someone." Bea wouldn't have chosen to run into him on the way to her date, but she didn't totally hate the idea of him seeing her with someone new.

"Ah. Well, have a nice lunch."

"Take care, Ben."

"You too."

Ben got in line, while Bea located Owen at a table in the middle of the room. He was easily recognizable by the Sunset Home logo on his fleece vest, but she probably would have pinpointed him anyway. He definitely had the look of a former athlete softening into early middle age, a little puffy but retaining the bearing of a jock. He stood to shake her hand, nearly crushing it. "I'll go put our order in. What would you like?"

"A turkey sandwich on sourdough, please. And a seltzer. Thank you."

"That sounds good. I'll get the same thing."

Owen ended up in line directly behind Ben, who made a face at her and then, to Bea's profound mortification, *turned around and introduced himself*. Oh god, she couldn't look. She couldn't hear them over the din of the cafe, and she wasn't sure whether that was a blessing or a curse. Ben got a cup of soup to go and smirked at her as he left the restaurant.

Owen returned to the table with their drinks. "I just met one of your coworkers."

"Mm," she said, hoping she sounded casual. "Yeah, that was Ben."

"He invited me to join his poker game."

She almost shot seltzer out of her nose, recovering by making it look like a cough. "Wrong pipe," she wheezed. Owen handed her a napkin.

Owen turned out to be perfectly nice: from his desire to work with the elderly ("I hurt myself playing football at the same time my grandma broke her hip, and we ended up going to physical therapy together."); to his daughters ("Jessica plays volleyball and is in choir, Alexandra wants to be a programmer and is in chess club."); to his divorce ("We just grew apart, I guess. Her new husband is a real nice guy, and we all went on a cruise together last year."). Everything about Owen was nice, the way a bowl of plain noodles with butter is nice. Bland, comforting, you can be absolutely sure it's not going to upset your stomach, but missing something. Still, he seemed to enjoy her company and after so many years on her own before Ben, it was nice to know she had options.

Heron

Heron only needed another forty-five minutes and she'd be done with her very last college assignment, the final paper for her Marriage and the Family class. Despite the notification that her thesis had passed with honors marks and she'd be graduating at least magna cum laude, Heron wanted her GPA to be as high as possible upon graduation. She was studying more diligently for finals than she had any other semester. Without wedding planning to distract her, or needing to help Charlie study, she could focus all her energy on her own classes.

She was in her favorite corner of the library, typing furiously about the gender pay gap and caregiver duty distribution, when she heard, "Hey."

She looked up. Charlie. "Oh, hey."

"I was in one of the study rooms, and I thought, I bet Heron's at her table, and here you are."

She shrugged. "Here I am. I'm actually almost done and I—"

He scraped out a chair and sat down. "So, listen, before we graduate, I wanted to say I'm sorry about all the stuff that went down this semester. I know some of it was my fault."

All of it was his fault, but saying so wouldn't make a difference, so she said, "Mm hmm."

"And I hope it didn't impact your grades too much. I've realized having so much personal turmoil during a time where your academic performance can impact your entire future isn't wise." He sounded like his father.

She gave him a weak, self-effacing smile. "That's probably true, but I'm graduating with honors." Personally, she was still only so-so, but she wasn't going to tell Charlie that. After her run in with Jason she hadn't been able to go around the back of the building without a fluttering heart and sweaty palms, but she was managing with exercises from her therapist.

Charlie chuckled bitterly and said, "Of course you are. Wouldn't want anything to get in your way."

She looked him in the eye and said evenly, "I found myself with a lot of spare time to study over spring break."

"Right."

He made no move to get up. She sighed and said, "How about you?"

"Not so good. I have a C average this semester, but I'll graduate. Apparently, I was lucky not to get expelled." He paused, as if waiting for her to say something.

Surely he didn't expect her to apologize? Heron remained quiet.

Two juniors walked past, girls who'd been in Ben's book arts class with Heron and Charlie last fall. "Hey Heron," they said, before cutting cold glares at Charlie. This sort of thing had been happening a lot lately. She'd been pleasantly surprised that campus sentiment seemed to be on her side.

Charlie seemed slightly flummoxed by the girls' open disdain but flashed them a political-candidate grin before continuing, "I can still go to Columbia though, so it's okay. Dad says they are usually pretty reluctant to withdraw an acceptance, especially for a legacy."

"That's good."

He stood. "I guess I'll see you around. Congratulations on the honors."

"Thanks."

Heron drummed her fingers on the home keys of her laptop, trying to remember the rest of the sentence she'd been in the middle of when Charlie appeared. Against her better judgement, she missed him and felt wistful about the loss of the version of this time she'd pictured for so long: graduation followed by a wedding, looking ahead to a bright future with Charlie. But the fun, romantic, spontaneous guy she'd been swept away by four years ago bore little resemblance to the person she'd just had a conversation with. She didn't expect to see that version of Charlie again.

Bea

Bea's perfectly nice lunch with Owen had led to a perfectly nice trip to a minor league baseball game. Now he was taking her home from a perfectly nice dinner date. While she was getting ready, her gaze had fallen on the blue velvet dress, but she'd pushed it aside in favor of slinky jeans, heeled sandals, and a silky, plum-colored top.

Owen walked her to her door and after she fished her keys out of her purse, he touched her cheek, leaned in, and kissed her. His other hand entwined with her free one, which, she thought objectively was a pretty good move. He was a good kisser, too. Not too much pressure, lips soft but not wet. It was right after he pulled away a little, then moved in again with tongue that she realized she didn't feel a thing. Not one single hint of the electricity that had thrummed through her body when Ben so much as touched her hand.

Gently, she put a hand on his chest. "Owen, stop."

His retreat was one of a man who'd spent a lot of time talking about consent with his teenage daughters. He let go of her hand and took an immediate step backwards. "Sorry. You seemed receptive."

"Yes. I mean, I was, but…It's just that I am not really feeling the chemistry. It's not you. You're great."

His face fell. "It's not me, it's you?"

Bea smiled in an attempt to lessen the blow. "Something like that. I have had a very nice time."

He waved her off, "It's fine."

"Can we be friends?"

With a smile that didn't reach his eyes, he said, "I have a lot of friends, Bea."

"Sorry."

"Yeah, me too." He turned and shuffled down her walkway, back to his car.

Inside, Bea checked her texts.

Sarah had already written to ask, "How'd the third date go???"

Bea answered, "No spark. Sent him home."

"Spark is key."

"Yeah."

The spark, she thought, as she fed Herschel and put on her pajamas, was the one thing she couldn't do for herself. She could find friends to have a meal with, to go to a baseball game with should she ever be inclined to repeat that experience. But she couldn't surprise herself the way Ben surprised her. No one could make her laugh, or laughed with her, the way he did. And he was definitely the only person who'd ever, with the simplest touch, made her feel like the actual current in her body had been dialed up.

Someone like Owen, who was pleasant and kind, might have been a good enough substitute, a little companionship to keep her from feeling lonely, now that her time with Ben had made her a little less inclined to be satisfied with her own company. But no, the experiment with Owen had only confirmed being alone was better than being with a person who didn't deliver the full package.

Bea hated how the time she'd spent with Ben made her independence seem less satisfying, shown her more was possible, only to leave a void after they were over. She knew she'd get over it in time, but she wasn't sure she wanted to.

Chapter Nineteen

Bea

Bea's velvet-trimmed doctoral gown had cost nearly four hundred dollars, and she wondered who on earth had decided to dress faculty in heavy dark fabrics for an outdoor ceremony in hot weather. It was still May, but the morning's temperature was already approaching ninety degrees. The students looked over-warm, too, in their flimsy, shiny black gowns, but at least they could fan themselves with their mortarboards. Bea's tam offered no such respite.

Rick was serving as a commencement marshal, as he had every year since before Bea was even a student, so she was the only representative from the astronomy department marching as part of the regular faculty procession. She recognized a little extra applause and a cheer in Len's voice as she took her seat to the side of the stage. The metal folding chair had been sitting in the sun all morning and when she sat, her robe released a smell of heated polyester, like a garment being ironed.

As the other faculty filed in behind her, she caught a familiar whiff of evergreen, and turned to look over her shoulder. They were seated in two long rows, and the procession had worked out to place Ben directly behind her. At the end of the aisle, she caught Rick's eye and flattened her mouth in a "seriously?" expression. Rick maintained a straight face in keeping with the solemnity of his duties, but she detected a hint of mischief in his eyes.

At a tap on her shoulder, Bea turned again.

"Hi," Ben whispered.

"Hi."

"Here, I brought two." He handed her a cold bottle of water.

Even holding it was a relief. She ran her chilled fingers over the back of her neck. "Thanks. You're a lifesaver."

"I try."

President Phillips' speech was focused on accountability and integrity, and Bea suspected it was an intentionally pointed message. Bryant had been elected to give the student address. Amid cheers, he urged his classmates to use their privilege to become agents of change. The guest speaker was a Silicon Valley CEO who had recently published a book on balancing personal and professional fulfillment. Bea kept her face neutral as she listened, thinking it was easy to strike a balance if you had an army of assistants at work and a salary that allowed you to hire household staff.

Still, this past year had made her wonder about her own balance. She'd always been happy living alone, always. Sharing her highs and lows with friends and extended family had been enough. Rick had taken her to a beautiful brunch when her tenure was approved, she'd celebrated with Heron and Sarah, too, and the following Sunday Len and Toni had opened a special bottle of champagne they'd brought back from a winery tour in France. All of that should be enough, and it was.

But, in February, when she'd left the meeting where her science division colleagues discussed their recommendation for her tenure, Ben had been waiting on the bench outside the building, ready to console or congratulate as needed. It was hard to shake the feeling she'd taken the comfort of having someone entirely in her corner, just hers, for granted. She'd thought their fight about Charlie meant he didn't understand her, but now wondered if he'd simply been unwilling to blindly agree when he truly believed she was wrong. Bea knew her passionate personality could sometimes overwhelm people. Ben deserved credit for not letting her get away with that.

Messiman was small enough that each student could be called in turn to come receive their diploma, as faculty stood in the receiving line to congratulate them. When Charlie's name was called, there were a few cheers and some clapping, but not as much as she might have expected. Even the SOD house had made a lot more noise for their members with names earlier in the alphabet. Bea was prepared to be gracious when he came to her part of the faculty line, but he brushed past without meeting her eye.

When Heron's name was called, there was a roar of cheering, mostly women's voices. Bea knew Heron had kept much to herself during most of her time as a student, but when she forced a partial turn-around of the conduct board's decision, she'd become something of a folk heroine on campus. A group of students had organized to demand that the changes to the code of conduct and associated procedures be substantial, all due to Heron.

As she approached the stage, Heron's shy smile opened into a brilliant grin. Pride welled deep within Bea. She'd fretted about Heron all year, first about Charlie's plans overtaking hers, then about her devastation after the videos. She was still a little worried about Heron's after-college plans, but Bea was confident she'd be just fine. Here she was, resilient, radiant, accomplished. Whatever she decided to tackle next, she'd be ready.

By the time they got through the rest of the alphabet, Bea's shoes were pinching her toes. Now that she had tenure maybe she could worry less about dressing the professorial part and start wearing sneakers like Ben. She chuckled a moment, thinking they'd make quite a pair about campus if they started dressing alike, before the pang of remembrance set in. They weren't a pair anymore.

Finally, finally, Elizabeth Zimmerman made her way down the receiving line, President Phillips made brief closing remarks, caps were thrown high, and they were done.

Heron

After the ceremony, Heron searched for her family in the crowd of black-gowned students and congratulating relatives. She found Bea, Toni, and her mother chatting in the shade in front of the library, then saw her dad coming down the path, holding two bouquets of apricot-colored roses.

"There she is!" said Toni, and they all clapped.

Heron's dad presented Bea with one of the bunches of flowers, "Your first commencement with full tenure deserves a little fanfare," he said. Then he enveloped Heron in a hug before presenting her own flowers. "I'm so proud of you, Birdie."

"Thanks, Dad. I couldn't have gotten here without you."

Bea said, "I'm positively braising in this robe. At least I was sitting in the shade. You must be dying, Heron. Let's take the obligatory photos so we can take this stuff off."

HOW TO ALIGN THE STARS

Len posed them under the oak tree in front of the library, taking shots from several angles before Toni finally said, "Enough," and pulled collapsible nylon bags for Heron and Bea to put their regalia in, and half-frozen bottles of water for everyone out of her bag.

"You don't miss a thing," Bea said.

"She's a marvel." Heron's father beamed at his wife. Felicia smiled limply.

With the robe gone, Heron felt much more comfortable, but Felicia said, "Len, you're not in any of these pictures. Let me take a couple."

Ben was ambling toward the library and Heron's dad called him over. "Take a photo of us all, will you?"

"Sure," said Ben, accepting the camera. He snapped a few shots.

When he handed the camera back, Toni said, "Are you coming to the party at the winery tonight? You're more than welcome."

"Oh," said Ben, "I don't want to intrude."

Heron glanced at Bea, who looked like a deer in headlights, but her cousin couldn't hide from Ben forever. "Please come," she said. "Your class was one of my favorites and it won't be the same without you."

"I'll see if I can drop by."

Heron thought it was Ben's answer that made Bea's eyebrows shoot up, but when Toni's expression also registered surprise, she turned to see what they were looking at. Charlie strode toward their group with purpose, a look of determination on his face, his parents and Emma trailing behind. Her stomach knotted, anticipating some new reprisal or embarrassment. He came to a hard stop, skidding to one knee in front of her, removing a ring box and holding it in front of her in one fluid motion that almost seemed choreographed.

His voice thick, he said, "Heron Hunter, I'm an idiot. I thought

I couldn't look past what happened in March, but now I realize it's nothing compared to what you are, every part of you — your grace, your strength, your kindness. When I asked you this question before, I didn't understand what I'd be losing if you said no. Now I do, and I'm not sure I could bear it. Heron Hunter, please be my wife."

He beamed up at her, the ring he'd demanded she return sparkling in its velvet box. Heron's stomach unfurled, but immediately twisted itself into a new knot. She hated disappointing people. But what other choice did she have?

She said, "Charlie. I'm so sorry, but I can't." She held out a hand to help him up, but he brushed it away, dropping to both knees and inching closer to her. Off-balance, Heron cast a glance around at the crowd that had formed, making eye contact with Bea, who looked like she might break into a nervous laugh, but whose eyes showed genuine concern. Heron knew a gesture would be all it took for her family to physically yank Charlie away, but she also felt confident she could handle this herself, discomforting as it was.

"I know I was wrong, Heron. I know. You have to forgive me. Please. I'll never doubt you again. I have it all worked out." He glanced back toward his father. "Dad says we can still use the city apartment. You can do whatever you want, grad school, anything! Don't we both deserve a second chance?"

It would be so easy, wouldn't it? One word from her and this spring could just be a hiccup, a small interruption before they continued down the path they'd been on. But that path wasn't leading anywhere she still wanted to go.

Heron stepped backward. "Charlie. No."

He shook his head as if he couldn't quite believe he'd heard her correctly. He dropped back, sitting on his heels.

"What?"

"No. I'm sorry."

Charlie's family looked on. Mrs. Brewster appeared to have indigestion, Mr. Brewster looked impatient, Emma uncomfortable.

Heron's own family's reactions were different. Bea's face was now an open book of complete disdain, Toni's mouth hung slightly open, her father looked like he was barely containing his rage, and her mother's brow furrowed with worry.

"But…you said you can't live without me."

She wished he'd stand up. "Well," she said, "I tried it, and it turns out I can."

"You need me."

"Son." Mr. Brewster gestured for Charlie to stand. A crowd had formed around them when Charlie took a knee, their classmates drawn to the spectacle like moths to a flame.

"No," she said, "you need *me*. I don't want that, Charlie. I've had a lot of time to think this spring. I'm not sure you ever loved me. You loved the idea of me. Maybe I loved the idea of you. Right now, what I need is to be on my own for a while. I miss you, but I'm a better person without you. If I ever get married, it will be to someone I can trust not to deliberately hurt me. That's never going to be you."

Charlie hoisted himself to his feet. "I can't believe you're doing this to me in front of everyone. You've ruined my graduation."

His graduation? What about hers? She wasn't going to let him ruin this for her. "Sorry. But I didn't choose the setting."

"Fine," Charlie hissed. He slapped the ring box shut and thrust it at his mother, who tucked it into her purse with a satisfied smile.

Charlie and his parents strode away, but Emma lingered a moment, nudging Heron with a shoulder, "Nicely done," she said. "I told him he was a fool to let you go and he owed you an apology. I didn't think that meant he'd try to get you back. But you know Charlie."

"Yeah, I guess I do."

"If you're in New York next year after all, look me up. We'll get a drink."

"I'll be in Seattle next year." Heron smiled. "But I'll keep in touch."

"What's this?"

Whoops. The surprise in her father's voice reminded Heron she'd been keeping her plans to herself until now.

"I was going to tell you later, Dad. I'll be moving to Seattle in July. I have an apartment picked out already," she looked pointedly at Felicia, not wanting her mother to assume she planned to live with her again. "And I'm taking the LSAT in June." She'd been consistently scoring near 170 on practice tests, and with her GPA admission was a pretty sure thing. All that work helping Charlie had paid off, apparently. Everything she had been through this spring had Heron thinking she should explore family law or policy work. When she imagined herself five years down this path, it felt right to her in a way all the other futures she'd considered — even marriage with Charlie — hadn't. She'd missed the cutoff for fall admissions but could build her savings up in the meantime.

"Wow," said Toni.

Bea applauded. "I couldn't be prouder of you, Bird."

"Do you have a job figured out?" asked Felicia.

"That's a good point, sweetie," her father said. "I still have a little money set aside for tuition, but you'll need to help cover living expenses."

"I've got something lined up."

Lucy from the bridal shop had been impressed with Heron's work on her gown and needed part-time help. It would be mostly weekends and evenings, which would work with her class schedule, and she might eventually even be able to take some dresses home to work on them during breaks from studying.

She grinned at her surprised family, "I guess I can't keep a secret too well."

Her mother took a tentative step toward the parking area, "I should get on the road if I want to beat the traffic over the pass."

"I wish you could stay a little longer, Mom."

"Sorry, sweetie, I have work in the morning. Besides, it sounds like we'll be neighbors pretty soon."

"Sure." Heron had intentionally chosen an apartment near the university rather than in Felicia's neighborhood. She'd be happy to see her mother every once in a while, but wasn't sure yet how much she wanted her mom to figure into her day-to-day. Ever since spring break, she had been thinking about what Felicia said about leaving because she couldn't stand her life anymore. Heron understood what Felicia was trying to tell her, but it would take some time to come to terms with the idea that she had been part of the life her mother couldn't bear. It would always be complicated between them. That was okay, but she would need to set the terms of her relationship with her mother carefully.

Bea

"We've got to go set up for the party," Len said. "Can we drop you at home, Bea?"

"I'll walk. I have a couple of things to take care of in my office. See you later."

Ben was still lingering on the steps of the library. He flagged her down as she passed. His robe was unzipped and he wore a Sub Pop t-shirt and his usual sneakers and jeans. He'd trimmed his beard drastically, but he needed a haircut. An unruly wave pooched out above his ear, and she resisted the urge to reach over and tuck it back.

"Hey, listen," he said. "I'm not gonna come to the party tonight. Heron will be so swept up in people congratulating her she won't even notice I'm not there."

Bea waved his words away. "Come. She wants you there. Besides, we're supposed to be friends now, right? A friend would come."

"I'll see. Maybe."

"It'll be a great party, you know." She considered offering him a ride, but that would be too much, too like old times, and bit her lip. Then she thought *to hell with it*, and said, "Do you need a ride?"

At the same time, Ben said, "Are you bringing Owen?"

She laughed. "Ah, no. That didn't work out."

"I'm sorry to hear. He seems like a nice guy."

"He is a nice guy. But—" She'd been about to tell Ben there hadn't been a spark with Owen. Admitting that to Sarah was one thing, but to Ben? Too much information. She pivoted mid-sentence, and asked instead, "Did he really come to your poker night?"

"Oh, yeah. I cleaned him out in the last pot, actually. He shook my hand. Last time I did that to Kevin he flipped the card table."

"Sounds about right."

"Anyway, if I can make it, I'll call a car."

"If you're sure. I'd better run. I extended the final paper deadline for a couple of students and need to make sure they're turned in. I'll see you later, maybe." She started down the path toward the science building.

"Hey, Bea?" he called after her and she turned. "I lied."

"What?"

"I lied. I'm not sorry it didn't work out with Owen."

Bea heard the words, but he was too far away for her to make out the expression on his face. She didn't reply, just turned around and continued toward her office. Despite herself, and despite her pinchy shoes, her step was a bit lighter.

As she went up the stairs, she was thinking about what Heron said to Charlie about not needing him. She'd gotten so comfortable with Ben over the winter, and everything felt so right and so wonderful, when they'd argued it was too much, too scary. Especially on top of seeing Heron comprehensively devastated by the person who was supposed to love her. If Bea was being completely honest with herself, she had been intentionally contrary that night, testing Ben to see where his loyalties lay. Of all the emotions she'd been having, anger at him was the easiest to express so she'd let herself be carried away by it. When his response wasn't perfect it was a good enough excuse for her to end things before she got in any deeper.

Before he broke her heart.

Well, wasn't that a bitch?

If Bea had as much faith in herself as much as she presumed to, she had to trust that she was worthy of unconditional love. But because she hadn't honestly believed herself lovable in that way, she hadn't believed in Ben's feelings for her, which had screwed things up for both of them. The question was, what to do about it now?

While she reeled from this lightbulb moment, Bea switched on her computer and checked her inbox. The overdue papers were in. Good. The last thing she wanted to do today was try to track down a student or give them a zero grade.

Then she clicked over to social media. Bea didn't follow many people, so Heron's post from the morning was still near the top of her feed. The caption said: *Congratulations to all my friends graduating today! Let the stars be your beacon. XO.*

She'd posted a set of images for different signs of the Zodiac, omitting, Bea noticed with satisfaction, Gemini — Charlie's sign. The square for Bea's sign, said:

SCORPIO: A new phase is about to begin. You like to hold on to things but try releasing them and let something new grow in their place. What is meant to endure will stay with you.

Honestly. What the hell did that even mean?

Bea stewed about it all the way home, finding herself sweaty enough from the walk on the baking sidewalks that she needed to freshen up for the party. She came to her decision in the shower. She owed Ben an apology, regardless. It was simply the right thing to do. If he showed up tonight, she would ask him if he'd be willing to try again. If he didn't come, she could interpret his absence as a statement of his boundaries, and she would respect them. She'd send him a note telling him she was sorry, but she wouldn't press for more.

So that was it, she'd leave it up to Ben, or to the universe or whatever. As she dressed, she thrummed with nervous energy, unsure whether she was hoping he would show up, or hoping he wouldn't.

Heron

The winery terrace was bathed in early evening sun, which had begun to slant over the vineyards. As Heron walked toward the party, she couldn't banish the thought that she had intended to make this walk as a bride. It would have been a dream wedding, with the ceremony among the trellises and the reception on the patio in the warm twilight. But now the idea seemed completely strange to her. Heron didn't fully understand how she had gone from despair about her broken engagement to contentment with her own company in the space of two months. Maybe it was the way she'd begun to form a picture of what marriage to Charlie would have been like—suspicion and inaccurate expectations of who she was gradually outweighing the fun and the sweet gestures he was so good at. She'd become so focused on the fairy tale, she hadn't seen the darker subtext of their story. If she looked at things through a certain lens, Jason had done her a favor.

A few guests had arrived so far; Bea, Maggie and her family, Bryant with his parents and little sisters, who flitted around Maggie vying for her attention.

"Before more people arrive," her dad said, "I'd like to have a toast with a special vintage. Heron, would you do the honors?" He pulled a bottle out of the ice bucket and presented it to her. It had to be his special reserve pinot gris, but he'd changed the label from what they'd discussed last fall. The name of the edition, "Wings," swirled across the top and the art was a drawing Heron had done in sixth grade; a girl, aloft, with broad fierce wings spread on either side of her, twice as big as she was. She remembered her teacher scoring the assignment badly because she had been meant to draw a realistic self-portrait. Heron had been indignant because she'd drawn herself exactly as she felt. A girl whose family called her Bird, unafraid of heights. It had taken her a long time to get back to feeling that way again.

"I love it, Dad. It's perfect." She tipped her head back to keep the happy tears that had sprung to her eyes from running down her cheeks and ruining her mascara before the party even got going. She uncorked the bottle and her father poured it into glasses, which Bea and Toni passed out.

Len held his glass up. "I don't want to get maudlin, so I'll keep this short and simple. Heron, I am so proud of everything you've accomplished this year. Parenting isn't easy. You want to protect your kid from anything that might hurt them, but you can't. I'll always be here for you, but this year you have proven you have the strength to thrive even when others are trying to tear you down. I believe you can do anything, honey. And you will."

"Hear hear!" said Bea, raising her glass.

Before anyone could drink, Heron raised her own glass and said, "I want to thank you all for supporting me this year. Knowing I had people behind me who believed in me and loved me unconditionally got me through. Thank you. And congratulations to Maggie and Bryant, too."

"To all the graduates!" said Toni.

The wine was dry and crisp, a refreshing kiss of acid and citrus on her lips. It tasted…hopeful, and it was perfect for her and for the day.

The DJ started the music as the rest of the guests began to arrive. A few faculty members, family friends, and more of Heron's newly graduated classmates, their families in tow.

Heron had the same conversation several times with the older party guests about her plans for the next year. At a certain point, her conversation partner's eyes would begin to glaze over, and they'd say something like "That's wonderful, dear," and drift away.

Bryant's mother, however, was the exception. "I think it's interesting," she said, "you don't mention money or prestige when you talk about being an attorney."

Heron felt her cheeks flush. "Financial security is nice, but I guess I'm more interested in the work. I'd also considered social work and I see practicing law, the way I would like to, as more of an extension of that. A different way to help people."

"I see," said Ms. Hardy. "Why don't you call me when you're ready for an internship? I'm at Sampson Climp Peterson's Seattle office. I'd love to have someone like you on my team."

"Wow. Thanks. I'll definitely call you." Of course, she had a lot of hard work ahead of her before she was ready for an internship, but Heron felt entirely up to the challenge. She was looking forward to it.

Bea

Bea scanned the party from her perch near the kitchen door, where she'd been helping Toni keep an eye on the buffet to see what needed to be restocked. The food was going fast, appetites returning as the heat of the day waned.

Heron flitted from group to group, making small talk and accepting congratulations. Bea was impressed by her poise and self-assuredness. This was the first time in years she'd seen Heron able to sparkle on her own in a social setting. She'd gotten so used to seeing her glued to Charlie's side like an accessory.

She was also looking for Ben. No sign of him yet, an hour into the party. Well, there was her answer. She was…relieved? Yeah. Relieved. Things seemed to be good between them the way they were now, the way they always should have been. Friendly, cordial, collegial. But surely, he would be here if he had any interest in rekindling their relationship.

Sarah was here though, finally, fresh from work, waving from the other side of the party. Bea slid off her bar stool and began weaving her way over to join her friend.

She was trying to squeeze around a cluster of Maggie's sorority sisters when she heard, somewhere to her left, "Hey, do you know where we can put gifts?" and she turned toward the voice. Ben. His hair was still damp, curling around his collar, and he wore faded jeans and his ubiquitous sneakers, but also an olive-green rumpled cotton shirt that brought out the mossy colors in his eyes. He'd pushed his sunglasses up on his head so they held his hair back — he really did need a haircut.

Her responding "Hey," came out like a sigh, then she caught her breath and said, "Inside. I'll show you."

As they walked, she said, "You didn't have to bring anything, you know. Heron will just be so happy you came."

"I wanted to." He held up what he was carrying to show her, a book. It was unwrapped except for a blue satin ribbon, so she could clearly see the title, "Vogue Pattern Book, February-March 1959." A woman in a shamrock-green suit smiled from the cover.

"She'll love it."

"I bought it in February," he said with a small smile. "I meant for it to be a birthday gift, but then you and I weren't talking in April and, well…awkward."

"Yep," she said. She led him through the doors of the tasting room, and the chill of the air-conditioned building hit them like a wall. When the door swung closed the chatter of the party reduced to a murmur. It was just the two of them in here, the cool, empty room providing a stark contrast to the sunny hum of the party. If she didn't take the chance to say her piece now, she would always regret being a coward.

Ben spoke before she did. "Sorry I was late. I had a hard time getting a car."

She took the book from his hands and put it on the table with the other gifts. "Yeah. Graduation weekend. That's why I tried to give you a ride."

"I figured you were being nice."

"You should know better."

"I do." He chuckled.

And here they were, falling into their old pattern. It would be so easy to breeze back out to the party, go their separate ways. But she'd hate herself tomorrow if she let that happen.

"Hey, listen, can we talk a minute?"

"Sure."

Bea went behind the counter and poured them each a glass of pinot gris while Ben watched, his expression a question. He eased onto one of the stools and she came around to sit, angled toward him, one stool between them for a buffer.

"I wanted to explain about what happened in April," she said. "It was awful—"

"Agreed, but—"

She held up a hand. "Please let me finish or I won't get through this. I was so shocked and hurting so much for Heron and angry on my own behalf, too. And I think I saw you as a member of Charlie's team in a way that wasn't fair to you, or accurate." He opened his mouth to speak again, and she stopped him with a look. "I know. I was too stuck in my own head and not paying attention to what you were actually saying or doing. I took things out on you that you shouldn't have been held accountable for. Please accept my apology."

They sat in silence for a moment before Ben said, "Oh. I can talk now?"

Her "Yes," came out accompanied by a nervous laugh.

"I thought you should have known I was on your side. And Heron's."

She grimaced. "I know. Sorry."

"I was getting to be part of this family and it felt so nice, and then suddenly I was an outsider again. I felt like you didn't really see what I was doing or saying, you saw what you expected me to do and say, in a way that didn't seem reasonable."

"Yeah." She looked down into her wine.

"So, you're right, it wasn't fair."

"Yes. I know. I'm sorry." For the first time, it occurred to her that he must have had a lonely spring, too.

Ben said, "I accept your apology. I have one to make, too."

Bea met his eyes, hoping her expression was open in a way that told him she was ready to hear whatever he had to say.

He continued. "I knew you needed space, deep down, I think. After that first argument, I knew still being at your place when you got home from dinner might send you over the edge, but I guess I felt I deserved acknowledgement of what I was trying to do to help. I picked that fight."

She laughed. "Oh no, my friend. I'm pretty sure *I* picked that fight."

"Maybe it was mutually picked. Anyway, I certainly didn't expect it to end things. Couples fight sometimes, Bea, they don't always see things the same way. As much as we had silly little disagreements, it was our first real fight and you went nuclear."

Bea took a deep breath. This was her opportunity. "I know. So, that's the other thing I wanted to say to you. I've been thinking, since I heard what Heron said to Charlie today about how she didn't need him anymore. In March, everything seemed like it was happening so fast. I was scared to lean on you when things were so awful, scared of…developing a dependence? I'd just seen that completely wreck Heron. And I guess maybe I felt like I needed to go cold turkey."

"I see. It's not entirely flattering to be compared to an addictive substance."

"But today I was thinking, I never needed you."

"Thanks?"

"I wanted you. I can do anything I need to do on my own."

"No doubt." He raised his glass and drank.

"But sometimes it's more fun when there's someone else around. And better if that person makes the hard things easier." That wasn't all, because while Ben did make things easier for her, he also challenged her. Didn't let her get away with anything. "The way you see through all of my bullshit, Ben, I didn't think I would like that. And sometimes it does piss me right off."

He chuckled in assent.

"But it's good for me. You're good for me. It wasn't easy to admit, even to myself, but knowing you see me as I am and you…

still like me…means everything."

"Yeah." A slow, easy smile spread across his face. "I still like you."

This was the point of no return. If she asked and he said no, could she live with it? She could, but she'd really, really rather not have to. Her stomach dropped, and she pushed the words out as quickly as possible before she lost her nerve. "Can we try again?"

The tiny muscles under his eyes tightened as he considered her question. She kept talking. Now that the dam had burst, she couldn't seem to stop. "I know I can be prickly, and I'm certain we'll fight again, but I've missed you so much and I think we made a mistake and everything good that happens seems less good without you and—"

"Bea." Ben scooted over onto the stool between them, closing the distance.

"What?"

"Shut up." Turned toward each other on stools meant to face forward, their legs pressed together so it was easy for Ben to slide his hand onto her hip as the other one tangled in her hair and pulled her face toward his. When their lips met, it felt like coming home after a long journey.

Several minutes later she straightened her dress and smoothed her hair, and said, "So, that's a yes, then?"

Ben's shrug was slow, exaggerated, infuriating, adorable. "Sure. I'm a glutton for punishment."

She balled up the cocktail napkin she'd been using to fix her lipstick and threw it at his face, but he caught it and shoved it into his pocket. He extended a hand and asked, "Shall we?"

Bea was fully prepared to offer a sheepish explanation for their reconciliation when they returned to the party arm in arm, but none of her loved ones seemed the slightest bit surprised to see them together.

Chapter Twenty

Three months later

Heron

In the photo Heron posted to her online story, long pieces of particleboard were laid out as logically as possible given the limited floorspace of her basement studio. She entered the text:

"The Billy bookcase is a bother."

Dave handed her an Allen wrench. "I think with these big sides, I'll hold it still and you do the bolts. Then we can switch because our wrists are going to get tired."

She laughed. "You sound like you have a lot of experience with furniture assembly."

"My fair share, yeah." He grinned.

Heron hadn't expected to reconnect with her high school boyfriend when she moved to Seattle, but she'd taken him to coffee to tell him about the video Jason had made of the two of them. As she explained she didn't mean to get him caught up in all of that, he'd listened sympathetically to her story of Jason and Charlie and everything that had happened to her in the past year. They'd seen each other a few more times for movies and festivals. Just as friends, but it was nice to have someone other than her mom to do things with and help her get oriented in the city. Everybody needs a patient friend when it's time to go to IKEA.

This bookcase was the finishing touch on her apartment. Her desk and sewing table were already here, positioned under the south-facing window for the best light. The view wasn't so bad, actually. High windows around almost the entire perimeter of the room made for plenty of light, and she looked out past flower beds to the sidewalk above, where she could watch people's feet go by. She'd filled the space with textiles in bright shades of goldenrod, violet, magenta, and jade to brighten the room up even more. And, the rent was cheap enough that she'd be able to afford it on her part-time salary from Lucy after classes started. For now, she'd also picked up a few shifts in the juniors' department at Nordstrom thanks to her mom.

Heron hadn't heard from Charlie after graduation, but she exchanged messages every so often with Emma, who told her he was seeing someone new, the daughter of family friends who would be starting at Barnard in the fall. She texted, "I'm sure you can imagine my mother's delight at such a stellar junior league candidate."

Heron could indeed imagine. She hoped Charlie was happy. It amazed her to realize she didn't feel much of anything about the news about him moving on — only a little surprise, given the fervor of his proposal to her at graduation.

From Maggie, who shared an apartment with Bryant halfway

between his grad school classes at USC and her student-teaching gig in Torrance, she'd heard Jason's do-over senior year wasn't working out quite according to his plans. Thanks largely in part to Bryant having a word with the president of the SOD chapter there, Jason's membership transfer had been rejected and he was apparently persona non grata at Greek functions. Heron felt mean for laughing when Maggie pointed out that he lacked the social skills to make friends any other way, but it was true and couldn't have happened to a more deserving person.

They finished the bookcase and Dave positioned it against the wall. For now, Heron only had a few of her own novels and books borrowed from the library, but it would be full of schoolbooks soon enough.

"Want to grab some tacos?" Dave asked.

"I would, but I have plans. Rain check? Thanks again for your help."

"Anytime. See ya."

Heron tied on her running shoes and headed west from her apartment. Her evening runs often took her to the path around Greenlake, but sometimes she just explored the city streets. This solitary time pounding the sidewalks had become her favorite part of the day. Alone with her thoughts, she liked the company she was in.

Bea

The volume of Ben's worldly possessions was exactly double the capacity of the pickup truck Bea borrowed from Len. It had only taken them two trips to move everything from his place to her house. The only furniture he'd wanted to keep was a table he made in junior high shop class, which was now in the corner of their guest room playing the part of a nightstand.

They had both wanted to be careful about the decision to live together, making sure it wasn't only for practical reasons, but with Ben there every night anyway and his landlord dropping hints about a rent increase to keep up with the demand for student housing, it only made sense to do it now, before fall semester started, when they both had time to devote to settling him in.

She was grateful for Sarah's tough love during her closet clean-out last spring, leaving plenty of room for Ben's austere wardrobe. Bea cleared her things from half the dresser and knelt to unzip Ben's suitcase.

"Hold on," he said, coming up the stairs with an armload of t-shirts on hangers. "I'll do that. You don't need to unpack my underwear."

"Really?" She flipped her hair over her shoulder in a show of mock coquetry and lowered her voice to a breathy Marilyn Monroe purr. "I thought you liked that."

"Seriously, Bea, I'll do it." He dropped the stack of clothes on the bed and moved to shut the suitcase.

"It's no bother, I'll just—oh!" Among the folded boxers, she felt something firm and flat. "Mr. Addison, there seems to be a package in your underpants."

He sank to the bed with an exasperated sigh. "This is not how I imagined this moment." The words were muffled, his face buried in his hands. Ben rubbed the back of his head, then slid off the bed, settling on a knee, one hand gently removing hers from the box she'd found in the suitcase and taking it in his own.

"This is a little anticlimactic," he said. With Bea already kneeling on the floor, now they were simply eye to eye. "Can you stand up or something?"

"No," she said, trying to keep the corners of her mouth from spreading into a grin. "I'm pretty comfortable where I am."

"Fine." He opened the box. Inside, instead of a solitaire, there were two matching bands. They were palladium, a simple design with a channel of small sapphires in hers, a groove in his. "Bea, I know you aren't into the idea of a traditional marriage or a traditional proposal, so that's not what I'm asking for. I want us to be partners. I love you, and I want to spend the rest of my life with you."

Bea couldn't keep a straight face anymore, she broke into a grin, then she giggled, stopping herself when she saw a shadow of hurt and doubt flicker across Ben's face. She couldn't resist kissing it away.

"I can't say this is exactly the reaction I anticipated," he said, "but I'm glad you're amused."

"It's not that. Wait." She reached up into her top dresser drawer and brought out a small box from the same local jeweler. This one contained two bands made of black tungsten, each set with one tiny lab-created diamond. "I was going to give you these at dinner."

Now it was Ben's turn to laugh. He took her head in his hands, kissing her forehead, the tip of her nose, her lips. "Can I consider that an answer?"

"I suppose."

Unpacking forgotten while they found each other, raucous laughter rang from the bedroom, surely disturbing the neighbors as boxes and piles of clothes were carelessly shoved aside.

An hour later they were exhausted. The late afternoon sun filtered through the sheer curtains, warming their bare skin.

Ben said, "Oh, shit. Are we engaged?"

"I guess we are."

"Hmm," Ben looked thoughtful. "I suppose we can each wear both rings, but whose are the engagement rings and whose are the wedding bands?"

"Yours are the engagement rings, obviously, since you cracked and asked first."

"I cracked? You were snooping through my things! I had a whole romantic evening planned."

"Please. Your idea of a romantic evening is using plates for the pizza. I was unpacking your suitcase. Look, I'm already a dutiful wife."

"Bite your tongue. That's the last thing I want."

They had a lot more unpacking to do, the work of settling Ben's possessions into Bea's house. Planning to do: a wedding, apparently; their life together. They both needed to get ready for the new school year, too. But it could all wait. She was content to lie here next to him, watching the cat settle into the square of sunlight puddling on the sheet, listening to the breeze ruffle the leaves outside the window, feeling it tickle her skin. Right now, Bea was perfectly happy to stay exactly where she was.

Coming Soon

Coming soon from Amy Dressler: **THE ADVISORY ROLE** is a loose retelling of Shakespeare's *As You Like It*. Follow us on social media for updates on this and other new works in progress.

Instagram: **@egretlakebooks**
Newsletter: **www.egretlakebooks.com**

Book Club Guide

1. Which character do you relate to the most? Why?

2. Bea and Heron each have strong opinions about the other's choices. Do you think Bea was right to voice her concerns about Heron's engagement? Do you think Heron was right to engineer the matchmaking scheme?

3. Have you ever had a piece of clothing like Bea's blue velvet dress that boosted your confidence or made you feel special in an unexpected way? Where and when did you wear it?

4. How do you think Felicia's choices affected Heron? What do you think their relationship will be like moving forward?

5. Practical Bea uses evidence and logic to make decisions, while Heron relies on emotions and supernatural guidance like tarot and horoscopes. How do you think these approaches have helped them or held them back?

6. Bea is a strong believer in body positivity but still harbors insecurities about her body and how she is perceived. Why do you think this is, and how do you think it impacted her relationship with Ben?

7. If someone were to release a special wine in your honor, what would it be called and what would the label look like? What kind of wine would it be?

8. How do you think Charlie's family influenced the way he treated Heron?

9. Why do you think Bea is much closer to Len, Heron, and Toni than her own parents?

10. Are you satisfied with the consequences Jason and Charlie faced for the videos? What do you think a fair outcome would have been?

11. Do you think Bea's dates with Owen helped her come to her final decision about Ben? How?

12. Did you expect Heron to say no to Charlie the second time he proposed? Why or why not? Do you think there was anything he could have done differently to get her back?

13. Based on Bea's reaction to the wedding expo she attended with Heron, what do you think Bea and Ben's wedding will be like?

14. If you were familiar with the play *Much Ado About Nothing* before reading this book, what do you think of the changes the author made to the story?

Shakespeare Reader Guide

1. Which characters from the book are most similar or different from Shakespeare's *Much Ado About Nothing* play, and why?

2. *Much Ado About Nothing* takes place in Italy, while *How to Align the Stars* takes place in wine country in Washington State. How do you think these settings support each story?

3. What cultural norms around marriage have changed between the time the Shakespeare play was written and modern day? What cultural norms have remained the same?

4. What "nothings" (rumors and tricks) were actually "somethings" in each story, and why?

5. Do you think these two unique stories are comedies or dramas? Why?

6. After reading the book, has your opinion about the ending of Shakespeare's play changed? Why or why not?

7. Why do you think author Amy Dressler chose to tell the story from the point of view of the two cousins?

8. What themes are shared by *How to Align the Stars* and *Much Ado About Nothing*?

9. *How to Align the Stars* takes place over the course of a year, while the events of *Much Ado About Nothing* only take a few days. How do these timelines impact each story?

10. How are Bea Hayes and Heron Hunter similar to Shakespeare's Beatrice and Hero? How are they different?

Acknowledgments

This book was made possible by feedback and support from Olivia Allison, Peter Amos, Meghan Miller Brawley, Sarah Hawkins, MaryKate Lypka, Nicole Roth, Jessica Robertson, and Jessica Rice Haller (who also deserves credit for tolerating my teenage obsession with the Kenneth Branagh/Emma Thompson film adaptation of Much Ado). The contributions you made are too numerous and valuable to list. Y'all know what you did. Thank you also to Bethmarie Fahey, Joelle Davis, and the Manuscript Academy Women's Fiction/Romance Intensive cohort for their feedback, encouragement, and camaraderie.

My fiction-writing life sprouted in Pam Binder's Popular Fiction course, and while it's a mercy to all of us that the book I was working on that year was lost to a hard-drive crash, Pam and the rest of the Pacific Northwest Writers Association have fostered an environment in which aspiring writers find growth and encouragement, for which I am ever grateful.

This book is in your hands because I bumped into Tess Jones in the ladies' room at a writing conference and she encouraged me to submit it. That was just the beginning of a process driven by Tess's expertise, enthusiasm, and collaborative spirit. I'm so proud to be part of this small press driven by and for the work of creative women.

To all of my Whitman friends, especially the women of 4-West and Theta Omicron, thank you for your kindness and friendship, now and then. I hope this book reflects our shared experiences in ways that make you smile.

Extended family is very important in this book, and that was easy for me to write thanks to the Plucker and Grande clans. Especially my cousin Leslie, who is the "adultier adult" I call when I need to talk to someone more grown up than me.

I owe a big piece of my sense of humor to my brother Graham, and a lot of the wine detail in this book to the influence of his wife, Michell.

For my parents, who made sure books would always be part of my life and that I grew up believing I could do anything with my brain I wanted to. Dad, thank you for your encouragement and for trying to answer my weird legal questions. Mom, it's the greatest sorrow not to be able to hand you a copy of this book. I miss you.

To my sister Karen, who insists she is going to see me on the Today Show someday — ha-ha. But thank you for believing in me, and also for all the pizza and tofu bowls. As well as the complicated cat-sitting, letting me shoot Instagram reels at your house, storing so many of our shared books, the raspberries, sending my blog link around, dropping me off at college and giving me all the ins and outs, and insisting I at least try going through Greek recruitment.

And finally, to my husband, who really did ruin my plans to be a merry spinster by showing me being half of a couple didn't mean I couldn't still be my whole self. I am so grateful to you for being such a good partner through this process and always. You're the love of my life, let's giggle together forever.

About the Author

How to Align the Stars is Amy Dressler's first novel, even though she has said being an author is her dream job since eighth grade. She has worked as a librarian, freelance pop culture writer, and in local government. As a literature major, theater nerd, and believer in the cathartic power of humor, Amy has always gravitated toward Shakespeare's comedies. Finding ways to transpose those stories into contemporary settings that highlight the heroines' emotional arcs is a fun — albeit emotionally fraught — puzzle. Like Beatrice, Amy enjoyed being single and was rather looking forward her future as an eccentric cat lady, but her plans changed when she met and fell hard for her husband. They are the eccentric cat couple of their suburban Seattle neighborhood.

FOLLOW AUTHOR AMY DRESSLER
www.AmyDressler.com

EXPLORE MORE BOOKS
www.EgretLakeBooks.com

If you like this book please leave a review on the platform where you purchased it. We appreciate our readers, thank you!

Instagram: @egretlakebooks
Newsletter: www.egretlakebooks.com

Made in United States
North Haven, CT
07 February 2025